J. H. Riddell

Above Suspicion

A Novel

J. H. Riddell

Above Suspicion
A Novel

ISBN/EAN: 9783337047276

Printed in Europe, USA, Canada, Australia, Japan

Cover: Foto ©Andreas Hilbeck / pixelio.de

More available books at **www.hansebooks.com**

ABOVE SUSPICION.

A Novel.

BY

MRS. J. H. RIDDELL,

AUTHOR OF

'GEORGE GEITH,' 'TOO MUCH ALONE,' 'HOME, SWEET HOME,'
'THE EARL'S PROMISE,' ETC.

LONDON:

HUTCHINSON & CO.,

34, PATERNOSTER ROW.

CONTENTS.

Contents.

Contents.   vii

 Contents.

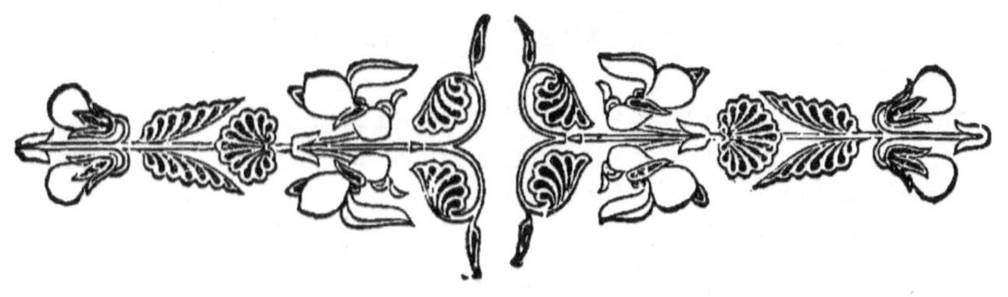

ABOVE SUSPICION.

CHAPTER I.

ABOUT WEST GREEN AND TOTTENHAM, AND THE SHOEING OF A HORSE.

SIXTEEN years ago no more rural village could have been found within five miles of the General Post Office than West Green. It was as utterly in the country as though situated a hundred miles from London, and by a natural consequence it was country in its ways, habits, and manners.

The various lanes leading to it from Stamford Hill, Tottenham, Hornsey, and Southgate were rural, which they certainly are not now. In those days Philip Lane was not a street, with houses all along one side, as is the case at present. Neither had any building societies invaded the sacred quiet of the road, bordered by wheat-fields and meadows, which led off to the Queen's Head, then as pretty a roadside public as the heart of a traveller need have desired to see—now refronted, redecorated, provided with tea gardens and other modern innovations of a like description.

As for Hanger Lane, no one had yet dreamed of the evil days to come, when mushroom villas should be built upon ground that not long before was regarded as an irreclaimable morass—when first a tavern and then a church (the two invariable pioneers of that which, for some unknown reason, we call civilization) appeared on the scene, and brought London following at their heels—when the common lands were enclosed and laid out in plots on which more houses were erected—when little by-roads were made leading to meadows then innocent of brick and mortar, but soon destined to be covered with small two-story tenements—when, in a word, Hanger Lane should be improved off the face of the earth, and in the interests of speculative builders (who had come entirely of their own accord to spoil it), called, as it is at present, St. Anne's Road.

Everything is done very quickly nowadays, and it has only taken sixteen years to change West Green from an extremely pretty village to an eminently undesirable suburb.

The familiar omnibus still passes through it twice a day, once going to London, once returning from it; but it does so empty of passengers; and if the proprietor could only find a loophole in a certain will which might enable him to cease running it altogether, he would esteem himself a very happy man.

A new station has been opened quite close to the village. New streets—hideous streets—debouch on the once pleasant green; the old horse-pond, which used periodically to overflow and spread half across the highway, is now fenced in with un·picturesque railing; and there is little left to tell of the pretty little hamlet which used, in the early spring, to look so sweet and countrified, with the hawthorn-bushes and the lilacs and laburnums all blossoming for flower.

Gone is the primitive post-office kept at a cottage, where a customer could purchase hot rolls on one side of the passage, and postage stamps in the parlour on the other—gone like the postmaster, who worked hard at his trade as a baker all the while he held that ill-paid appointment under Government; and the pretty young girls his daughters, who were, oh! so very pretty, but who, like their father, died one after another of consumption. Gone too are the old residents who lived in the few eligible houses dotted round and about the green.

The old village is still there, but it is huddled up amongst Streets, and Villas, and Places, and Groves, and all the other devices of modern investors; and those who can remember West Green in the olden time, and to whom the memory of it returns softly and gratefully like the recollection of some sunny picture, may well wish never to look upon it again.

So far I have spoken of the place as it was within my own recollection, when, after traversing part of Hanger Lane, any one coming from London turned off along a road exactly opposite to an old picturesque wooden house, shaded from the road by chestnut-trees and evergreens, and, wending his way under branching elms, emerged finally upon the green, and in front of the Black Boy public house. But at the period this story opens, West Green was a much more retired spot than at the date indicated—Eighteen hundred and fifty-nine.

Tottenham High Cross, as it is styled in the ancient histories, was itself a very quiet and secluded country town. The northern coaches had ceased running through it, and in lieu thereof the Great Eastern Railway had cut a line parallel with the old highway straight through the valley of the Lea. In accordance, however, with those principles to which for so many years the Great Eastern Railway Company have remained faithful—the latest development of which principles can be inspected at the new Bishopsgate Station, where no provision has been made for an up-platform—they carefully placed the Tottenham Station so far from the town as to be practically useless to all the inhabitants save those who lived round and about the Hale; and therefore, to all intents and purposes, Tottenham was a more out-of-the-world place after trains began to run to it than it was before. For which reason, any person, whether labourer, skilled workman, or trader, who could form a connection among the independent gentry, the City magnates, and the Quaker families who then tenanted the great brick mansions which are still to be met with in that neighbourhood, had a very fair chance indeed of making a comfortable living, and in many cases of putting by sums of money which seemed large in the primeval days of which I am writing. It was a much easier thing, in fact, for a man to drop on his feet in remote ages dating a generation back than is the case at present. There was more space for people then. If a person had special knowledge on any subject, he could find some one who wanted to use him; and if he were clever as an artificer, if he were ready and active, and civil and reasonable, why, he might compass a good deal in the way of success, as success counted then.

In the opinion of West Green, where he lived, and its neighbour Tottenham, where he had lived, Miles Barthorne had compassed a success quite unprecedented in the memory of the oldest inhabitant.

There were, as is usual, various versions of his antecedents. According to some, he had appeared traversing the mail road to London without a shoe to his foot or a coat to his back. According to others, he was attired like a gentleman when he made his first great *coup*, and had so drawn greater attention to himself than would have proved the case had he appeared in the conventional rags and been possessed of the regulation two-pence-halfpenny which mean future civic honours and the applause of kings and aldermen.

Miles Barthorne, however, made his first step along a road which conducted him ultimately neither to the Mansion House nor St. James's, in the garb of a well-to-do traveller. He was not clad in purple and fine linen, but there was no evidence of poverty in the man's dress or appearance.

Having elected to walk to London—which even now might, on occasion, be a wise procedure for those coming to seek their fortune in the metropolis—he was trudging through Tottenham, when his attention was attracted by a concourse of idlers surrounding a man and horse and smithy.

The horse had cast a shoe and could go no farther; the smith was ill, and his men were out; the traveller was angry, and the farrier's wife tearful. All this Miles Barthorne grasped as he stood and listened to the expostulations and the lamentations; and when he had grasped it, he made his way through the gaping, staring throng, and doffing his cap to the traveller, said:

"With your leave, sir, and that of the sick man's wife, I can put your horse's shoe on if she lends me the use of the forge and her husband's tools."

"You!" remarked the rider, in amazement.

"You, good gentleman!" supplemented the farrier's wife.

In answer to the first remark, Miles Barthorne pulled off his coat and turned up his shirt-sleeves, thereby exhibiting a breadth of chest and development of muscle calculated to inspire confidence in the breast of the owner of the horse which had cast a shoe; and at the same time, in reply to Mrs. Dorman, the smith's wife, he said:

"I am not a gentleman, though if every one had his rights I

suppose I should be; I was brought up like one. Nevertheless, I can shoe a horse as well as your husband, let him shoe
as well as he may."

And with that he picked up hoof after hoof of the steed,
which all this time stood quiet enough, perhaps liking the excitement as well as the rest, which is the nature of some
animals. When he had set down the last, which happened to
be the near hind foot, he said with a smile:

"Have you the shoe, sir?"

"No, that I have not," was the reply. "He cast it somewhere on the road—where, I have no idea."

"Then you had better have a new set all round. Look
here;" and with a "Woa!" which conciliated the horse, he
held up the animal's feet one after the other, for inspection.
"Come, sir, they won't cost you more than a shilling apiece,
and you and your beast will travel all the happier. I am a
stranger hereabouts, and know not the name of any good inn;
but if there be such, I will bring the horse to you in an hour's
time—no less—no more."

"Agreed," was the answer. "I will go back to the Rose and
Crown, and you can bring the horse there as you propose."

Now, the shoeing of that horse proved an immense sensation
to the population.

The news spread that in Dorman's smithy a strange man was
shoeing a horse for a traveller, and straightway every idler
flocked to see, and criticised the work freely.

"Hey, lad, where wert thou apprenticed?" asked an old
carter. "Who ever heard of shoeing a horse with cold iron?"

"Wiser folks than thou wilt ever be," answered Miles Barthorne, with a quick mimicry, which set the spectators in a roar.
"When thou goest to the cobbler, does he make thy foot to fit
his shoe, or his shoe to fit thy foot? I deal with my horses as
he does with thy feet; though had I such feet as thine to shoe,
they would drive me distraught." And so he went on talking,
blowing, hammering, cooling, nailing, till the town was in an
uproar between delight and dismay.

When he had finished he sought out Mrs. Dorman, and would
have placed four shillings in her hand, but the woman refused
it, saying:

"My husband would like to speak with you, sir, if you can
spare a minute."

To which he replied, "I will be back when I have taken the horse to its owner and got the money he agreed to pay."

Saying which, he clapped the saddle on the animal, drew up the girths, slipped on the bridle, and then, having previously inquired his way to the Rose and Crown, jumped on the horse's back and set off, not at a gallop, but at a quiet trot, to the Rose and Crown, where he received four shillings for Mrs. Dorman's benefit, and half-a-crown for the benefit of himself.

"You are a likely fellow," said the traveller, looking Barthorne over from head to foot, "and should do some good for yourself in life."

"I shall try to do so," was the reply. Already Miles Barthorne understood fortune had done him a friendly turn, and that he had travelled a considerable number of miles that day along the road to success.

CHAPTER II.

MR. DORMAN MAKES TWO DISCOVERIES.

MILES BARTHORNE retraced his way to the smith's shop, followed thither by curious glances from the older inhabitants and a train of boys and children of both sexes. He had been accustomed, however, to that peculiarity of country life which causes persons to take more interest in the most trivial affairs of their neighbours than in the serious affairs of their own, and he was not therefore disconcerted by the attention paid him, as might have been the case had he chanced to have been born in London.

When he arrived at the smith's house, he found Mrs. Dorman waiting his return.

"Will you please step this way, sir?" she said. "My husband bid me tell you his sickness was nothing catching."

"If it had been, I should not be afraid of catching it," Barthorne answered, a little contemptuously. "But what does ail him, mistress?"

"A weakness of the chest," was the reply. "He caught a cold last winter, and has never been the same man since. Sometimes he can scarcely draw his breath for pain."

"A bad complaint for a man who has to stand much over the fire," commented the stranger, as he felt his way up the dark staircase, and followed Mrs. Dorman along a narrow passage, at the end of which she opened the door of a room where the sick man lay.

Though the apartment was small, the furniture it contained indicated that the smith had been well to do, and was still in fairly comfortable circumstances.

Barthorne cast a rapid glance around, and guessed this fact; while the woman, stepping up to the four-post bedstead with its heavy moreen curtains, announced his presence by saying:

"This is the gentleman who shod the traveller's horse."

"Ay," said the other feebly; "would you mind coming a bit nearer, sir? Polly, had not you better be minding the shop? Women," he added, as the door closed behind her, speaking apologetically to the stranger, "are like children—they aye want to stay where they are least wanted."

"If every one were of my mind they would be wanted nowhere," answered Barthorne, with an abrupt decision of manner remarkable in so young a man.

"You have been crossed in love, most like," conjectured the smith.

"If I have not been crossed in that, I have in something else," was the answer. "But you wanted to speak to me. What have you to say?"

"I want to thank you for your kindness," began Dorman, with a certain hesitation.

"I do not see why you should," replied the stranger. "I was on my way to look for work, and work offered; and I have been well paid for it. See!" And he took four shillings from his pocket, and laid them on the coverlet. "That is your share," he said; and then he took out the half-crown, and spun it in the air, dexterously catching it as it came down. "And this is mine," he finished.

The sick man looked at him thoughtfully.

"I should not have taken you for a smith," he said.

"I am one, though, by trade," answered Barthorne. "I served a regular apprenticeship. See, here is my character from my master;" and he pulled out a pocket-book, and from it drew out a letter, which Dorman read slowly and with difficulty twice over.

"Seven years as apprentice, three as foreman," he spelled out.

"That is right," agreed the other, "and ready now to take any berth that offers at the forge, or bench, or vice. I can work at them all."

Once again Dorman looked curiously, almost suspiciously, at the dark gipsy face, the thick black hair, the stalwart frame of the man who sat beside his bed.

"Would you take service with me?" he asked, when he had quite finished his scrutiny.

"I have no objection to try your service," returned the other carelessly. "I can leave if I do not find it or you to my taste. I had, indeed, purposed going on to London; but I dare say this country will be more to my mind than the close city streets, at this time of the year especially."

And he walked, as he concluded, to the window, which commanded a view over market gardens, and the valley of the Lea, and the wide expanse of land lying under the summer sunshine between Tottenham and the blue hills of Essex.

"You have not spoken about wages," suggested the smith.

"And neither need you till I have been with you a week. At the end of that time you will know what I can do, and I shall know whether we are likely to suit each other. For that week you can pay me what you like."

"You are a queer customer, I think," remarked Dorman.

"That will not signify to you if you find me a good workman," retorted the stranger.

When, in the course of further conversation, Barthorne asked his new employer if he could recommend him a decent lodging —inns, the stranger explained, were not much to his taste— Dorman said hospitably that his wife could no doubt manage to house him, for a time at all events; but the other shook his head.

"Had I never lived under the same roof with Hal Glendy," ae remarked, "I might, had it so pleased me, have gone on working for him till the crack of doom.   No, master, thank you all the same ; but, in my humble opinion, master, and man, and mistress, are best separate out of working hours."

"You are too far-sighted for me," replied the sick man, wearily, "and I cannot say I just understand your notions or your talk clearly ; but, as you observe, if you work, that is all I need care about ; and if you are, as I suppose, too high in your way to be altogether neighbourly, why, no offence on either side. If none has been given, none has been taken."

"None has been given to me, at any rate," returned the younger man, with more heartiness of manner than he had yet exhibited ; "and so long as I work for you at all, I will work well and honestly. There is my hand on it ; " and he stretched out a hand hard and brown, and yet, for that of a man who had followed such a calling, singularly small.

As the blacksmith took it in his, he said, "Why, it is no bigger than a woman's.   It is lost like in mine."

"It can do some work, though," answered Barthorne, smiling, "as you shall see."

And Mr. Dorman did see.   Before the end of three month his trade had doubled ; and though he could not do much him self, money had never been so plentiful.

When he made up his books each week, which he did, I regret to say, for the sake of greater quietness, every Sunday morning, his heart sank within him lest his new man should give warning.   He had paid him liberally and treated him well, and allowed him to discharge idle hands and take on others at his pleasure, but still Dorman felt such a treasure was not likely to remain with him for ever on unequal terms ; and he would have proposed "going shares" with him, or even suggested that they should become "pardners," but for that vague uneasy feeling of "not understanding so queer a fellow" which had oppressed him at their first interview.

And indeed it was not for want of conjugal spurring that the blacksmith held back.   Mrs. Dorman was always urging upon him the expediency of securing Barthorne.

"You will find he will be snapped up by somebody who understands his value," she was in the habit of remarking ; and Mr. Dorman, who recognized the likelihood of her prophecy being fulfilled, always promised to "think the matter over."

"These sort of things ain't to be done in a hurry, Polly," he would say, refilling his pipe; and she would say, with a snort and a flounce :

"Well, you will find his going can be done in a hurry some fine morning, and then perhaps you will be sorry you did not turn yourself round quicker."

"That may all be, Polly," he agreed philosophically; "but, upon the other hand, it may not."

Which proposition being unanswerable, drove Mrs. Dorman to the verge of despair.

How long Mr. Dorman might have dallied with the question, had his man not broached it himself, it is impossible to conjecture.

One dreary Saturday in December, said Barthorne, heating his horse-shoes in the fire, to his master idly blowing the bellows—which, though an undignified, was a congenial occupation :

"I wish you would go to church to-morrow morning; I want to speak to you."

"All right!" agreed the other; "but do you really mean to church?"

"Yes," was the answer; "and I can walk part of the way home with you; only remember to say nothing about this indoors, or else Mrs. Dorman will be wanting to make one of the party, and three are no company, so far as I ever heard."

"I will say nothing about the matter to her," Dorman replied, and he kept his word; for he had an intuitive feeling that Barthorne wanted to speak to him concerning business which might be best transacted without assistance from the lady, who certainly ruled Dorman's domestic roast.

"Let us walk towards White Hart Lane," suggested the man, and the master assenting, they left the old churchyard behind, and paced slowly, having stood aside to permit those of the congregation whose way home led them along the same path to take precedence of them, over the damp fields in the direction Barthorne had indicated.

When they were left quite alone, when the meadow path held no more sign of life than the walk leading round the ivy-covered tower, Barthorne opened his mouth.

"Have you ever thought of selling your business?" he asked.

"No, I hain't," replied Mr. Dorman.

"Will you think of selling it now?"

"I see no call to do so," was the answer.

For half a dozen yards they paced on together in silence, then Barthorne inquired:

"Am I to take that as final?"

"I dunno what you mean by final," said Mr. Dorman, sullenly.

"What I mean by final is, that you have not thought of selling your business, and that you will not think of doing so," explained Barthorne.

"I see no call why I should," repeated Mr. Dorman.

"Well, there is no particular reason, certainly," was the reply, "except that if you will not sell your business, I can take it from you without purchase. I have but to open another place, and all your customers will come flocking to me. I need not pay you a penny for goodwill, for I have the good-will of the neighbourhood already; but you treated me fairly, and I don't want to treat you unfairly. Your health is not good, and it is not likely to be much better so long as you remain near London. Shouldn't you like a change? Come, I will make you a bid: I will give you fifty pounds for your business, and take the lease and tools and fixtures at a sum to be agreed on between us—your furniture I do not want. Will you strike a bargain?"

"I had liefer have you for a pardner," exclaimed Mr. Dorman, breaking out into a profuse perspiration caused by the agony he experienced in making the proposition, and the fear he felt that his man might accept his offer.

But on the latter score he need have suffered no uneasiness; nothing on earth save heaven was farther from Barthorne's mind than any compromise of the sort, and he said so frankly.

"I will either be your successor or your opponent," he replied. "Think the matter over for four and twenty hours, and then let me know whether we are to be friends or foes—at peace or at war."

"I have treated you fairly," expostulated the smith.

"And I have worked for you honestly," retorted his man.

"And I think we might do a good stroke together as pardners," suggested Mr. Dorman.

"Perhaps we might; but I won't be your partner," replied Barthorne.

"Will you tell me why?"

“For one reason, I would rather be working for myself than for myself and another.”

“And what is the next reason?”

“None that I need tell to you,” was the curt reply.

And with matters remaining in this unsatisfactory state, they parted—Barthorne professing an intention of walking back by Wood Green, and Mr. Dorman, only too glad to be rid of his company, declaring he would take the shortest way home, which for once chanced to be by following the high-road.

He was not a strong man, and he knew he had not the faintest chance of success if his new man started an opposition smithy. Nevertheless, his heart clung to Tottenham and his smith's shop, and even for fifty pounds he was loth to leave either.

Nor was Mrs. Dorman one whit behind her husband in lamentations and regrets.

So earnestly she besought him to make any sacrifice rather than leave the neighbourhood, that Dorman went that night to bed determined to offer Barthorne even two-thirds of the profits, rather than separate his fortunes from those of the new-comer.

Whether it was owing to the fact of his having partaken of a hot supper late, or of his having retired to rest early, Mr. Dorman never could tell; but hours before daylight the next morning, he woke with a sense of horrible oppression about his chest —with a feeling of some dreadful misery having come upon him about his heart.

For a few seconds he lay battling with his waking mind against his sleeping, as people often do in such extremity, then he turned and felt for something human and tangible to reassure him; but he felt vacancy—his wife's place was empty.

“Polly,” he said, “Polly dear;” but Polly never answered.

Then—he never could tell afterwards what made him do it, though he understood an impulse beyond his own power of self-control was urging him on—he got up, and partly dressed, and stole like a thief along the passage, and down the staircase, and across the parlour, and so into a little office beyond adjoining the shop.

Yes, his intuition had been right—the door of communication was ajar, and the forge fire alight. He could hear his wife's voice, and the whoo-of of the bellows. Oh! that thrice-accursed Barthorne. He would have his life. Standing there in the darkness, Dorman swore to himself, nothing save the spilling of that strange man's blood could cool the fever raging in his own. But he would not be in a hurry; he had never been in a hurry yet —not even in proposing to the woman who was false to him; so he waited for a minute, first to recover his breath, and then to decide on his future conduct, and while he waited he heard his wife say:

"I don't know why you are so cruel to me."

"I am not a bit cruel to you," was the sharp reply, uttered in a pause of the bellows-blowing. "I'd be cruel to you if I took you at your word, and let you leave a better man than I ever was or shall be for the sake of a stranger you have taken a fancy to. But it is of no use your plaguing my life out in this way. If I loved you as much as I do not love you—if I hated your husband as much as I like and respect the man, I would not ask you to leave him for anything you could offer. I have my work cut out, and I do not intend that any woman shall come between me and its execution. Now, will you stand back? if you do not the sparks may burn you."

"I wish they might," she answered, "and then you would be sorry for your hard-heartedness."

"I should not be sorry if they burnt you to death, mistress," he said angrily. "If there had never been women like you to tempt men, I should not have been hammering on a smith's anvil now. By ——," and he swore an oath which sounded fearful to the weak and shuddering listener, "if I was your husband I'd thrash this nonsense out of you, if I killed you in the process."

"I would rather be killed by you than kissed by him," she answered with an unconscious alliteration.

Barthorne flung his irons back into the fire, and, advancing straight to where she stood crying and sobbing, took her by the shoulder.

"Now, look here," he said, "I have had more than enough of this love-making; and if you went on with it for ever you would never win a love-look from me. I don't like you—I didn't like you from the first day we met. I am a trifle too dark myself to care for brown eyes and black hair. When I fall in love, which at present I never intend to do, it shall be with a woman whose eyes are blue as heaven, and whose cheeks are as white as snow. So now good morning and good bye. I shall take the liberty of screwing a bolt on the inside of this door while I remain here, and if you give me any further trouble I shall tell your husband why I found it necessary to do so.

"Great heavens!" he added, as she went along the passage, her progress facilitated by a push from him, "that men should peril their interests for such cattle—for such cattle!" and he was so overwhelmed with the absurdity of the idea, that he sat down on the anvil and let his fire out while he thought the matter over.

"I don't believe one bit about the serpent tempting Eve," he considered. "I believe she must have been one of those stealing, artful sort of women, who, finding her husband a fool, as he undoubtedly was, and the serpent clever, as he certainly must have been, played up to him, and manœuvred about till she got his secret, when, woman-like, she pitched him over. Well, I suppose they are necessary evils, but they are evils. Till I am laid in my coffin it will always baffle me to comprehend why God made women. There, now, that woman has made me neglect my work."

And he rose and re-kindled his fire, and did what his hand found to do, unconscious of the misery which that morning had brought to one heart he would willingly have kept from trouble. For he really did like his master. And when, my reader, you come to know what the man's nature had been and was, you may be inclined to score a few points in his favour on that account. The same day, when he went to his dinner, Dorman followed him to his lodging.

"I have been thinking," he began, "about that there offer o' yourn, and p'rhaps, as I ain't so handy as I were, I might do worse nor close on it."

"I think you might," was the calm reply.

"Well, then, I will, and so no more need be said. Fifty pounds for the goodwill; and lease and plant we can agree upon, and I will go away and interfere with ye never more."

"That is it," said Barthorne in confirmation.

"And, neighbour, so long as we are talking, I want to tell you I heard what passed between you and my wife this morning."

"More is the pity," was the comment.

"And I bear you no ill-will, mate, for the evil you have wrought—though, God knows, I understand you as little now

as I did the first day you crossed my threshold. I canno' tell
how it has all come to pass—I canno'. I married my wife for
love, and she married me for the same—or I thought she did.
Since we came together she has never lacked bite nor sup ; she
has lived on the best; she has two silk gowns now, and her
watch and chain like a lady, and—and——"

At this point he buried his face in his hands and sobbed aloud,
Barthorne never interposing; but when he had indulged his
grief for more than a sufficient period, his successor slapped
him on the shoulder, and said :

"Take her away from here—take her among her own people,
if she has any ; she will outlive this folly, and be to you a better
wife in the future than she ever was before she understood all
men might not be of your mind. And as for the bother and
the shame, friend, I would have kept both from you if I could ;
and I am not likely, unless your mistress trouble me hereafter,
to make either public."

"Heaven bless you for that !"

"Amen. Have you anything **more to say ?**" seeing his visitor
hesitate.

"Nothing, except this. This forenoon I met a man from your
parts, and asked him if he had known a smith called Barthorne
at Spindlethorpe. In answer he said, 'No. A man of the name
of Glendy was the only smith at Spindlethorpe, but I might
have made a mistake. Four miles off, at Abbotsleigh, there was
a place owned by a Squire Barthorne——' "

"Yes ?" interrogated his man.

"Was that Squire kith or kin to you ?" asked Dorman.

"I do not know which Squire you are talking about," was the
reply; "but a Squire of Abbotsleigh was my father. You have
the mystery and its solution at last," he observed with bitterness.

Whereupon Mr. Dorman, suddenly oppressed by the atmosphere of gentility by which he had unconsciously been surrounded
for so many months, beat an unceremonious retreat.

CHAPTER III.

MILES BARTHORNE'S PARENTAGE.

THERE were persons residing in and around Abbotsleigh who would have said Miles Barthorne had no right to so call himself; but in this they were wrong. He had as much right to that name as to any other. Conversely, however, he had as much right to any other as to that, which, after all, is not a nice kind of inheritance for any man.

Had Lucy Sanson been as prudent as she was pretty, no scandal would have attached itself to the memory of Squire Miles Barthorne, who slept as quietly in the family vault as Lucy did in her grave in a foreign land.

There could be no question but that the Squire would have married her had she played her cards properly; but she did not play them with the slightest wisdom, and the result proved Miles, junior, who, except by the Squire's favour, could not be regarded as his eldest son, or, in fact, as any son at all.

How this came to pass was as follows. The Squire's mother, a Scotch lady, had brought with her to the Hall a maid called Glendy, Presbyterian, prim, precise, honest beyond belief, disagreeable beyond the power of expression.

She arrived at Abbotsleigh when she was very young, and she stayed there, first as lady's-maid and then as housekeeper, till her hair was grey; stayed there till her mistress died, and her son first married, and then died also. When that event occurred, Miss Glendy gave and received notice to quit—the letters of dismissal and resignation crossing each other—and retired with her savings to spend the remainder of her days with a niece, the sad widow of a dissenting minister.

Before her mistress died, however, Miss Glendy urged many of her own relations to come south and taste of the rich sweetness of English pastures. And they came—some to do well, and some to do ill; some to tire of the pleasant land, and seek further change in distant countries; some to die; some to marry. Amongst the latter were two girls—one, Bessie, who married a small farmer named Sanson, and another, Jean, who, being of a serious, not to say discontented, turn of mind, attracted the attention of a Methodist preacher, who ultimately asked her to become his wife.

Of the men we need concern ourselves only with Hal Glendy, son of Miss Glendy's favourite brother, who, having settled in the north of Ireland, refused to leave his adopted home, but eventually sent his firstborn to Abbotsleigh as deputy, and bade him look after his aunt's savings, which the youth failed to do, though he came of Irish folk on the one side, and of Scotch on the other.

Nevertheless, he prospered. He had the best work in all that part of the country. The gentry liked him, and he did remarkably well both for himself and those belonging to him. He it was who first made any stir about his pretty Cousin Lucy living at the Hall. Perhaps he knew that of the new Squire recently come into his estate which made him think the young woman might find a better service elsewhere. Perhaps jealousy quickened his perceptions. Be all this as it may, he did not approve of Lucy remaining at the Hall after Mrs. Barthorne's death; and he told his aunt this, and his aunt bade him show his face again in any house where she lived at his peril.

For Miss Glendy had as high a notion of the pride of station in men as she had of the power of virtue in women. For no earthly consideration would Miss Glendy, even in her most youthful days, have permitted herself to be chucked under the chin, or kissed, or even complimented, and if she did not credit the whole of her sex with a like circumspectness, at all events she considered no child of a Glendy would ever suffer any undue familiarity. And supposing—even supposing any Glendy capable of so far forgetting her genealogy and her training, she felt quite certain the son of her dead lady was too true a gentleman ever to speak familiarly to a servant.

At her approach Squire Miles had always shrunk away appalled. He called her, in his juvenile days, "Old Whalebones;" but then, who dare have repeated this utterance to Miss Glendy? And when he grew older, weak and foolish as the man was, he had sense enough to understand it would be well to retain so discreet a housekeeper in his service; and, accordingly, no duchess ever received higher honour than did Miss Glendy from the young heir. She would as soon have thought—this is unquestionably true—of Mr. Miles making love to her as of his making love to her niece.

But he did make love to pretty Lucy Sanson, nevertheless; and, as has been said before, there is not the slightest doubt he would have gone further, and made her mistress of the Hall, had she been wise as she was fair.

When it all came to the knowledge of her friends—as it had to do before the birth of Miles—the dissenting minister took her home, and Miss Glendy wished to resign her situation, but Mr. Barthorne was penitent, and declared his intention of marrying their niece.

Perhaps he might have done so even then, had Lucy proved true to herself and her relatives; but she failed in her part; and one day — sick to death, probably, of the monotony of her uncle's house, weary of his homilies, and unable longer to endure the uncertainty of her position—she yielded to her lover's persuasions, and slipped quietly away with him to France, leaving uncle, aunt, and child to brave popular opinion as they might.

Mr. Mason, being a thorough Christian and truly moral man, took her defection seriously to heart—indeed, people said he never recovered the shock of finding upon what empty air he had spent his exhortations. Miss Glendy, equally moral, bore herself with more equanimity.

"Something must be done for the child," she said; so she had him brought to the Hall, hired a nurse for him, and treated Miles in all respects as though he had been born in lawful wedlock, and was next rightful heir to Abbotsleigh Hall.

There Lucy never returned. She and the Squire passed two years travelling about from city to city, at the end of which time she died at a little roadside inn, after giving birth to a dead child—her second—a girl.

The Squire did not immediately retrace his steps to England. He visited the Holy Land; he spent some time in Norway; he travelled through Spain, and when he finally recrossed the threshold of the paternal mansion, Miles—little Miles—was a sturdy handsome lad of six, able to read very well indeed, and still better able to ride.

He was introduced cautiously to the Squire, who first tolerated his presence, and then took notice of him.

"He will make the child his heir," Miss Glendy decided, and her heart beat high at the thought.

But the Squire made no sign of such adoption; with the boy as with the mother, he drifted. He did not send the child away, neither did he arrange for his proper training.

Almost out of pity—and perhaps with an eye to possible benefits in the future—the rector of Abbotsleigh saw to his education. The boy was clever. Any father might have been proud of such a son; and it is quite possible the Squire would in time have taken to the lad, and left him the lands of Abbotsleigh, which were quite free and unentailed, had it not so fell out that at the house of a relative—of his nearest male relative, indeed—he met with one of those women whom the younger Miles abhorred afterwards with all his soul—soft, stealing, plausible, cunning—a mere nursery governess in the eyes of Mrs. John Barthorne; the loveliest, and the sweetest, and the gentlest creature God had ever made, in the opinion of Squire Miles.

This creature, lovely, sweet, and gentle, understood her admirer's nature much better than poor Lucy had done. She fell no victim. This time the Squire was lotted off and bought in at a very low price indeed. Miles Barthorne, Esquire, of Abbotsleigh Hall, married the governess in his cousin's family, and took her abroad as he had taken Lucy.

History repeats itself. There is a wonderful sameness in the record of most human lives. There was a wonderful sameness in the life of Miles Barthorne, only this time it was he who died abroad. He died very suddenly at Florence—so suddenly that he could not make his will, long deferred, or do anything, save, when almost in the death struggle, entreat his wife to "see to the boy."

Squire Miles was thought worthy of Christian burial in Protestant England: so his remains, not having been wrecked by the way, were brought to Abbotsleigh, where his dust was laid with the dust of his fathers, and where Mr. John Barthorne followed as chief mourner.

Miles, junior, aged fourteen, was nowhere. He had been brought up—Mrs. Barthorne number two being childless—as the heir; unacknowledged, perhaps, but still certainly; and now he could not even attend the funeral. The man who had wrought the sin was dead, and none might repair his error.

When Miss Glendy knew there was no will, she tendered her resignation, which Mrs. Barthorne had anticipated by a letter of her own.

No more education for Miles—no more ponies—no more Latin and Greek.

"Cast out the son of the bondwoman," was Mrs. Barthorne's dictum ; and, coincident with her return, Miles was cast out neck and crop from the pleasant lands of Abbotsleigh.

For her life Mrs. Barthorne had the house of Abbotsleigh and five hundred a year—everything else went to Mr. John Barthorne. To him, not unsuccessfully, an appeal was made for the illegitimate child. The applicant, Hal Glendy, who went over to state the case, received a cheque for fifty pounds, and some useful advice anent bringing up the boy to an honest calling.

Next day he had a long talk with his nephew, told him in plain English his position, and asked would he learn a trade— would he learn all he could teach him? The boy slept upon the proposition, and said—yes; he liked his uncle, and he did not like his Aunt Glendy. So his uncle bound him apprentice, but not under the name of Barthorne.

To Hal Glendy the cognomen was odious. "You are my nephew, Mick Sanson, now," he said, and Miles assented, for he was yet young, and the bile in his nature had not begun to stir.

For which reason, far and near, the boy, as he grew older and the story of his birth became more remote, was known as "Black Mick."

So far as anybody could tell, he had no name of his own— neither Barthorne nor Sanson. He was simply Glendy's nephew, or Black Mick.

Curiously enough, whenever any pity chanced to be expressed for the youth, it was certain to be by some of the gentry in the neighbourhood, who thought Miles' a hard case, and considered the widow and Mr. John Barthorne might between them have devised some scheme for bringing up the son of the dead man to a profession.

They had seen the child riding about on his rough pony, when the sturdy, handsome boy stood a very fair chance of being left all his father's possessions, and they did not consider that merely because Squire Miles died without a will, Miles, junior, should have been put to work at the forge.

For this reason, when business took these gentlemen to Glendy's yard, they had always a kindly word and pleasant look for the smith's nephew; and when he went to work at any of the large houses in the neighbourhood of his old home, the ladies went a little out of their way to speak civilly to the youth who had been treated, as they considered, so harshly by Mr. Barthorne.

Indeed, to speak truly, the memory of that very frail young woman, Lucy Sanson, was much less displeasing to them than the presence of Mrs. Barthorne. Lucy, at all events, had not been sufficiently artful to induce the Squire to marry her, and this woman, not a bit better born, probably, and certainly not possessed of a tenth part of Lucy's beauty, had insisted on church, and clergy, and ring, and proper settlements like any countess.

Of course the ladies of Spindlethorpe and Abbotsleigh, and the other neighbourhoods adjacent thereto, never reduced their real feelings into such exceedingly plain language as the above, and consequently they found Miles a convenient peg on which to hang their dislike of the Squire's widow.

"She might have had some pity for the boy," they declared, which she certainly might, though it by no means follows that those who were warmest in expressing their opinions would have acted a more Christian part themselves.

"We find it so easy to tell other people how they ought to act," as the rector who had educated Miles, and who had privately remonstrated with Mrs. Barthorne concerning her treatment of the boy, slily remarked when public opinion set, as it did at frequent intervals, very strongly against the widow.

As Miles grew to manhood, the gentry were more than ever decided that it was a scandal to see the young man shoeing horses, and going about the country carrying a basket of tools; and they felt quite satisfied in their own minds that Mrs. Barthorne must feel thoroughly ashamed of herself when she met her stepson.

It is extremely improbable she did anything of the sort; but the sight of Miles became in course of time a source of serious annoyance to her.

When she cast out the boy, she forgot that, in the ordinary course of things, he would grow to be a man, and it was not pleasant for her to be stared at and elbowed by a stalwart young fellow who was the very image of her late husband, and who lost no opportunity of thrusting himself in her way.

Spite of the remonstrances of his friend the rector, he made a point of attending Abbotsleigh Church, and he attended it to such purpose that Mrs. Barthorne's pew became finally tenantless.   She tried speaking to the young man, and said to him in the church porch:

"How do you do, Miles?"

For answer he folded his arms and stared her out of countenance.

About Abbotsleigh the people ceased touching their hats to her, and she had to send fifteen miles if she wanted a lock re-. paired or a horse shod; for Hal Glendy would permit no man in his employ to work at the Hall.

Each month which added to Miles' age made the neighbourhood less tolerable to Mrs. Barthorne.

Out of pure insolence the young fellow had commenced his system of persecution, but eventually he pursued it with an object.

"I will drive her out of the neighbourhood," he said to his uncle.

"Better let her alone and stick to your work," was the answer.

"I do stick to my work," replied Miles, "but I will not let her alone."

And the upshot of it all was that Mrs. Barthorne eventually, finding that the state of her health necessitated change of air, let the Hall, and departed bag and baggage, to revisit Abbotsleigh no more.

From the time of her departure public interest in the late Squire's son began to abate. There was not the slightest chance of his ever being anything better than a blacksmith now. The Squire could not rise from his grave. John Barthorne had a large family of his own; and really fifty pounds was not an illiberal gift, when the circumstances were reconsidered. The Hall was let to strangers, who had never heard of the Barthorne scandal; and Glendy was willing enough to allow the horses belonging to the new-comers to be shod in his yard, and to send over and execute any work in his line which the incoming tenants wished to entrust to him.

Glendy had a very good business indeed, the gentry said. He was making money fast and investing it prudently. No doubt young Sanson would be his heir. He was unmarried, and had no nearer relative. Further, Miss Glendy had amassed no contemptible amount of savings during her residence at the Hall.

Miles therefore stood a very fair chance of becoming hereafter a well-to-do master smith. It had been a good thing his learning a trade—better, perhaps, than if Mr. John Barthorne had educated and sent him to college.

Hal Glendy was a far more prosperous man than many who considered themselves his social superiors. Altogether, the thorn of Mrs. Barthorne's presence being removed from the flesh of the good people round and about Abbotsleigh, society began to make itself comfortable about the young man Miles.

After all, the story was a very old one, and the boy had fared much better than might have been expected; and it was time the whole affair was forgotten—in which opinion Hal Glendy most heartily coincided.

As for Miles, no one asked what he thought of his position. No one dreamed of the wild aspirations that had grown with his growth and strengthened with his strength.

He meant to make money, and buy the Hall and land immediately adjoining, if he could do no more. For him the face of woman had no charm. There was only one thing on earth he desired, and that thing was sufficient wealth to enable him to take back his name and become Squire Barthorne of the Hall.

His uncle's business was increasing steadily and rapidly. It would not be hard to make a fortune out of their trade, Miles decided.

Visions of a foundry had often crossed his mind. Mentally he had built ranges and ranges of workshops, and heard the chink of a hundred hammers. He with his education, which he had never forgotten, his uncle with his keen shrewdness— an integral part of his nature—between them could they not rear a trade? Could they not make their hundreds thousands, and their thousands tens of thousands, as other men, no cleverer, no wiser, no more industrious, had done before?

And thus, while working at his trade, he built his air castle.

When he had got it perfect—ay, even to the cloud-capped pinnacles—it was swept in a moment away. The work of all his young life had to be begun over again.

He had mistaken the foundation on which he built; and it

was necessary to reconstruct the whole edifice, and go on labouring, labouring through the years till the turrets of his fresh palace should touch cloudland again.

For five and twenty years Hal Glendy had remained faithful to the memory of his first love, Lucy Sanson. At the end of that quarter of a century he met a very young woman who had no objection to become an old man's darling, and married her.

Miles thought this hard upon him; and perhaps it was : but a harder trial was in store.

With an intuition by no means rare in her sex, Mrs. Glendy took it into her pretty head that she did not like her husband's nephew, which was all the more singular, since women generally admired his handsome face.

But Mrs. Glendy's instinct told her this man would prove an enemy; and she gave her husband no rest till he intimated to Miles it was best they should part company.

He did not do this ungenerously, however. He gave Miles the fifty pounds handed to him by Mr. John Barthorne, with the interest at five per cent. for ten years added. Further, he gave him twenty-five pounds and a watch and chain as a present from himself, together with the written recommendation already mentioned—and not without tears, for the lad had been very dear to him, and the mother dearer—and a dead love, like a dead sorrow, can never be quite forgotten—he bade Miles Barthorne goodbye and God speed.

Miles had insisted on being styled Barthorne in his uncle's letter of advice to all whom the character of his nephew might concern.

"For a woman my father left me a beggar," observed Mr. Miles Barthorne bitterly, and quite truly. "And for a woman you send me adrift to make for whatever land I can. I will enter that land in my own name. I have been known by one of your choosing long enough."

"See that you bring disgrace on neither," said his uncle sadly.

"Even in that case I am not likely to trouble you again," the young man answered; and so left Spindlethorpe.

—◆—

CHAPTER IV.

MILES BARTHORNE MARRIES IN HASTE.

FOR three years Miles Barthorne continued shoeing horses—increasing his staff of men and extending his business. At the end of that time he sold his plant, premises, and connection, and retired from the smithing trade and Tottenham to a small cottage situate at West Green, which he had bought for an old song.

The public mind at Tottenham was much exercised to account for this proceeding. Fortunes were in those day made at Tottenham. The resident gentry in the neighbourhood patronized the local tradespeople, and did not rush to London for their supplies, as is in all neighbourhoods too much the case at present ; and the butcher and the grocer, the baker and the candlestick-maker, were by consequence well-to-do and substantial householders and house proprietors. Further, the resident gentry were wealthy. No stable but held its pair of carriage horses, whilst there were many stables that held many more ; and as the new smith invented a new system of doing business which found great favour in the eyes of those who had been perpetually harassed by the ever-recurring remark, "If you please, sir, the bay horse must be shod," or "John has just taken the chestnut mare to the forge," uttered at the precise instant when the bay horse or the chestnut mare was most urgently wanted, he had at the time when he sold his "going concern" the pick and choice of the best work in the neighbourhood.

Mr. Barthorne it was who originated the contract system of shoeing horses. He roughed and shod for so much a head per annum, sent his own men for the animals, and sent his own men back with them. For an additional annual sum he saw to their general health, and would have engaged to feed them likewise, had he for a moment supposed the oats supplied would ever have found the way to their mangers.

There are things a man cannot effect ; and one is commanding the honesty of any human being who has to do with horses.

At that point Barthorne drew the line.   He shod and he phy-
sicked, there he stopped. Being, after his fashion, a representative man, it is not a matter for wonder that amongst all ranks
and by all classes his relinquishment of a paying business was
freely canvassed. Fat Quakers remarked to their demure wives
"that it was very strange, but doubtless friend Miles knew his
own affairs best."   Irritable gentlemen, not of the Quaker per-
suasion, wondered "what the —— Barthorne could be thinking
of;" whilst in bar-parlours wiseacres said "there was no depen-
dence to be placed on strangers;" and their wives running in
next door to gossip, declared "Master Barthorne had never
been the same since he married."

For he had married, six months previous to the time when he
sold his business, a quiet-looking, pale-faced, grey-eyed young
woman, possessed of a pretty graceful figure, light brown hair,
two dimples, and a mouth exactly like a cat's. She managed
this feature remarkably well, but still it conferred upon her a
peculiarity of appearance for which most persons were puzzled
to account.   With all she was not a bad-looking person.   She
was pre-eminently that which in a certain rank is known as
"genteel-looking," the accent being laid strongly on the "gen."
She dressed well, walked well, spoke well, and was by the neighbourhood generally considered "above her station."

Miles chanced to see her at the house of one of his patrons,
where, being a poor though publicly acknowleged relation of the
mistress of the establishment, she filled the position of nursery
governess.   And a wretched life she led while in that position;
so wretched that, although Barthorne was, in her estimation,
"only a blacksmith," and after a fashion she considered herself
a "lady," she accepted his advances without disdain and thankfully agreed to become his wife, which he made her despite his
former resolve of remaining single till he could marry to advance
his interests.

To resolve, however, is one thing—to perform, another.
Practically Miles Barthorne found his single estate a drawback
to his worldly prosperity; not merely, being young and good-
looking, did it compel him to have his domestic affairs managed
by hags who were neither pleasing to look at nor desirable in
their habits, but he found that ladies discovered he proved a
bone of contention and a fertile source of idleness amongst their
female servants.

He was not the man to encourage smiles and covert glances from cooks or housemaids, but his studied reserve inflamed the hearts of all the fair creatures who came in contact with him, and it is not too much to say he might have had his choice of at least a hundred personable women, some of them possessed of a not contemptible amount of money in the savings bank.

Now, Barthorne did not like being made love to. Had his lot been cast in a higher circle, he would have fallen a prey to no match-making mother, to no young beauty eager for a settlement.

In all ranks there are a few men to be found utterly insensible to flattery, who read a woman through and through as they might a book, and who can tell as accurately what she is worth as a judicious buyer can the probable value of a field of standing wheat.

This man Barthorne, who plays a prominent part in the story I have to tell, was probably as great a scoundrel as any one could, in the length of a midsummer day, meet in the streets of London, but his wickedness did not take the form of an undue love of women. Rather, as has been indicated, his nature was unredeemed by any love for any woman. He had his ideal, possibly, but so far his and her paths had not crossed. Given him his ideal, it is quite possible he might have developed higher qualities, for not unfrequently the worse a man the greater his veneration for a woman, pure, gentle, gracious, beautiful.

As from the bottom of a well one can see the stars in daylight, so from the depth of a man's wickedness he can discern the beauty of virtue when possessed by a woman.

It was, therefore, from no particular love of Miss Lucy Chappell that he asked her to marry him. He wanted a wife, and just then she was the only person likely to suit in that capacity who presented herself. On the other hand, it is fair to say that, so far as she was capable of caring for anything, Miss Lucy did care for the handsome and audacious smith. Of course, being a properly constituted young woman, had any person of a like appearance in a higher rank appeared and proposed, Miss Lucy would have accepted him ; but no more eligible suitor crossing the stage, she conceived a very sufficient affection for him, which, as years went on, developed into jealousy of every woman he looked at.

It is quite possible, however, that Miles, placed as he then was, might have hesitated before asking her to marry him, had he not chanced, while waiting for the master of the house in order to explain a disputed item in the quarterly account, to hear Lucy's mistress engaged in giving that young person a "tongue-thrashing," as the lower orders graphically style that merciless lecture some women are so well able to inflict. In the course of this verbal chastisement his own name was mentioned more than once, the mistress declaring she would not have her house disgraced by the governess of her children speaking familiarly to a tradesman, to a person who she believed shod horses himself.

To this Lucy answered deprecatingly, she had never spoken to Mr. Barthorne at all except to say "Good morning:" or "Good afternoon;" which remark only added fuel to the flame, and started the indignant lady off on another furious canter, beginning with the words:

"*Mr.* Barthorne, indeed! What next, I wonder!"

"I will marry that girl," said Barthorne to himself; and he did.

For the time being he gave up shoeing horses, and walked about every day in the glory of his Sunday garments, in which he did not look uncomfortable, as is the manner of his class, but as Miss Chappell mentally observed, "quite like a gentleman."

First he threw himself across her path when she was walking out with the children; but ere long he persuaded her to meet him in the pleasant, quiet lanes round and about Edmonton, or in the still more lonely field-paths which are so numerous in the country lying to the north of London.

It ought to have been a happy wooing, according to the old proverb, for it was a very speedy one. Within three months of the time when Barthorne heard his patron's wife finding fault with her governess for having spoken civilly to him, he was married to her in Tottenham Old Church, Lucy's only brother acting the part of father.

After the ceremony Mrs. Barthorne, who was not deficient in courage, returned to the house of her employer, broke the news of her change of state, said she hoped the step she had taken would cause no "ill-will," remarked that she should send for her boxes, which were already packed, stated that "Mr. Barthorne and she intended to spend their honeymoon at the

Isle of Wight," and finally, having stricken her relative almost dumb with indignation, left the place with all colours flying.

Within ten minutes after her departure a messenger was dispatched to Barthorne, requesting that his bill might be at once sent in—his bill up to that date. Barthorne laughed, and returned it by the man ; but nothing further came of the matter. On his return home, the owner of the establishment did not find it convenient to send a cheque for the amount; and accordingly things drifted on as usual, and Barthorne's men still continued to shoe and dose the horses of Mrs. Barthorne's kinswoman's husband until Barthorne sold his business, and gave rise to those remarks and conjectures to which reference has already been made.

The mind of Tottenham, then, was exercised concerning Miles Barthorne. Tottenham could not understand why he should sell his business. Tottenham failed entirely to comprehend why he or any one found the air of West Green better suited to his taste than the air of Tottenham. Finally, Tottenham, which considered it had made the stranger, felt disgusted at his desertion of it.

And yet the secret was really a very simple one. For three years Miles Barthorne had tried whether it was possible to make a fortune out of a farrier's business ; at the end of that time he decided his fortune could never be made out of it in Tottenham.

He was young, and when men are young they think they have not a moment to lose: when men are old they think, conversely, and fortunately, that time will wait for their lagging feet. Further, the dead, certain level of his existence seemed killing him; and beyond all, he had, one winter's day, in crossing the field-path leading from West Green to White Hart Lane, slipped in getting over one of the stiles, which were made purposely quite as inconvenient then as they are made inconvenient now, and strained himself severely—so severely, indeed, that he finally understood a long time must elapse before he could do a heavy day's work at " the fire," or be in any respect the strong man who had halted at Tottenham *en route* to London.

Further, he made the discovery all persons who have to do with labour make sooner or later, viz., that while it is possible to make a large amount, comparatively, of profit out of a couple of workmen, and a very fair per-centage out of a large amount of capital when a vast number of hands are employed, a medium trade—a lower middle-class sort of factory—always must prove eminently unsatisfactory to an ambitious employer.

His connection had spread, and was spreading; but when Barthorne came to count his gains, he found the result utterly disproportionate to the risk and the anxiety. Bad debts he had not many; but of bad workmen he had a surfeit—men who, the moment his back was turned, lit their pipes and sent out for beer, and shod the horses badly, and confided their return to some boy, who galloped them along the highway as if running a race with John Gilpin. And, lastly, he hated being a master smith; he loathed the sort of position it conferred. As a workman, people had regarded him as an anomaly; as a farrier employing labour, they were disposed to consider he occupied his proper sphere.

"I would rather work hard at contracts, with one or two men under me, than go on with this sort of thing," he remarked to his wife; and she, though secretly mortified, dared offer no opposition to his whim.

She had indeed looked forward to a phaeton, in which he should drive round and take his orders and collect his accounts, she, dressed in all her best, sitting by his side; she had dreamt of her husband abandoning work altogether, leaving that to his men, to the end that his hand might become nearly as white and soft as her own; she had seen visions of annual visits to the seaside, where, in a black satin gown, and gold chain well spread out over a silk velvet mantle, she should ruffle it with her betters, as she had done on that memorable journey to the Isle of Wight. And now, as she once observed to her husband, "It turned out she had married a man determined to be no more than a common labourer."

"But still who will give you more luxuries than any clerk at his thirty shillings in the City," replied Barthorne; "and if you behave yourself, and be a good girl, and do as you are told, you shall be a lady some day, you shall, by —— !"

For Mr. Barthorne, unconventional though he might be, had already imbibed the London idea that a lady is a person who dresses every day in purple and fine linen, who employs her elegant leisure in doing nothing, who drives out in a handsome carriage, drawn by a pair of high-stepping horses, and whom it is competent for the fluctuations of the Stock Exchange to unmake, as, generally speaking, the fluctuations of the Stock Exchange have made her.

———◆———

CHAPTER V.

EXPLAINS A LITTLE DIFFICULTY.

ABOUT thirteen years after Miles Barthorne's entry into Tottenham, and ten after he disposed of his business and retired to his small cottage at West Green, the ruling minds which held watch and ward over the well-being of the Mint were much exercised to discover that a new species of illicit coining was, and had been for a considerable period, going on. The peculiarity of the spurious money was that it all appeared to be made of perfectly good metal; and it so admirably counterfeited the productions of the Mint that no one except an expert could have detected the fraud.

That this coinage did not emanate from any ordinary gang of forgers, was well known to the authorities; but the authorities would have been much better pleased could they for a moment have supposed such a thing possible, as the chances of detecting the criminals might then have been much greater.

Over and over again the powers that then were discussed the question as to who the person could be that found such a course of crime remunerative. First, the Jews were suspected : a theory was put forward that some "fence," belonging to one either of the known or lost tribes, had discovered it would be more remunerative to deal with stolen goods in the form of crown pieces and sovereigns than in the shape of melted tankards and irrecognizable teapots; and till this theory had been thoroughly discussed and exhausted it seemed plausible enough. There could be no doubt but that tankards would find a more ready circulation in the guise of lawful coin of the realm than of stolen goods ; there could equally be no question that whatever wickedness it was in the power of man to do in order to make money, some unscrupulous Jew might safely be trusted to think of. Besides, what Christian could know so well as a Jew where to lay his hand on the men and the machinery necessary to carry out such a purpose? "A person would require, in the first instance," so argued those who believed in a larger amount of original sin having come out of the Garden of Eden for the benefit of the Jews than that entailed upon the Christians, " a cheap stock of gold and silver, and a knowledge where to replace such stock is needed. Now, all that is A B C to those descendants of the tribes who receive stolen metals ; in the next place, it would be necessary to give these metals into the hands of a chemist able to make them pure, as we find these crowns and sovereigns to be. Now, who so likely to find such a chemist amongst his brethren as a Jew? When all that is effected, he must provide a secret place for transmuting the precious metals into coin. Who would have better facilities for finding such room or building than a Jew? And last, but not least, who could more readily find some poor wretch, probably in his power, able to supply the requisite moulds, which we all see must have been made by an expert at his trade? The manipulation is a mere *bagatelle.* If men are, for the sake of a very poor living, willing to run the risk of manufacturing and issuing base coin, men could easily be found to make genuine coin, with the distribution of which it is evident, as we know the bulk of this money comes from abroad, the makers are not entrusted."

Now, there was a certain plausibility about this theory, and the way in which its parent presented it to his friends in council ; and as one theory is good till another is told, this was held to be the true explanation of the case until another gentleman adopted the wise course of undertaking to refute his friend's notion without attempting to advance one of his own.

" It is neat," he said, " but it won't hold water. Bring experience to bear on the subject, and what do we find? Why, that a Jew never cares to bring a number of capable instruments together to do his work. He may have a hundred people doing his bidding, but he never engages them in any undertaking where they could combine together and pitch him over. Here you have at least half a dozen interests cognizant of each other, and yet employed to benefit one man, and that man a 'fence.' Besides, it is agreed on all hands that this money is pure. Believe me, the Jew doesn't exist who in such a case could refrain from putting base metal with the pure. It is a simple impossibility. Clever as your friends are, my dear sir, believe me, that sovereign"—and the speaker rang one on the table—"emanated from the brain of no Hebrew. A German might claim the credit of it—if we can suppose a German possessed of sufficient capital willing to run the risk. I cannot suppose it, however, and I am therefore at sea."

After that, official opinion ran up and down the gamut, now inclined to attribute the coinage to some gigantic conspiracy, and again willing to suppose it originated with some clever tenant, who, having unearthed a mass of buried treasure, wished to conceal his discovery from the lord of the manor.

Though an annoying, it was a simple matter, after all. For obvious reasons it never could be extended indefinitely. A man who could sell gold in bulk honestly would never think of troubling himself to convert the metal into sovereigns. It was an extremely easy matter for the Mint to re-melt the coins, and send them out again with the stamp of authority on them. A few thousand sovereigns per annum increased the yearly loss by a sum too trifling to mention. Nevertheless, the authorities governing the Mint did not like the circumstance, and, lest the practice should spread, made little stir about the matter.

A few confidential detectives were instructed that such coinage was in circulation, and the detectives really tried their best to discover what villain it might be who was sending into the market genuine silver and gold. Smashers had good terms offered to them if they would turn informers, which, in good truth, they would have been only too glad to do had the secret lain with them. But, one and all, they were in the same story. They had no story to tell. They knew of no one who possessed hidden stores of the precious metals. They were only acquainted with men who cut their dies pretty well, but not so well as those exhibited to them. They could not say whether there was in London a "master smasher" able to employ skilled labour and supply men like themselves with moulds and materials. They had never heard of him, at all events. With a shrug, and **a** wink, and a significant thumb over the left shoulder, they thought if there was such a one he "would not find it pay—no, not at all."

Nevertheless, the detectives persevered. They kept their eyes on Whitechapel, and bestowed fond glances on Clerkenwell and the environs of Gray's Inn Lane. They travelled down East as far as Bromley, and they went West to Marylebone. They did not omit to investigate suspicious localities round Lambeth, and they extended their search far down the Old Kent Road. For a long period one most respectable but eccentric house-holder, residing near Ball's Pond Gate, unconsciously received an extraordinary amount of attention from one of the force; whilst a widow at Homerton and a bachelor at Hackney were about the same period subjected to a strict system of *espionage*, under the impression that one made the bullets while the other fired them.

And all the time the real culprits were upon the most friendly terms with the police of their respective districts; for no human being could have imagined that Walter Chappell, head manager to Nelson Brothers, of Soho, on the one part, and Miles Barthorne, plumber, gasfitter, locksmith, and contractor for general repairs, on the other hand, between them devised and agreed to carry on this precious scheme.

And yet such was the fact. In a modest little cottage at West Green, all overgrown with creepers, in the garden of which during the summer months Miles Barthorne might, evening after evening, have been seen watering his roses, and tying up his carnations, and hoeing amongst flower-beds, these deeds of coining were done. The man who had for so long a time persistently wooed fortune now seemed on the point of winning her. Honestly he had tried at first to gain her smiles; dishonestly he finally decided she was alone to be possessed.

Still young, he might hope to compass all his fancy had pictured as desirable. If not Squire Barthorne of Abbotsleigh, he might yet be Squire Barthorne of a fairer domain. Other men as unscrupulous—more unscrupulous than he—made fortunes, bought properties, retired from trade, married their daughters, sent their sons to the universities, and became magistrates, members of Parliament, and deputy lieutenants.

All this he intended to do, with the exception of sending out his sons, for he had none. His family consisted of only one daughter, a large-eyed, sallow-skinned, dark-haired, precocious girl, in whose features her mother failed to trace the promise of future beauty; while her father—a better judge of such matters —declared she would be the image of that naughty Molly Barthorne, so celebrated in Court annals, who, in the palmy days of Abbotsleigh, caused nobles to sigh, and write inane verses in praise of madam's dimples; whilst great ladies wept—not without reason, perhaps—over her graces of person and her lack of virtue.

Following the family traditions, this child had, much against Mrs. Barthorne's wish, been called Mabella—not a bad name, perhaps, for a child in any rank, since so easy to speak in full, and so much more easy to shorten into Mab.

Since, however, neither father nor mother elected to shorten it at all, the child's name gave great offence to those who had the privilege of being neighbours to the Barthornes; though whether the Barthornes could have called their daughter by any name capable of satisfying the West Greenians may well be doubted.

"Drat them Barthornes, says I," remarked a voluble matron about the period indicated at the beginning of this chapter, "making such a goddess of that yellow-faced thing, all eyes and hair, with her double rat-tats at the door, and her ' pa ' and her ' ma,' as if they were all gentlefolks together. And, then, missis in her grey silk gownd on Sundays, and grey bonnet trimmed with pink and a white feather, if you please ; and her poor man going off every morning to his work just as regular as my Bill. But, if you think of it, he's every bit as bad as she, giving his five shillings to this and his half a crown to that, just, as my Bill says, to get the blind side of the clergy and suchlike. And no doubt he finds it all to his account ; for they don't owe a farden to nobody—not a farden, if you believe me. But, for my part, I hate such ways. And Bill says, for all Miles Barthorne was a master smith, and sold his business—no one knows why—and does live in his own house, and holds his head so high, it will all come home to him some day ; for such lofty and mighty airs ain't suitable to the likes of us." From which it will be seen that Miles Barthorne was not popular; and, indeed, had he been endowed with all the qualities which, in the thirteenth chapter of First Corinthians, St. Paul so eloquently enumerates, with charity at the back of them, he could not have pleased West Green.

West Green did not like strangers, and he was a stranger. West Green liked people it could understand, and it could not understand Miles Barthorne. West Green liked people who were not above taking a friendly glass at the bar of the Black Boy, and Barthorne never drank with any one at any bar, and had his beer in by the cask, "like a gentleman."

Further, in a vain endeavour to curry favour with people who detested him because he was prosperous, he had been weak enough to lend here half a sovereign, and there a couple of pounds, to keep the wolf hunger, or that worse wolf the bailiff, out of his neighbours' houses; and the result proved precisely what might have been expected. When he demurred about the second half-sovereign, and refused the next two pounds, the would-be borrowers, who had never repaid the original loans, mentally stigmatized him as a close-fisted curmudgeon, or as a time-serving hypocrite, as the mood was on them.

There were many who, like Bill's wife, said " it would come home to him." Nevertheless, when the vague " it " did come home, these were the first to remember his good works. At that period, however, Barthorne was not in a position to know much about their compassion or to extract any comfort from it had he been aware the human being existed who pitied him.

When the good people of West Green came to speak with bated breath of his known virtues and his supposed vices, the object of so much animadversion was lying in gaol upon a somewhat serious charge. Not that of coining, be it remarked. No one in authority ever, except vaguely, imagined Barthorne had anything to do with that little business. If other secrets leaked out, the secret of the good money was preserved almost intact. Into that which eventually proved his stumbling-block Miles Barthorne drifted quite by accident. Great crimes, I apprehend, usually originate in very small beginnings, and the beginning of Barthorne's wickedness was as small as can well be imagined.

When Miss Mabel was about four years of age, her Uncle Walter, who always made much of the child, promised to give her a medal, and to let her see him make it.

Barthorne had about that time taken in exchange from one of his customers a considerable amount of copper, and out of this copper Walter Chappell moulded missy's ornament. He bored a hole in it, and hung it, suspended by a ribbon, about the child's neck.

After she had gone to bed and fallen asleep, the medal still clasped in her little hands, Miles asked his brother-in-law how he made that thing he gave Mabel.

"Out of your copper," answered the other. "I hope you are not angry. The value of the thing is not more than two-pence."

"Oh, I am not angry, of course. Use as much of it as you like, only I felt curious, that was all."

That was not all, as subsequent events proved. Barthorne turned the matter over in his active mind. He thought about it while walking to and from his work. He thought about it when directing the two men he employed. He lay awake at night, and considered the question in all its bearings, and finally, when missy had so long outlived her fourth birthday as to be nearer her fifth, when the medal had long been lost and re-placed by one of those superb watches which in those days were sold for a shilling, and in these can be bought, with the addition of a guard chain, for a penny, Miles opened his mind to his brother-in-law.

The young man had about this period managed to get into two scrapes—one concerning a horse which did not win as he had expected, and another about a girl upon whose character, like that of the horse, he chanced to place too much depen-dence. In each case money was needful to extricate him from his difficulty, and in the extremity he made use of funds belonging to his employers. When another horse happened to be " no-where," and it became absolutely necessary to replace the sum abstracted, Chappell was forced to confide in his sister's hus-band, and ask his assistance to save him from disgrace and ruin; and this assistance Barthorne gave willingly enough, tagging on to his favour, however, the stipulation that the younger man should lend his skill as a die-sinker to enable Barthorne to make both their fortunes.

The downward path is one easy enough to travel at the outset; and so Chappell discovered. Ere long he not merely gave his skill, but gave it eagerly. He liked the money Bar-thorne freely handed to him; he liked the excitement this illegitimate trade produced in his life. He did not pause to ask where Barthorne procured his materials He did not inquire how the money was coined or who disposed of it. And, in truth, in the earlier stages of the business, any questions of this sort would have elicited little information, for Barthorne then was merely experimenting, considering his plans, and developing his resources, placing his men for the battle, and considering the possible cost of defeat, the probable gains of victory.

When the fight against law began in earnest, Chappell was too deeply in debt, and too completely involved in the plot, ever to dream of drawing back if he had wished to do so. But as has been said, he did not wish anything of the kind. He believed two men never engaged in a safer speculation, or one more certain of carrying them ultimately to the pinnacle of prosperity.

"We shall be able to do better yet, my boy," said Barthorne, slapping him on the back. "When I can perfect the milling machine, and find out how to separate the alloy by some quicker and simpler method, we may consider ourselves made men."

Nevertheless, the shortest road to success generally takes years to travel. The milling machine never was made quite perfect, and the separation of the alloy proved a matter of time, during the course of which many difficulties had to be encountered and overcome ; and accordingly it came to pass that missy, for whose special benefit the original copper medal had been struck, was eight years of age before her Uncle Walter and her Papa Miles had got their machinery well at work.

By the time, however, that the company was in full swing, that little cottage at West Green was turning out illicit coin at the rate of some thousands a year ; but Barthorne never ceased working at his trade, while Chappell, promoted to a salary of three pounds a week, acted as manager to the firm with whom he had been apprenticed, and the employers of both would, if put upon oath, have sworn to the pair being most respectable men, which no doubt they would have been had temptation not chanced to cross their path. As matters stood, they were very far indeed from being respectable ; but this only proves how very cautious people ought to be about vouching for the good character of any one. Which perhaps is the reason why people like to speak so ill of their neighbours, since there are those who hold the semblance of sincerity to be a more Christian virtue than the reality of charity.

This is beside the story I have undertaken to tell. Miles Barthorne, whatever his other faults, was held by those who came in contact with him to be a respectable, well-to-do, clever-honest man. He had played and was playing his double gamo with admirable coolness, courage, and address; and it is per, bable that he might have gone on playing it successfully for years, or till he chose to retire from business with an ample fortune, but for one of those unfortunate accidents which occasionally upset the worldly vehicle in which the wisest and best of our celebrated criminals are travelling post to success.

The accident which happened to Miles Barthorne was, though a remote, a very awkward one. A man took it into his head to die—what was worse, he elected to be murdered.

----♦----

CHAPTER VI.

A NOBLE IS BROUGHT TO NINEPENCE.

ANY one who, even so recently as ten years back, had a visiting acquaintance with the suburbs of London, must be aware that nowhere round the outskirts of the metropolis were such fine, roomy old mansions to be met with as to the north, north-west, and north-east of the City.

The reason may not be hard to find. As a rule, householders, like witches, did not in the old days voluntarily cross water, and the Thames was a line of demarcation which the merchant princes of former times avoided when practicable. Far out west, noblemen and rich commoners built themselves residences; but the City men of long ago looked themselves out convenient sites on which to build their country palaces. Hackney at one time was a salubrious village which the citizens much affected when in search of pure air; and the old red brick houses with stone facings, which are fast being pulled down or converted into asylums, bear testimony that the citizens who there congregated possessed incomes by no means contemptible.

Round and about the now Victoria Park there used to be mansions in which one might have lodged any illustrious foreign visitor. Stoke Newington, and particularly that portion of Stoke Newington called Church Street, was abundantly provided with spacious and comfortable houses, whilst Hornsey, Highgate, Finchley, and Hampstead were rich in fine old residences, surrounded by great forest trees and well-grown shrubs, and gardens secluded within goodly walls, on which grew nectarines, and peaches, and juicy pears, and Hawthornden apples, and other desirable fruits too many to enumerate.

Perhaps, however, Highgate could boast a larger number of such pleasant homes than any of the other districts mentioned; and it was to one of these that a certain Sir Alexander Kelvey, who had made a fortune in India, retired to spend the remainder of his days. Sir Alexander had left Scotland a very poor lad, and returned to England a very rich elderly man.

He had achieved great success in life. He had risen to be a chief justice, and to have the honour of knighthood conferred upon him, at a time when Misters were not transformed into Sirs so indiscriminately as is the case at present. He came back laden with testimonials. He had great vases of silver and gold. He might have ate off the precious metals at every meal had he been so disposed; but in his age he retained the simple habits of his country and his youth, and his hoards of plate were never exhibited save as a curiosity to some intimate friend, or on the occasion of one of those rare banquets at which Sir Alexander—who was a widower—and an elderly maiden sister dispensed stately hospitality to old Indian friends and esteemed London acquaintances.

The care of his treasures was entrusted to his butler—a man grown grey in his service. For years he had kept the key of the strong room, which contained articles of almost incalculable value; but the responsibility seemed to have sat lightly upon him, for although a Scotchman and a Presbyterian, no more jovial person could have been met within a circuit of half a dozen miles than the butler of Hillview, as Sir Alexander's place was called.

The butler's brother was head gardener at Hillview. He had a small cottage in the kitchen garden, and "did for himself" as regards matters domestic; but there was very little to do, for he took most of his meals in the house, and, when not reading some quaint work of an old divine, or a well-thumbed book about gardening, spent his evenings either in the servants' hall, or else in talking alone with his brother concerning former times, and dead friends, and the days of their far-away youth.

This was the man who had been murdered—brutally murdered. Hillview, during the absence of its owner, chanced to be undergoing extensive alterations and repairs, and a labourer who happened to be the first at work on that especial morning found the unfortunate gardener lying on the grass in the flower-garden, his right hand clenched as if to defend himself, and his skull cleft open, evidently with a blow from a spade, which latter was found amongst a clump of rhododendrons close at hand. The body was quite warm, though the doctor, who quickly arrived on the spot, declared life must have been extinct for about three hours. Most probably, therefore, he had met with his death in the early dawn.

It was a summer's morning, and the sun shone brightly over the scared group collected round the body. As for M'Callum, the butler, he was like a man distraught. The affection each of the brothers bore for the other was of no ordinary nature. Natives of a country where family ties are stronger, perhaps, than in any other land, they had the further bond between them of standing utterly alone in the world. All other relations, near and remote, were dead. As they often said, "If they went back to the old place they would have to seek their welcome in the kirkyard; living creature there was none to greet them."

"He was all I had," sobbed M'Callum, who had been roused from his sleep to hear of the murder; and the man knelt upon the grass—the sun slanting upon his grey hairs—and wept like a child.

There was not much work done that day at Hillview; but a large amount of beer was consumed. The painters and the paperhangers hung about in knots, discussing the question, and considering it from every possible and impossible point of view. At intervals the carpenters and masons joined them, while Barthorne, who had contracted to heat the house and lay gas into all the principal rooms, found it so difficult to keep his own men together, that he directed them to leave off work at twelve o'clock, and himself retraced his way home about the same time.

He had, at an earlier period, spoken a few words of earnest sympathy to M'Callum, still distraught with grief, still unable to grasp the reality of his loss.

"We little thought of this last night," he remarked to Barthorne. "When he was ready with his joke about your 'brew,' we had small notion we would never hear his voice again. Who could have done so black a deed? He never harmed even a worm—I have seen him throw them away, that his spade might not cut them—and there is not the value of a sixpence missing out of his bit house."

"Did not I hear somebody say a pane of glass in one of the library windows had been cut out?" asked Barthorne.

"Ay, there was some talk of that, I mind," answered the other; "but I had forgot. I can remember nothing but him. Well, well! we are all in the hands of the Lord, and He won't suffer my poor brother's blood to call out for vengeance in vain."

The next day came, and with it the coroner's inquest. Nothing fresh had been elicited, no trace, not the slightest, of the murderer had been discovered.

The weather being exceptionally fine and dry, no mark of footsteps was to be found; and though the grass showed evidence of a struggle, the police were able to make little out of that fact. As nothing in the interior of the house appeared to have been disturbed, the theory advanced at the inquest, and accepted by the jury and society, was, that the deceased had interrupted an intending burglar in his felonious attempt, and that he had lost his life in trying to intercept the thief in his flight.

Then came the question, who was the thief?

The police racked their brains to think of any suspicious characters who had of late been seen loitering about the neighbourhood, and one or two people were taken up who had never even known that such a place as Hillview was in existence. Out of his savings M'Callum offered a reward of one hundred pounds for such information as should lead to the detection of the criminal. But no information came; and meanwhile, the poor fellow who had been "wilfully murdered," according to the verdict of the coroner's jury, "by some person or persons unknown," lay in his decent, comfortable cottage—quiet enough —sleeping that sleep which knows no waking—here.

Mr. M'Callum had not been able quite to make up his mind as to the precise spot of earth his brother might have selected to occupy till the Day of Judgment, had five minutes' speech been permitted him before he died; and Mr. M'Callum was much exercised in spirit accordingly.

Sudden death was not an idea which had ever suggested itself to either of them. They came of a hardy stock—of a race that died of old age, of fever, of inflammation, of severe colds —but not of apoplexy, heart disease, or any other of those short sharp maladies, rapid in their action as a cannon-ball, and as unexpected, which summon the members composing some families to appear in eternity without a moment's grace being allowed for preparation.

Highgate Cemetery was adjacent; but then his brother did not "just care" for cemeteries. Despite his taste for trim lawns, and smooth walks, and well-kept shrubberies, M'Callum knew his heart had always kept a loving memory of a certain kirkyard, where, amidst waving grass and rank weeds, a grey stone solemnly set forth that underneath, in the full hope of a glorious resurrection, one Mary Maxwell, aged eighteen years, lay at rest.

For her sake he had remained single all the years of his life, and consequently his brother leaned to the opinion that David might like his body to be laid in some snug spot of ground adjacent to that sunny corner, close beside the grey stone wall separating God's Acre from the lonely acres beyond, where his betrothed was buried.

This was the sentimental view of the question. The other view was, that David had never cared to give needless trouble, and that doubtless, "poor lad" (so the grey-haired man spoke in his deep trouble of one but two years his junior—thereby proving that death is the only elixir capable of restoring our youth), "he knew now full well he was as near Mary in one burying-place as another."

"He always spoke of Hornsey churchyard as a fair, quiet sort of spot," thought M'Callum at last, "and I'll e'en see if a bit of ground can be spared for him there."

It would puzzle any present Mr. M‘Callum to find a bit of ground to spare for a stranger in that dear old churchyard now; but the matter was capable of arrangement then, and the murdered man was finally interred where the earliest sunbeams fell athwart his grave.

Once there was a headstone above his resting-place, setting forth that David M‘Callum, who died by the hand of some unknown assassin, on the 16th day of June, 18—, lay beneath.

"Vengeance is mine; I will repay, saith the Lord," was the text following the above inscription; but M‘Callum did not live to see the verification of the statement.

The mills of time grind so slowly, though they do grind so exceeding small, that if we cannot pin our faith upon the experience of others, we are extremely likely to find ourselves eventually destitute of faith altogether.

Before David M‘Callum, however, was laid in his grave, a curious thing occurred. The night before the coffin was screwed down, his brother James dreamed a singular dream, or said he dreamt it, which came to the same thing.

He thought he was lying in bed fast asleep, when he was awakened by some one shaking him, and found his brother standing at his side.

"You needn't be looking among strangers for my murderer, James," this unlooked-for visitor remarked. "He is in this house every day, and——"

At this point James M‘Callum averred he started up "in a white sweat, with every hair on his head standing straight on end;" and the dream, he further stated, produced such an effect upon him, that, "in the darkness of night," he resolved to ask every man employed about the place to lay a hand on his brother's body, and solemnly declare he was not the murderer.

Now, upon the face of it this did not appear a pleasant request to comply with, and the men looked doubtfully one at another, till at last a young carpenter, laying aside his plane, offered to lead the way.

"Poor old chap," he said, "I wish our touching him could bring him back among us. I am sure nobody who ever knew what a good fellow he was would have hurt a hair of his head."

"Brayvo, Tom," cried his mates. "If it is any satisfaction to you, Mr. M‘Callum, we will all go and pass our word over his body—though it did seem a bit queer at first," they added.

And so, solemnly, man after man stretched out his hand and touched the corpse, making at the same time asseveration that he had no act or part in the murder.

When all assembled had performed this ceremony, which, before it was ended, had assumed an importance impossible to have been predicted, a whisper went round that one person had not laid hand on the body of David M'Callum, and that person was Miles Barthorne.

"There is no call to trouble him," remarked the bereaved brother, looking with dull, lack-lustre eyes—eyes in which the hope of revenge seemed to be quenched—at the assemblage.

But still the whisper continued.

"We will have Barthorne," decided the young carpenter already mentioned. "Just for the form of the thing—just to prove your dream false, Mr. M'Callum, we must have the word of every man who was about the premises."

And with his young active step he went in search of Barthorne, whom he found in the basement measuring up some quantities.

"Will you step down to the cottage for a minute?" said the self-elected messenger.

"Why should I?" asked Barthorne.

"You know old M'Callum has had a dream about his brother, and——"

"Has had the devil!" remarked Barthorne, folding up his rule, and preparing to obey the summons.

"Well, it is natural he should take on," observed the young fellow, "for David was one in a hundred. Once at home, when we were awfully down on our luck—all out of work—and mother lying dying, the dear old boy brought us one night a bottle of wine and a couple of good mutton chops, and left them and half a sovereign behind him ; and if I knew——"

But already Barthorne was out of hearing.

"What a surly, stand-aloof gentleman it is !" soliloquized the carpenter, as he slowly retraced his steps to the cottage.

There he found every one in a state of excitement. No man about the place had, after the first amazement wore off, attached the slightest importance to the ordeal suggested by M'Callum.

They had touched the body to humour the o'd man, who, when he beheld hand after hand laid unhesitatingly upon the dead man's heart, began to think he had been "but foolish" after all.

He had felt it was a useless piece of formality sending for Barthorne; but when Barthorne, striding into the place, declared he would countenance no such superstitious absurdity, that nothing on earth should persuade him to lend himself to so gross a piece of fooling, the butler began to think his brother's " warning " had not been given in vain.

" It take it very hard," he said, " that any one who knew and respected my murdered brother should call my natural desire to bring justice home, fooling. This is not a meet word to use in the presence of the dead."

" Don't talk nonsense, M'Callum," interposed Barthorne ruthlessly. " The dead cannot hear you, and the living can. There is not a man present upon whom you have failed to fasten an insult by your ridiculous request. You have branded a lot of innocent people as possible murderers. And for what purpose? You cannot be such a simpleton, I take it, as to imagine, if the murderer were present and laid his hand on your brother's wounds, blood would gush out."

" I believe his blood cries aloud, and that the Almighty will hear that cry," was the reply. " I believe that the crime will be brought home yet—that it is being brought home even now."

" The sooner the better," replied Miles Barthorne. " But, meantime, you ought to discontinue this indecent mummery. As I said before, I will have nothing to do with it. I pity your sorrow, but when sorrow degenerates into drivelling, it is needful to draw a line."

A murmur of approval greeted this speech. Those who at first had thought very badly of Miles Barthorne because he refused to touch the dead man, now found that his utterances exactly embodied their own opinions. In truth, the sort of suspicion cast upon those employed at Hillview was eminently unpleasant, when each individual came to think the matter over in cool blood.

" There is a great deal of sense in what Barthorne says," one remarked to another. But the young carpenter merely observed: " He might have humoured poor old M'Callum. I don't think he 'd have slept the worse for getting off his high horse for once."

Which was indeed very true. People seldom lose much by being courteous and considerate.

All Miles Barthorne gained by his move was that his fellows

remembered in after time he alone refused to touch the body, while James M'Callum went about the house and grounds muttering to himself :

" He said it was one about the house, and Barthorne would not lay a hand on him : Barthorne is the man."

Really a most unpleasant conclusion for one human being to arrive at concerning another.

After David M'Callum's funeral, after Barthorne had completed his work and withdrawn his men, the butler made a sickening discovery. The gold plate and the silver plate were gone. The lock of the strong room was intact—there was not a sign of violence to be observed—but the gold and the silver had vanished : how, M'Callum could not imagine ; when, he decided must have been the night of his brother's death.

He had informed Sir Alexander of the murder, and Sir Alexander was on his way back to England in consequence. Knowing this, knowing also how little good the police had effected, and feeling sensibly the truth of nis own country proverb that the " silent sow sups the most brose," M'Callum waited his master's return. That Sir Alexander should suspect him of having made away with the plate was an idea which, to the credit both of master and servant, never entered his mind.

He had sense enough to know the plate was gone past recall, but he understood the criminal might remain within reach, and that the quieter affairs were kept the more likelihood there was of their being able to lay hands on him.

Except he alone, no human being beside the thief knew of those treasures being abstracted, and his object was to persuade the thief that he, M'Callum, still remained in ignorance of the fact.

Accordingly he kept his own counsel, and carried a load of care about with him until Sir Alexander's arrival.

The morning after his master's return he told him everything which had occurred ; and said boldly, for reasons hereafter to be given, that he believed Barthorne had stolen the plate and murdered his brother.

Now, the ex-judge, in virtue of his position, was a cautious man ; and mere beliefs are occasionally difficult things to prove.

There was a vagueness about M'Callum's statements — an utter absence of succinctness about his narrative ; " but yet," thought the judge, " such apparently disjointed pieces of evidence are precisely those which, well fitted, make up a very fair map of criminal proceeding."

Now, Sir Alexander had peculiar means of obtaining authentic information about any man whose antecedents he wished to study, and ere long he knew much which was important about Miles Barthorne. He traced him back from Tottenham to Spindlethorpe, and forward from Tottenham to West Green. He found that wherever Miles Barthorne had been permitted the run of the house, there was, sooner or later, a burglary committed.

"I will have his house searched," decided Sir Alexander; and he applied for a warrant accordingly.

When the officers entered, Miles Barthorne was sitting at tea with his wife, his brother-in-law, and his little girl, now arrived at the discreet age of eleven. Certainly guilt was not stamped on the faces of any one of the party, and when the men, awkwardly enough, explained their errand and apologized for troubling him, he cheerily told them to search away, "they would not find anything contraband in his house."

There were two men, and one stayed downstairs while the other proceeded to examine the upper rooms, Mrs. Barthorne fidgeting in her chair the while, and at length she would have left the parlour, but that Barthorne stopped her.

"Sit still," he muttered. "What the —— are you afraid of? Do you suppose, if my house was searched for ever, any one could find in it an article not honestly paid for and come by?"

As if in answer to this speech, the man who had gone upstairs came down again, and, looking very white and excited, held out a card-case and a pair of filigree earrings, asking Barthorne if he could account for their possession.

There ensued a dead silence, during which Barthorne surveyed the articles; then he said, "I know nothing about them," and cast a look at his wife which a demon might have tried in vain to surpass in devilishness of expression.

"I am afraid we shall have to trouble you to come with us," remarked one of the policemen.

"All right," replied Barthorne, rising and putting on his hat.

"And you too, ma'am," said the other, turning to Mrs. Barthorne.

She went upstairs to put on her bonnet, the officer accompanying her.

While she was engaged in "dressing" Miles took off his hat again, and brushing it round and round, said to Walter Chappell:

"If I am not back in time to finish the work for Phillips' job, will you see to it? Everything ought to be ready for the morning," and he looked meaningly at his brother-in-law.

"Yes; I will see to it," was the reply, uttered almost carelessly.

"Good bye for the present, then," said Barthorne, stretching out his hand, which Chappell grasped in silence.

At this juncture Mrs. Barthorne reappeared, and her husband intimated his readiness to depart.

"All is up with me. Remember!" whispered Miles to his brother-in-law, turning his head as he passed through the doorway. And with that utterance he left his home—never again to recross its threshold.

CHAPTER VII.

IN WHICH MAB COMES TO THE RESCUE.

WALTER CHAPPELL remained standing at the door of the cottage long after his sister and her husband had passed out of sight.

He was stunned by the suddenness and completeness of the calamity. He could scarcely realize what had occurred. It seemed incredible to him that Barthorne, a free man half an hour previously, was now a prisoner almost as good as convicted. This was not a case of mere suspicion; there was a certainty about the whole business which left not the merest loophole for hope to creep through.

That card-case, those filigree earrings must, he knew, prove damning evidence against his brother-in-law.

" And all through Lucy's folly," he thought.

For the third time in Miles Barthorne's experience a woman had upset the coach in which he meant to reach the goal of his life.

Feminine acquisitiveness—feminine vanity—feminine disregard of warning—feminine disbelief in the possibility of any danger not immediately apparent and immediate, had induced Mrs. Barthorne to rescue those articles which her husband laid out for destruction. She had purloined them from a (to him) useless heap, destined to be consumed in the smithy fire.

With all his foresight and calculation, Barthorne never imagined the possibility of such a casualty as this. He could have made affidavit that all the London detectives might search his house and find nothing compromising in it. He had been careful and cautious to an extent that Chappell often ridiculed, and to no purpose. From a totally unexpected quarter the blow had come. Those accursed knick-knacks, the like of which he would cheerfully have bought for his wife could he have imagined her soul longed for them, had compassed his ruin as effectually as chests full of plate, as cupboards filled with valuables belonging to other people.

" It was all up with him," as he said, and in a dim, confused kind of way Walter Chappell began to wonder if it would soon be all up with him also—if he might not be dragged into the affair as an accomplice, and haled off to jail, there to await his trial for all the sins he had committed.

If ever a man was suddenly converted, that man was Walter Chappell. If ever a man's eyes were opened to a perception of the deformity of wickedness, Walter Chappell's were in that hour.

Fear came upon him, and produced instant conviction that, after all, honesty was the best policy. He turned sick with dread ; and though he promised no votive offerings to his patron saint, no stained window or communion service to Tottenham Old Church—no gifts to the poor of the parish, or almshouse for necessitous widows—he did make a vow that, if he only escaped from the peril which menaced him, he would turn over a new leaf, forswear his evil ways, lead a better life, and never make another sovereign or crown-piece save in the way of legitimate trade.

"It is a bad job," remarked the policeman who still stayed in the house. "That is true enough; but fretting about things makes them no better."

"I am certain he had no notion anything of the sort was in his house," answered Chappell, more because he desired to make some reply than for any other reason.

The policeman shook his head and smiled. "Likely not," he said. "People don't generally keep such things lying about loose, if they know where they came from. I should say, now, he *had* no notion anything of the sort was in his house."

"Are you going to stay here long?" asked the other desperately.

"Well, yes. I suspect my mate can't be back yet awhile, and it will take a tidyish time to search the premises thoroughly. We haven't found much so far, you see."

"I do not believe there is anything more to find," answered Chappell; "and I have no doubt my sister will be able to account satisfactorily for having those articles in her possession. She is fond of jewellery and bargains, and——"

"Perhaps you don't happen to know where that there card-case and those slight-looking earrings came from?"

"No, that I don't," returned Chappell. "She never showed them to me; and I do not know how or where she got them."

"Where she got them is a different matter; though, perhaps, I could give a guess as to that also," was the reply. "But I do know where they came from. They were among a lot of things stolen last winter from Lane House, Enfield Chase. We have been looking out for some trace of them ever since. Tortoise-shell card-case, inlaid with mother-of-pearl—design, rose, thistle, and shamrock, lined with pink velvet—silver hinge and snap, and initials engraved on a silver plate at the top."

"But that proves nothing. She might have bought it from any one."

"She might; but then, you see, she will have to prove that."

"I thought," said Chappell, a little scornfully, "there was some saying about every man being considered innocent till he was proved guilty."

"I have heard a saying to that purpose myself," was the calm reply; "but I fancy it a great deal simpler to consider every man guilty till he is proved innocent. That is what we all do, at any rate."

"Well, talking about it won't mend the matter," remarked Chappell, "and standing idle won't clear either of them. I 'll just finish the work he spoke of, and then go and see some lawyer."

And so saying, he flung off his coat and waistcoat, turned up his shirt-sleeves, lit the forge fire, and commenced his labours.

"I didn't know you were a smith," remarked the policeman, leaning against the door-lintel, and idly looking on.

"Neither am I; but I have helped Barthorne now and then, and can do any simple work like this;" and Chappell, as he spoke, chucked about a dozen bits of steel into the fire.

"What are you making?" asked the other.

"Only a bar for a fender just now. I shall have to finish some chimney-rods before I go home."

"Well, that is queer, too," observed the policeman.

If he had only known how queer it was, this story would never have been written. Had he known that Chappell's laboured breathing arose not from the severity of his toil, but from the agony of apprehension he was experiencing, Policeman Blank's promotion had proved a very rapid affair; but, as matters stood, he had really not the faintest idea that before his very eyes the whole plant of a coiner was being destroyed.

He had been sent to Barthorne's to search for silver and gold and other valuables, and it never occurred to him that the bits of metal Chappell picked so carelessly from amongst the coal-dust on the forge, were moulds that had been employed to convert stolen goods into sterling coin. Even to the milling machine, which Chappell picked carelessly off the lathe, everything was destroyed before the policeman's eyes.

Then, when the whole mass was red hot, Chappell said:

"I must look after the child before I do any more."

"The child!" repeated Policeman Blank, with a sudden sense of having neglected his duty. "Where is she?"

"We had better go and see," answered her uncle. "Poor little thing! I forgot all about her."

They passed together through the kitchen, which was empty. Then they entered the parlour, furnished with some preten- sions to taste as well as comfort. The front door was still bolted, as the policeman had fastened it when he went into the forge with Chappell.

"Mab!" cried her uncle; but there came no answer, till they entered the bed-room where the discovery had been made which resulted in such a loss to Barthorne.

There, with the evening sun shining in upon her, lighting up everything in the room, and bathing the trees at Harringhay in a flood of golden colour, lay the child huddled up on the counterpane, her face hidden amongst the pillows, her right arm under her head, her left flung listlessly down, in an attitude of utter and hopeless grief.

As the two men entered she started up, and, pushing her hair back from her face, stained and swollen with weeping, asked:

"Did you want me, uncle? I—I——" And then she broke down, and began to cry bitterly.

"Don't do that, Mab," entreated Chappell. "Be a good girl, and dry your eyes, and I will take you to your mamma to-night."

But Mab only shook her head in reply; and then it suddenly dawned upon Walter Chappell that by some means she understood all that had been going on; that this child, for whose pleasure he made the copper medal—the suggester of such sin and misery—knew enough to convict her father and himself—to hang them, even, he thought, for Chappell's knowledge of the laws of his country was as limited as that possessed by nine hundred and ninety-nine persons out of every thousand.

He had been hot enough coming out of the forge; but now he turned as cold as ice. In a moment it was given to him to behold Nemesis in the shape of a thin, sallow-faced, dark-eyed child. First his sister, then his sister's daughter. Like Miles Barthorne, Walter Chappell felt it was too much, and so answered irritably:

"Well, at any rate, stop crying, for heaven's sake, and I will take you home with me till your mother comes back."

It was noticeable that Chappell did not say father and mother; but Policeman Blank, who had children of his own, and whose heart was stirred with a great compassion for the small creature who was in such great trouble, was not a clever individual, and had no eyes or thought for anything save Mab, for whom he felt the profoundest pity.

"Why, that is the best thing you can do with the poor dear," he remarked approvingly. "Take her away with you. She could not stay here all alone; and the neighbours might only torment her, even if they did take her in."

"I shan't trouble anybody to take in my sister's child, you may be sure of that," said Chappell a little indignantly.

He was more confident now. If once he could get Mab away, and ascertain exactly how much she knew, he might make some effort for his own preservation.

"Don't cry any more than you can help, Mab. I shall have finished some work I am doing for your father in half an hour at the outside, and then we will go away to London together. You will like to go with Uncle Walter, won't you, dear?" he asked, with more tenderness in his tone than he had yet evinced when addressing her. She was a person to conciliate now. She had ceased, in his eyes, to be a mere child; she was a possible witness; and already Mab unconsciously reaped a certain benefit from her change of position.

"Yes," she answered, "I shall like to go with you, if I may."

"Then have your bonnet on in half an hour," said Walter Chappell, "and then we will start for London together."

Often afterwards he wondered how he did it—wondered how he had been able to speak so quietly, to act so naturally, to think so rapidly. He wondered how he was calm enough to talk as he did, to finish his work, even to the chimney-stays he had talked about, to ask the policeman to give him a helping hand by holding the iron he was fashioning, to suggest the desirability of beer to that functionary, and request him to draw from one of the casks which had given offence to Barthorne's neighbours sufficient to quench the thirst of both.

Shortly afterwards Chappell and his niece left the house— not much too soon, as it turned out subsequently, for they had not bade the policeman "Good evening," and been gone fifteen minutes, before the more diligent officer who found the card-case returned, and hearing of their departure, said breathlessly:

"You never let Chappell go without following him!"

"What should I follow Chappell for?" was the answer. "There is nothing against the man."

"That is as it may be," was the reply. "At any rate, I must go back and hear what is to be done now. Don't let anybody in till I come back again, on any pretence whatsoever."

"All right," answered the other, and closed and bolted the door.

Meanwhile Walter Chappell and his companion were walking to London. He had asked which she should like best, to take the omnibus at the High Cross, or walk to the Cock at Highbury. Without a minute's hesitation, she answered: .

"Oh! walk, please, uncle; and do let us go across the fields."

So, hand in hand, they walked down the Black Boy Lane and along that path which is a short cut over the triangular bit of common which abuts on Hanger Lane; and then they climbed the stile which gives access to a path leading away to the Green Lanes, and at the end of the path, crossing the main road at the Tile Kilns, they wended their way over the New River, and so to Hornsey Wood House, since pulled down, in order that the new Finsbury Park might not retain a vestige of anything old, picturesque, or romantic about it.

When they had passed the old tavern—a drawing of which may be seen by the curious in Hone's "Everyday Book"—and turned sharp off to their left and entered the path which formerly led straight down to the Seven Sisters Road, the girl, after first looking cautiously round, to make sure no one was near at hand, said:

"I have got something, uncle; what must I do with it?" and she drew out of her small pocket a curious foreign-looking dagger, the handle of which was rich in ornament, the design being marked here and there by precious stones, not, perhaps, of intrinsically great value, but which conferred an imposing appearance of brilliancy on the pattern.

Chappell had never seen this before. He turned the weapon over in his hand, looking at it curiously, then asked:

"Where did you get this, Mab?"

"I knew mamma had it hidden away," answered the child. "I saw her take it; I saw her hide it. She told me I must never tell any one. She and papa had a quarrel that morning. She wanted to keep it, and said no one would ever be the wiser; and he asked her if she was mad, to think of such a thing; and he took it away and put it—you know where; and then some one came to speak to him about work, and while he was outside she took it out again and hid it. After the men came this evening I remembered, and when they were gone"—there was a break in the narrative for a moment—"when the one man and papa and mamma were gone, I crept upstairs and looked for it, and when everything was quiet, I thought I would go out and throw it into some ditch; but when I came down I found the door bolted, and I dared not unfasten it. So I went upstairs again, and lay down on the bed, and said my prayers, and all the hymns and good verses that would stay in my head, over and over again. I said them till I was nearly silly, and then you came, uncle."

Prayers, hymns, verses, with any good in them! Could such utterances really have been in a house where sin had taken up a permanent habitation? Prayers, hymns, verses. Vaguely Walter Chappell found himself mentally repeating, in a sort of amazed wonder, those three words, whilst all the time his mind was busy conjecturing where the dagger had come from, marvelling how he should dispose of it, and puzzling himself as to what he ought to do with his niece.

When once again, after crossing the Seven Sisters Road, they came upon the course of the New River, he paused, uncertain whether to drop the weapon into the water or not. Again, however, his good genius, which had come to his rescue more than once that evening, stood his friend.

He was well known to many persons by sight along that route. He had traversed the road, indeed, far too often to suppose it possible for even a small action of the kind to escape notice from some chance acquaintance who might be near enough to recognize him. No; he must run no risks. He must carry the accursed thing on with him still farther into the heart of the great metropolis, and there, where even temporary possession could never be brought home to him, lose this fresh evidence of his sister's folly and cupidity.

"Shall I take it, uncle?" asked the girl, as they continued their course after that lingering look at the waters of Sir Hugh Myddelton. "I am not afraid now."

He stopped, and pulling her a little forward, so that he could see her face distinctly, said :

"Mab, you frighten me. In heaven's name, when and where have you learnt all your wisdom?"

"I could not help learning," she answered simply, tears filling her great dark eyes as she spoke. "I could not help hearing and knowing. Many and many a night, when you all thought I was asleep, and you were busy, I have cried till I could cry

no longer, with my head under the bed-clothes, for fear mamma
would hear me and be angry."

"Did you know what we were doing, Mab?" he inquired,
with an irrepressible shudder.

"Yes; you were making money," she replied; "and mamma
was always saying to me, when you had made enough we should
go away and have carriages, and horses, and servants, and live
like ladies and gentlemen; and used to be angry with me for being
frightened when papa was out late at night. I always was afraid
something dreadful had happened to him. I did not know what;
but now something dreadful has happened," and the child, who
had forgotten her sorrow for a minute, began to cry again quietly,
but, nevertheless, bitterly.

Chappell did not make an effort to console her. It was growing dark as they emerged from Highbury Terrace and entered
the Holloway Road, through those iron gates which stood
opposite to the old station of the North London Railway. He
knew she would attract little if any notice from the passers-by.
Nevertheless, perhaps with that certain instinct of self-preserva-
tion which acts as an additional sense to so many persons whose
ordinary complement of senses would, in extremity, serve them
but little, he selected the least frequented side of the road leading to London, and walked far away from the shops under the
shade of the trees which make that part of Islington seem so
rural to persons accustomed to the more modern suburbs, where
groves of brick and mortar have taken the place of forest trees,
and porticoes of a more or less pretentious design, with flights
of stone steps leading to nowhere in particular, and great bay
windows, affording opportunities for a fine view of over the way
and up and down the crescent, have elbowed creepers, and
climbing roses, and clustering vines out of fashion.

When they had walked some distance along Islington High
Street, always keeping, as I have said, on the darkest side of
that wide thoroughfare, Chappell suddenly changed his course,
and struck right across into Barnsbury. In one of the loneliest
and quietest roads which still abound in that locality, he dropped
the dagger, then doubling and twisting, the pair retraced their
steps and made straight for the Angel.

Arrived there, he crossed the then Pentonville Road, and,
almost following the crow's flight, walked on towards Clerkenwell.

Where he had lodged in the days of his apprenticeship he still remained, and the mere lapse of time, to say nothing of his own uniformly good behaviour in that familiar home, had given him a pleasant sort of proprietorship in the house, where he came and went with a sense of greater freedom than if it had been his own.

For a man is never quite free to come or to go when he has a mother, or wife, or sister, or housekeeper, or servants, to scrutinize his proceedings, whereas the old lady with whom Chappell lodged had her own affairs to attend to, and never attempted to obtain a vested interest in the young man's business.

He paid his way, and gave her very little trouble, and she, honest soul, never troubled her head as to what time he reached home at night, or whether, indeed, he ever reached it at all.

It was in one of those large houses in Red Lion Street which are now let out in suites at five and six shillings a week for work-rooms and tenth-rate offices, that Walter Chappell had resided ever since he first went to Nelson Brothers.

He had began with one small room on the third floor, and he now occupied three rooms on the first.

Mab Barthorne knew her uncle's house well. She had spent many a pleasant hour there. She and her father and mother had often taken tea in the cheerful drawing-room before going to the theatre, or Astley's, or any one of the other places of amusement, visiting which was the only relaxation Barthorne permitted himself.

She was familiar with every print on the walls, with every book in the room; no drawer had been safe from her investigation, no cupboard in her uncle's small domain held anything capable of concealment from her inquiring spirit. But now as Mab crawled wearily up the staircase, her little shawl awry, her bonnet only kept on the back of her neck by the strength of the strings which tied it, her handkerchief wet as if it had come out of a washtub, and her gloves damp with holding her handkerchief, she felt as if life even in Red Lion Street was not worth having.

One of the things the world, so wise in many matters, will never know for certain, is the age at which a precocious child begins to have a keen knowledge of good and evil, so far as good and evil affect itself and those belonging to it.

Now, essentially Mab Barthorne was a precocious child—precocious in her sensibility, precocious in her sense.

For many a long day she had carried about a woman's heart in a child's body. No need to tell her to be cautious and reticent—no need to put her on guard about babbling home affairs to the multitude. As Walter Chappell recalled the nature of the deed she had performed that evening, the words she had used in speaking of her own fears and trouble, he felt he might safely leave Mab to choose her own course for herself; that any warnings he could give would only bewilder her, and tend to disturb that subtle instinct which already had stood her father —still unconscious of the benefit—in such stead.

All he insisted upon was that she should eat a biscuit and drink a little hot negus before going to bed.

"You must swallow it," he said, holding the glass, which she had already rejected, again towards her. "I cannot have you laid up on my hands now. They are too full as it is."

"Can they do anything to you, uncle?" she whispered, clasping her hands round his neck as she bade him good night, putting her lips close to his ear to ask the question.

"I think not. I hope not," he answered. "I knew nothing of the card-case or the earrings. I did not know till to-night where they came from."

"Did you know nothing of all the silver and gold we used to have at our house?"

"I knew it was there, my dear, that was all."

"Then how did you help papa to make money, if——"

He checked the inevitable question he felt coming, and said:

"Do not let us speak of it any more, Mab, now. Some day, when you are older, when you can understand everything more fully, I will tell you the whole truth; but I will tell you one thing, my dear, now—that if it pleases God that no harm comes to me through this matter, I will try to be a better man in the future than I have been in the past; yes, whether harm comes or not, I will try hard."

And thus Walter Chappell published the vow he had made standing beside the cottage door at West Green.

After his niece was in bed and asleep, he started off in search of a lawyer to undertake Barthorne's defence. He knew of one residing in Guildford Street, willing to attend business at any hour of the day or night: to him — avoiding the House of Correction on his way—Chappell accordingly went. By the time he had told the solicitor all he wished to tell him—or ever, in fact, meant to tell any one concerning the business—and had again reached Red Lion Street, it was growing late, or rather early, for eleven o'clock had struck by St. James', Clerkenwell, before he left his lodgings for Mr. Westroe's house, and as he turned out of Snow Hill, which route he had selected on his way home, he heard St. Sepulchre's chime out first the four quarters making a perfect hour, and then solemnly ONE.

Entering Red Lion Street, not from Clerkenwell Green or St. John's Gate side, but from an obscure little lane running almost parallel with Cow Cross Street, Chappell noticed a man standing on the opposite side of the way, looking up at the windows of the house he occupied.

With a steady tread, Chappell paced on towards Clerkenwell Green, and then made his way down the alley leading to St. John's Square, and thence to Red Lion Street.

The man was still on the opposite side of the way, engaged at the moment in an apparent attempt to light a pipe.

Then the young man knew he was suspected and watched.

"Let them watch," he thought, "they can prove nothing against me now."

About the same hour when Chappell made that mental observation the policeman left in charge of Barthorne's cottage at West Green, feeling, after a long sleep in an arm-chair, somewhat stiff and chilly, rose in order to stretch himself, and walked towards the door, with the intention of looking out and seeing what sort of night it was.

As he stood, only half awake, fumbling first for the latch and then for the bolt, there was a report as if a cannon had been fired off at his ear, there was a flash of light in the smithy, followed by a crashing of bricks as if fifty Irish labourers had let their hods fall from the top of a three-story house.

It seemed as if a whole pane of glass could not be left in the cottage, and, in a panic of fear, the man somehow opened the door and rushed out into the night.

When morning dawned it was found that the whole of Barthorne's forge had been blown out. There was a huge rent in the side of the smithy, the bellows were in ribbons, of the forge not one brick remained on another. The tools were scattered about in all directions, and the glass in the skylight lay shivered round the garden and the adjacent fields.

How it was blown up the authorities never could discover; why it was blown up, those most interested in Barthorne's secrets were utterly unable to imagine : not a trace of anything sus·picious was found amongst the *débris*, save some particles of copper adhering to fragments of fire-clay. The police had a theory that Barthorne must nave possessed a hidden furnace, where all the plate he was supposed to have stolen was at once melted down ; and this idea received confirmation from the fact that, beyond the card-case and the filigree earrings, no article of value, save what the accused had legitimately pur·chased, could be found on his premises, and that the most diligent inquiry, and enormous offers of reward, failed to dis·cover where any of the stolen goods had been disposed of— save in one instance, and that exception only proved the rule.

Four days after Miles Barthorne's arrest, a poor old woman was given in charge for attempting to pawn a certain foreign dagger, she being unable to account satisfactorily for its pos·session.

Before the magistrate she repeated the statement she had made when a police officer was sent for by the pawnbroker.

"I found it, your honour," she sobbed. "I picked it up in a street leading out of the Liverpool Road ; I don't remember the name of the street, but I was coming back from doing a hard day's washing, your worship, and the lady would speak to my character."

"Now, will you be silent?" interrupted the magistrate ; then turning to the constable, he said, "Some special importance attaches to this dagger, I think ?"

"Yes, your worship," answered the constable. "It is one of the articles stolen from Hillview House, Sir Alexander Kelvey's place at Highgate, the time David M'Callum was murdered."

Walter Chappell, reading the *Times* at the chop-house where he usually dined, came suddenly upon this paragraph.

He laid down his knife and fork, left the paper on the table, paid his reckoning in silence, and walked out into the open air.

The fact of the murder and the fact of the robbery had not been made known previously in connection one with the other.

But now in a moment the dagger he himself had dropped

supplied a hitherto missing link, which, truth to tell, he **in some** vague sort of way had always dreaded to find.

Mab's premature wisdom had saved her father's life—that life so nearly risked by his wife's folly.

But Miles Barthorne was a murderer.　Through all the business of the day—through the hours of the night, when he lay awake and restless, in the snatches of troubled sleep that came to him at intervals, that refrain rung through his brain, till his mind grew sick and tired with its persistence as much as with its horror.

Miles Barthorne was a murderer.　The man who was lying in jail upon a comparatively trivial charge had blood on his hands—the blood of a fellow-creature who had never wronged him or his.

Though a thousand witnesses came forward to prove an *alibi*, Walter Chappell felt he never could be persuaded of his innocence.

"He murdered the man," thought Chappell: "and if that dagger had been found in his house, they would have hung him to a certainty."

As matters turned out afterwards, however, Barthorne's accomplice in outwitting the authorities at the Mint felt that if Mab had left the weapon where her mother hid it away, the lives of many people would subsequently have proved much **more** endurable than they did.

CHAPTER VIII.

SENTENCED.

To Miles Barthorne the agonies of years were concentrated in the short time which elapsed before he knew that his forge was destroyed, and that nothing to inculpate him in the Highgate murder had been, after diligent search, discovered by the police in his house. If his wife, notwithstanding her knowledge of the peril incurred, could have been such a simpleton—he put the last word differently, and prefaced his version with a couple of strong adjectives—as to hide away two such trumpery articles as those on the strength of which he had been taken in charge, Barthorne's common sense told him there was nothing else—nothing which she might have refrained from secreting.

Once again a woman's hand had dashed the cup of success from his lips. Through the act of a woman, and that woman his wife, every hope of his existence was destroyed; and it might be also—well, this was not a contingency on which he cared to dwell, though at intervals it would force its presence upon him, and compel him to think of that morning's work at Highgate—of the dead man's living brother—of a charge different from theft—of an attentive jury and a stern judge—the verdict, "guilty," and the sentence, "to be hanged by the neck till you are dead."

Not a nice sort of possibility, this, for a man to have to try to shun, with nothing to distract his attention, nothing to divert his thoughts, nothing to lean against save uncertainty, nothing to be quite sure of except that he stood in a position of fearful peril. There have been men, it is said, whose hair has turned grey in a single night containing less misery than Miles Barthorne endured for nights and days, which seemed to lengthen themselves out into an eternity of torture.

If M'Callum had but known all his brother's murderer passed through after his arrest, he must have felt satisfied. David, sleeping in Hornsey Churchyard, was amply revenged. The mills of Time already had Barthorne between their stones, and imperceptibly, it is true, but still certainly, were grinding his heart. He could not have suffered as he did had the human fiat gone forth. No condemned cell ever contained a wretch who suffered such fear as Barthorne had to bear and show no sign. But relief came at last. After two remands he was committed for trial with no fresh evidence against him.

Walter Chappell had been taken into custody, and, after one remand, discharged, with a remark from the magistrate, that although he thought the police had not, under the circumstances, exceeded their duty in arresting him, he felt bound to say he left the court without a stain on his character—which was certainly very gratifying to Mr. Walter Chappell.

Mr. Westroe, acting for him, remarked to his client that he might deem himself extremely lucky; for it was the fact that the lawyer never for one moment thought of believing Chappell innocent. He considered it not only possible, but probable, that the older and cleverer criminal had drawn the younger into the commission of sins he would never have eliminated out of the shallows of his own imagination; but although Chappell declared with many an asseveration that he had neither head nor hand in any of the robberies of which Barthorne was suspected, Mr. Westroe's opinion did not waver in the least.

The day of the trial came, and every available seat in the poking court was filled with people who had known Barthorne either privately or in the way of business. Tottenham sent its representatives, and West Green also. M‘Callum headed a select party from Highgate; and gentlemen who had availed themselves of Barthorne's skill as a workman, appeared as interested listeners, anxious to hear whether, in the course of the trial, any light would be thrown on the manner in which their own plate-chests had been emptied.

Barthorne's first London friend, the Tottenham smith, had come up from his country home to give evidence as to the prisoner's good character whilst in his employment, and probably his wife would have accompanied him, had he given her the faintest inkling of the nature of the business which took him to town.

Taking public opinion round, those whose goods had not been stolen, or who possessed no goods to steal, felt some sympathy for the man; but no one felt any sympathy for the woman. She had never been popular—never tried to make herself popular. Wives spoke of her as a "stuck-up piece of goods," and husbands considered it a "main hard thing that a fellow who worked as Barthorne had worked should be sent to jail because a woman fancied a card-case she could never use, and a pair of earrings she could never wear."

Indeed, had it not been for that ugly doubt as to whether Barthorne were not a murderer as well as a thief, popular feeling would have been entirely in his favour.

Certainly since he first came to Tottenham people never spoke so well of him as when he stood in the dock at the Old Bailey.

Nothing had been found in his house except the card-case and the earrings, and who knew how Mrs. Barthorne had come to be possessed of them? Bets were laid as to whether he would get off or not; and there was much speculation as to what the nature of the sentence might be, in the event of a conviction.

In any case, let the result of the trial be what it would, the Barthornes could never again hold up their heads about West Green—which idea so pleased those whom their prosperity had irritated, that the bulk of the interested court hoped Barthorne would be able to make a good defence.

But in this hope they were doomed to disappointment.

Barthorne pleaded "Guilty," Mrs. Barthorne pleaded "Not Guilty."

For very sufficient reasons Mr. Westroe had advised both husband and wife to answer "Guilty;" but Mrs. Barthorne declined following his counsel, and engaged separate professional assistance for herself.

The result proved her superior wisdom; for an intelligent jury found that there was no evidence to convict her, and returned a verdict of acquittal.

There was a stir and murmur in the court after the foreman announced the decision to which himself and his eleven brethren had arrived—a stir and murmur, not of approval; but the crier, in a rich beery voice, shouted out "Silence!" and the sounds died away.

Indeed, there was almost a dead silence while Miles Barthorne, now alone in the dock, stood awaiting his sentence.

After a long preamble from the judge it came at last: To be transported for seven years.

Seven years! The words fell like a blow on Barthorne. He turned white to his lips, and the court, judge, jury, and spectators, swam round before his eyes.

One of the turnkeys, thinking him about to faint, put out a hand to catch him, and the action, slight though it was, steadied the man's nerves.

"Let me alone, will you?" he said in a savage whisper. "I don't deserve it, but I can bear it;" and then, without once glancing round the audience, without taking one last look at freedom ere going into servitude, he turned and went away from the gaze of those who had known and envied him at the time when he lived at West Green—a time that seemed now farther distant than the days of his childhood.

The game had almost brought him fortune—the play had nearly been successful. If David M'Callum had not met him that morning, or if he could so far have shaken off the superstitious repugnance he felt to touching the corpse as to bring himself to lay even a finger on the dead man's body, suspicion had never fallen upon him.

Or if—and this was even a bitterer thought—he had either not married, or married a different woman, suspicion might have fallen, and still done him no great harm.

"Yes," he thought, "from childhood until now women have cursed my life. If ever a woman works evil for me again, it will be my own fault—that I swear."

Whilst he lay in prison, the woman whose act had brought this last calamity upon him was searching London for some trace of her brother and her child.

Both had disappeared. They were vanished as utterly as though the waters of oblivion had closed over their heads.

Through his solicitor, Barthorne sent her a message, charging her not to come near him.

"Voluntarily," he remarked to Chappell before the trial, "I will never see your sister again."

"And certainly you will not see much of my sister's brother," added Chappell mentally.

Mrs. Barthorne, however, was determined to see her husband again, and, armed with an order, repaired to the prison where he waited till the time should come for him to leave England.

She threw herself on her knees before him, and in an agony of grief besought his forgiveness.

"I will go to Australia also," she sobbed; "I would go to the world's end with you. I will do anything you tell me, if you will only forgive me."

Miles Barthorne listened to her with a set, hard face. When she had quite finished her petition, when she had exhausted her lamentations and tired herself with weeping, he said :

"Will no one take this woman away before I kill her?" and then with a shiver, as his own sentence recalled something he was always trying to forget, he retreated to the farthest corner of his cell, and stood there, with his eyes averted, while the turnkeys carried his wife into the passage, and, locking the door, parted them.

For months she haunted Mr. Westroe's offices, in hopes of hearing something of her child and brother, but Mr. Westroe was as ignorant of their whereabouts as she. At the end of a year, however, she obtained a clue which induced her to think Walter Chappell and the child had gone to America ; and thither, not being destitute of money, she started in quest of them.

And thus the family dropped out from amongst the acquaintances who had known them in their days of apparent prosperity. Their very name became an almost forgotten word. Strangers came and strangers went about West Green and Tottenham, and the story of the handsome smith was remembered but by a very few old inhabitants of those neighbourhoods.

In or near London, it is not difficult to compass being forgotten. The tide of human life flows so fast through the great metropolis, that a man's memory scarcely lasts so long in the recollection of his fellows as a name written on the sand remains legible on the sea-shore.

And indeed, even at Abbotsleigh and around Spindlethorpe, Miles, the illegitimate son of the old Squire, had dropped out of mind.

Glendy was dead; his widow had sold his business, and left that part of the country.

Mrs. Barthorne was dead likewise, and another Squire than John—who gave fifty pounds to enable the discarded heir to learn an honest trade—reigned at the Hall.

The years which, to contemplate in prospective, seemed so long and so capable of bringing wealth and position to the son of the bond-woman, had flitted by silently and swiftly, and the result was that, with oceans stretching between himself and

England, Barthorne was working out the days and the months of his heavy sentence, whilst the very fact of his ever having existed was an almost forgotten memory.

Not by one man, however. James M'Callum remembered: the blood of his dead brother still, to his morbid fancy, seemed crying aloud for vengeance on his murderer.

—

CHAPTER IX.

THE REV. DIONYSIUS AND MRS. WRIGHT.

ABOUT six years after the day when Miles Barthorne received his sentence of expatriation, when the story of his sin and his punishment, and the other story of his suspected sin and punishment still deferred, remained only in those short and significant records which can be inspected free at the Old Bailey, and in the memories of a few people connected with the criminal, the Reverend Dionysius Wright, Rector of Fisherton-on-Thames, found himself in a difficulty.

Inclusively at the same time Selina, wife of the above, found herself in a difficulty also.

To the Reverend Dionysius and Mrs. Wright this experience was no novelty. From the first year of their marriage they had found themselves at intervals in precisely the same position.

Difficulty, pecuniary difficulty, had for years ate with them, drank with them, slept and walked with them, boarded and lodged with them; it pervaded the air they breathed, and was part and parcel of their being. Had a legacy been bequeathed to them, and the possibility of paying their way for a time without anxiety been presented, they would have felt out of their natural element, got rid of their money, and plunged into the old slough of debt, as soon as might be. Therefore, it was not the fact of impecuniosity which troubled the reverend gentleman so grievously. It was merely that, for once in his varied experience, he really could perceive no way of relieving, even temporarily, his embarrassments.

It is not at all likely that when the Rev. Dionysius started in life he voluntarily chose the path he had for years and years been traversing, yet he drifted into it very early in his career, and it was now too late, as he himself sometimes said with a sigh, to retrace his steps.

Despondency, however, was not the failing of Mrs. Wright. She had a fixed belief, that if her husband could only induce his creditors to wait a little longer, and still a little, help would come.

Help had come so often, and from such unlooked-for quarters, that Mrs. Wright was sometimes wont to declare it would be downright rebellion against Providence to imagine it would not arrive once more, all in Heaven's good time.

"You may depend upon it, Dion," she said, in a tone of solemn conviction, "that although we cannot hear its footsteps, assistance is on its way to us even now."

In the same manner as we are told orphanages and other charitable institutions are occasionally supported entirely by the power of faith, so hitherto Mr. and Mrs. Wright had, by means of faith in their fellow-creatures and the goodness of Providence, managed somehow to pay baker and butcher, and other tradespeople, when the day came on which those individuals declared, severally and collectively, they would not wait another hour for their money.

But a crisis had at length occurred. It commenced about eighteen months after Mr. Wright's induction to the living of Fisherton. A bill which had been renewed and held over, and renewed and held over again, for a series of periods of which the Reverend Dion's memory could retain no accurate recollection, was now—in consequence of the original possessor's death —in the hands of a very different man, of a man who "considcred business was business," who did not intend to let him-self be cheated " by Jew or Gentile, parson or layman," who " meant to have his money by fair means or foul," and who gave the Rector of Fisherton to understand that some definite understanding on the subject must be arrived at.

As a definite understanding on the subject of money, unless he were to be the recipient, was the last thing on earth poor Mr. Wright ever desired, he tried to stave the matter off, and actually did succeed in doing this for a period of nearly ten weeks.

At the end of that time came a lawyer's letter. Mr. Wright called to see the lawyer, and obtained a fortnight's longer grace. No remittance, however, arriving, even when a week longer than the fortnight had passed, a writ was served upon the Rector, and in twelve days more judgment was obtained against him. Then of course all the household goods—all the well-worn furniture, all the patternless carpets, all the faded curtains, the old out-of-tune six-octave square pianoforte, and other miscel-laneous effects—including a half-length portrait of Mr. Wright, in gown and bands, holding a prayer-book in his hand, having to his right an oriel window, and to his left an old-fashioned cabinet, decorated with sundry vases and pieces of old china; and another half-length portrait, this time of Mrs. Wright, in curls and a low dress, holding a lace handkerchief and a rose in her left hand, whilst with the right she was gathering jessamine from the outside of the oriel window above referred to,—all these things, representing to the clergyman and his wife the comforts and elegances of a refined home, as well as the luxuries of departed days, were at the mercy of the destroyer.

But the destroyer was merciful ; though Mrs. Wright, in the privacy of her husband's study, called him a brute, and declared the wretch had so unnerved her she could scarcely say her prayers, he really did act so very badly.

In consideration of Mr. Wright handing his solicitor ten pounds down, and signing promissory notes payable at intervals extending over a year, he agreed to give further time. The ten pounds, however, only covered the costs ; so the debt remained as much as ever, *plus* the interest.

"Dear dear dear ! dear dear!" said Mr. Wright, with a little click of the tongue which sufficiently bespoke his nationality without the help of the soft pleasant accent and cheerful brogue that, added to his good-tempered face and genial manner, had carried the Rector through so many difficulties and enabled him to clear triumphantly many an awkward fence. "Now, to think of that money having gone all for nothing—positively for nothing, Selina—and the poor dears wanting new dresses so badly, and you looking like a ghost for need of a glass of decent wine."

"Don't trouble yourself about me or the children, Dion," said Mrs. Wright, in a tone meant to be valiant, but which broke towards the end of the sentence into a hysterical whimper; "you have enough to bear without us—though I must say it seems strange and hard to think we find it so much more difficult to make the two ends meet since you have been a rector than ever we did in the days when you were only a curate."

This was one of the pleasant fictions with which Mrs. Wright entertained her family and friends.

Since they came together she and her husband had never fitted their expenditure to their income, but in lieu thereof they had fitted the incomes of very many other people to their expenditure, and the children's dresses and the decent glass of wine so pathetically referred to by Mr. Wright had, as natural consequences, generally been obtainable.

To do Mr. and Mrs. Wright strict justice, during their whole married life it did not once occur to either of them that the words "for worse" and "for poorer" could have any meaning applicable to themselves. In every single respect, save that they were always in debt, they lived better and fared more sumptuously than their parents had done before them. They had really never been in what could be called absolute poverty, save such as was caused by their own bad management; but the reason, beyond bad management, of the chronic difficulties in which they were involved, was that neither understood the meaning of the sentence "doing without."

They could do without, of course, when they were compelled to do so ; but given that Mrs. Wright had five pounds—a not unusual occurrence, by the way—and she was quite certain to spend the greater part of the amount on a fancy, not a necessary.

In a word, she worked herself up over their debts and their duns to a state of nervous excitement which even the typical glass of wine failed to subdue, and all the while the beer went unpaid for; and in like manner, when the doctor's tonics proved unavailing, Mr. Wright was wont, in the happy days when people spoke of him as a struggling curate, to bring her home mock turtle from Scarlett's and grapes from Moses'—the time a noisy butcher was clamouring for payment for the family sirloin, and the greengrocer thought people ought not to eat a peck of potatoes a day if they never intended settling for them.

Upon what principle it was that the Rev. Dionysius and Mrs. Wright had made up their minds society was bound to maintain them no one ever could tell, unless, indeed, it was because they had a quiver full of children.

So exclusively personal an affair might not in the hands of less skilful manipulators have proved a peg strong enough whereon to hang claims for money, clothes, food, house-rent, taxes, and any other trifles which they found necessary to their comfort and well-being; but the Wrights were very skilful.

Had the mandate to replenish the earth been just issued, had the Deluge only just subsided, had there been no surplus population, had babies not been appearing at extremely short intervals upon the face of the earth for nearly six thousand years, had there seemed any immediate danger of the human race coming to an untimely end, the Wrights could not possibly have comported themselves more like benefactors to the world than was the case.

"God has been very good to them," said an old nurse, who, after living with Mrs. Wright's mother for a score of years, came over to see that Miss Selena's children were properly cared for. "He took seven to Himself."

Which was quite true. Nevertheless, after deducting the defunct seven, nine remained. "Of as fine boys and girls as you would wish to see," the Rev. Dion was wont to remark.

Whether they were fine or not might, despite the reverend gentleman's dictum, be a matter of opinion; but there can be no doubt that scarcely any one ever did wish to see them.

Of their mother's *savoir-faire*—of their father's joviality—of the combined light-heartedness of both parents, they had not inherited a trace.

Excepting during the Sunday services, the life of an ordinary clergyman is essentially one of small things. The doings, and sayings, and affairs of persons whose doings, sayings, and affairs are usually and discreetly ignored, form, as many of us are unhappily aware, the staple of conversation in most parsonages—and the gossip of daily life is not always edifying for children to hear. Further, the young Wrights were priggish and self-conscious, as the sons and daughters of clergymen often are in their innocent teens—a little proud also, and very much disposed to give themselves airs on the strength of their pedigree.

Wherever they went—and in the way of his profession Mr. Wright had to make many homes for his family—the young ladies and gentlemen were rather apt to hold their heads very high, and to turn unequivocal cold shoulders to persons whom they were pleased to consider as not quite on a level with themselves.

"Comes from the mother's family," Mr. Wright was wont to explain apologetically when any of these pleasant ways gave offence in quarters where it was desirable offence should not be given. "Poor dear old Mr. Curran was the proudest man I ever met—most ridiculously proud—Irish pride, you understand. Though Irish myself, and come of decent enough people—Admiral Wright, who did such good service at Trafalgar, was my father's cousin, and my mother's aunt married a nephew of the fourth Lord Castlebar—I am thankful to say I know nothing of the feeling; self-respect is enough for me. But, as I was saying, my children inherit the failing from their mother's family: poor dears! the world will soon teach them better. They will understand, ere many years pass, how much happier it would have been for them if their father had been a cheesemonger, or something of that sort, than a clergyman possessed of a few poor talents which he has tried not to hide in a napkin."

Whatever claim Mr. Wright's progenitors may have had to social consideration in the days of the Admiral and Lord Castlebar's nephew, it is quite certain there was not much in his own youthful reminiscences calculated to justify so slighting an observation, even concerning a man who wore an apron and stood behind a counter.

But many a mile stretched between Ireland and England, and many a year between Mr. Wright's boyhood and the time when he was presented to the living of Fisherton.

"A poor thing," he said confidentially. "His Lordship might just as well have given me one nearer town and worth a couple of hundred a year more."

But this really was scarcely grateful on the part of Mr. Wright, considering he had written to "His Lordship"—in whose gift the living was—with tears in his eyes, a letter of thanks, part of which ran as follows :—

"Your Lordship's note, received this morning, and read with feelings of mingled thankfulness and astonishment, marks the beginning of a new epoch in the life of myself and family.

"The cruel bugbear which has hitherto haunted my life, prostrating my energies and nullifying my efforts for the benefit of my fellow-creatures, has been banished by your Lordship for ever. I see a future of as utter peace and contentment as this poor world can afford stretching out before me, like sunshine lighting up a fair valley. The prayers of myself and my family will ascend night and morning for the prosperity and happiness, temporal and eternal, of my noble and generous patron, to whom I beg to subscribe myself,

"His Lordship's devoted and grateful servant,
"DIONYSIUS WRIGHT."

And, after all, poor Mr. Wright did not find himself in a land of peace ; he was met in the fair valley with that serious difficulty of which I shall have more to say in the next chapter.

—◦—

CHAPTER X.

"JUST LIKE AN INSPIRATION."

THE Rev. Mr. Wright had some curious ideas on the subject of time. When he was expecting money, weeks lengthened themselves out into months. When any one else was expecting money from him, months shrank into weeks.

"I give you my honour," he was wont to remark, "it does not seem ten days since I signed that note which you tell me is now due. Oh! of course you are right. I do not dispute the accuracy of your statement for a moment, but I really am taken quite by surprise." And then Mr. Wright would gently move aside the obnoxious document his creditor wished him to examine, and say, "Dear, dear, dear! what am I to do? Cannot you suggest any way out of the difficulty, my good, kind friend?"

Sometimes the good, kind friend would offer to renew the bill, but sometimes he resolutely refused to suggest any way out of the difficulty, except that Mr. Wright should hand him over the amount due, in which latter case Mr. Wright had to appeal to one of his many other good, kind friends, and repeat his statement concerning the extraordinary way in which the three or four months had fled by, supplementing that lamentation with an emphatic statement that he ought to have received his own salary or the interest on his wife's fortune four weeks previous to the moment when he was speaking, and that neither had yet been remitted to him.

It would have been a most extraordinary thing if the interest on Mrs. Wright's modest portion had reached him, seeing that within six months of their marriage they had transferred it for a period of five years—a process which at the end of that period bore repetition, and had gone on bearing repetition during the nineteen summers and winters of what they both were in the habit of calling their "happy wedded life."

And indeed they had been very happy till they came to Fisherton. When they first came to Fisherton they were very happy also. They laid out all sorts of plans for the future.

"First and foremost," said the genial Dionysius, "we must repay every farthing the generous Samaritans have lent or given for our use."

"I don't think I should, dear," remarked Mrs. Wright. "I am sure none of them ever gave with any idea of return. They knew perfectly well how we were situated. I am certain we never made any false pretences. Whatever they spared to us was lent to the Lord; and we know He won't forget it to them."

"And He has not forgotten us, Selina," Mr. Wright replied, a little severely, pointing at the same time to the rectory garden, which sloped down to the Thames. "And we must not forget that some of our benefactors gave out of their little instead of their abundance.”

“Very well, Dion; I suppose you know best,” said Mrs. Wright, in a tone which implied she supposed nothing of the sort. She was a more practical person in some respects than he, and knew perfectly well a moonlight view of the river would not provide butcher’s meat for a growing-up family.

In the first excitement of his new position, with sovereigns in his pocket, she thought it possible her husband might be so Quixotic as to send back money to people “who did not expect it, and who did not need it;” but her doubt of Mr. Wright’s personal prudence was not well founded.

It is quite true that he did actually procure a post-office order for five shillings, and send that order to a very dear friend who had lent it to him the day he received his Lordship’s letter; but there Mr. Wright’s voluntary honesty began and ended. And perhaps it was quite as well for the good Samaritans that he stopped at that point, as he certainly would eventually have made his repayments then the basis for future operations on a much more extensive scale.

Never, probably, before in their lives had Mr. and Mrs. Wright been so flush of money as when they took up their residence at Fisherton. A grateful congregation had presented the Reverend Dionysius with a purse containing one hundred and eighty sovereigns, as a token of their affection and esteem, and to the husband and wife it seemed that such a sum was practically inexhaustible. They acted as if it were so, at all events. Mr. Wright thought that his poor dear Selina required a thorough change of air, and poor dear Selina was quite certain he wanted change more than she did. As for the children, it went without saying that they needed change more than anybody; and so the whole family travelled to the seaside; and it was the joint opinion of Mr. and Mrs. Wright that the man who could see the innocent enjoyment of the young people and grudge it to them must possess a heart hard as the nether millstone. They arrived at this decision in consequence of a tailor, who happened unfortunately to have selected the same watering-place for his holiday, remarking to Mr. Wright that he—the tailor—thought that if a man could afford to hire flys and boats, he might manage to pay his debts.

“There must be a bitter drop in every cup,” said Mrs. Wright;

and there can be no doubt that the democratic and disgusting practice of tradespeople going out of town, just as if they were their own customers instead of mere shopkeepers, was a very bitter drop in hers.

" It is really very hard," she often observed, " that, go where one will, one can never get away from London."

At Fisherton, at all events, Mr. Wright found he could not get away from London. There his debts followed him, and as he dared not commence his new life in a strange place amongst fresh people, in the capacity of spiritual shepherd-in-chief, with writs hovering about his door and bailiffs waylaying him along the footpaths, he had to make a virtue of necessity—pay as much as he could in cash, and give promissory notes for the balance.

What was left of the hundred and eighty pounds, after Mr. and Mrs. Wright returned from their holiday, did not go far in the way of setting their worldly affairs in order.

" They could just as easily have made it another hundred," sighed Mr. Wright, whose gratitude never survived the spending of the last given, begged, or borrowed sovereign. " What would another hundred have been to them?—nothing. And I am sure I worked in that parish like a galley-slave."

And this was quite true. In whatever parish Mr. Wright chanced to be placed, he did not stint his labour ; but then other clergymen worked hard also, while for them was not even the purse—to say nothing of the hundred and eighty sovereigns. At all events, nothing now remained of that testimonial for which Mr. Wright had with tears thanked his beloved friends. The old debts had only been reduced about one-fifth, and it was clear, even to the mind of Mr. Wright himself, that he never could manage to feed and clothe his family, to get rid of his old creditors—who, he said to Mrs. Wright, were " mere leeches, sucking his heart's blood "—to maintain a respectable appearance before the world, and to provide a few little luxuries for Selina, his wife, on three hundred and fifty pounds a year and a free house.

" Other people do it, though," he remarked to his better half.

" But *how ?* " asked Mrs. Wright significantly. " By pinching, and saving, and practising all sorts of meannesses, calculated to bring the Church into disrepute. I am sure, Dion, you would not have done half so much good amongst the poor as has been the case, had you gone about in shabby old clothes and cotton gloves like poor Mr. Seymour; or if I had allowed the children to wear checked pinafores, and helped with the housework, as little Mrs. Manners boasts that hers do. I say a clergyman is worse than useless unless he is a gentleman also; and to be thought a gentleman in England a man must, at any inconvenience, maintain a respectable appearance. We have been wonderfully supported, and I can see no reason why we should fail now. There are other livings in England beside Fisherton, and, if we can only manage to preserve our position here as we have done everywhere else so far, I am positive you won't be forgotten. Wherever we may be placed, a man of your talents cannot hide his light under a bushel."

Which sounded pleasant in Mr. Wright's ears. When he was busy making up his charitable accounts, or writing begging letters for the support of the schools, the lying-in charity, the Dorcas club, the mothers' improvement society, or any other one of the admirable institutions he, in conjunction with his wife, always established wherever they went, it was Mrs. Wright's practice to sit in his study, and indulge in long statements, such as that just recorded.

As she could not preach, and did not write books, and was sufficiently domestic to have no inclination to lecture in public, she contented herself with instructing her husband on various subjects wherein she considered his views wavering or unsound.

There were times, for instance, when poor Mr. Wright, who had personally to endure the insolence of creditors, the threats of lawyers, the dread of arrest, and the horror of impending bankruptcy, could have found it in his heart to wear cotton gloves, and permit his children to appear in checked pinafores, had such sacrifices been necessary in order to compass deliverance from debt.

There had been moments in his life when he doubted the expediency of having friends to stay in the house; and when he marvelled whether, with her superior mind and wonderful store of accomplishments, his wife might not have instructed her girls, and so saved the expense of that visiting governess, whose quarter days appeared to Mr. Wright to come round every three weeks.

But at such moments Mrs. Wright was at hand to point out the error of his ways, and to prove to him that if he ever wished to be rich, prosperous, and respected—if he desired his girls to marry well and his sons to succeed in life, he must be prepared to face even worse difficulties in order to maintain that place in society which Mrs. Wright piqued herself, and justly, upon having maintained intact, for nineteen years, through storm and sunshine, good report of the poor, and bad report of malicious grocers and bakers, and other people of the same rank in life, who " seemed," so Mrs. Wright was wont to declare, with a sigh, " to have no gratitude in them."

And no doubt Mrs. Wright was quite right in what she said. If social consideration could make up to a man for the loss of all self-respect, of all honest pride, of every scrap of independent feeling—for the misery of being dunned, for the disgrace of debt, for the discomfort of having to regard every rich acquaintance he made as a mere sponge, which he must eventually squeeze—Mr. Wright had his reward.

He was bidden to great houses, and received there as a welcome guest. He had game sent him till the very children grew sick of the taste of it. Choice wines were often left at his house, with a polite note hoping Mrs. Wright would find the particular vintage aid in restoring her to health. Interest was made to get his children into the Charterhouse, or the Navy, or anywhere else " off his hands." Whilst all the time Jones, in the next parish, or it might sometimes be even in the same, honestly paying his way, and finding it a grievous struggle to do so, was left out in the cold with never an invitation to dinner to bless himself withal; whilst his wife had to struggle through her illnesses as best she could, and nurse the children, and pay their school bills, and clothe them respectably, without help from anybody—unless, indeed, Mr. Wright sent round a pheasant, or a few grapes, or a bottle of old port, with his very kind regards.

For they were not mean, these people — nay, they were generous with everything except their own money. With the goods of others they were very generous indeed; the sick and needy never left the door of any house they inhabited, empty-handed. Moreover, they carried from parish to parish a lengthening string of dependants with them; having, for instance, at Fisherton a series of humble visitors who stayed at the rectory a few days or a few weeks, as the case might be : the consumptive dressmaker from St. Giles' ; that poor rheumatic laundress from Blackfriars; "that honest old creature Dobbs," whose acquaintance they had made in the north of London; and "that most unfortunate of schoolmasters, Brooks," for whom Mr. Wright had conceived a compassionate sort of attachment whilst both men were temporarily enjoying the questionable comforts of the Cripplegate Hotel; all of which produced a great effect in fresh neighbourhoods in favour of the new-comers.

"That is what I call Christianity," Mr. Cleaver would at such seasons declare, when some pauper delivered an order from Mr. or Mrs. Wright for so many pounds of gravy-beef to be supplied to the bearer and charged to their account; but at the end of a twelvemonth the butcher generally expressed himself differently.

"Don't talk about your Christianity to me," he frequently entreated. "Christianity is acting right between man and man, ain't it? Christianity is paying its way honest. Christianity ain't sending children out with lies in their mouths, that 'mamma is ill in bed,' or 'papa is busy with his sermon, and can't be disturbed,' when a man calls and asks civilly for his own. Give to the poor, indeed! Who gives, I'd like to know? You and me. And we get none of the thanks. It is easy enough to give if you put your hand in another man's pocket and take his money or his goods to give with."

And really there was a considerable amount of justice in this, which Mr. and Mrs. Wright called "the tradesman's view of the case."

"Just as if we were swindlers, and never intended to pay our lawful debts," remarked the lady; and the gentleman followed suit, though perhaps with less indignation. It may have struck him that a long-deferred "some time" means occasionally to a shopkeeper, who cannot carry his day-books and ledgers into Eternity with him, very much the same thing as "never."

There was one creditor of Mr. Wright's, however, who did not intend to wait for his money till Eternity, nor even for a very long period of time—that same creditor to whom reference was made in the last chapter, as holding various promissory notes signed by the Rector of Fisherton.

With their accustomed rapidity, when anything disagreeable was borne on their wings, the weeks and the months flew round; and Mr. Wright assured the clerk who presented his first "pro-

mise to pay," under the new arrangement, that he had never
been so much surprised in his life.

"I am sure I thought the bill was due next month," he said.
"I cannot imagine how I could have made such a mistake.
Dear me! I am very sorry. I would not have disappointed
your worthy employer upon any consideration."

And he was so very sorry; so grieved for the vain journey
the young man had undertaken; so remorseful about his own
lack of method; so hospitably insistent upon his unwelcome
guest having something to eat, if only a mouthful of bread and
cheese and a glass of porter—that the clerk returned to London
perfectly charmed with the Rector, and willing to take a hundred
affidavits, if necessary, as to his utter good faith and honesty.

The solicitor, who had some experience of Mr. Wright, only
laughed, and said:

"Well, write to say he shall have the month, but that the
money must be then forthcoming."

At the end of the month, Mrs. Wright wrote to say, her husband was not at home; that doubtless the matter had escaped
his memory. The moment he returned, it should be attended
to.

"We shall have to go through the previous ceremonies once
again, I see that plainly," remarked the lawyer. And, without
communicating again with Mr. Wright, he "most unhandsomely,"
as the poor clergyman phrased his conduct, served him with
another writ.

The man who put it into Mr. Wright's hands, finding him in
the first instance "not at home," had left a message that he
wanted to see him about the possibility of having a relative interred at Fisherton; and when the Rector discovered the *ruse*,
he rose equal to the occasion, and read the fellow such a lecture
concerning the enormity of his sin as he had never listened to
since he left school.

"I am sorry to have done wrong, sir," he said penitently and
respectfully; "but I was bound to see you, and I didn't want
to be wasting my time hanging about the village."

"My poor fellow," answered Mr. Wright, with infinite compassion, "if you had only mentioned that you came from such
and such an office in London—if you had hinted in the remotest
manner at your real business, I trust I need not say I am too
much of a gentleman to have given you needless trouble. There

—there—I don't want to add to the distress I am sure you now experience.　Only, remember my words—nothing pays so well, even in this world, as perfect straightforwardness and childlike sincerity.　My compliments to your employer, and I will see him about this unpleasant affair."

Which Mr. Wright did.　He saw the solicitor, and the solicitor saw his client.　The solicitor said his client was inexorable. Mr. Wright then saw the client, who said he had placed the matter in his solicitor's hands, and did not intend to interfere.

Mr. Wright then posted back to the solicitor, who had, following the clergyman's example, gone out of town and was not expected back for a fortnight.

Mr. Wright at once demanded to see the managing clerk, who assured him his instructions were to "go on," and that he had no alternative.

Hearing this, the Rector asked for pen, ink, and paper, and straightway wrote a letter which might have melted the heart even of that tailor who viewed with distaste the spectacle of the Masters and Misses Wright disporting themselves by the sad sea waves.

It did not move this inhuman lawyer, however, who, holding on the even tenor of his legal way, at the end of the orthodox period took out judgment against the Rector, and then, without "with your leave," or "by your leave," sent down a very humble and yet very powerful visitor to the rectory.

Now, if he could not get rid of this visitor without having those effects already honourably mentioned sold by auction, Mr. Wright knew that his hour was come; and it may safely be said the Rector moved heaven and earth to raise the required amount. But he could not do it.　For the first time since he and Selina, daughter of Theophilus Curran, became man and wife, her letters and his letters, her entreaties and his entreaties, proved unavailing.　Five pounds was the total result of all their appeals ; and as that amount—to quote Mr. Wright's own statement—was "worse than useless," Mrs. Wright spent it in purchasing some extremely pretty summer dresses for herself and her two eldest girls, which dresses she sent to the Fisherton milliner, stating they must be finished in time for General Grace's picnic party on the First.

"That will restore confidence, dear," she said to the **Rev.** Dion, "if the people in the village suspect anything."

The Rev. Dion groaned. He knew well enough the village suspected nothing. Accustomed as Fisherton was to the sight of Lazarus and all his sores at the rectory, they simply regarded the new-comer in the light of another London pauper, to whom it pleased Mr. Wright to extend hospitality.

The village did not require to have its confidence restored, but its clergyman did. Mr. Wright could not see his way. Mr. Wright had found that out of sight meant out of mind. Mr. Wright believed people thought three hundred and fifty pounds per annum—a paltry seven pounds a week (and two weeks with nothing)—must be a ducal revenue.

"I can't understand it at all," sighed Mr. Wright. "There was a time when, if distress came, I had but to ask and have; and now—now, when one's whole future trembles in the scale, there is not a friend to come forward—not a friend who will come forward when he is asked."

But Mr. Wright did understand perfectly. Perpetually advancing, he and his wife had taken no thought for retreat, but pillaged the whole country through which their route lay; and now, when they wanted to try back, no greenness of verdure greeted their return.

If Mrs. Wright wilfully shut her eyes to facts, Mr. Wright was unable to do so. He recognized now the truth that the testimonial over which he had shed tears, not merely of gratitude, but of pride, was as much an offering of gratitude to Providence as of love to himself; that while the parishioners felt bound to acknowledge his services, they were heartily glad to get rid of an active and impecunious curate. The rich men, delighted to pay their last black-mail, hasted to pay it voluntarily; whilst the poor followed the lead of their betters, never questioning.

He could not disguise from himself the fact that he had worked the mine of friendship down almost to the last piece of gold it contained.

People had liked—people had been kind to him; but he had tired them out; and if they failed to say in so many plain words that he was a very lucky fellow to have dropped into Fisherton, their manner implied the same thing, and Mr. Wright felt the implication bitterly. For he did not consider Fisherton equal to his deserts. Fisherton, with a certain income from his living, and an uncertain income from friends, old or new, might have been tolerable; but Fisherton sufficiently remote from London to have no rich merchant residents, but only a population living on their settled incomes or small settled earnings—a population "without a spare ten pounds among them"—filled the Rector with dismay.

No more of the leeks and cucumbers of the goodly city for husband and wife—no more share of great men's plenty. Only three hundred and fifty pounds a year—less income-tax; old debts to pay off; fresh credit to any large extent not easily procurable; and "a man in possession."

It was the last evening but one before his creditor meant to turn the final screw on the Rector. Properly speaking, every chair and table could legally have been sold some days before; but Mr. Wright had pleaded so hard for another week's grace, and paid so liberally for having it granted, that Reuben, the sheriff's officer, who happened to have the matter in hand, had, on his own responsibility, granted him longer indulgence than was the wont of that merciless Jew.

Now, however, Reuben had told him he could not give him a minute after ten o'clock on the day but one following.

"They are sendin' in to me about it," explained Mr. Reuben to Mr. Wright, "and I must either have the money, or——"

"Dear, dear, dear!" said the unfortunate Rector, mentally ending the sentence; "it will ruin me."

"Come, sir, don't take on so," entreated Mr. Reuben, who had been acquainted (professionally) with the Rector for many years, and found him "quite the gentleman." "You will get through it all right, never fear. Why, you have got through far worse trouble, to my knowledge."

Mr. Wright was aware of that, but still he did not see how he was to get through this trouble. For the first time in his memory he was placed in a parish where there was not a creature to whom he dare proclaim his need. He might just as well, he felt, be sold up at once as take any one of the Christian friends he addressed each Sunday into his confidence.

"If there had only been a Jew in my district," he thought, "or even a rich dissenter, I might have received assistance." As matters stood Mr. Wright saw no sign of assistance anywhere, and returned to Fisherton almost broken-hearted.

The rectory looked very pretty in the light of the summer's evening; the Rector thought he had never seen it look so pretty.

The church, too, appeared as he passed it more picturesque than usual ; and the graveyard, with its billows of green grass, and its few headstones, seemed inviting in its quiet and repose.

"If it was not for Selina and the children, I should not mind if Reuben were 'taking my body' there this moment," the un-fortunate man muttered as he stood contemplating the resting-place of those whose last bed had there been prepared for them. "And, indeed, perhaps Selina and the children would do far better without me : my day seems over."

And then, suddenly remembering his profession, he struck himself lightly on the chest with his closed hand—a trick that had now become habitual with him—"Wright's roll-call to duty," as an acquaintance styled it—and saying, "God forgive me ! After all His mercies too !" he strode on, head erect, umbrella shouldered, to face Selina and tell her the bad result of his day in town.

He found his wife wrapped up in a thin shawl, which once upon a time had been elegant as well as light. That shawl was a sign of misery with poor Mrs. Wright. When she felt "very poorly," or when she was "very wretched," she adjusted that shawl about her long neck and falling shoulders, and bemoaned herself as the Israelites did in sackcloth and ashes.

But, wretched or not, she never reproached Dionysius. She blamed others, but never herself or him ; and if he ever dreaded telling her of his want of success, it was only because he could not endure the sight of her disappointment. Curtain lectures were things for which the perpetual excitement of their lives left no margin. Perhaps that was the balance of happiness for Mr. Wright. Heaven knows, if he had been cursed with a shrew at home, as he was cursed with duns abroad, he might have wished himself underground. As it was, Mrs. Wright, wrapped up as has been stated, met him at the rectory gate.

"Well, my dear, any good news ?" she asked.

"None," he answered ; "worse than none. Reuben either won't or can't give longer than till ten on Friday morning. He says I have got through worse troubles ; and that is true ; but we had friends then : we have no friends now."

His voice faltered a little. Perhaps he thought at the mo-ment of that Eastern story concerning the beggar who received a daily alms for so long a time from his wealthy neighbour, that at last he came to consider it in the light of an annuity.

"Don't give up yet, Dion," said his wife. "Help may come to-morrow. We have *all* to-morrow, remember, and who can tell what a day may bring forth? Think what a day has often brought forth for us!"

At that moment Mr. Wright was inclined to look so gloomily on life, that the only events his memory could recall as having been brought forth by a day were unexpected demands for money; but he could not bear to add to his wife's distress— outwardly represented by the shawl — and so refrained from answer.

"Have you dined?" she inquired. It was an unusual thing for Mr. Wright to return from London luncheonless or dinner-less, but something in his manner caused her to imagine he had assisted at neither meal.

"I have had all the dinner I want," he replied: "a roll and a glass of ale."

"But you must eat, or you will be knocked up," she persisted. "There is some nice cold roast beef—or shall I send for a chop, or would you like tea and a rasher of bacon? I think the tea might perhaps do you the most good; but——"

"I am neither hungry nor thirsty, dear," he answered; "but still I should like a cup of strong coffee with a tea-spoonful of brandy in it—only one spoonful, mind!" he called after his wife, who was inclined sometimes to put a liberal interpretation on Mr. Wright's wishes in such matters.

Left alone, the Rector sat down beside the window of his study, and looked out over the garden towards the Thames; then, with a groan, he closed his eyes, and leaning back in his chair, fell into a reverie.

From the next room came the maddening sound of "prac-tising." One of his daughters was essaying "Il mio Tesoro," playing about one correct note in seven, and trying back per-petually, in order to see if her next venture would be more successful than the last.

Mr. Wright endured the noise as long as he could; but at last the irritation it caused him became so great, that he was just rising to ask Miss Maria to postpone her performance, when Mrs. Wright reappeared with the coffee.

"What an in——ahem !—comparable instrument the piano is, when it does not chance to be in the same house with one," remarked Mr. Wright sarcastically.

"I will tell her to stop," said Mrs. Wright. "But you know, dear, the children must practise."

"I don't see why they must do so when I am at home," he answered.

Which was rather unreasonable on Mr. Wright's part, considering he was at home the greater part of each day, and in and out of the house perpetually during those hours he devoted to his parish.

"You have put a great deal too much brandy in this coffee," he said, when his wife returned after silencing Maria's musical efforts.

"Only a spoonful, dear!" she answered, Jesuitically.

"It must have been a gravy-spoon," he persisted; which, indeed, was short of the truth; but still he finished the cup, and when he had finished, said he felt better for it, and went straight up to his dressing-room.

"You are not going out again, Dion, are you?" asked Mrs. Wright five minutes after, meeting him in the hall, fresh cravated, brushed, with no speck of London dust visible about his person.

"Yes, indeed I am," he replied. "I am going to Riversdale, to ask Mr. Irwin to help us. I don't know why the idea should have occurred to me, or why it never did before, but I assure you it came just like an inspiration."

"Do you think he will lend you the money?" said Mrs. Wright, doubtfully.

"I don't know. I mean to try, at any rate," answered the Rector. "He can but refuse."

Which last was a phrase very often on the lips of Mr. and Mrs. Wright.

CHAPTER XI.

CONCERNING AN UNEXPECTED PROPOSITION.

THERE were good reasons why Mrs. Wright should feel dubious about the success of her husband's application to Mr. Irwin. In the first place, he was not a resident in Fisherton or any of the adjoining parishes, having only taken Riversdale for a couple of months during the temporary absence of Sir John and Lady Giles, who were in the habit of making as much money out of their residence as they possibly could. Mr. Irwin had therefore nothing whatever to do with the neighbourhood ; and the wildest imagination could not conceive that he was likely to take much interest in Mr. Wright, considering he had never seen him except twice, once while fishing in the vicinity of Fisherton rectory, and once when they met accidentally at a dinner-party given by a gentleman resident at Richmond.

Mrs. Wright had called upon Mrs. Irwin, who had not seen fit to return the visit. Mr. Wright had called upon Mr. Irwin, but failed to find him at home, and a like result ensued when Mr. Irwin called upon the Rector. The acquaintance, therefore, was not of a character to raise undue expectations on the subject of assistance. Nevertheless, Mrs. Wright could not but remember how frequently total strangers had come to their rescue, when friends seemed inclined to hold aloof; and it was quite possible, she considered, Mr. Irwin might be the something brought forth that day.

She was very low, however. For weeks she had eaten little and slept less ; and accordingly, after her husband's departure, she took his chair by the open window, and cried for a time, and then felt better.

Meanwhile Mr. Wright, tired as he was, walked rapidly on towards Riversdale. He had two miles of flat, uninteresting country in which to reconsider his intention, but he never faltered about the matter. He did not know anything concerning Mr. Irwin's position. Whether he was rich or whether he was comparatively poor, the Rector had not an idea. He had one fixed determination, however—if money was to be had out of the gentleman, he, Mr. Wright, would have it.

It was growing quite dusk by the time he reached Riversdale; but Mr. Irwin still sat over his wine, not drinking much, but thinking deeply. Mr. Wright, who was asked into the dining-room, rejoiced at sight of the decanters, first, because he felt he needed a glass or so of sound dry sherry, such as he prophetically believed to be on the table, and secondly, because he knew by experience how much easier and pleasanter it is to talk to a man who has just dined, than to one who has not.

Mr. Irwin—a tall, melancholy-looking man, with a large beard and moustache—greeted the Rector courteously, and remarked, in reply to Mr. Wright's apologies for intruding upon him at so unusual an hour, that a pleasure late was better than a pleasure never. "And, indeed," he went on, "I am so little here during visiting hours, that, excepting in the evenings, it is difficult to find me at home."

"I am very glad I came to-night, then, instead of to-morrow," said Mr. Wright; "for I am here to ask a favour."

It was one of Mr. Wright's principles to plunge into business at once. He had studied the art of requesting assistance and mastered it more completely than he had ever done divinity.

"You may depend upon one thing," he confided to a friend, "that it is an entire mistake to defer the evil moment. No amount of preparation can reconcile a man to the fact that you want money; and the only consequence of preparation is, that it gives him time to make up his mind to say 'No.' Further, it has a bad effect in this way: if you tag on a request to the end of an interview, it makes your friends suspicious about all your visits, for they never can tell what may be at the bottom of your pleasant chat. No; take my advice—ask for what you want, and get 'Yes' if you can, and take 'No' if you can't. It is only fair to let a man know the worst at once, and have the matter done with. I always do this when I am begging for a church, or a school, or a charity, or—or anything," added Mr. Wright; "and I believe I may say I have not generally come away empty-handed."

Carrying this theory into practice, the Rector, in two minutes after he entered Mr. Irwin's dining-room, had broken the ice.

Mr. Irwin knew he wanted something, and said that he should be most happy to assist Mr. Wright if in his power.

Of course this might mean much, or it might mean little ; and Mr. Wright was too old a campaigner to suffer his hopes to be excited by such a conventional expression. Nevertheless, it answered his purpose to appear to read the words literally, and accordingly, with a deprecating motion of the hand, he entreated Mr. Irwin not to be so hasty in committing himself.

"Because," went on the Rector, "the request I have to make is so extraordinary—on the face of it so almost audacious, that I can hardly be surprised if you utterly refuse to assist me."

"I have already expressed my willingness to further your wishes if in my power," answered Mr. Irwin. "Until I know what it is you want, I can scarcely say more or less."

This was not so encouraging, and it confused Mr. Wright a little.

"Perhaps I ought to explain——" he was beginning, when Mr. Irwin interrupted him :

"If you will excuse my saying so, I think not. If I cannot advance your views, you may regret having entered into useless explanation ; if I can, there may be no necessity for explanation at all."

"You are quite right," agreed the Rector, taking his cue from the other in a moment. "I want you to lend me fifty pounds—if you can do so without inconvenience."

"Yes——" said Mr. Irwin, thoughtfully.

That "Yes" did not mean acquiescence, or refusal, or anything except that he understood the nature of the request.

"An abominable ' Yes,'" as Mr. Wright explained afterwards to his wife, "calculated to take all the courage out of a man, and entirely to stop any remarks of an entreating nature he might otherwise have felt disposed to utter."

Mr. Irwin did not say another word for a couple of minutes, which seemed to Mr. Wright like two years. He did not even look at his visitor, but kept his eyes bent on the table, studying —so thought the Rector—how to word his refusal civilly. At last he raised his head and spoke :

"I think I can manage to do what you want—indeed, I will do it. But still, if not unpleasant to you, I should like to know why you require a loan of the kind, and ask it from a comparative stranger ?"

Was the room reeling round? Had his ears played him false? Was the peril really averted? With one hand Mr.

Wright grasped the arm of the chair in which he sat, with the other he tried to unfasten his neckcloth, and failed.

Mr. Irwin rose, and undid it for him, then opened one of the windows, and pouring out a glass of water, held it to the clergyman's lips.

"You are better now," he said, when Mr. Wright raised his head from the back of the easy chair and looked, with a wistful, bewildered expression, in the face of the man who at that moment represented to him temporal salvation. "Take some wine. I will just leave you while I get my cheque-book. I will return immediately."

Left alone, Mr. Wright, indifferent for once to the fascinations of dry sherry, leaned his head upon both his hands, and tried to realize the fact that deliverance had come at last. Never before, never, could he remember having been so totally prostrated by good fortune.

The agony, so long protracted—the relief, so long delayed, had proved too much even for Mr. Wright; but no stoicism or fluency could have served his turn one-half so well as the physical effect Mr. Irwin beheld produced upon a strong man by mental reaction. About words there might be much doubt, but about that semi-faint there could not lie the suspicion of doubt.

When Mr. Irwin returned he brought back in his hand an open cheque for fifty pounds, which he gave to Mr. Wright.

"Now," he said, reseating himself, "if you like to tell me all about your anxiety, well; if not, we will not speak of it any more."

There was nothing in the world Mr. Wright liked better than talking about his own troubles to a new listener; so, beginning at the beginning, he presented Mr. Irwin with a comprehensive view of his life as a husband, a curate, and a rector. He gave his host a succinct account of the origin and progress of the especial trouble which induced him to come to Riversdale. And Mr. Irwin paid undivided attention to the narrative, and drew his own conclusions from it—some of which were right, and some of which were wrong.

With the fifty-pound cheque safely lodged in his purse, with a good glass of wine beside him, and a sympathizing listener, rich enough to help and willing to do so, as he had already proved, the haunting figure of the unwelcome guest located at the rectory was already growing dim in Mr. Wright's memory, and Dionysius was himself again.

Mr. Irwin felt irresistibly attracted towards his visitor. The apparent frankness and the real buoyancy of his nature were very pleasant to the man who hearkened to the Rector's exposition; and it was quite half an hour before he effectually stopped the flow of Mr. Wright's eloquence by inquiring:

"Will you forgive my asking what you mean to do when the next instalment of this debt is due?"

Now, if Mr. Wright had spoken out his mind, he would have answered he thought it extremely probable the dear, kind friend, who sat facing him, might be induced to come to the rescue once again; but judging that Mr. Irwin would probably consider such an amount of candour premature, he merely said that he intended to put aside sufficient to pay this importunate creditor and get rid of him, no matter who else went to the wall.

"If we have all to live on bread and water," finished Mr. Wright, buttoning up his coat, preparatory to facing the night air, "we will be prepared for him next time, please God!"

Mr. Irwin smiled—he could not help doing so. There was such a discrepancy between Mr. Wright's appearance and the fare indicated, that he could not but admire the final saving appeal by which the Rector left a way out of the difficulty; since, if Providence did not approve, even a diet of bread and water would naturally be insufficient to enable the family to meet their engagements.

Mr. Wright saw the smile, and involuntarily his own face reflected it.

"But, upon my honour, I am quite in earnest," he said, answering Mr. Irwin's unspoken thought. "I would not endure what I have endured latterly if any personal privation could secure me from such a trial."

"That I can well believe," agreed the other, who, indeed, could not conceive of any human being in his senses running such a risk a second time.

"I suppose you will be in town to-morrow?" suggested Mr. Irwin, as he walked slowly beside his visitor to the outer gates.

Mr. Wright replied that such was his intention.

"I wish, then," said Mr. Irwin, "that if you happen to be passing my office, you would give me the opportunity of a little conversation. I think I might be able to put something in your way that may prove an acceptable addition to your income."

And with that they parted, Mr. Irwin to smoke a solitary cigar whilst he paced up and down beside the river, Mr. Wright to traverse the two miles home as unweariedly as though he had been treading on air.

"Il mio Tesoro" was in full progress when he re-entered the rectory, another daughter having taken possession of the music-stool; but if the first performer in Europe had been playing the air, Mr. Wright could not have hummed a vague second to the air with greater approval and enjoyment.

"Very good—very good indeed, my child," he said, patting his sixth-born on the shoulder, which, perhaps, was a little hard on Maria, seeing her sister played even worse than she. "Selina, my love, one moment——"

And husband and wife passed together into the study.

"Oh! Dion, you have got it!" she said, and then began to sob hysterically, while Mr. Wright stood silent, so great and overpowering was the sense of merciful deliverance which again came over him.

It was Mrs. Wright who first spoke.

"We ought never to be faithless again. It seems to me we are worse than heathens ever to doubt, even in our greatest extremity." And she paused, expecting her husband to agree in the sentiment expressed.

But Mr. Wright held his peace. He must have been much less astute than was actually the case if, in spite of all his efforts at self-deception, it had not occasionally occurred to him that a creed which contained no sentence concerning personal works might be as dangerous, though apparently less presumptuous, than one composed entirely of faith in them.

Next morning the Rector was early astir.

"Let me have a cup of coffee, Mary," he said to the cook; "and don't disturb your mistress. I want to catch the eight o'clock train. Tell her I shall be back as soon as possible."

So, Mr. Wright. If there were anything beautiful in that house, it was the consideration of wife for husband—of husband for wife—of both for children. Short-sighted they may have been in many respects, but selfish personally as regarded each other most undoubtedly they were not.

Against the outside world they warred with genial manners

and pleasant faces; but at home they were at peace, which was perhaps the reason why the outside world, seeing so little domestic union elsewhere, was inclined to forget to be merciful to their offences.

That was a very different journey from the one he had undertaken the previous morning, and Mr. Wright's spirits rose accordingly. It was quite a sight to behold the way in which he returned the greetings of those of his parishioners he happened to meet on his way to the station; and when he handed Mr. Irwin's cheque over the counter, the tone in which he said "Short, if you please," was that of a man accustomed to deal with thousands.

After he had settled with Reuben, who laughed knowingly when he saw the note, and remarked, "It was fortunate when a man had good friends," Mr. Wright betook himself to Eastcheap, where Mr. Irwin's offices were situated.

Asking for his new friend, he was ushered into a small office, where an old man sat, with his hat on, writing at a shabby baize-covered table. At sight of Mr. Wright's portly figure he removed his hat, and greeted the visitor with:

"Servant, sir. What can I have the pleasure of doing for you?"

"I beg your pardon," answered Mr. Wright, in his most courtly manner, "but I expected to find another Mr. Irwin."

"My son-in-law, perhaps," suggested the other. "Here, Hammond!" he shouted to a clerk in the warehouse, "take this gentleman up to Mr. Walter's room. Good morning, sir;" and he put on his hat again and resumed his correspondence.

The premises occupied by Messrs. Irwin were old, dilapidated, and quaint. The house, or rather houses, in which they carried on their business had evidently been at some time not remote inhabited as private dwellings, and the apartments now used as workrooms and offices were wainscoted, whilst over the ancient mantelpieces were panels curiously festooned with carved flowers and leaves, from amongst which peeped forth the faces of fat Cupids, black with smoke, grimed with the dirt of years.

"I have been thinking over our conversation last night," said Mr. Irwin, after hearing Mr. Wright's account of his interview with Reuben, "and wondering whether you would entertain an idea which suggested itself to me at the time. I want to find a suitable residence for a young lady—my niece, in fact.

She is now, and has for some years past, been at a school in France; but I am desirious to make some different arrangement for her future. When you were speaking of the difficulty you experienced in making both ends meet, it crossed my mind that perhaps Mrs. Wright would not object to receive her. I would pay a hundred a year for her board, and so forth, exclusive of any sum which might be necessary for lessons. She is a nice, quiet girl, and, except myself, utterly alone in the world."

He looked at Mr. Wright as he concluded, and, despite the clergyman's usual command of countenance, read in his face utter, blank disappointment.

The truth was, Mr. Wright had gone to Eastcheap expecting some great piece of preferment. A lectureship was the most modest idea he conceived of Mr. Irwin's intentions, while a possible bishopric had gleamed with the morning sun upon him.

And to have all of these visions reduced to the proposal of taking a vague girl into his house for the sum of a paltry hundred a year tried the Rector's powers of dissimulation too severely.

"You do not like the idea, I see," remarked Mr. Irwin. "I can well understand your objection. Let us say no more about my proposal."

"My dear sir—my kind friend—pray do me justice. Even if your proposition were disagreeable, which it is not, I should not be so ungrateful, so stupid as to decline it without full consideration. You took me by surprise, that was all; and to be quite candid, it appeared to me that there might be difficulties in the way of such an arrangement. I should, however, like to talk the matter over with Mrs. Wright. After all, it is an affair which belongs more to her department than to mine."

"Of course," answered Mr. Irwin; "but pray remember one thing—don't take the girl because you imagine I have any claim upon you. I want the affair to be conducted upon a strictly business footing; and if Mrs. Wright can manage, in the event of her consenting to take charge of my niece, to give a little motherly love to a most desolate child, I shall be very grateful to her. That is all. Let me have your decision in a week."

"Do I understand that the young lady is an orphan?" inquired Mr. Wright.

"She is utterly alone in the world, excepting myself," was the answer. "She has neither sister nor brother, nor any one," finished Mr. Irwin.

"She is his own child," thought Mr. Wright; but he only said, "Poor dear! how sad! How my wife would love her if we are only able to get over those little difficulties which, as you can well understand, our peculiar position could not fail to cause— domestic details and so forth—but I won't trouble you about such matters. This day week, then—Oh! by-the-bye, I have brought you an acknowledgment of that money"—and he placed a sealed letter in Mr. Irwin's hands. "I never can thank you sufficiently. Good bye—good bye—don't come downstairs with me on any account. Good bye!" and the Rector was gone.

Mr. Irwin stood for a minute after his departure, looking with bent brows at the letter Mr. Wright had given him : then he broke the seal and read the epistle. After he had done so his face cleared ; and saying, "They will take her," he put the letter and acknowledgment in a private drawer and locked it.

Mr. Wright's epistle was commendably short, but it was un-deniably judicious.

"MY VERY DEAR SIR" (so the note began),

"It is my duty to send you a formal acknowledgment of the generous loan which has rescued myself and my family from disgrace and ruin ; for I may at some time be in a position to refund the amount ; although if I am you shall have no occasion to put it in force. God bless and preserve you, my kind bene-factor.

"Ever your grateful and obliged,
"DIONYSIUS WRIGHT."

The Rector returned home not quite satisfied with his own conduct about Mr. Irwin's offer.

"Selina will put me right," he considered. "We will talk it over to-night when the children are out of the way. I won't go into the subject till we can discuss it fully."

The first thing to do was to get rid of Mr. Reuben's man ; and the Rector accordingly sent for him to the study, where he delivered his employer's note, which ran as follows :

"DAVIS,

"Quit possession.
"G. REUBEN."

"I am sure I am very glad indeed, sir, to see this," said the man.

"Thank you, I know you are," answered the Rector, loftily. "Here is a trifle for yourself;" and he put half a crown into his hand.

The man looked at it and then at Mr. Wright.

"Well?" said the Rector.

"If you remember, sir, I have come in for family prayers—and gone twice to church to save appearances, although I had no right to leave the house—and I thought, sir, perhaps you would take all that into consideration. Prayers is things I have not been accustomed to; and I can safely say that go to church before I never did to oblige any gentleman living."

"Shocking—shocking—shocking!" commented the Rector; "I really did hope better things of you, Davis;" then, seeing an expression in the man's face which intimated he had thought better things of the Rector, he gave him another half-crown, and said he hoped he would not get chattering with any one on his way to the station.

That night Mr. and Mrs. Wright thoroughly enjoyed their evening meal.

The children, old and young, were in bed, and the house was perfectly quiet before Mr. Wright repeated to his wife the conversation which had taken place between himself and Mr. Irwin.

"You don't mean to say you hesitated, Dion!" exclaimed the wiser half, in astonishment.

"Well, you see, my dear——"

"I don't see at all, and I won't see anything, except that you ought to have closed with the offer at once. I wish you could make some excuse, and go to him to-morrow and say we shall be only too glad to have her."

"I can make an excuse," said Mr. Wright, "and save our own dignity as well. Trust me for that, Selina."

CHAPTER XII.

MR. IRWIN WAXES COMMUNICATIVE.

About noon on the following day Mr. Irwin was somewhat surprised to see the Rector of Fisherton enter his office once again.

"Now, pray, pray do not rise," began the reverend gentleman, hat in one hand, umbrella under his arm, enforcing his entreaty with a persuasive pastoral grasp of his new friend's nearest shoulder.

"I have not come to disturb you, or to take up the time of a man to whom time is money. I just want to ask one question, and then I will be off."

He stood on the hearthrug, looking the embodiment of clerical respectability. A novice in the deceptive nature of such appearances might have taken his note of hand as good for a thousand pounds; and even Mr. Irwin, who had seen something of the world and the people in it, found no little difficulty in realizing the fact that, but for his interposition, the rectory goods would have been advertised for sale in that morning's papers.

As if adversity were a cold bath, and a plunge in its waters refreshing, the Rector had come up out of its depths cheerful, rubicund, smiling. The whiteness of his shirt was immaculate, the tie of his cravat a marvel of accuracy of design and neatness of execution, the fit of his coat precisely what the fit of the Rector of Fisherton's coat should have been, whilst his hat was new undeniably. Mr. Wright had, indeed, bought it by the way.

Yes, here was the man Mr. Irwin needed—a man it seemed impossible wholly to dislike, and equally impossible wholly to respect—a man whom fate could not buffet out of countenance, and who would do anything he honestly could in a decent, even if doubtful, sort of way, to add to his income—a man who would not ask too many questions if it were necessary for him to hold his peace—who could talk, if talk were required, from his mouth, and keep silence if he understood silence meant profit.

So thought Mr. Irwin ; and yet the Rector's first move seemed to indicate some error in his premisses or his conclusions.

"I mentioned that little matter to Mrs. Wright last night," said the reverend gentleman, who had four different ways of designating his better half, according as circumstances required.

"Yes," answered Mr. Irwin, taking refuge behind that detestable monosyllable, as Mr. Wright considered it.

"And of course we feel we should be only too delighted to meet your views, even if such a course did not promise pecuniary advantage to ourselves; but there is one thing — one question——"

"Yes," repeated Mr. Irwin.

"Really, now I am here, it seems such a ridiculous inquiry that I think I shall just go home again, leaving it unmade," said Mr. Wright, who had never in the whole of his varied life believed that one word, and that word "yes," could have proved such a barrier to conversation.

"If I were in your place I should not do anything of the kind," replied Mr. Irwin. "You came here, as I understand, to ask some question, which now appears to you superfluous. Under any circumstances I should put it."

"You are very good, I am sure. As you advise perfect candour, I will put it. Is there—was there anything peculiar about the birth of the young lady in whose welfare you are so deeply interested ? "

The question was so different from anything Mr. Irwin had anticipated, that he stared at his visitor in blank amazement.

"I am not her mother," he answered ; "but I have no reason to doubt she came into the world much as other children do, however that may be."

"That is not what I mean," said the Rector, thinking, with a coid shudder, that he had perhaps taken a wrong tack, and that Mr. Irwin was aware of it.

"What do you mean, then ? "

"Well, I feel an awkwardness in putting the query into plain words. Cannot you assist me a little ? "

"I confess I cannot, unless you help me to understand what you want to know. Have you got an idea that the girl is queer in any way ? Because, if you have, I can answer you. She is as sane as either of us, and a dear, good little creature beside."

"I give you my word such a notion never crossed my mind,"

said Mr. Wright, heartily. "The fact is, I imagined—that is, I did not imagine, but I thought I should like to know whether the young lady's parents were—married."

"Certainly they were. I was present at the marriage."

"You have taken a load off my mind," exclaimed the Rector, holding out his hand, and shaking Mr. Irwin's till that gentleman's fingers tingled. "I am so thankful, though of course I never really felt any apprehension. I am so glad. My dear wife will be so relieved. We shall be delighted to try to fill the place of parents to your orphan niece."

Mr. Irwin took his hand, which the Rector had at length released, into his own custody, and folding its fellow over it, said:

"As a matter of curiosity, I wish you would tell me how my niece's legitimacy can prove any relief to Mrs. Wright."

"With the greatest pleasure," answered the Rector. "Like myself, my wife is an Irishwoman—that is, I would say——"

"Never mind the bull, Mr. Wright. You will only correct it, I foresee, by saying an Irishman. Mrs. Wright being, like you, an Irishwoman, what follows?"

"Well, you know what Irishwomen are."

"I do in the States. I cannot compliment you on your compatriots there."

"I do not know anything about them in the States," said Mr. Wright a little impatiently.

"What you wish to say, I suppose," suggested Mr. Irwin, "is that Irishwomen are usually supposed to have a higher standard of morals, and are more capable of acting up to it, than the women of other countries."

"That is it," agreed the Rector; "only you should not have interpolated 'supposed' into your sentence. They have, sir; they are."

"I am quite willing to take your word on both points, Mr. Wright," said Mr. Irwin. "Except as 'helps,' I have no acquaintance with their virtues or vices. Still I ask, what then?"

"Why, only this. My poor dear has passed through sufficient trouble and experienced sufficient sorrow to make her tolerant and pitiful to any sinner. And I think I may safely say, no outcast from society, no deserted creature, no poor wretch plunged in sin and misery, would appeal to her won a ily heart in vain. Nevertheless, she has her crotchets. Her father, though one of the kindest men who ever lived, was full of them; and further, all ladies—Mrs. Irwin, whom I have not the honour of knowing, of course excepted—have their whims and fancies."

"You need not except Mrs. Irwin. She has her whims and fancies, which, like a good husband, I respect," was the reply.

"Dear, dear! I am sorry to hear you say that," remarked Mr. Wright, with more earnest sympathy than Selina might altogether have approved. "Well, then, talking to a family man—a man blessed, no doubt, with a wife in every respect as admirable as mine, but still aware, from experience, of the peculiarities of the better sex—I may say Mrs. Wright has very strong opinions on the subject we have been discussing. And though I do not mean to say she would decline the responsibility of taking charge of a—hem!—child born out of wedlock, still, she would accept the trust in fear and trembling, lest the sin of the mother might be entailed on the child."

"Do I understand you to say that Mrs. Wright believes, if a woman goes wrong, her child, differently placed, differently educated, differently guarded, kept from temptation, is likely, out of sheer depravity, to go wrong too?"

"You put the matter strongly," suggested the Rector.

"Do I put it too strongly?" asked Mr. Irwin.

"I do not know that you do," was the reply. "I told you my wife had her prejudices."

"Well, it is a very strange notion," said Mr. Irwin thoughtfully.

"I do not believe," began the Rector, clearing his throat, "that the idea of mental as well as bodily maladies being hereditary is so singular a one as you seem to imagine. You are a good churchman, as I know, and therefore I need scarcely do more than remind you——"

"Does Mrs Wright think other sins, besides that of bringing an unfortunate infant into the world which has no place and no name ready for it, are transmitted from parents to children?" asked Mr. Irwin, cutting ruthlessly across the Rector's meditated discourse. "Take murder, for instance. There was a man hung at Newgate last Monday. Suppose him to have left a child: do you imagine it likely that child will commit murder also?"

"I trust not, but I should consider the probability of his taking away life greater than in the case of one of my own boys, for instance."

"Given, that one of your boys and he were so situated as to start with the same advantages or disadvantages——"

"They could not start the same, he being his father's son, and my boy being my son," and Mr. Wright stood virtuously upright, internally thanking God and glorifying himself that his children were not as other children, inasmuch as they called him father, and his wife Selina mother.

"It is a curious speculation," said Mr. Irwin, at length, lifting his head and looking thoughtfully in the Rector's self-satisfied face. "I will not say you are wrong, but I hope you are not right, or else it would be a dreary prospect for philanthropists and social reformers."

"We are all bound to do what lies in our power to make this sinful world better," remarked Mr. Wright; "and by the blessing of Providence, philanthropists, and we poor clergymen, and true Christians like yourself, are able to effect some good even amongst the most depraved classes of society; but it would be worse than folly to shut our eyes to the fact that vice is hereditary—or, if you prefer a milder expression, that most weaknesses are constitutional and capable of transmission. As we say in Ireland, 'The dirty drop will come out,' and it will, too. I could give you fifty instances in which money, and education, and association have been employed to counteract its influence in vain."

"We have digressed considerably from the subject of my niece," remarked Mr. Irwin. "Am I to understand all obstacles are now removed, or is there any other question you wish to put to me?"

"None, not one," answered the Rector, inflating his chest and rising a little on his toes to give greater emphasis to the utter confidence he reposed in the respectability of Mr. Irwin and Mr. Irwin's relations.

"So far, so good," said that gentleman; "but now there is an explanation I wish to give to you. It is a necessary explanation, or I should not make it; it is not altogether pleasant, and therefore I must beg that you will regard it as confidential."

"You may say anything to me," replied Mr. Wright. "In the interests of a friend, I can be secret as the grave—silent as the dead——"

"I wish you would sit down," suggested Mr. Irwin.

"My dear friend, why did you not mention that wish sooner?"

replied the Rector, seating himself with alacrity. "I know how disagreeable it is to talk up to a man. And now tell me your difficulty—but stop. First, am I, or am I not, to mention the matter to my wife?"

"I think that from so admirable a wife and discreet a lady you ought to have no secrets," was the answer.

"Of my own I have none," said the Rector, which was indeed very true, for Mrs. Wright would never have permitted him to indulge in such a luxury; "unless it may be when I occasionally attempt a pious fraud and try to make worldly matters look brighter than they really are, so as not to worry the poor soul unnecessarily; but, bless you, she always finds out that I have been deceiving her. A friend's secret, however, I would, if he desired it, keep safe in my own bosom." And Mr. Wright thereupon tapped his chest, which was certainly capacious enough for the purpose indicated.

"We will not exclude Mrs. Wright in this instance," said Mr. Irwin. "What I wish to tell you is that my wife is not aware of my niece's existence."

"She *is* his daughter," thought the Rector, feeling now quite confident upon that point. "Probably the offspring of some youthful, wretched *mésalliance.*"

"You don't mean it?" he remarked aloud.

"I do mean it," persisted the other. "I have never mentioned her name to my wife, and if I can avoid doing so, I never shall name it. Some years ago—it does not matter how many —I found myself in the possession of a considerable sum of money, part of which I held in trust for other people, and a portion of which I might have fairly appropriated to my own use. But I had reason for supposing—indeed, for knowing— the money had been acquired by questionable means; and I resolved to employ none of it beyond what might be absolutely needful for the necessities of my position, for my personal pleasure or advancement in life."

"A resolution which did you honour," observed the Rector; and a glow of conscious rectitude flushed his face as he mentally considered how much he should like to be placed in a position where he could not only make such a resolve, but keep it.

"In furtherance of this design," continued Mr. Irwin, "I went to America, where I obtained employment in the house of Irwin and Son, die-sinkers. Mr. Irwin was an Englishman, originally engaged in business with his brother in the very premises where I am now speaking to you."

"I follow your words," said Mr. Wright, as the speaker paused. "I shall understand their meaning presently."

"In the particular class of work to which he had devoted his life I was not inexperienced—indeed, I may say without vanity, there are few men who knew more of its mysteries than I; and Mr. Irwin, whose heart was in his trade, took a fancy to me, and eventually placed me in a lucrative and responsible position. All this time, however, I was his clerk—his servant—what you will that signifies dependence and inequality of rank; and I did not encroach on his kindness—I did not intrude myself on his notice—because he was good enough to think me of service in his business. After I had been with him for some time, a terrible affliction befell him. His son—his only son—died. He had loved that son well as his child; but I do think he loved him more as the future representative of Irwin and Son. He moped about, and hugged his grief, and neglected his business, and during that period I managed everything for him—managed so well, that his connection, instead of falling off, extended—the reputation of his house grew. He had one other child, a daughter. Now you begin to comprehend my story. I should not, situated as I was, have dreamed of aspiring to her hand; but she honoured me with her regard, her father more than approved of the arrangement, and by marriage I stepped into the name and the place of the dead son.

"Absent from England, and likely to remain absent for ever, I made no mention to father or daughter of the few relations I possessed. Within a couple of years of my marriage, however, the brother with whom Mr. Irwin had originally been in partnership here died childless, and his fortune and his business passed to the man with whom he had quarrelled forty years previously. Immediately upon this event he was seized with that *maladie du pays* which, sooner or later, afflicts every true-born Briton, and nothing would content him but to dispose of the American business, and return to London and Eastcheap. How earnestly I entreated he would let me have the American business, I could not tell you; but he refused. His whim was to make his name world-known in connection with this establishment, and it was not for me, who owe everything almost I possess to his generosity, to cross such a fancy."

"Certainly not," agreed Mr. Wright promptly, remembering, no doubt, that if old Mr. Irwin's whim had not chanced to bring him across the Atlantic, the rectory would most probably have been stripped of some of its choicest treasures. "The gentleman I had the pleasure of seeing yesterday, then, no doubt is your respected father-in-law?"

"Yes; eccentric, but admirable—a just man, a staunch friend, an affectionate father. Happy in his business, in the home he makes in London with us, and happy, above all, in his grandchildren—in one especially, a boy, who is hereafter to compass wonders in the way of commercial achievement. A cheerful interior, you will think. Yet there is a slight shadow lying over it. My wife's health is wretched. I do not know what is the matter with her, neither do the doctors, neither does she herself. If she had been a poor woman, and compelled to exert herself, it is possible her health might have been better. As matters stand, she has sunk into a state of physical helplessness and mental irritability, which compels us to avoid subjecting her to the slightest annoyance. Were I differently situated—were I a free man, even if a much less wealthy—were my wife strong, and able to share any trouble with me, our house, of course, would be the most fitting home for my niece to come to."

"I understand your position—I recognize the difficulty. You *could not* take her to your own home," remarked Mr. Wright, thinking of his wife Selina, and the hundred a year she had already in the dead of night verbally appropriated to many domestic needs.

"You do not understand all my difficulty yet," continued Mr. Irwin. "I never could have mentioned the existence of this girl, to whom I am, in fact, sole guardian, without entering into a number of details which, for various reasons, are to me fraught with very great pain; and it would be utterly impossible for me to open the subject now without introducing an apple of discord into my home."

"Utterly," agreed Mr. Wright. Sorry indeed would he have been, if similarly situated, to take such an apple and present it for Selina's acceptance.

"Therefore I judged it better to look out for some family with whom I could place my little niece," finished Mr. Irwin. "I advertised my requirements, and have had many interviews with various persons in consequence; but all proved more or less unsatisfactory, and I had almost made up my mind to allow her to remain at school for another year, when you came to Riversdale."

"A most providential visit for me," murmured the Rector, with a lively memory of the fifty pounds, and a still livelier faith in other fifties he trusted were yet to follow.

"I trust it may prove providential for my niece," said Mr. Irwin, "for she is a very lonely little woman."

"Poor dear!" ejaculated Mr. Wright. "It shall not be our fault, Mr. Irwin, if she is not happy in our humble home—that I promise you."

"Thank you," said Mr. Irwin. "I am sure you will fulfil your promise;" and the pair shook hands once more.

"By-the-bye," remarked the Rector, returning after he reached the first landing, and putting his head inside the door again, "you have not yet told me the young lady's name."

"Miles," was the reply.

"Not her Christian name, surely!" exclaimed Mr. Wright, to whom the cognomen was familiar enough in his own dear land.

"That is Bella."

"Bella Miles," repeated the Rector. "I shall not forget. Much obliged. Good morning."

——◆——

CHAPTER XIII.

MR. WRIGHT WONDERS WHAT SELINA WILL SAY.

IT seemed as if, after all, Miss Bella Miles, kept so studiously from disturbing the domestic peace—if peace such an armed neutrality could be called—of Mr. and Mrs. Irwin, was to

prove, even before she appeared at Fisherton, an apple of discord between the Rector and his wife.

There were many things Mrs. Wright wanted to do on the
strength of her coming, which even Mr. Wright's slight knowledge of Mr. Irwin's character and position taught him could
not be done; and when he ventured to suggest difficulties, Selina
waxed fractious.

"Of course we must refurnish a bed-room for her," said Mrs.
Wright.   "She can sleep in it when no one is staying here;
and it will do for best bed-chamber when Colonel Leschelles,
or any one else very particular, comes for a few days.   And we
had better have good articles when we are buying—they always
prove the cheapest in the long run."

"You cannot get them without ready money," ventured Mr.
Wright; "and where that is to come from perhaps you know.
I confess I do not."

"It shall come from Mr. Irwin," she replied, standing well to
her guns.

"I don't think it will," said the Rector; "at any rate, I should
not select the things till you have his cheque in your purse to
pay for them.   But of course you know best."

Which remark putting the lady on her mettle, she at once
went to her desk, and in an extremely clear, pretty, and feminine hand, wrote a clever little note to Mr. Irwin, assuring him
of the pleasure she should feel in welcoming his niece to the
rectory, and adding a hope that in time the young girl "may
become as much attached to me as I am sure I shall be to
her."   After this statement, which had no insincerity about it,
since Mrs. Wright's power of attaching herself to unlikely ob-
jects was indeed as boundless, and oftentimes as foolish, as her
charity, the Rector's wife went on to say:

"So as to be certain to have everything ready for her recep-
tion by the time you mentioned to Mr. Wright, I am just order-
ing furniture for her room—ours being too heavy and old-fashioned, not to say shabby, to please a young lady whose tastes
have been formed abroad.   I hope to have all bright and pretty
to greet her on her arrival here.   Again assuring you that nothing
love and care can do to promote her happiness shall be wanting
on my part,   "Believe me,
                        "Yours very sincerely,
                          "SELINA WRIGHT."

"Good heavens! they will refurnish the rectory on the strength of that hundred a year," was Mr. Irwin's first thought; while once again the reality of the unwelcome visitor whose presence had driven Mr. Wright to Riversdale seemed an utter impossibility. "Could the Rector and his wife be sane?" he wondered. "Was it credible that, within ten days of having his goods rescued from the sheriff, Mr. and Mrs. Wright were actually talking of purchasing more goods, which in their turn would, no doubt, if this was the way the family at Fisherton meant to live on bread and water, be watched and guarded, when the next instalment of the old debt became overdue, by another emissary from Mr. Gath Reuben, sheriff's officer?

"Instead of benefiting, I shall be ruining them," considered Mr. Irwin. "What ought I to do in the matter?" and he was perplexing himself on this point, when it suddenly crossed his mind that the Wrights were sane enough; that Mrs. Wright had apprised him of her hospitable intentions, with a view of getting the money to pay for them out of his purse; and that the sooner he made her understand he had no intention of letting her do anything of the sort, the better it would prove for all parties interested.

Having so decided, he took pen in hand, and, in writing which exactly resembled copperplate, replied to Mrs. Wright's note as follows :—

"512 Eastcheap. London,
"29th July, 18—.

"My dear Madam,

"I hasten to express my thanks for your very kind note, just received. Bella will, I trust, do her utmost to merit your good opinion, and to deserve the affection you are so generous as to offer. But pray do not make any alteration in the arrangements of your house on her account. Believe me, she will be more than satisfied with the present appointments of any room it may be most convenient for you to assign her. A girl who has been for years the inmate of a French school can have had no opportunity of acquiring a taste for luxuries; and, situated as she is, it would be most undesirable for her ever to do so. With assurances of my respect, and gratitude for all your kind intentions with regard to my niece's comfort and happiness,

"I have the honour to remain

"Yours faithfully,
"W. C. Irwin."

At the period of the world's history of which I write, the morning's post at Fisherton came heralded by the sound of a bugle. On the especial morning when Mr. Irwin's missive arrived at the rectory—breakfast happening to be rather later than usual—Mrs. Wright was dispensing weak tea to the family generally, when the letters were brought in.

Copperplate penmanship being apt, as all the world knows, to occupy a considerable amount of space, Mr. Irwin's epistle felt bulky enough to have contained half a dozen cheques, for which reason Mrs. Wright laid it down beside her cup, with a satisfied little pat, and looked across at her husband with a look which said, "The grey mare has again proved the better horse."

Before he had finished his breakfast, Mr. Wright was called away to speak to one of his churchwardens; and by the time that individual had said his say and departed, the children were fed and out in the garden.

Cheerfully the Rector stepped back into the parlour, exclaiming, as he entered :

"Well, my dear, how much has our good friend sent you?"

"Read for yourself," said Mrs. Wright, handing him the note, with an air of resignation. "You need not talk to me about the man being a gentleman—and writing such a hand, too, like a clerk's!"

"I can tell you I thought I had never seen a nicer hand than his when he signed that cheque," observed her husband.

"Oh! that is all past and done with," retorted Mrs. Wright, whose gratitude for past favours was even more evanescent than that of the Reverend Dion. "It is quite clear to me we have a Jew to deal with—yes, a Jew Christian—and we shall not be at all the better for Miss or her hundred a year—having to keep an extra servant, too."

Now, this was one of the points over which she and her husband had argued not a little, and, consequently, the reverend gentleman at once replied that he could see no reason, or rhyme either, in keeping another servant.

"We have a pair already," he remarked, not without reason on his side, "and between them they get through less work than when we had only one. Given that we take on a third, we shall have to keep them, and do all the work ourselves."

"I wish you had to do my work for a day—only one," said

Mrs. Wright; "and you would not talk so glibly about three servants being unnecessary."

Having delivered herself of which sentiment, Mrs. Wright took her parasol, strolled out into the garden, found a comfortable seat, and was soon absorbed in a new novel. Never, in their poorest days, had the Rector's wife failed to pay her subscription to a well-stocked library.

"It was essential to their position to keep *au courant* with what was going on in the literary world," she said. And to do Mrs. Wright justice, she read a greater number and variety of books than any reviewer.

Curiously enough, all the things Mrs. Wright considered it incumbent upon her to perform, in order to maintain that position necessary to their well-being and success in life, were those for which she had a natural taste. Ill-conditioned people said she never believed in a duty unless it chanced to be a pleasure likewise; to which the lady herself, on one occasion, retorted, that it was only right to feel duty a pleasure.

"I am sure I try to do so," finished the Rector's wife; and on this principle she found that duty demanded a third servant in addition to the two, whose wages, though paid in a scrambling, irregular sort of fashion, they were scarcely able to manage.

"She must assist with the needlework, and get up your shirts, dear," explained Mrs. Wright, when demonstrating that a third servant would prove a saving instead of an expense. "We must not employ a laundress then at all, even for your shirts."

The meekest of men domestically, Mr. Wright nevertheless rebelled at this. "Help with the needlework she may," he said, "but get up my linen she never shall. I do not object to a shabby coat occasionally; but wear shirts looking as if they were mangled, and cravats like wisps, I will not; remember that, Selina."

Whereupon Selina observed that he always thwarted her in any scheme she proposed for reducing the domestic expenditure.

"I am not sure," thought Mr. Wright, as he walked through his parish, head well up, chest protruded, umbrella shouldered —"I am not sure" (he pronounced the latter word shu-ah) "whether Providence did not intend the shortness of money, at which I have so often repined, as a blessing. There is an under-current of mercy in many of those misfortunes poor humanity finds it so hard to endure ; and it may be that I have purchased domestic happiness at the cheap price of chronic insolvency. It may be, God forgive me the ungracious thought! that Selina, if easy in her mind about pecuniary matters, might develop some faults of another kind, fatal to that peace which has hitherto brooded over our home."

Before the next Sunday Mr. Wright had eliminated a sermon from this idea. Having, for a wonder, received no dunning or threatening letters during the whole week, he was able to give more thought than usual to the subject he proposed treating ; and he wrote what he wanted to say carefully, and blotted out freely, the result being a very good discourse, to which Mrs. Wright listened with pleased though critical ears.

" I am certain, Dion," she said, as they walked home together in the summer twilight—it was at evening service the Rector preached the sermon in question—"that no one in the church could have failed to take some good for him or herself out of your words to-night. It was all so true and yet so plain. I have not your facility of expression, Dion, nor, of course, your grasp of mind, but I declare that often, in a vague sort of way, I have thought the evils we consider most unendurable are really blessings in disguise. For instance (I know you will not misunderstand what I say), it has sometimes occurred to me, if we had not been obliged to struggle for a large family and contend with poverty, you might not have been one-half so amiable as you are ; you might have been unreasonable, inclined to be captious and irritable about trifles. Now, Dion, what are you laughing at? I am not jesting. I really do not think you could bear the sun of prosperity as well as you have done the winds of adversity."

" I should like to be tried, my dear," answered the Rector, forgetting to practise the virtue himself had inculcated, and then he laughed again ; but he did not dare tell his wife that the same idea about her had given birth to his sermon.

" It is really very funny," he said to himself, as he put his manuscript away with a goodly company of other documents of the same nature. " I shall never be able to preach that sermon again with gravity—never ! "

For Mr. Wright had brought a certain sense of humour into the world with him ; and not all the years spent in borrowing and begging money, to keep wolves away from the domestic hearth, had been able to destroy his appreciation of any circumstance which struck him as ludicrous.

The furniture was not bought, but the new maid was hired; and then arose another little misunderstanding between the Rector and his wife.

Mr. and Mrs. Irwin were going to Paris, and it was Mr. Irwin's wish that his new friend should repair to the same place, at the same time, in order that Miss Miles might be committed to his charge by her uncle, and brought back to Fisherton by the Rector of that "favourite summer resort"—see local guide-book.

Mr. Irwin, of course, was to hand Mr. Wright a sufficient sum to cover his travelling and hotel expenses. And Mr. Wright, happy at the prospect of such a holiday as a schoolboy, delightedly closed with the proposal, and returned home, never doubting but that Selina would be delighted also to hear of the pleasure in store for her husband. To his astonishment, Mrs. Wright at once objected to the whole scheme.

"I do not think it would be at all proper, Dion, for you to be wandering about the Continent alone with a young lady," she began.

"But, my dear," he interrupted, "I have no idea of wandering about the Continent with a young lady. I shall bring her straight home."

"If it be necessary for any one to go, I am the proper person," persisted Mrs. Wright.

"Come, Selina, that is good!" cried the Rector. "If it is not the correct thing for me to travel from Paris to London with a chit no older than one of my own girls, I am quite positive it would be most improper for you to be running over Paris with Mr. Irwin."

"Don't be immoral, Dion," entreated his wife.

"My dear, if any immorality has been suggested, most certainly I am not the one to blame. So far as I am concerned, you are welcome to go on this trip instead of me; but I do not think Mrs. Grundy would be satisfied with such a proceeding, and I am quite certain Mr. Irwin would not."

"I must beg of you not to mention Mr. Irwin to me," said Mrs. Wright. "He is not a gentleman, I am convinced. No gentleman would have so completely ignored me throughout this whole arrangement as he has done. But I am determined to assert my position. I shall go to Paris to fetch that girl."

"If such is your resolve," remarked Mr. Wright, "we shall have to travel together, for, most decidedly, I mean to fetch that girl."

Which was a very strong position for the Rector, who usually deferred to his wife, to take up.

"Very well; let us arrange to do so," she said, after a minute's pause. "I dare say we can manage to get the money somehow."

Cash was short enough at the rectory just then. But the state of the funds did not stop Mrs. Wright's contemplated journey. She packed her trunk, she made some shiftless arrangements for the well-being of her children, and then she caught a severe cold—so severe that the doctor forbade her leaving her room, and Mr. Wright consequently set out for Paris alone, enjoyed himself there for four days thoroughly, and on the fifth was introduced by Mr. Irwin to his niece.

"I tell Bella she has grown quite a woman since I saw her," said Mr. Irwin, with a grave smile. "I must not call her my little niece any longer, must I, Mr. Wright?"

But Mr. Wright did not answer. For the moment he was struck literally dumb. He had expected to see an unformed, shy, retiring school miss; and suddenly there was presented to his astonished gaze a most beautiful girl-woman, the most beautiful girl, the Rector decided, he had ever seen; a young girl possessed of a charming voice, and still more charming manners— who seemed to pervade the room with her beauty, and who filled Mr. Wright's heart with a terrible apprehension.

"What will Selina say?" he thought. "What are we to do in our house with a creature like this?"

CHAPTER XIV.

THE FIRST EVENING.

HAD Mr. Wright known as much about women as he did about many things—say writs, for example—he would not have spoiled the pleasure of his homeward journey by speculating on what Selina might say.

Men are very catholic in their ideas of beauty. If a face is pretty and a figure good, it matters little to the masculine mind whether the owner be tall or short, plump or slight, fair or dark, pensive or *piquant.* A woman, on the contrary, has, as a rule, only one standard, and that is herself. The world—the usages of society—the little commonplace experiences of every-day life —the natural and charming deceitfulness of her sex, teach her to try to disguise this peculiarity even from other women ; and therefore it is that we so often hear the phrases " sweet," " charming," " pretty, fragile creature," " such a grand face," and other expressions of a similar character, which might well deceive any one unaccustomed to look behind the curtain.

Sitting behind that curtain, however, in the *abandon* of dressing-gown and whatever may be the present substitute for curl-papers—or *tête-à-tête* at five-o'clock tea—or dreamily chatting by the sea-side while the waves ripple in and out upon the sand— or drawn into the still closer confidence engendered by a wet afternoon in a country house,—woman, talked to by woman, knows " all about it." She learns how Mrs. Juno " is distrustful of small snake-like women ; " how interesting Miss Hysteria wonders what people can like 'n Diana ; how Light-hair thinks there is always something staring about black eyes ; while Black-eyes says, " for her part," she believes " there never yet was a straightforward woman to be found under the outward guise of a pretty doll."

We hear a great deal about the attraction of physical antagonism ; but the reader may be certain this attraction never exists in the same sex. A woman's ideal of a hero may be as opposite to herself as night is to day; but her true ideal of a heroine will be the creature she has seen reflected back from her mirror every day since, perched on tiptoe, she first beheld her own face in the looking-glass.

Precisely the same remark would hold good with regard to men, were it not that men are not interested in men in the same way as women are in women.

To most men, every man he meets is a possible source of profit; to all women, every woman assumes the form of a past, present, or future rival. If she cannot talk better she can dress better; if she cannot do either she can "look sweet," and so deceive humanity. If she takes a different line altogether, and expresses depreciatory opinions of mankind—not including its feminine portion—then male vanity is tickled and male curiosity aroused, and, like David, her victims are tens, whilst those of her non-admiring lady friends are units.

All of which facts poor Mr. Wright, through that masculine love of generalization which is the snare of his sex, overlooked altogether.

Simply he saw that Bella Miles was beautiful exceedingly; and he therefore worried himself all the way from Paris to London over the consideration that Selina would not like it. Why he thought this, he must have failed to inform an inquirer. All he could have said, if examined on oath, amounted to no more than: "Though my dear Selina has more than the virtues of her sex, she has also a few of its failings, and sometimes she does not care for pretty women."

Which was quite true. But then he left out of calculation the fact that Mrs. Wright might not consider Miss Miles pretty. If that idea had only occurred to him, how happy he might have felt *vis-à-vis* to a girl with great dark eyes, clear olive complexion, wonderful black hair, a rare beautiful smile, and an almost foreign accent.

"We shall be good friends, I hope," he said, in his pompous, priestly, genially patronizing manner.

"Dear sir, no doubt," she answered; "it must be so easy to feel good friends towards you."

"You must not flatter me, my child," he replied, pleased, nevertheless, with her words; and then he laid his hand softly on the girl's head, and stroked her dark hair thoughtfully, the while he saw her expression alter, and the sunlight that had glanced across her face change to shadow.

How many times in the after days he beheld the same change turn the dark eyes, from sunlit waters to pools of darkness, it sickens him now to remember.

For, liking him, she proved so good and so true : not one of his own children, charming as the Rector thought they were, served him with so sweet an alacrity as she.

From the hour they met first in Paris, till the end, he found no change—no shadow of turning in his new *protégée*—whilst she——?

If you asked Mr. Wright how she found him, he would answer impatiently :

"I was a man beset. What is the use of looking back? If I did wrong, I am sorry for it."

And he is, without any "if" about the matter. Between Mr. Wright's self, and God, there lies knowledge of a story the Rector would give all he now possesses to be able to remember as untrue. To him, in the watches of the night, there come dark eyes, and low-toned voice laden with reproaches—eyes, the language of which he ought to have been able to understand ; voice, musical with the burden of an unspoken sorrow. A life laid in his hand, as it were, to answer for—laid there by chance, as it seemed, but really, as he afterwards understood, by no chance at all ; which he used for his own purposes ; which he marred because he, a servant of the Almighty, had found himself the slave to debt, and could furnish nor eyes, nor ears, nor understanding, save how best to keep creditors at bay, and continue the shiftless, harassed life he had led every day since the first hour of his marriage.

It is of no use his mentioning these visitations to Selina, his wife.

An admirable woman still, no doubt : good to the poor, fond of her children, attached to her husband, lenient to the peccadilloes of her servants,—nevertheless quite persuaded that Mr. Irwin was very little better than a swindler ; and Bella Miles a bad, unprincipled, deceitful girl, who ought never to have been permitted to sit, clothed in wickedness and duplicity, by any Christian hearth.

At the particular Christian hearth mentally referred to by

Mrs. Wright, Mr. Wright and Miss Miles arrived in time for that composite meal, a "meat dinner."

Thinking, probably, that Miss Miles might consider there was safety in a multitude, Mrs. Wright had elected for the whole of her family to greet the new arrival ; and accordingly, from Miss Maria down to the "puling infant," represented by Rosa, the latest arrow in the rectorial quiver, all the children sat round the table, staring at the new-comer with that delicate consideration which obtains amongst young animals of the human species.

Under such circumstances Miss Miles naturally became nervous. She spoke French when she should have spoken English ; and then when she apologized, the middle-sized children giggled, and the elder smiled with that air of superiority natural in the offspring of clergymen of any denomination in England ; whilst the small fry set her with their round eyes, and mouths like the letter O, and wondered to themselves why she did not eat cake when it was pressed upon her—or, as an Irishwoman, then priestess of the culinary department at Fisherton Rectory, remarked subsequently, "Make a baste of herself like the rest o' them."

"Curran, dear," said Mrs. Wright, addressing one of her numerous offspring, "run away to the kitchen and tell Nurse Mary to send us some more butter ; don't drop it by the way, that is a good boy."

The good boy so addressed involuntarily let one leg slip from the front to the side of his seat, but made no further sign of hearing, every sense being apparently absorbed in staring at the stranger.

"Curran, did you hear me ?" asked his mother, languidly.

"What do you mean, sir, by not doing what your mamma tells you ?" inquired Mr. Wright, who always supported the maternal authority. "Sit still, my dear," added the Rector to his guest, who had involuntarily risen to do Mrs. Wright's bidding—the only creature at the table who seemed willing to perform an errand ; "we do not expect you to fetch butter from the pantry—which, indeed, our servants ought to do, as they are paid for it," added poor Mr. Wright, with a reflective sigh.

"Ah ! Dion," said Mrs. Wright, plaintively, "Miss Miles can understand, I am sure, what servants have to do in a house like ours. Run, Curran, and perhaps I may find something nice for you about twelve to-morrow."

Thus entreated, Curran, who had no fear before his eyes of anything which might have made him move much more rapidly, slid down from his chair and repaired to the kitchen, having first fortified himself for going into the wilderness by seizing a great hunch of bread.

Armed with this, he made his way to the servants' quarter, where he gave a full account of his impressions of Miss Miles to an appreciative audience.

"Jus' like sloes," said one who had first seen the young lady, referring to her eyes.

"A skin like a wild Indian," added another, who had heard Mrs. Wright express an opinion adverse to Miss Miles' complexion; and so the kitchen criticism proceeded, while the parlour waited for its butter.

"Maria, ring the bell," said Mr. Wright at length; whereupon Miss Maria rose and rang a sharp summons, which fetched the new servant from the conversational abysses in which she had been plunged.

"Did not Master Curran tell you we wanted some more butter?" asked Mrs. Wright.

"No, ma'am; and there isn't any more in the house," was the concise answer; at which Miss Miles blushed crimson, just as though she had consumed the reserve fund herself.

"Hey! ho hum!" sang Mr. Wright to himself, gently tapping his chest.

Spite of the debt and the humiliation, and the work and the worry, and the mental wear and tear, these little *contretemps* were not of infrequent occurrence, and the Rector might have become accustomed to them. But the Rector could not become accustomed to them, so cut short Mrs. Wright's indignant remonstrance with the servant upon the iniquity of allowing "things to run out without informing her, Mrs. W., of the fact," by saying:

"You can go, Mary." Then turning to Miss Miles, he added, "Such accidents will happen."

Which was quite true, as Miss Miles found before she had been two days in the house.

Tea finished, and all the children fed, Mrs. Wright proposed an adjournment to the drawing-room, where, after having looked out over the garden, on which a drizzling rain was falling, and advanced various topics for conversation and exhausted them all, and talked at great length of Paris—which Mr. Wright called, in honour of his recent visit, Pa-ree—the Rector, who sometimes declared "he knew nothing of music, and wished every one else in the world was in like case," merely as a new device for passing time, and as a polite attention to their new inmate, asked Miss Miles to play.

Miss Miles immediately rose to comply with this request—rose blushing, as was her wont.

"Shall Maria fetch your music down for you, dear?" suggested Mrs. Wright; "or will you look over the girls' pieces and see if there are any you know?"

"Thank you," answered Miss Miles, "but I can manage without the notes, I think."

"The true way—the true way," commented Mr. Wright, watching her as she took up her position before the Broadwood square, which was always open on every working day, and very frequently not closed at night.

"You will find it a little out of tune, I am afraid," remarked Mrs. Wright.

"It is, rather," agreed Miss Miles, as she ran her fingers over the keys; and indeed, even had the instrument been young as it was old, it could scarcely have proved otherwise. The practice of Kalkbrenner's Exercises for a few hours per diem, to say nothing of agonized attempts to hammer out operatic airs "simply arranged for young beginners," and national melodies arranged for no one in particular, had naturally exercised a somewhat detrimental influence upon the hammers.

"Now, Curran," said Mrs. Wright, "if you do not keep quiet, I shall send you out of the room;" whereupon Curran made a hideous face at Rosie, who immediately burst into shrill shrieks of laughter.

"You naughty boy!" Mrs. Wright was beginning, when the opening bars of the piece Miss Miles had selected literally stopped her utterance.

No "trying back" now—no fumbling amongst the intricacies of unfamiliar notes—no mistakes between sharps and flats—no slurring over difficult passages.

A thorough musician had her hands on the keys, and the old piano knew this, and gave out under her touch such tone and power as time and ill-usage had still left in its frame.

Ordinarily, it was a cracked, vibrating-stringed, feeble-voiced instrument, the notes of which rattled, while suffering at the hands of the Misses Wright, like loose teeth ; but that evening it seemed to have renewed its youth once more, and answered to the clamour of martial music — to the hurrying of many feet —to the steady, stately march of an advancing army—to the melody of exultation and the lament of sorrow.

For suddenly the key changed into a minor, and then the piano told a story of such woe and such tenderness—of such sweet sadness, such subtle longing regret—that its own weakness and age were forgotten in the pathetic beauty of the recited tale.

"Exquisite ! exquisite ! — char — ming !" exclaimed Mr. Wright, who did indeed consider he had listened to a performance as wonderful as unexpected.

"Thank you," said Mrs. Wright ; and the Rector, looking at her, knew something was wrong.

"What is the name of that ?" asked Miss Maria, who had hung about the piano, trying, perhaps, to "catch the knack," as fond mothers sometimes counsel their darlings to do.

As for Rosie and Curran, they both sat with their eyes and mouths wide open, precisely as they might have sat had the house been coming down about their ears. They were frightened into good behaviour. When that old piano, which they had thumped with no gentle hands themselves, took to making such a noise, what might not happen next?

"And all without any turning over, too," secretly thought Curran, who had hitherto regarded that part of the performance as essential to success.

"You sing, I am sure," said Mr. Wright, as Miss Miles, after dreamily touching a few chords, was about to leave the instrument. "If you are not too tired, pray favour us with one little song."

Miss Miles laughed, and resumed her seat. For a few seconds her fingers wandered over the notes, as if uncertain of the air they should select ; then she began the accompaniment to that which, if not the sweetest of all Irish melodies, is, at all events, sweet exceedingly—"Luggelaw," mated by Moore to words flowing and graceful.

The drawing-room at Fisherton was one well adapted for hearing music to advantage, and in the silence of that summer's evening the singer's voice throbbed through the apartment, filling each remote corner with melody and pathos.

For the moment after the last note died away there ensued **a** dead silence, which Mrs. Wright broke by saying :

"You have an exquisite voice, and sing beautifully. Dion, will you ring for candles? I think it must be nearly time for prayers. Maria, close the piano ;" which was a blow to Maria, as she had been hovering about the instrument, in hopes of being requested to play " Il mio Tesoro."

Mrs. Wright, however, was a clever woman, and thought it better to defer the revelation of her daughter's accomplishments to some future occasion.

She had expected a Miss Miles, but not the Miss Miles who appeared at Fisherton.

She had expected a vague " miss," with little vanities, little affectations, little knowledge, a smattering of learning ; but for this girl-woman she was not prepared ; and Mrs. Wright felt she must reconsider the position.

And for this reason Mrs. Wright, when discomfited over Miss Miles' instrumental performances, and astonished at her singing, fell back upon her own lines, and suggested that safest of all manœuvres, prayers.

Which stopped further hostilities and surprises for the time, and gave her the night to organize and reflect.

" Well, my dear," said the Reverend Dion, when, the family all in bed, he and his wife sat *tête-à-tête* in the study—Mr. Wright imbibing that tumbler of punch, made out of the best Irish whisky—whisky the friend who sent it knew had never paid the Queen a halfpenny—which often wooed sleep to visit the rectorial pillow, when otherwise she might have been requested long enough and vainly enough to do so—" Well, my dear, and what do you think of Miss Bella Miles ? "

" I do not know what to think," answered Mrs. Wright.

" Of course, of course," agreed the Rector. " It is indeed early to form an opinion as to her heart and disposition." Here Mr. Wright handed his wife a wineglassful of the subtle beverage contained in his own tumbler. " What do you think of her looks ? " he ventured.

" Well, I don't think she is quite my style, Dion," answered the lady, with an engaging rounding of one shoulder, and the old trick of lifting her chin in the air, and casting her eyes over it, or trying to do so, which had rendered Miss Curran so irresistible at hunt and yacht balls in the days when she had lovers galore, and proposers were as few as primroses at Christmas. "Some people—some men "—this last statement with a shake of the worn curls, and a smile that long and severe service had not deprived of all its coquettish charm—"admire that sort of face, I am aware ; but still, Dion dear, confess that, beside our Maria, for instance, Miss Miles lacks that sweet, guileless look which seems to me—but perhaps I am foolish—to be the exclusive possession of a girl who has been carefully brought up at home, under the eye of a loving mother——"

"Ah, my dear ! there are few mothers like you," said Mr. Wright, which was perhaps fortunate, if England were to support her population.   "And I knew you would feel attached to this poor orphan girl.   She has nice manners, I think."

"Unformed," remarked Mrs. Wright.

"Well, she has not been accustomed to society," observed the Rector.   "You will form her, Selina."

"I will do my best for her in every way," said Mrs. Wright. "But, do you know, she strikes me as being very reserved—and —and—odd."

"Perhaps so," was the reply.   "She is in a strange place, and no doubt things do seem odd to her at first."

"That may be ; and yet I think no Irish girl would have risen from table as she did to-night when I spoke about that butter."

"I think I once knew an Irish girl who would have run on any one's errand when I used to sit at her father's table," said Mr. Wright, throwing a dash of sentiment into his voice as he looked at his wife and mixed himself another tumbler.

"You foolish Dion !   Are you so fond of your old wife still that you care to remember those times ?"

"If I had not you and the children to be fond of, how could I bear my life ?" he answered gallantly, forgetful of the fact that without either he might at least have been free from debt ; and for reply she laid her hand on his, and Mr. Wright knew an impending storm had been averted, and that Miss Miles' advent would pass over without boisterous weather ensuing.

"She will be of use to the girls in their music," remarked Mr. Wright, after a pause.   "They can play duets, and that sort of thing together, eh ? "

"I am not quite sure," said the lady, doubtfully, "whether her style of playing is quite correct in a private person.   Professionals, and those kind of people," added Mrs. Wright, with a wave of her hand towards the window, signifying that "those kind" dwelt somewhere outside Fisherton Rectory, "have to deal in effects; but I doubt whether I should care to have a child of ours exhibiting herself as Miss Miles did this evening. It is all very fine and Frenchified, no doubt; but I am afraid it is not feminine. And beyond all things, Dion, I should like our girls to be feminine."

If Mr. Wright had expressed his secret feelings at that moment, he would have said that he thought their girls were too feminine already, in the way of fine-ladyism and uselessness; but it was a rule of husband and wife, and not a bad one, to praise their offspring and each other, for which reason he murmured, "Bless them all," including mentally in that blessing the lonely girl, to whom his heart, or at least as much of it as debt had left under his own control, had gone out in sympathy.

"Do you think her French will be any good?" he inquired after a pause, the "her" referring, as Mrs. Wright understood, to Miss Miles.

"I must first see what books she has brought with her," explained Mrs. Wright, as though a young lady leaving school were likely to have a library of immoral novels hidden in her trunks. The Rector's wife had been reading up Racine and Molière, "La Henriade" and "Charles the Twelfth," as a good preliminary to conversing with Miss Miles in the language of Voltaire; but, after five minutes of the young lady's society, she decided to eschew every tongue save English.

More especially as she had her doubts about Miss Mile English. Mrs. Wright was a very shrewd and observant woman, and after she had lain down in bed and Mr. Wright was more than half asleep, she woke him up by saying:

"I wonder, Dion, if that girl is quite right about her I's?"

"About her what?" asked poor Mr. Wright, divided in his mind between burglary and the breaking of the Seventh Commandment.

"About the letter H," explained Mrs. Wright. "It seemed to me she made a mess of it once or twice this evening, more especially when she was singing. I am quite certain she said:

'Then came that voice when all forsaken
This 'eart long 'ad sleeping lain.'"

"Tush! that is French," retorted Mr. Wright, fresh from Paris. "I do wish you would let me go to sleep."

And thus exhorted, Mrs. Wright said no more—then.

Within three days, however, she was able to assure the Reverend Dion her instincts had, as usual, been true. In this wise knowledge came to her. Fine weather and sunshine once again prevailed, and whilst Mrs. Wright sat on her garden-chair reading the latest novel of that year, Miss Miles at a little distance squatted on the grass, her fingers employed on some delicate embroidery, her thoughts probably far enough away.

After they had remained thus silent for about half an hour, Master Curran, stealing softly across the lawn, came with a bound behind Miss Miles, and, with a sudden "Bo-o!" clasped both hands round her neck. Then came the revelation.

"Don't you—don't you, Curran!" cried the girl, in an access of nervous irritation. "You know I can't a-bear to be frightened."

Mrs. Wright dropped her book and took up her eye-glass.

"My dear child," she asked, "where did you learn English?"

Miss Miles made no reply: but her head drooped over her work, her fingers flew more rapidly in and out of the fine cambric, and a glow spread from throat to forehead.

That night Mrs. Wright, not without a certain sense of triumph, informed her husband she considered it would be only her duty to cease conversing in French entirely, to the end that Miss Miles might be taught "how English is spoken in a certain rank of English society."

CHAPTER XV.

A SPECIMEN DAY AT FISHERTON.

TIME passed on, and Miss Miles had settled down into her place at Fisherton Rectory. She was already one of the family. The boys called her Bella, and the girls "dear," and Mr. and Mrs. Wright called her both. Mrs. Wright had borrowed all her money, and the young ladies had tried on each separate article of dress she possessed, and admired some of her few ornaments so much that she requested their acceptance of those which took their fancy.

Mr. Irwin had sent down a new piano for her benefit; and though a rule was made that the instrument should be locked and the key kept either in the pocket of Mrs. Wright or Miss Miles, still the key was so generally not in Miss Miles' custody and out of that of Mrs. Wright, that the rule became nugatory, and the children worked their sweet will upon this full-compass Collard, as they had done upon the old six-and-a-half-octave Broadwood.

Occasionally Mr. Wright would remonstrate when he found Curran playing a tune with one sticky finger which left black marks on the note, or Rosie thumping the new keys with all the might of her little fat fists; but remonstrating in that house produced much the same effect as addressing the wind, and Miss Miles knew this, and wished Mr. Wright would not speak about the matter.

On the new instrument Maria and her sisters practised, and Miss Miles helped them with their music, and "put them in the way"—so Mrs. Wright defined the matter—of learning fresh pieces; and some duets were procured, of which Maria played the bass and Miss Miles the treble, and when Mr. Wright was easy in his mind, which was not often, he beat time approvingly, and said "the performance was char-ming."

As for French, Miss Miles would have talked it willingly enough, had any one wished to hear her discourse in that language, which she soon found no one did,

"Had it been Latin, now, or Greek," said Mr. Wright, with a merry twinkle in his eye, which showed that the humour of the position was not lost upon him, "I could have met you upon equal ground ; but French is too modern a language, and parley-vousing would be more of a toil than a pleasure to me."

Nevertheless Mr. Wright picked up a few French phrases from their visitor, and produced them upon occasion, not without effect. As for Mrs. Wright, she directed herself to the improvement of Miss Miles' English.

"You had better, my love," she said to that young lady, "write me each day a letter recording the events of the previous day, and then I will mark any errors I may find, and leave you to correct them."

Which was very good policy on the part of Mrs. Wright, as in many cases she would scarcely have known how to correct them herself.

Each morning, directly after breakfast, or at least as soon after breakfast as the Rector started on his round of parochial visiting, Miss Miles took possession of his study and wrote her letter to Mrs. Wright. When, as happened not unfrequently, Mr. Wright came back to indite some forgotten epistle, or to search for some paper, or to look for some book, he always said :

"Scribbling still, my dear ! why, what a wealth of incident you must find at Fisherton," or made other remarks of a similarly innocent description.

There were some events, however, which Miss Miles did not chronicle. She did not state the number of buttons she sewed on the Rector's shirts ; the state of order in which she kept his gloves, the rents she repaired in his surplices, the strings she stitched on his bands. It was not much she had it in her power to do for the Rector ; but what she did perform seemed very pleasant to a man who had always before been compelled to pause in his dressing, to shout for Selina or one of the servants to come to his assistance. No shouting now was required. Even to the loop on his umbrella, to the stitch needed where the silk had given from the wire, Miss Miles saw to his little wants.

And the Rector, who liked to go out looking trim and neat, faultless as regarded his linen, and sound in gloves as in orthodoxy, felt grateful to the girl who, paying them money for her keep, still did work which no servant had ever thought it worth her while to perform.

Naturally Mr. Irwin felt anxious to know how his niece liked her new home, how she got on with her studies, how she amused herself, what acquaintances she made, and so forth. And by way of answering all his questions, which were neither few nor far between, the young lady hit upon the device of sending him each week her letters to Mrs. Wright, which letters answered all the purposes of an objective diary.

Mrs. Wright had at a very early period of the exercises noticed that nothing of a subjective character occurred even in a single passage. Miss Miles might have been the reporter of a daily paper, so much did she say about others, and so little about herself. For the gushing sentimentalism of sweet seventeen Mrs. Wright looked in vain ; for any evidence of thought she scanned the written pages without success. An observant girl, able to remember the events of each day and chronicle them faithfully, but able at the same time to keep her opinion of those events well in the background.

"She is deep," decided Mrs. Wright, "and I fancy has a vein of sarcasm about her. Now, what does she mean by some passages in this letter?"—which the lady knew was meant as much for Mr. Irwin's information as for her own perusal.

"Tuesday.

"MY DEAR MRS. WRIGHT,

"I woke up early yesterday morning, and having got out of bed to look at the first snow of the season, decided on dressing and going downstairs. There, to my amazement, I found Nurse Mary, who explained the extraordinary *phenomonen* by stating 'she had not slept a wink all night with the toothache.'

"I asked her why she did not have the tooth out, and she replied that 'she did not want to lose her mark of mouth before her time.'

"When I offered to make some creosote out of a *Times* newspaper and cure her toothache, she received the suggestion with incredulity, and asked if I thought myself cleverer than Doctor Ryan, who said there was no cure for toothache except having the tooth out, unless it might be 'filling the mouth with cold water and sitting on the fire till it boiled.'

"We had a cup of tea together beside the kitchen fire, and the consequence of our mutual early rising proved to be that Mr. Wright was not called till half an hour later than usual.

"Wrote my letter to you before breakfast. After breakfast we were all very busy perfecting Colonel Leschelles' room. We made it quite smart with chintz and muslin, almost too beautiful, Nurse thinks, for sleeping purposes.

"Contradictory accounts are given of this Colonel Leschelles. Maria, *she* says he is at least a hundred, that he dyes his hair and wears stays, that he cannot endure the sight of a young person, and that the boys always light a bonfire when he leaves the house. Rosie, on the contrary, declares he is a 'sweet sweet man;' and Clara informed me as a strict secret that she is engaged to marry him when she is sixteen, that he has promised not to grow a day older until she has attained that age, and that it is agreed she is to have as much Everton toffee and as many peaches as she can eat. Curran declines to express any opinion till he knows what sort of a present the Colonel means to make him this Christmas. Mr. Wright speaks warmly of the coming visitor as 'a fine old English gentleman,' but Julia declares he ought to be sent to Madame Tussaud's in the character of an ancient beau. He is expected to arrive laden with gifts on Christmas Eve.

"After we had done up his room (the looking-glass is dressed with new book muslin tied back with blue ribbon to match the blue convolvulus on the chintz) it was time for dinner.

"Mr. Wright being in London, Curran offered to say grace in his stead, and though Mrs. Wright declined to allow this, he insisted at a later period upon telling us what he meant to have said. He had heard Roderick repeating it to Frank.

> 'One word's as good as ten,
> Go ahead—Amen.'

"For this misdemeanour he was deprived of his pudding, when he at once made matters worse by saying he was very glad not to have to eat it. If we knew what Cook had put in it, we would not eat it either.

"When dinner was finished we went to the vestry to finish our wreaths, etc., for decorating the church. Many ladies *where* there, young and old. Miss Faint has arrived at the conclusion that holly pricks her fingers, and Miss Bolton is of opinion Mr.

Wright ought to have a curate; she says a parish is dull without one, and that coming and going they make a pleasant change.

" We returned home tired and thirsty to tea, and found Mr. Wright at home with Curran beside him eating bread and jam. The child had waited for his papa at the gate, and stolen a march by telling him about his delinquencies, which Mr. Wright, upon promise of better behaviour, forgave; Curran then demanded bread and jam.

" Nurse waylaid me on the stairs to say if I really thought that 'concrete' would do her any good, she 'did not mind' letting me try it.

" Five minutes afterwards Mr. Wright rang the bell to know if the house was on fire.

" Two minutes later and Nurse was screaming out that I had poisoned and destroyed her, and entreating in a breath that her master would save her soul and preserve her life.

"As Roderick remarked—it was Satan casting out Beelzebub. This morning she declares the pain has moved out of her tooth on to her tongue.

" I think I have now exhausted all the news you would think it desirable for me to chronicle, and trusting your headache is much better,   " Believe me, dear Mrs. Wright,

" Yours affectionately,

" B. Miles."

Pencil in hand, Mrs. Wright sat pondering this letter rather than correcting it.

In addition to the news reported by hers affectionately B. Miles, there had been two annoying affairs with the servants and three persistent and most offensive duns. Mr. Wright had returned from London out of sorts, and Mrs. Wright had, as implied, gone to bed with a headache. All these things, except only the headache, Miss Miles had omitted, but quite enough remained in her letter to decide Mrs. Wright on selecting some other form of education than that of correspondence.

" It was my own fault," the Rector's wife argued. " I ought never to have suggested the reproduction of domestic and family gossip. Had I done my duty properly, I should have insisted on her writing an essay every day, and so educated her powers of thought instead of her powers of observation, which are far too keen already."

"My dear," she said, bringing forward once again the graces of her youth that had, according to Mr. Wright, turned the heads of all the marriageable and eligible men of Dublin in the days when she too was in her teens, "I think you have now so much improved your colloquial English that these letters may be discontinued. You had better take a fortnight's holiday, and then after the new year has fairly set in, we can consider the subjects upon which it will be most to your mental advantage to write."

In reply, Miss Miles simply bowed, and, taking her manuscript, corrected those passages which Mrs. Wright had pencilled as being capable of improvement.

"You have amended your errors very quickly and well," said Mrs. Wright, glancing over the sheet and handing it back again.

Miss Miles, with a pleasant "Thank you," received the letter, and at once tore it into slips, and placed the morsels under the grate.

"My dear," cried Mrs. Wright, "what are you doing?"

"Only burning some useless paper," answered Miss Miles quietly.

Mrs. Wright paused for a minute, then she remarked, "I hope, Bella—I do hope—you have not a bad temper."

"I hope not," was the reply. "I do not think I have. I only burnt this letter because I fancied—forgive me if I am wrong—you did not want my uncle to read it."

"My child, you are very foolish," said Mrs. Wright in her most matronly manner. "I trust nothing ever occurs at Fisherton Rectory which I should care for the whole world knowing."

"And if there were," retorted Miss Miles, her cheeks aflame and her head erect, "I trust you know such things would never be repeated by me. I have never mentioned even the merest trifle to my uncle I thought you and Mr. Wright might like me to keep secret. If I know little else, I know, at least, when to remain silent." And then and there she burst into a passion of tears.

"Bella—Bella, what is the matter?" exclaimed Mrs. Wright. "What have I said or done to cause you such grief?"

"Nothing—nothing," replied the girl for answer. "Only sometimes I cannot forget. I cannot."

"Forget what?" asked Mrs. Wright.

"Do not ask me. Nothing I can tell you or any one," was the answer. And Miss Miles left the room, leaving Mrs. Wright in a state of bewilderment impossible to describe.

"I have it," at length decided that astute lady. "Her mother or her father was mad, and she knows it. She has all the cleverness and secrecy of insanity, and the malady will break out some day in her. I must speak to Dion about this."

But when she did speak to Dion, he only said, "Pshaw! Selina, the girl has all her wits, believe me. There is a mystery, doubtless, but we were not sent into the world to solve it. Let us make what we can out of Mr. Irwin, and thank Heaven for the windfall, without troubling ourselves too much concerning the ins and outs of affairs that are no business of ours."

CHAPTER XVI.

INTRODUCES COLONEL LESCHELLES.

COLONEL LESCHELLES, for whose benefit the spare bed-room of Fisherton Rectory—Miss Miles' bed-room, in short—had been duly prepared, as narrated by that young lady, was an old friend of the Wrights—so old a friend, indeed, that the Rector declared the date of his first acquaintance with the Colonel was enshrouded in the mists of memory.

This is a good way some people have of forgetting the number of years which could be counted since they first made the acquaintance of this distinguished statesman or that admirable millionaire. They could tell to a day, I will warrant, when they first met poor Tom Styles, or Jack Oakes forced his company upon them; but it is really so long since they first knew Rothschild, and Baring, and the rest of the plutocracy, that the exact date has been rubbed, by the mere action of time, off Recollection's tablets.

It would not have required, however, any extraordinary amount of thought to enable Mr. Wright to state precisely the Christmas Eve on which he made Colonel Leschelles' acquaintance.

Had he chosen to do so, he could have told any inquirer the date, year, and hour when he set eyes for the first time on that gallant officer. He was at that period curate in a parish situated well away to the east of London, in the middle of the marshes, with no resident vicar, one resident Squire, a scattered population of about a couple of hundred souls, an old church, a full graveyard—ague to the south, fever to the north, bronchitis to the east, and rheumatism and consumption pervading the west almost exclusively, and spreading to the other three quarters when inclination or business called one or both diseases thither.

"For eleven weary months," to quote Mr. Wright's own words, "I vegetated in that slough of despond, most part of the time wifeless and childless. Except in the summer, I preached to about half a dozen of a congregation; there was not an educated man in the parish but one, and he was an atheist. As for the Squire, he had not an idea beyond horses, dogs, fat cattle, and good investments. He had plenty of money; but he spent as little as he could. He never entertained. During the whole time I had charge he never asked me to his house, or offered me a glass of wine when I called. The stipend, however, was good, as well it might be, and the duty light—if it had been heavy, I could not have performed it. I kept my health wonderfully, and Selina and the children kept theirs, at a distance. I lived at the vicarage, and the woman who was left in care of the furniture attended to my wants. Besides this woman, who was deaf, I never exchanged a word with any human being after my rounds were finished for the day, and the curtains were drawn and the shutters closed. Sometimes, when the flat marsh lands were covered deep in snow, or lay under water, and the wind came howling up from the German Ocean across those dreary wilds, I have sat by the fire in the old vicar's study, and imagined how a man might hang himself, or take to drink, or go mad, living alone in such a spot."

Even to such a spot, however, Christmas Eve came—such a Christmas Eve! The wind, after having blown for about three months from the east, as is the habit of the wind in these forlorn regions, suddenly changed to the south, and brought with it, on the Twenty-fourth of December, in that especial year of grace, such a fall of snow as was unparalleled in the memory of the oldest inhabitant, a certain Job Groom, who had, as man and boy, worked upon the farm and lands owned by Squire Olier and Squire Olier's forefathers for sixty-five years.

"There had been a very heavy fall of snow," so said Job, "the night Master Samuel was born;" and now there came a heavier fall, and Master Samuel, the Squire, was—quite in his prime, as it seemed to Job—dying; and, unless the weather changed greatly, Job did not see how he was ever to be buried. Job could remember that at the time of the heavy snow, when Master Samuel was born, graves could not be dug at all; and Job, sorry for his master's impending death, was still more sorry he should have selected such weather for flitting from this world to the next.

So Squire Olier lay dying. His house stood low, even for that low-lying district; and he had drunk heavily for many years past, in order to banish ague; and perhaps also because he liked strong liquors. The doctor, who came from the nearest town to attend him, said that he had drunk too much, and that brandy and hollands had between them signed his death-warrant.

Upon the other hand, the doctor said if he had not drunk so much he would probably not have lived so long. He made this remark to Mr. Wright while he and that gentleman were having something hot in the dining-room upon the especial Christmas Eve of which I am speaking, when Squire Olier was speeding to eternity with greater haste than he had ever ridden on his good horse Rochester back from hounds or market, with the sharp east wind cutting his head off, or the driving sleet beating in his eyes and blinding him.

"I shall not go just yet," said the doctor; "though I can be of no more use, I am afraid, still I may just as well wait for half an hour. Who succeeds, do you know?"

"It depends on his will," answered the Curate. "The place is his own, to bequeath to you or me, if he were so inclined. The heir he fixed on, however, offended him, and he has sent. I know, for I wrote the letter at his request, to some man—an officer not long returned from India—that I fancy he had half a notion of willing most of his property to. But the Colonel tarries; and if he had not tarried, I suppose our poor friend has been in no fit state to execute a will for days past."

They sat silent for a time over the fire in that dark wainscoted room. Without, the snow continued to fall softly; upstairs the Squire lay insensible. In the kitchen, servants, house and farm, huddled together round the hearth, reading warnings in the blaze of the wood fire, and seeing winding-sheets in the guttering candles. At every sound they started; and when occasionally one of the two women attending on the dying Squire crept downstairs, they looked at her as if she had come from another world.

There was no mistress at the farm, there had never been in Squire Samuel's time, and the servants spoke in hushed tones of some cruel disappointment in early life, which had kept the once young master single, and changed the whole course and meaning of his life.

In the parlour, the doctor and clergyman touched on the same subject; and Mr. Wright said he understood the lady— dead and dust long before—had been a sister of this very Colonel Leschelles, and a cousin of Mr. Olier's.

"Though he has lived the life of a boor, he comes of a good family, I believe," added the Curate; and he was about to enlarge upon the theme when the doctor said "Hush!" and rising, walked towards the door, which was opened at that moment by one of the watchers.

"Will you come upstairs, please, sir?" she asked. "He is very bad."

Thereupon doctor and clergyman proceeded to the sick-chamber, where they found Squire Olier so bad that he never could be worse.

The doctor did what lay in his power to soothe him; but his power was literally *nil*.

"It is almost the last struggle," he whispered to Mr. Wright. "All will soon be over."

And still the snow fell softly, and the graves in the distant

churchyard were covered, like the dead, from sight; and Mr.
Wright, with a great sense of pity for the human loneliness ot
the dying man, knelt by the bedside and prayed, till the doctor,
touching his shoulder, said :

"He has gone, poor fellow! He is past any help of ours."

At the same instant there was a peal at the front-door bell,
immediately followed by a rush of cold air into the house and a
sound of talking in the hall. Then, as Mr. Wright descended
the staircase, a servant met him and announced that Colonel
Leschelles had come.

Mr. Wright, re-entering the parlour, found standing before
the fire a tall, thin man — military, unquestionably— elderly,
presumably—a man who came to the point at once by asking :

"Am I in time?"

"He is dead!" answered the Curate; and for a minute not
a word was uttered. Then the Colonel spoke :

"I received a letter written by a Mr. Wright——"

"I am Mr. Wright," explained the Curate.

"But only late last night, as it has been following me from
place to place," continued the Colonel, acknowledging the information with a bow. "I have been travelling ever since.
I should like to have seen him alive once more. Poor Samuel!
we were good friends many a long year ago."

And there ensued another pause, broken this time by Mr.
Wright, who told the officer his cousin had been virtually dead
for some days previously, and that no speed he could have made,
even had the letter reached him in regular course, would have
enabled him to arrive in time.

"I am glad to know that," replied the other; "for I should
have liked to comply with his last request, if possible."

At this juncture the doctor came in to tell Mr. Wright he was
going, and to say he would inform Mr. Olier's solicitor of his
client's death. Then the doctor inquired if it was Colonel Leschelles' intention to remain in the house.

"I suppose I must," said the Colonel ruefully. "If I were
ever so much tempted to desert my post, I do not think, considering the road we have travelled, I should feel inclined to
retrace it. I hired a conveyance to bring me here, and I suppose the driver can put up for the night. It is not weather in
which to turn a dog out, or——"

"Anybody except a doctor," finished the other. "Doctors

are supposed to be weatherproof; but if I mean to get home at all, I must be off now."

"Better stay at the vicarage," suggested Mr. Wright.

"Only wish I could," was the reply: "if I did my wife would be fancying all manner of evil; and, besides, some patient will be sure to want me. Patients always do fall ill on Church holidays and snowy nights. But take the Colonel home with you, Mr. Wright. He will be far better and more comfortable away from here. Take him with you."

"Ay, that I will, if he is only willing to come," said Mr. Wright, laying a persuasive hand on the officer's sleeve as the doctor left the room. "Listen to me, Colonel: you will be miserable here, I know. The servants are upset; and if they were not, they would not be of much use to you. You can be of no service to our poor friend upstairs. Come with me to the vicarage, where I am, in the absence of my wife and children, leading a bachelor life. You can be as much alone as you like. The house is warm, if it is nothing else. I can give you a snug bit of supper to-night, and cut you a slice out of as fine a turkey as ever came to table to-morrow. Say you will come. Upon my honour I shall be as glad of your company as I should of that of my own brother."

Which, if the Colonel had known everything, would not have seemed a strong way of putting the matter. Nevertheless Mr. Wright was quite in earnest over his invitation. He would have killed a fatted calf for his guest's benefit, had such an animal been running loose about the vicarage straw-yard, rather than let his captive go.

Colonel Leschelles looked round the dark parlour; he surveyed the gloomy wainscot of the room, the heavy, old-fashioned haircloth-covered chairs, the worn sofa, the unsnuffed candles, the hearth strewn with wood-ashes, and thought of what an evening, companionless, in that house was likely to prove, with no living soul he could ask to relieve his loneliness downstairs, with the memory of the dead lying stiff and silent upstairs; and he decided in favour of the vicarage.

"You are very kind," he said, speaking to Mr. Wright; "and I will avail myself of your proffered hospitality; but first I should like to see IT."

"You would like to be alone, probably," suggested Mr. Wright, as he led the way upstairs.

"Yes, if you please," was the answer. And so the two men who had parted in youth met again in age.

With the memories which thronged through Colonel Leschelles' mind, as he stood looking at the face no longer distorted with pain, over which the peace of death was rapidly stealing, we have no concern. There was no remorse, at any rate, in the officer's heart. The quarrel, in whatever cause it may have originated, was not of his seeking, and at any time he would have made it up. Further, he had obeyed his cousin's request the moment he received his message, and he had been ready, knowing nothing of the dead man's pecuniary intentions towards himself, to hold out the right hand of fellowship, and tell his kinsman that in his heart there rankled no bitterness, no feeling save good-will and charity.

All too late, however, thought the Colonel, as he stood regarding the changed face of the cousin who had loved his sister; and it was consequently a grave man and a depressed who, half an hour later, apologized to Mr. Wright for having detained him for so long a time, and signified his readiness to accompany the Curate home.

That night Mr. Wright, depressed and out of sorts himself, let his visitor alone. He gave him good cheer, it is true; but he did not enter into much conversation. What talk they had was about the late Squire and his relatives, and the life he had led, and the life he might have led; and as neither found any one of those topics entertaining, they bade each other good night, and went to bed early.

Next morning both arose in better spirits, and looked out over a white world glittering and sparkling under the beams of a winter sun.

"The finest Christmas Day I can ever remember," said Mr. Wright, rubbing his hands, and looking at the ruddy glow of the fire, and listening contentedly to the bubbling of the urn. "The labourers from the farm were at work by daybreak, and have cut a road to the church, so we may get something of a congregation, after all. Will you come with me, or keep at home beside the fire?"

The Colonel elected to go with Mr. Wright, who picked out a very good sermon from a pile already yellow with age, and delivered it admirably. He touched very feelingly upon the death that had taken place so recently; and though he said little concerning the late Squire, still he said as much as it was possible for any one to say in his praise.

After service was over, Mr. Wright and his visitor returned to the vicarage, where, in due time, that turkey spoken of in commendatory terms was placed smoking on the board.

"You see your dinner?" remarked Mr. Wright; and the Colonel was fain to remark he saw a very good dinner indeed, which was rendered none the worse by the addition of some capital punch, in the brewing of which Mr. Wright was a proficient. The punch-bowl was not produced till the old cook had removed the remains of the turkey, and disappeared with the almost untasted pudding. Then Mr. Wright produced "his materials," and compounded a beverage which the Colonel declared to be "perfect," and which he sipped, looking at the upheaped fire and listening to Mr. Wright's talk.

In those days the Curate could talk. Debt had not then been sitting upon him for so long a time as was the case at Fisherton. Children had come and gone; but his mental elasticity was almost as great as ever. Duns had been pressing, and Selina's health was often delicate; but the buoyancy of his youth still remained, and the evil days which came upon him at last, of regarding all men as mere possible chances from which to borrow money, had not yet arrived.

So Mr. Wright, who was perhaps always a little more loquacious to any chance guest, or at any hospitable table, when Selina and the dear children were absent, and he living *en garçon*, unfolded his experience budget for Colonel Leschelles' benefit.

He wanted to rouse the officer from his depression, and he did it. He wished to see him laugh, or, if that were impossible, smile; and he made him both laugh and smile.

He told him of Dublin life, and of his own life at Trinity— then so merry and witty a college—recited profane anecdotes concerning bishops and archbishops; told how the Church in Ireland had been neglected, and expressed his own conviction that it was hard to feel energetic in a country where nineteen-twentieths of the population were either Presbyterians or Roman Catholics; had his fling at the absentee clergy, who he said were even worse than the absentee landlords; citing, as an example, the case of a rector who, starting in the morning with the bishop of the diocese on a visit to his parish, drove about till evening without finding it, gravely assuring his lordship, when compelled to give up the search, he had been "once there, and was quite astonished he could not remember the way to it again."

"And yet there was a considerable amount of Christian feeling at that time among the various denominations," continued Mr. Wright, "which I doubt does not prevail now.

"No dinner-party then was complete without the priest, and good stories they gave, never fear, in return for their entertainment. No men were such story-tellers as they. Why, every gentleman's house was open to the priests, who were right jolly fellows, until after Catholic Emancipation; well educated and gentlemanly too, many of them, which is more than could be said nowadays. If the dissenting ministers were not asked to mix freely with the landed gentry, it was only because in country districts many of them had come from the plough, and because the better educated and those born in town were just like Samson's foxes, running amuck against Churchmen and Romanists alike.

"Still, even between the Presbyterians and the Church people —the Regium Donum and the Tithes, as we used to dub them —a kindly feeling sometimes prevailed. I remember once, when I was a boy, staying with some relatives of mine in the north. They were Presbyterians, stiff-necked as the perverse generation, and bigoted as Mussulmans, so, of course, I had to go to 'meeting' with them, and stand out those interminable prayers, and sit while psalms fifty verses long were sung in unison through their noses, and listen to sermons which they said were full of pith, but which seemed to me full only of repetitions.

"We used to muster a goodly company, for there was only one Roman Catholic family in the parish, and not more than fifty Church people. All the women went to meeting with their Bibles wrapped round in unfolded pocket-handkerchiefs, and all the men wore black clothes about three sizes too large for them.

"The men and the women walked in separate detachments. Four or so of one sex walked together, taking up the entire sidewalk, and sometimes the whole road, and then came four or less of the other sex walking by themselves.

"They were very strict in all the relations of life, and part of their religion was to keep the footpath against all comers.

"The clergyman of the parish was of course non-resident. He lived many miles distant, near a pleasant town, where he had a nice house, good society, and a fine library.

" It is said that a matter-of-fact bishop once wrote to him to know whether he considered his books or the souls of his flock of the most importance, to which he slyly replied :

" ' I apprehend, my lord, there can be no doubt about the matter. My books, of course.'

" He and his clerk rode over the hills to perform one service on Sundays, that is, unless the day happened to be very wet indeed, in which case, after waiting for half an hour, the congregation quietly dispersed, some going to ' meeting,' others home, and those who had friends pretty well to do near at hand accepting invitations to ' take an air of the fire ' and a drop of something to keep the cold out.

" By all ranks the Rector was greatly liked. When he did come among his people, he was pleasant to them, and to the dissenters and the one Roman Catholic family. He had a royal memory, and never made mistakes about names. He was ready with a joke for the mothers, with a kind word with the men, with a sly compliment for the girls, and pats on the head, and sometimes halfpence, for the curly-pated, barefooted, straight-limbed children disporting themselves in the village horse-pond and the familiar gutters. True, the minister often had a rap at the clergyman of the Established Church for taking money and doing no work, but his people did not attach much importance to these remarks. Paying for their sittings, being asked to contribute to collections, being called upon for money when their children had to be baptized or themselves married, seemed much harder to them than the payment of tithes, which usually came out of their landlords' pockets.

" At all times the Rector was willing to christen for nothing, marry for nothing, ay, and often as not to give the newly-wedded a trifle with which to begin housekeeing ; and so, as I have said, he was popular, more especially as it was well known he ' could take his glass just like one of themselves.'

" To a parish some few miles distant had come a clergyman of quite another stamp. An Englishman with an English wife, both of whom were cordially hated : he, for wanting to make converts ; she, for wishing the people to keep themselves and their houses clean. He gave blankets and tracts to the Roman Catholics, and their priest told them to burn the tracts and keep the blankets, adding, ' God knows, poor souls ! this weather you have need of them.'

"He gave straw bonnets and cotton frocks to the Presbyterian children, and was astonished to find they donned those articles of attire only in order to attend the Sunday-schools attached to their own meeting-house.

"He preached alternate Sundays against the Roman Catholics and the dissenters, and was not sparing upon those of his own cloth who folded their hands in idleness, and said 'peace when there was no peace.'

"This was the man who stood waiting for the Rector of our parish one stormy winter's morning, and who, as the old clerical cob came in sight, advanced to meet his friend.

"'How do, Agnew?' he began. 'My steeple was blown down last night, and as we could not possibly have any service, I thought I would come over and preach for you.'

"'I am sure I am greatly obliged to you,' answered our Rector. In telling the story afterwards, which he did at many a dinner-table, he said he would as soon have seen the gentleman with a cloven hoof as the man who greeted him. Nay, I am wrong, he said he would rather have seen *Il Diavolo;* but, however, he felt he must put a good face on the matter, and so he got off his cob, and the clerk dismounted from his pony, and they all went into the vestry together, where the Englishman proceeded to robe himself decorously, while our Rector flung on his surplice, as was his fashion, anyhow.

"'You don't get much of a congregation here, I suppose?' remarked the stranger.

"'Oh! pretty well; all things considered, I cannot complain.'

"'There don't seem many here yet,' said the Englishman, peeping through the chinks of the vestry door.

. "'We always give them a few minutes' grace,' observed the Rector; 'and I dare say they will be late such a boisterous morning as this.'

"Having made which excuse, he passed out into the church-yard, and accosted a member of the constabulary force who chanced at that moment to be passing the vestry window.

"'Mr. Jeckey,' says he, 'I am in an awful fix. Here's the Rev. Mr. Maude come to spy out the nakedness of the land. If Mr. Cathers won't help me, I am disgraced for ever. Just run round to the meeting-house and tell Mr. Cathers *if he'll lend me his congregation* I'll be eternally obliged to him.'

"Like an arrow from the bow sped Mr. Jeckey on his errand. The Presbyterian service had been begun before he reached the meeting-house; indeed, it had proceeded so far that Mr. Cathers had finished his extempore prayer and given out the psalm, which we were all singing as well as we knew how.

"But never recked Mr. Jeckey of that. Down the aisle he tramped unheeding, not a man stirring to stop his progress. Up the pulpit steps he strode, and whispered the position in Mr. Cathers' ear.

"We were all dying of curiosity, but still we sang on—sang our fiercest, till Mr. Cathers, having taken the sense of Mr. Jeckey's communication into his brain, raised one hand, in order to silence our voices and obtain attention for himself.

"'My friends,' he said, 'our worthy Rector is in a serious strait. You all know, or have heard, of the English clergyman who is disturbing the peace of Ballinascraw. Without message or notice of any kind he has come this morning to take the church duty here, and, as a personal favour, our Rector asks you all to go and listen to his sermon. If you will do so, I shall feel obliged. In any case, there will be no service here, as I mean to go and sit under him for this once myself.'

"So," proceeded Mr. Wright, "we all rose in a body and repaired to church, the minister heading us; and Mr. Maude looked upon such a congregation as had never gladdened his eyes in his own parish. The pews were packed, the aisles were full, the clerk could not beg, borrow, or steal prayer-books sufficient for one in six; but the dissenters did their best. They watched what the others did, and knelt at the right places, and got up not often at the wrong. If they sat during the singing when they should have stood, that was nothing unusual even among Church people; and I am bound to say they listened to Mr. Maude consigning the Roman Catholics to the lowest depths and describing the iniquities of the Scarlet Lady with an appreciative ear.

"When Mr. Maude took off his gown, he did it with the air of a man who feels he looks like a dog with his tail between his legs.

'I had no idea you had such a congregation,' he said to our Rector.

"'It was larger than usual to-day,' said the Rector modestly, 'I suppose the news of your coming had got wind.'

"And something else got wind too," finished Mr. Wright.

"It was too good a story to be kept quiet, telling as it did as much against the Englishman as our Rector.

"Besides, our Rector felt it ought not to be lost. He gave a supper on the strength of it to all the parish, and was better liked than ever afterwards.

"Moreover, he told the story at various dinner-parties, and the laugh was so loud and so long against Maude that he exchanged his living with a man who has since gone over bodily to Rome, and been succeeded by a vicar of moderate views, who is the happy father of nine daughters.

"No straw bonnets or cotton frocks are given away in the parish now, I believe, and the pigs live in the cottagers' houses, and the children in the gutters outside the houses without let or hindrance from the wife of any one, lay or clerical."

CHAPTER XVII.

COLONEL LESCHELLES IS ASTONISHED.

WITH stories, quotations, and oftentimes more serious conversation on subjects of which even worldly men must occasionally take thought, Mr. Wright beguiled his visitor until the morning came round when all that remained of the Squire was to be laid in the ground.

To the brilliant sunshine which had made such brightness on Christmas Day, even in the Essex marshes, there succeeded a dull leaden sky, giving promise of more snow, and more after that.

In due time the promise was fulfilled. The heavens were opened, and snow fell for two days and nights without cessation.

"God bless me!" said the Curate, looking out at the untrodden road and the churchyard, where the graves were buried under a mysterious pall of white, soft flakes, "I don't know— I don't, indeed, know how we are going to bury that poor fellow at all."

And, indeed, had his relations not been hungering and thirsting to know the contents of his will, in all probability the body of Squire Olier might have lain quietly enough in his own room at the Grange till the weather moderated ; but as matters stood each man and each woman interested in the testamentary disposition of his property felt it was unseemly for him to keep the rightful owner out of possession beyond eight days. Accordingly, at the end of that time, the late Squire's remains were carried to the churchyard, where, by dint of bribes, and by liberal allowances of strong liquors, a grave had been prepared; and, while the mourners stood ankle-deep in snow, which had already drifted again over the ground cleared for them to occupy —while the sleet soaked through Mr. Wright's surplice, and wetted the leaves of the open prayer-book—while the wind moaned over the mournful expanse of lands stretching away to the river and the German Ocean, and the hair of those gathered round the place where their dear brother departed was to be wrapped up till eternity, was dripping as if they had one and all just emerged from a bath, the Curate read the funeral service over all that was left of Squire Olier.

A few minutes, and the words, few and solemn, had been spoken, dust was gone down again into the dust, ashes were returned to ashes. Ere long, one dark mound could be distinguished in the churchyard, looking like a rent in a white mantle over a black dress ; but soon the falling snow covered that away from sight also. From a window in the vicarage Mr. Wright noticed the flakes falling thick and soft on the Squire's grave.

"Poor fellow!" he thought, "his was a lonely life, and he is even more lonely in death than men are usually. By this time those harpies know how the property is left."

Which was correct. By that time the harpies, who had stopped for a few minutes at the vicarage, on their return from the funeral, to swallow some brandy, were in the wainscoted parlour, where Mr. Wright had received Colonel Leschelles, listening to the last codicil in the late Squire's will. In it was left, in token of kindness and good-will, a hundred guineas to Louis Leschelles, his cousin. As for the bulk of the estate, it was willed to a certain Charles Olier, hateful, for many reasons, to most of his kinsfolk. Being in Norway at the time of Squire Olier's death, he did not chance to be present. So those to whom no legacies were left—and their number seemed legion —were forced to vent their anger on the only person within their reach, Colonel Leschelles.

"What right had he to a hundred guineas, or to a hundred pence?" they asked each other, and eventually asked him.

"I must decline to answer that question," said the Colonel, stiffly, who, having heard from Mr. Wright that Squire Olier's estate might have been his almost for the picking up, felt, perhaps, a little natural disappointment at having been, if remembered at all, remembered to so little purpose; and then, after bowing to the assembled company, he left the room, and made his way back to the vicarage, where he had consented to remain for another night.

"Well?" said the Curate interrogatively, as he opened the door to welcome his visitor.

"Charles Olier has the property. There are the usual legacies. Several worthy people seem mightily disappointed, and I am a richer man by a hundred guineas than I was a fortnight ago."

"Charles Olier!" exclaimed Mr. Wright. "Why, he has the name of being a second Elwes. They say he would skin a—— Ahem!" finished the Curate, who had for the moment allowed excitement to triumph over rigid decorum.

"And sell the hide," finished the Colonel. "Yes, what is said is quite true, I am afraid."

"You might have had the place," went on the Curate, "if—"

"If 'ifs and ands' you remember," quoted Colonel Leschelles with a smile. "Yes, I suppose I might if an 'if' and an 'and' had both been different. As matters stand, however, it is a matter of no consequence to me. That which we have never expected it can be no disappointment not to receive, and, I am thankful to say, I have enough, and more than enough, to satisfy all my wants."

That night the Curate—feeling, probably, the fact of Squire Olier being buried, and his will read, had removed a weight from his mind—proved himself a more agreeable companion than ever; in fact, so agreeable did he continue to make Colonel Leschelles think him that the gallant officer voluntarily promised to spend Christmas with Mr. Wright, in whatever part of the three kingdoms that gentleman might be, so long as the Colonel remained in England.

"And I only wish I had a fat rectory in my gift," added the officer: "you should have it without the asking."

Whereupon Mr. Wright, with a sly twinkle in his eyes, quoted the last line of the epigram which commences—

> "A vicar long ill who treasured up wealth,
> Bade his curate each Sunday to pray for his health,"

and ends with the curate's reply to a somewhat impertinent inquirer into the state of his own feelings—

> "I've ne'er prayed for Death, though I have for his Living."

Within a few weeks after Colonel Leschelles' departure there arrived at the vicarage a note from Mr. Wright's late visitor, accompanied by a gold watch and chain, of which the Curate's acceptance was requested in a few kindly and well-chosen words.

It is needless to say the Curate accepted the gift in a note containing many words.

"A most appropriate present," thought Mr. Wright, laying aside the turnip-shaped, white-faced silver repeater, inherited from his father, he had hitherto been fain to wear; and indeed so it proved.

"The watch and chain were always," so the Curate often remarked to Mrs. Wright, "as good as twenty pounds to them;" and before many years had elapsed twenty pounds had been so often raised upon the articles that one facetious jeweller remarked to his foreman, "he thought they might be trusted to come to his shop alone."

If Mr. Wright had ever calculated the price he paid for that money, he would have found it considerably exceeded the probable first cost of the trinkets.

In whatever straits the family found themselves about Christmas-time—and their straits then were occasionally very grievous

—money was generally procured to rescue Mr. Wright's watch from the accommodating Israelite who held it in charge for so large a portion of each year; or if that were impossible, he at least liberated his chain from the enemy's hands, and attached to it the old-fashioned repeater, which, not being worth a sixpence, was always at home and available when its more valuable relative was detained abroad on particular business.

Of course, on such occasions, Colonel Leschelles knew well enough the second calling of the watchmaker who was "regulating" his present; but, being a man of the world, he took the Wrights as he found them, and acknowledged to his own heart that many persons with whom he was acquainted, and who took care of their jewellery for themselves, were not one-half so pleasant, or so hospitable, or so lively as the impecunious clergyman and his wife.

Long before Mr. Wright became Rector of Fisherton, Colonel Leschelles had been made free of the state of his affairs. At a very early period of their acquaintance, Mr. Wright had requested his good friend—"whom I hope eventually to call my old friend," added that accomplished letter-writer in a parenthesis—"to lend him an amount which, though it would seem, no doubt, ridiculously small to one blessed with such abundance," meant temporal salvation to the Curate, his dear Selina, his children, including a recently arrived baby, and every creature connected with the establishment. "In a sentence," said Mr. Wright, after having devoted many sentences to the explanation, "I am goaded almost to madness by the want—remember little things are great to little people—of twenty-five pounds. I know, my dear Colonel, you are just the man to help a friend at such a pinch, and will not despise him for this frank confession. I enclose my I O U for the amount, which I shall repay, D.V., in three months, with thanks and interest at five per cent. per annum, and shall feel eternally obliged if you will send me your cheque, open if possible, by return of post."

To which the Colonel diplomatically replied, that as he had few good friends, and could not afford to lose the regard of any one of those few, on principle he always refused to *lend* money.

"If a man," he explained, "lent money, it could only be in the expectation of having it repaid at some not remote period, when it might be most unpleasant to the borrower to have the subject mentioned. At the same time," he added, "I am always anxious to help a friend if it lies in my power to do so, and therefore, with much regret that I am unable to send the whole amount you name, I enclose my cheque for ten pounds, which I beg you will consider as in every respect your own, and deal with accordingly."

"He is no fool, Selina," was Mr. Wright's comment on this epistle. "He knows no gentleman can ask another to *give* him money, and that after such a letter I can never trouble him again."

"But you are surely not going to return the cheque?" cried out Mrs. Wright in alarm.

"No, my dear; I am going to keep it as a *personal favour* to him. From *any other* man I could not, of course, accept ten pounds as a gift. Why, he is a comparative stranger!"

"Almost a total stranger," agreed Mrs. Wright; and then the humour of the thing struck her, and, being slightly hysterical, she laughed long and heartily at Dion's way of "putting things."

When Mr. Wright took possession of the living of Fisherton, Colonel Leschelles was older than had been the case when he first met the clergyman in Essex marshes. If he did not note the fact, the Reverend Dionysius and his better half were more astute.

Already they were thinking about his will and the legacy he might leave to them or one of the dear children; and once when Mr. Wright was carving the Christmas turkey, he caught himself considering how much the Colonel had aged, and wondering how he would cut up, and who were likely to get the best slices.

"God forgive me!" thought poor Mr. Wright, thumping himself on the chest; "I am no better than those Olier vultures who, smelling the carcase afar off, gathered hoping to have share of the spoil."

From which it will **be** seen that the Rector had moments of self-accusation and repentance, and that, although he generally went about the world thanking the Lord he and Selina were not as other men and women, it sometimes did occur to him that they were not a whit better than the publicans and sinners who contributed to their need.

On the Christmas Eve following Miss Miles' arrival at Fisherton, the Rector was, however, for once able to meet his visitor with a cheerful face which masked no ugly thoughts of legacies or creditors.

Everything in this life is comparative, and for the Rector to have no writs or summonses pressing immediately for attention meant probably as much ease of mind as it does to a millionaire to have secured a picture at his own price, or to have outbidden a rival in the matter of some precious edition.

Colonel Leschelles arrived about five o'clock, and it was as good as a puppet-show to see the Rector's greeting.

He did not say a word in the first fulness of rejoicing. With his head turned a little on one side, he clasped the Colonel's hand with a pressure which implied, " I am too glad to see you to be able to tell you how happy I feel to have you here once more ;" and, indeed, his manner did convey all this, and more.

"God bless you !" he murmured at length. " Welcome again to Fisherton. Come in, come in ! Don't stay out in the cold. Let me settle with the man. There, now we have got you to ourselves again. Selina ! Where's Selina? My dear, the Colonel has come."

Considering that Selina had been expecting his arrival for half an hour previously, the visitor's appearance could scarcely have proved a surprise to Mrs. Wright ; but, coming out of the drawing-room, arrayed, in honour of the Colonel, in a silk dress, made with a low bodice and short sleeves, a scarf over her shoulders, bracelets of no particular material, or beauty, or worth, on her arms, her back hair wreathed round a comb in a variety of singular and charming devices, and the eternal curls falling in a graceful, not to say pathetic, manner on each side of her face, Mrs. Wright really acted a pleasant little by-play of surprise admirably.

With a heightened colour, and a smile which was sweet as well as plaintive, and a light of greeting in her eyes, which no affectation could have kindled, she took his hand in both of hers, and, saying in her pretty Irish accent—that accent which sounds so sweet falling from the lips of a gentlewoman when she does not give one too much of it—" I am very glad to see you indeed," lifted her eyes for a moment to the Colonel's face, then modestly withdrew them from a contemplation of his features ; but that moment told her a tale.

" My dear," she said to the Rev. Dion, while Colonel Leschelles, making his toilet in the apartment vacated by Miss

Miles, was thinking that, with his figure, by Jove, he might pass for not more than forty or forty-five when the weather was mild and he was not pulled up with that confounded rheumatism, "My dear, he gets awfully old. I think he must have added at least twenty years to his age since I saw him last."

"Pooh!" was the Rector's answer. "You only think so because you have been latterly looking continually upon young faces. The Colonel can't put back the clock, even with the help of tight frock-coats and leaden combs; but it is not running on with him, and so much the better. Good people are scarce, and we cannot afford to part with one of them—before his appointed time," added the Rector, with that sudden recollection of his vocation which was sometimes so absurd, and yet always so genuine.

Excepting upon Christmas and New Year Days, which were, of course, regarded by the young people at Fisherton as occasions when they had an immemorial right to make the lives of visitors a weariness to them, Mr. and Mrs. Wright did not cluster their olive-branches round the family mahogany at the same hour when Colonel Leschelles solemnly partook of dinner.

In truth, he would not have come to them if they had to his dulled senses introduced the prattle of children, and expected him to listen to it.

The Colonel did not love any children. Elderly gentlemen, fond of their own personal comfort, mental or physical, rarely are; and he certainly had in his creed no saving clause which exempted the juvenile Wrights from a place in his bad books.

As has before been hinted, these young people were not charming, save in the estimation of their parents; and Colonel Leschelles was not their parent of either sex, for which deliverance the misguided man thanked God.

If the truth must be told, as it ought always to be in fiction, Mr. Wright was secretly pleased by the consequences of his friend's idiosyncrasy.

Mr. Wright loved his children, but he also loved his dinner; and after a man has carved for a dozen, his own share of the repast is not usually eaten with much relish.

He was too wise a husband, however, to hint anything of this feeling to Selina, but it is a fact that the triangular meal eaten in company with Colonel Leschelles and Mrs. Wright was very grateful to the Rector. More especially as the Colonel, under pretence of having been ordered to drink the produce of some especial vineyards, provided his own wine—and more of it than he could have consumed himself had he stayed at Fisherton for three months.

Mr. Wright candidly confessed that he did like a glass of sound port, or a sip of thoroughly good dry sherry, but beyond these things he far preferred the Colonel's Madeira, which was stated, Heaven knows with what truth, to have been twice round the Cape.

The Madeira itself never spoke of its travels—on the principle, perhaps, that "good wine needs no bush."

Further, in the pop of a champagne cork there was something which brought out all the hidden virtues of Mr. Wright's nature.

The way in which he spoke of his dear friend, when the first glass had been swallowed and approved, might have converted a misanthrope ; whilst the way in which he seconded the Colonel's hint that Mrs. Wright had no wine, and pressed a second bumper on Selina, with a little nod of the head, and a cunning, "Now, now, my love! drink it up; it will do you good," was simply indescribable.

"What!" he would exclaim, "get into your head? Nonsense! I'll be bound your head is far too wise a one to let it do anything of the kind. You are tired out ; that is what you are, and you want something to put new life into you. Come, don't put a slight upon our good friend's magnificent wine. You won't get anything like this in a hurry again—take my word for that, and I taste a good deal of what is called first-quality champagne when I am asked to dine at great men's tables."

Apparently shocked by this barefaced flattery, Mrs. Wright would say, "Hush, Dion! Colonel Leschelles is not accustomed to your Irish frankness." To which Mr. Wright would reply :

"Ah, my dear, you'll never make an Englishman of me. I must say out my mind ; and I don't think it much matters what I say before our kind friend here. He has known me too long not to understand me thoroughly."

And indeed this was quite true. The Colonel did understand Mr. Wright thoroughly, and could have said pretty accurately what the Rector's pretty speeches were worth.

Nevertheless, he liked to stay with the Wrights. He liked being looked up to, and he liked being flattered. There are many people who, without being aware of the fact, are of one mind with Colonel Leschelles on these matters.

"Don't you think, Dion," said Mrs. Wright to her husband, a few days before that Christmas Eve of which this story is now treating, "that Maria might as well dine with us while the Colonel is here? She is getting old enough to appear in company, and she would balance the table nicely."

"I am afraid we mustn't risk it," answered the Rector. "In the first place, Colonel Leschelles might not like the change; in the next, we should be sowing seeds of disunion between Maria and her sister; and, in the third place, you can't have Maria without having Bella Miles, and five would be no number at all.

"I could explain the matter to Bella," remarked Mrs. Wright.

"I don't think you could," was the reply. "If we are to have a fourth person at dinner, that fourth should be Mr. Irwin's niece."

Whereupon Mrs. Wright took refuge in her usual remark— "I suppose you know best, dear!"

"I am sure I do in this instance," said the Rev. Dion valiantly.

There were times when he openly took precedence of his wife's intellect, and shook hands with himself without disguise in her presence. But he did not thus thwart Mrs. Wright very frequently. As a rule he deferred to Selina's superior judgment, and then took his own way, privately if possible, apologetically if necessary.

So it was settled that Maria should not dine with her elders; and the Colonel had therefore his repast in peace and quietness.

After dinner—that is to say, after the soup and the fish and all the other courses had come and gone—after dessert had been trifled with, and all the wines tried with judicial slowness and calmness—after coffee had been served, and the Colonel had declared he never tasted such coffee out of France as that to be met with at Fisherton—Mr. Wright said:

"Should you like to step up and see the decorations in our church? The ladies are just putting the finishing touches to them. We shall show something out of the common to-morrow, I can assure you."

"My dear Wright," answered the Colonel, "I have no doubt the decorations will be everything they ought to be in your church; but I would not leave your hospitable fireside to-night for all the wreaths, and crosses, and mottoes, and holly and laurel in Christendom."

"Just as you like," cheerfully agreed the Rector. "But I must go my rounds. I must inspect my fair regiment. Each profession has its toils as well as its pleasures."

"I know who would have commanded, had my regiment been composed of ladies," remarked Colonel Leschelles. "But don't delay duty on my account. I will have a chat with Mrs. Wright in your absence. I always like talking to Mrs. Wright."

"And Mrs. Wright always likes talking to you," said the Rector, with his accustomed heartiness. "She is out of the way of congenial society here. As she says, from one month's end to another, not a soul calls with whom she can exchange an idea."

With which compliment to the grasp of the Colonel's intellect, implied and understood, Mr. Wright went off to church, leaving his wife *tête-à-tête* with their visitor.

"Dion!" called Mrs. Wright after him, "mind you bring the girls back with you. Maria has got a cold already, and we must not have any invalids in the house at Christmas-time."

"Well, my dear, that can only be as Heaven pleases," answered the Rector; "but I will bring them back with me, never fear."

That, however, was precisely the thing he failed to do. Accompanied by his daughters, he returned in about an hour to the rectory, when he informed Mrs. Wright that Bella's uncle had called at the church and gone with her for a stroll by moonlight.

"I wonder if he will come here for supper," said Selina, care on her brow and housewifely anxiety in her heart.

"I should not think so," replied the Rector. "He will want to catch the nine o'clock train if he means to get back to town to-night; but, in any case, we can but give him the best we have in our larder. You may be quite sure Irwin is not the man to suspect us of want of hospitality."

"He must be a very extraordinary man if he could do anything of the sort," remarked Colonel Leschelles.

In return for which observation, Mrs. Wright cast upon him a grateful glance, and said softly, "Thank you."

Time passed on, but Miss Bella did not return. Nine o'clock came—a quarter-past—half-past—and still no Bella.

"I wonder where the girl can be!" marvelled Mr. Wright. "Her uncle would never take her to London without letting us know."

"Perhaps he is staying somewhere in the neighbourhood," suggested Mrs. Wright.

"I think I will go up as far as the station," said the Rector. "The Colonel won't miss me while he is showing you the presents he has brought for the children."

"Really, it is too bad of Mr. Irwin," said Mrs. Wright, who had never forgiven that gentleman for not rising to the bait of refurnishing Bella's bed-room. "He ought to know better than keep the girl out until this time of night."

"We are all of us old enough to know better, Selina," answered the Rector, taking his arm which he had just put into the sleeve of his top-coat out of it again; "and, after all, I don't see that there can be any use in my going to the station. He must, as you say, be staying in the neighbourhood somewhere. He would never leave her to walk home alone."

"I should be very sorry to answer for what Mr. Irwin might or might not do," commented Mrs. Wright, seated before the drawing-room fire, and screening her face from the blaze with a great feather fan brought by an admiring *protégé* from foreign parts.

"I think I will go, too," remarked the Rector in the hall, putting on his top-coat again.

"Ha! here they are at last," he added delightedly, as a pattering on the gravel announced that some one was coming up the drive.

"Why, Bella, my dear," he went on, flinging open the door and looking out incredulously into the night, "where is your uncle? Is he not with you? Have you come home alone?"

"Oh, Mr. Wright, I hope you will not be displeased," she began; "but we walked farther than we intended, and he had only just time to catch the last train. He wanted to come home with me, but I did not know where he could stay for the night, and besides, he wished to go to London; so I told him I would run all the way home; but I did not: I came back slowly, and that is the reason why I am so late."

"Gracious heavens, child? what is the matter?—what has happened?" asked Mr. Wright, noticing that she could scarcely restrain her tears, and that her face looked white and troubled.

Dreadful visions of Mr. Irwin's bankruptcy, insolvency, and ruin were vouchsafed to the Rector as he led her into the drawing-room and closed the door. In imagination he read: "A large failure is announced to-day in the City, that of Irwin and Son, die-sinkers, Eastcheap," and dire fears assailed him of the stoppage of that bank, so lately discovered, from which he had hoped cheques would continue to flow as naturally as manna once fell from heaven.

For a minute Miss Miles, coming out of the faint moonlight into the drawing-room, which the dancing fire and many wax candles made brilliant, seemed too much blinded and frightened to speak. Then, recovering composure, and seeing two pairs of anxious eyes fixed on her, she said:

"There is nothing the matter—at least there is, for old Mr. Irwin died yesterday. But it is not that," she added, "it was not that which made me foolish. Uncle and I were talking about long ago, and I could not help crying as I came home. And oh! may I go to bed, please?" she went on, addressing Mrs. Wright; "I have a dreadful headache, and I do not want to see anybody."

"Certainly, dear, go at once," replied Mrs. Wright, kissing the girl with a sudden impulse of affection and pity, which caress Bella returned with interest.

"Good night," she said, turning to Mr. Wright, who stood by, relieved but astonished.

He opened the door for her to pass out, and laying his hand on her shoulder, answered her words by saying:

"Bless you, my child!"

Then he went back to Selina, and exclaimed twice with great solemnity:

"Poor old Mr. Irwin! dear—dear—dear!"

Meantime Miss Miles, stealing off to Mr. Wright's dressing-room, which had for the nonce been appropriated to her use, was encountered suddenly by Colonel Leschelles, coming, laden with gifts, out of the blue-and-white apartment her skilful fingers had helped to embellish.

For a moment the light of the candle he carried fell full on her face, while he, standing still, made way for her to pass.

With a little timid half-curtsey and a "Good night, sir," spoken, in the confusion of the moment, in French, she tripped nervously away along the passage, leaving the Colonel still standing look-

ing after her in amazement, his candle held aloft, and his
astonishment finding vent in a muttered exclamation:

"I have seen that girl before," he thought; "but where?"

CHAPTER XVIII.

WHAT MR. IRWIN CAME TO TELL.

WHEN, earlier on that same Christmas Eve, Mr. Irwin looked
into Fisherton Church to ascertain if his niece were there, a very
pretty sight met his eyes.

Gas had not then penetrated farther into Fisherton than the
railway station, distant some mile and a half, and it was by the
light of many candles that the ladies, young and old, who had
undertaken the care of the decorations, were fastening up mottes,
twining wreaths round pillars, affixing lettered banners to the
walls—were, in a word, engaged in putting the old building
into gala attire.

There is a certain picturesqueness about candlelight, which
gas emulates in vain. The long, deep shadows—the small spaces
cleared out of utter darkness—the corners filled with blackness
—the changing of figures from flesh and blood to unreal phan-
toms as they pass into the shade—the roof seen indistinctly,
and looking consequently twice as lofty as it is in reality—the
uncertainty as to what is hidden behind the pillars, and a sense
of wonderment concerning the chancel, looking so dim and far
away in the gathering gloom—all these things go to make up

an interior, the secrets and fancies composing which gas sweeps ruthlessly away.

I marvel now what has become of the imaginings which childhood—in the days when Fisherton Church had to trust to the candle-maker for evening illumination—was wont to conjure up out of the old tomb to the right of the chancel, on which, under a stone canopy, lay the figure of a knight clad in complete armour, or of that other monument surrounded by praying children, and surmounted by a score of fat-cheeked cherubs bearing the body of Dame Ursula Berton, resting on rocky clouds, straight away to heaven.

When, last Christmastide, the present generation of young ladies assembled to put the finishing strokes to their labours, I am afraid the old church, though doing much credit to their taste and skill, lost, by reason of flaring gaslights, most of its romance.

Youth, beauty, and grace are eternal, and yet, as the fashion of the settings in which we behold them vary, so may those who have had their taste moulded in days gone down many and many a year ago into the grave of time, be pardoned if the conceits of a former age seem to them more lovely than the bald framing of this.

To the end of his life Mr. Irwin, at all events, will never forget Fisherton Church as he looked into it for the first and the last time by night ; never forget the sweet scent of the flowers, and the faint, unfamiliar, almost sickening odour of the evergreens, the flitting figures of the young girls, now tripping away into darkness, now posing themselves unconsciously into some picturesque attitude, whilst all the time the gloom of the pointed arches refused to receive even a gleam of light, and the ancient pillars seemed to submit themselves unwillingly to the hands of the beautifiers.

Around the font, admiring the work of her deft white fingers, stood a group of matrons and elderly ladies, who were expressing in no measured terms their admiration of Miss Miles' taste and skill.

" Not a flower or leaf but Christmas roses in the whole thing, I declare ! " one voluble mother remarked, as she reluctantly moved towards the door; "and look at it ! If you had showered down stars from the firmament on a green meadow, it could not be more like life itself."

"Do you know whether Miss Miles is engaged?" asked a gentleman standing in the shadow at this juncture, addressing the speaker, who had been uttering her admiration to no one in particular.

"Lawks, sir, how you did frighten me!" remarked the worthy woman. "I made sure it was a ghost a-speaking. Miss Miles, sir, she have just a-finished that there font, and though I say it, as perhaps shouldn't, being Fisherton bred and born, I don't think to-morrow will see such another font in all England. Did you want Miss Miles, sir?"

"Yes; if you could say to her, without putting yourself to inconvenience, that her uncle is here, I should feel very much obliged."

A moment after his niece sprang forward to where he stood.

"I am so glad—so glad to see you, uncle! I did not think you would be down before the end of the week. Come and look at my work. I did it all, every bit, myself."

"I have seen it," he answered. "I have been looking at it and you for the last quarter of an hour."

"And never spoke a word to me," she pouted.

"There were plenty to speak and say pleasant things besides me, my dear," he said gravely and fondly; "and I liked to listen to your praises. It makes me so happy to think I acted wisely in bringing you here."

"I am sure you did," she agreed. "I have learnt a great deal at Fisherton—more, in some ways, than I could have done in twenty years at school. You are going to the rectory, of course?"

"No," was the reply. "I want to have a chat with you. It is a moonlight night, if not a very bright one—not like the moon-lights we remember elsewhere. Let us have a walk."

"I will just tell the girls where I am gone, in case Mr. Wright wants me, and be with you in a moment."

And through the light and shade he watched her figure flitting up the aisle, and away to the reading-desk, where the Misses Wright received her communication with the most polite in-difference.

Red Indians and our upper ten thousand have, it is said, one charming trait in common—that of possessing the faculty of seeming to be surprised at and interested in nothing. If this be, as we are credibly assured it is, the perfection of good breeding, clergymen's children must have close affinity to the *crème de la crème* of society and barbarism.

Personally, I have no more acquaintance with braves and their squaws than I have with dukes and duchesses; but it has been my privilege to mix pretty freely with the sons and daughters of men holding rank of some sort in the Church, and I can safely say I have seldom met one who could be prevailed upon to evince a human interest in the affairs of any living being who was not directly or indirectly connected with themselves, or their papa's parish, or their papa's prospects.

This is, of course, while they remain in the parental nest. The world, fortunately, possesses a potent recipe for eliminating spiritual and social conceit out of the first-born even of a bishop; and there comes a time when the greatest prig nurtured in a rural parish becomes not merely tolerable, but agreeable in his manners.

But there is a middle passage to be encountered before this delectable land, where children born in rectories and vicarages become amenable to the laws of ordinary society, is reached, and clerical children may be met on equal terms by those destitute of ecclesiastical position.

The young Wrights were embarked on that passage, and woe to the unfortunate traveller who chanced to be in the vessel with them.

To all intents and purposes, they were ensconced in the cabin, while all the rest of their world had been only able to pay steerage fares. It is nice, this, for the clerical offspring, while it lasts; but it is nice also for the laity to remember it cannot last for ever. At first Miss Miles had writhed under the contemptuous indifference of Mr. Wright's dear children to anything except themselves and their own belongings; but time reconciles us to most things, and Maria's coolly-uttered "very well," in answer to her delighted communication, did not damp her spirits in the least.

"This is lovely!" she said to her uncle, clasping both hands round his arm as they left the church. "Only think of our having such a good time all to ourselves!"

"I am afraid you will not think it so good a time, after all," he answered; "for I have something unpleasant to tell you."

Instantly the smile left her lips, and the light faded out of her eyes.

“About—about—my father?” she faltered.

. “No, not about him—at least, I have news of him. He is going to the diggings.”

“Does he speak of coming home?”

“No. He says he will never come home unless he can return a rich man, which is not very likely.”

“I do not know that,” said the girl faintly.

Then ensued a silence for a few minutes, which Mr. Irwin broke by saying:

“My father-in-law is dead.”

“Dead!” she repeated. “When? What did he die of?”

“A fit of passion,” was the answer, spoken coldly and almost sullenly. “We had a quarrel about ten days ago, and when he was in the middle of a bitter and unjust sentence he fell back insensible; and though he lived for over a week, he never fully recovered consciousness.”

“How horrible! What a dreadful thing for you!”

“It would have been a dreadful thing for me if he had recovered consciousness,” replied Mr. Irwin. “He would have left me, comparatively speaking, a beggar. I wish, Bella—I wish with all my heart—I could say I felt sorry when I saw him lying dead. Had he lived, I must have left the firm, separated from my wife—that misfortune I could have survived, however—parted, for the time at least, from my children, and begun the world all over again.”

“Why, what happened?—what could have happened?” she inquired, shivering, though she was warmly clad, and the night not particularly cold.

“I will tell you,” he answered; “in fact, I must tell you, for our interests are identical, and besides, it is a relief to speak out to some one. Always I have been to a certain extent in my father-in-law’s power, and occasionally he made me feel the fact. Still, on the whole, we got on pretty well together. He liked keeping the reins in his own hands, but he was liberal enough in pecuniary matters; and though he never let me forget that the money was his, still he did not grudge me an ample share of it.”

He paused for a moment, and then continued:

“Some short time since we had a dispute with one of our customers about an account. He wanted, as I considered, to evade a just claim, and I was, therefore, firm about the matter

—firmer than I should otherwise have been about a larger amount."

"Yes, uncle?" said his niece, inquiringly.

"At last we threatened legal proceedings, and he then sent his attorney to our office to endeavour to effect some compromise.

"My partner left the management of the affair to me, and I rejected all offers of arrangement. After the lawyer had called two or three times his manner suddenly changed. He dared me to bring any case into court; he threatened me; he said, with a cunning insolence, for which I could have struck him, 'Those who live in glass houses should not throw stones;' and when I asked him what he meant, he said, 'I thought there was something familiar to me about you, spite of your beard and your Yankee twang; but I was not sure of the matter until the other day, when I happened to meet a lady coming up the stairs, whom I remembered perfectly. Come, you had better give up your point. You won't like going into court, I know, and being asked if you ever stood in the dock yourself. Put pride in your pocket, Mr. Irwin, and prove yourself as discreet as you have been fortunate.'"

"And what did you do, uncle?" she asked.

"I behaved like a simpleton. I told him to do his best or his worst. I said I was more resolved than ever to insist on our rights; and then I opened the door, and remarked that if he did not leave the office at once I would kick him out of it."

"And he?" inquired the girl.

"He laughed in my face. He said I should perhaps sing to a different tune before many days were over; and then he ran downstairs, stopping at the first landing to make a mocking bow."

"Uncle, who was the lady?" asked Miss Miles.

"Can't you guess, my child?" he said, pityingly, and then went on speaking more rapidly: "Yes; she found me out— traced me by some means. I warned her not to come to the office. I entreated her not to ruin me as she ruined her husband. I told her I would do anything—anything that lay in my power for her welfare—if she would only keep quiet, and let me have the chance of keeping that horrid past out of sight. She promised me faithfully to keep our relationship a secret, and then, because I could not go to see her the very day she wished, came three times to the office—three times, I assure you, in as many hours."

"She ought not to have done it; she ought to have considered you," murmured his niece.

"She ought. I have done all I could for her, but she is just the same as ever. If she wants a thing, she thinks the world ought to stand still while she gets it. When I remonstrated with her on her imprudence, she laughed and said: 'Nobody will notice me. No one could recognize me;' and she would not even draw down her veil."

"Why did she want to see you so particularly?" asked the girl.

"She wanted me to find her money to go to Australia."

"But you will not do so! Oh! don't let her go there!" entreated his companion.

"I shall come to that part of my story presently," said Mr. Irwin. "Let me tell you what that precious lawyer did. He went to my father-in-law, and raked up all the old tale; told how I had been connected with your father; told how he was transported, and how I had been taken into custody; explained how my sister had been acquitted, though no living being could doubt her complicity; said I had been obliged to leave the country, that I was no better than a thief, and that I was still the companion of thieves, with much more to the same effect. He, a clerk at that time, had, it appears, been engaged in the case, and knew all about it.

"That same evening, when all the clerks but one had gone— thank God he did not go—-Mr. Irwin came up to my private office and opened fire.

"First of all, he asked me if what he heard was true. Had my brother-in-law been a common workman—had he been taken up for theft—had he been convicted—had my sister been charged with him—had I myself been suspected of being an accomplice? To these questions I had to answer 'Yes.' I tried to explain, to soften, to make the best of a bad business—all in vain. I could not alter facts, and he broke out.

"He said I had come to him in a false character—under false pretences—that I had basely betrayed the confidence he reposed in me, and repaid his kindness by inveigling his daughter into forming an attachment for a mere adventurer—a common swindler. I thought he would exhaust his vehemence at last, so I finally sat silent. This he mistook for defiance. 'You think, I suppose,' he said, 'that I cannot sever my connection with you. If there is justice in England, I will have it. You shall not say I sent you off penniless, but you shall not have a halfpenny more than I choose to give. You may smile' (I had done nothing of the sort), 'but I shall prove as good as my word. I shall make my will to-night, and tie up every farthing, so that you can never riot on my hard-earned money. I shall take steps for a separation between you and my daughter. I shall——'

"'You need not trouble yourself to explain your intentions further,' I broke in at this juncture. 'I shall never make any demand upon you in the future. I shall never see you or your daughter again.' And with that I was about to leave the office, when he broke into the most frightful paroxysm of rage imaginable.

"'Don't go!' he shouted. 'Don't dare to go! I have not half done with you. I have not said a quarter I mean to say. I will send the police after you if you——'

"I shall never know what he imagined I was going to do," finished Mr. Irwin in a broken and agitated voice, "for at that moment he made a movement, as if trying to clutch the air, and fell back in a fit.

"I ran to him, and unfastened his cravat. I shouted for Tucker to come and stay with him while I went for a doctor. I raced through the streets like a madman, and at last procured medical assistance in the person of a young surgeon.

"When he looked at him he shook his head. 'You had better not try to move him, sir,' he said. 'Make up a bed here and give him a chance. I should like to meet a doctor upon the case. There may be some hope, but my own impression is he will never speak again.'

"We did all we could for him. The doctor came—many doctors came, but all confirmed the surgeon's opinion. Everything money could buy was bought. Everything skill could suggest was tried. His daughter came, but fainted directly, and had to be sent away again. We had two nurses, and I myself seldom left him. On the eighth day he died.

"He never spoke another conscious word. He never made the threatened will. He died intestate, as I understand from his solicitors; and if that be the case, nothing can now affect my pecuniary position; but I am afraid I shall not be able to hold up my head in the City again.

"I met that horrid lawyer again to-day, and he said, with a grin, 'It is better to be born lucky than rich; is it not, Mr. Walter Chappell Irwin? It is fortunate when refractory relations die just in the nick of time.'"

"Oh! uncle, uncle!" cried out Bella Miles, "don't offend that man any more. Make terms with him. Do anything to make him keep quiet!"

———

CHAPTER XIX.

UNCLE AND NIECE.

"I AM afraid it is impossible to make terms with the fellow without buying him," said Mr. Irwin, in answer to his niece's entreaty; "and there is nothing of which I have such a dread as putting myself into the power of any human being."

"But if you are in his power already?" she suggested.

"I should be putting myself more in his power if I began paying him for silence."

"In what way?"

"Why, his demands would go on increasing till the burden became unendurable—besides, there may be fifty other people who recollect me perfectly."

"I thought you said he would not have recognized you, had it not been for the unfortunate meeting with—my mother."

"He had some remembrance of me before that. Oh, Bella! what would I not give to be able to begin my life over again with my present experience! I think the happiest man upon earth must be he who, having no past he is afraid to remember, can walk in the present, and on to face the future, without dread."

She did not answer. She was thinking how frequently the same idea had occurred to her: how enviable, spite of its cares, its shifts, its debts, and its humiliations, Mr. Wright's lot had often seemed when contrasted with her own.

A life which held nothing in it to be concealed was her notion of an existence to be envied.

We have each and all our ideal of perfect happiness. Mr. Wright's was to have always five pounds in his pocket, and no duns at his gates. Miss Miles', to be able to speak freely without fear, and to feel she could answer any question concerning her parents and her childhood without falsehood.

To some of the old Barthornes—to some of the loyal gentlemen, and fair, faithful daughters of Abbotsleigh—this girl had gone back for the qualities which made her shrink when she was forced to back up the fiction of her orphan condition with one untruth after another.

There had been a time when she thought her uncle would have done wisely to tell the Rev. Mr. Wright and Selina his wife the story of her life as it really was; but she thought so no longer. Life at Fisherton, which had taught her much, had proved to her that there are some things concerning which silence is wisdom—silence is a necessity. Even as a servant, she now understood the terrible past would, if revealed, have power to destroy every blossom of happiness existence held.

She had no choice except to be careful and secret; but every vein in her heart loathed the deception she was forced to practise. Never till the end came, when deception was no longer needful, did her lips utter glibly the falsehoods her position compelled them to frame. Neither did she seek to justify her own lack of verity by dwelling on the shortcomings of others.

Not a day passed at Fisherton without some polite fiction being uttered by gracious, plausible Mrs. Wright, who was wont to say there was only one sin she humanly considered unpardonable, and that was lying; whilst as for poor Mr. Wright, the fibs he told, the "false glosses" he put on, the mendacious

statements he backed almost with tears, would have been absurd, had they not been pitiable also.

And yet, in this atmosphere, Bella kept her faith intact in all
things good, true, and lovely. Perhaps, by reason of her own
fault, she dared not judge the faults of others. This virtue is
not a common one. It is so much easier to see the mote than
to feel the beam, that we may well excuse poor Mrs. Wright for
frequently expressing her sorrow at finding people "so false."

But as for Bella, never once in Fisherton Church, when Mr.
Wright was declaring the weightier matters of the law, did this
girl—in whom I hope some of my readers feel an interest—
mentally thrust his words back to his condemnation. Nay,
rather, when she fell on her knees and shut out the congregation, and thought of all the sermon had taught her, her cry to
God was "Have mercy on me, a sinner," rather than "I thank
Thee that I am not as these."

"Uncle," she began at last, "do you remember promising
long ago that you would some day tell me about the work you
used to do at West Green?"

"I hoped you had forgotten all that," he said.

"I never forget. I wish—I wish I could," she answered. "I
should be so happy if it were possible to fancy those times only
a bad dream."

"We will not recall them," he replied.

"But there are some things I want to understand," she persisted. "I lie awake at night, and try to patch and put together
all I can recollect of what happened when I was a child. I
have often had the question on my lips before, but did not like
to put it ; now, however, that we have got upon the subject, I
must ask you just one thing, uncle : what was the work, so still
and quiet, that kept you up hours after all our neighbours were
in bed?"

"It was coining," he said doggedly. "Don't look so frightened—we did not send out bad money, but good ; and had
your father contented himself with doing what he told me he
intended to do—buy old silver and gold cheap—I don't know
that much harm could have come of the matter ; but he did not
content himself with that, as you are aware. Your mother's
folly and his own obstinacy ruined him.

"Often and often I told him what the end must be ; but he
always laughed at my cautions, and said he would give any one

leave to find him out who could. I do not see, however, that any good purpose can be served by our discussing that terrible past. Ever since the night you and I walked together into London, I have tried, God knows, to lead an honest life. I have striven to make atonement where atonement was possible. Every penny of the money which fell to my share, and that was in my possession when the crash came, I have divided amongst those I had any reason to suppose suffered through our malpractices. First or last, I have never used any of your father's share in order to pay for your education, and latterly I have not touched it even to provide for your mother. As for your father, Bella, he has paid a heavy penalty for his sins, and I think we may let them rest. What I hope and trust and pray now is that he may not return to England—that neither of us may ever set eyes on him again. The best news I could hear would be that he was dead, and the story of his crime and its punishment buried with him."

She was crying, silently and secretly, but in the moonlight he could see the tears streaming down her cheeks.

"Come, dear," he said, "let us turn back and have no more of this melancholy talk. You are not responsible for his faults, and we must prevent his sins being ever visited on you. The day may come when you will have to decide for yourself, whether you will cast in your lot with either of your parents—which would be certain destruction to your happiness—or whether you will strike out in life independent of both. It is possible, now Mr. Irwin is dead, that I may eventually be able to adopt you as my own daughter, and take you to my own home. That is what I should like to do; but for the present you must remain here. You are happy at the rectory, I hope and believe?"

"Quite—oh, yes!—quite," she said, her voice a little unsteady and broken with tears.

"And you are learning the usages of society, and all that sort of thing, which may be useful to you hereafter?"

"Yes—I think so."

"As for your mother, Bella," he went on, "she is just what she always was. She was a foolish young woman, and now she is a foolish middle-aged woman. Her latest idea is to go out to Australia and join your father. She says she is certain he would not refuse to be reconciled after all these years. But I think her real reason for undertaking the journey is that she believes he is married to some one else. She was always jealous when she had him under her eye, and she is naturally more jealous now he is beyond her supervision. She did not say much about you. She asked if she could see you, and offered to go to France for the purpose; but when I reminded her of the promise your father exacted from me that I should not permit any communication, she seemed quite satisfied. At the same time, it would not surprise me if she went to every school in and about Paris to try and find you."

"But, uncle, you are surely not going to let her sail for Australia!" exclaimed the girl.

"My dear Bella, how can I prevent her going to Australia, or any other place she takes a fancy to visit? She has money from me, of course, and she can spend it in paying rent or paying for her passage, just as she pleases. The only thing I could do would be to say: 'As you are determined to have your own way, I will make that way as unpleasant to you as possible;' and this is precisely what I should not care to do. For a few pounds more she can travel comfortably instead of uncomfortably; and as it is not in the least degree likely she will find her husband when she gets to Australia, why, no harm will be done, and she will be out of my way for some time, at all events."

"Why should she not find him?" asked his niece.

"Because Australia is a big country, and she does not happen to know where he is in it. You may be very sure I did not give her the address to which he told me to write. She has an idea that Australia is something like New York, where, if you remember, she followed me and found me."

"But if they do meet, something dreadful will happen," said the girl. "He will never forgive her—I feel quite certain of that."

"And if I were in his place, I do not think I could forgive her either. Knowing what she must have known——" He stopped abruptly.

"Go on, please," entreated his niece. "What was it she did know? Was it what I so often fancied—what I have been afraid even to think about?"

"Why, she knew, of course—she must have known—that most of the things which came into the house were stolen," said Mr. Irwin, a little confusedly.

"And what else?" persisted his companion.

"What else should there be? Was not that enough?"

"It is a long time ago," she said; "and, what with the voyage to America and the fever I had, I often get confused when trying to recall things that happened when I was young. But there comes back to me occasionally a terrible notion—I cannot remember when it first took firm hold of me—that I heard people talk about a dreadful murder; and with that murder I associate the dagger we dropped that night we walked across the quiet fields I have never seen since, and then through the London streets. Am I right? Was not some man killed at Highgate?"

He did not immediately answer—when he did, it was in a constrained tone.

"Yes—I think there was a man found dead about that time."

"Was it ever known who killed him?"

"Never, I believe."

"Uncle, do you know?"

"I do not," he answered.

"Do you suspect? Was it my father? Did we drop the clue in that silent street off the Liverpool Road?"

There ensued a dead silence. For the first time Walter Chappell felt a sickening desire to defend his brother-in-law's character—for the first time he searched about for excuses—for the first time he felt inclined to act as his advocate.

"Uncle, you do not speak," she said at last softly.

"My dear," he answered, "you press me hard and sore. I cannot tell you a lie; and yet, if I must speak, I am only able to say—what must pierce you to the heart. I believe that night you saved your father's life. I think, had that dagger been found in his house he would not have been transported—he would have died in front of Newgate. But, Bella, remember this: he did not do the deed, if it was done by him, in cold blood. I never mentioned the subject to him—I never will, except in case of the direst necessity. But my reading of the matter is this: He had constant access to the house. For days, as I take it—perhaps for weeks—he had been removing gold and silver plate and ornaments from the strong room. On the morning when M'Callum died he had probably just removed some valuable articles, and being met with the spoil, in a moment of desperation he killed the man who had the misfortune to encounter him. I have thought the matter over and over, and can come to no other conclusion than that he did kill M'Callum in order to escape the precise doom which afterwards overtook him.　He was in too great a hurry to be rich, Bella.　I trace every ill which has befallen him to one master passion—ambition."

And then, taking the girl's cold hand in his, he told her the story of her father's birth, education, expectations, disappointment.

With more tenderness than he had ever thought to employ when speaking of a man he feared and almost hated, he who had turned from the error of his ways recited the wrongs of this Ishmael who considered himself to have been so harshly treated.

He spoke of him as, had circumstances happened otherwise, he might have been —a wealthy country squire, clever, well informed, highly considered ; and then he presented her with the reverse of the picture.　He showed her the youth, brought up to consider himself the heir, cast out from his father's house, working as a common smith—with all the blood in his veins turning to gall—with all his boyish hopes dispelled—with all the idols he had worshipped shattered.

And so he talked on till he was almost too late for his train ; and she, after running a few yards on her way to the rectory, slackened her pace to weep almost frantically, for pity, over the father she trusted she might never see more—for sorrow, that she herself had not died when she lay sick of that terrible fever in New York.

CHAPTER XX.

ROSIE'S DÉBÛT.

If **Mr.** Wright had gone to bed on Christmas Eve with even a vague fear as to the solvency of Mr. Irwin, junior, and any doubt concerning the profitable "cutting up" of old Mr. Irwin's estates, his direst forebodings must on Christmas morning have been entirely dissipated.

Beside the hot water lay two packets, small, sealed, suggestive —one directed to Mrs. Wright, the other to the Rev. D. Wright, both in Bella Miles' handwriting.

The first contained a plain but handsome bracelet, with Mr. Irwin's kind regards and best wishes; the second a ring, with Bella Miles' earnest hope that the Rev. Dion might spend a happy Christmas, and enjoy many happy New Years.

"Really most graceful," said the Rector, turning the ring over and over, referring, it is scarcely necessary to say, to the thoughtfulness of the donor.

"I am sure I never expected Mr. Irwin to think of me," re-marked Mrs. Wright, sitting up in bed, and clasping the bracelet round her arm, which, though fair and soft, had lost much of the shapely plumpness of youth. "I call this a very handsome gift indeed."

"That it is," agreed the Rector heartily; "and the very thing you were in want of. You have needed a decent bracelet badly enough this many a year past, Selina."

Which was indeed quite true, jewellery happening not to be one of the sins of extravagance that Mrs. Wright affected.

At the first stir of wakened life in their parents' apartment came the children, eager to display their gifts, with which they were laden—gifts from aunts in Ireland, who had stinted them-selves to send toys, and presents of all sorts, to boys and girls already overstocked with books, and boxes, and dolls, and trumpets, and so forth.

Some indiscreet friend had forwarded Curran a drum, in which Roderick, with a wise foresight, had already punctured a few holes to facilitate the speedy demise of its powers of giving annoyance; and Rosie was making morning hideous by producing appalling sounds from the interior of a barking dog.

But Miss Miles' presents exceeded those of all other donors in value and appropriateness.

Roderick, it is true, was slow to disclose the wonders of his dressing-case, because amongst them were a pair of razors; but the other sons and daughters of the house of Wright eagerly displayed writing-desks, and silver pencils, and small brooches, and necklaces, and knives, and boxes full of *bonbons*, which Bella had purchased.

"Now, now, now!" exclaimed Mr. Wright at last. If he was a fond parent, he was also a fidgety man, and liked to have ample leisure for making his toilet, eating his breakfast, looking out his sermon, and walking at a moderate pace to church. "Take these things away, and be off, every one of you. Do you think I can brush my hair with all you young plagues swarming about me?"

"Yes, run away, dears," echoed the plagues' mamma. "Curran, I hope you gave Bella a pretty kiss for her kindness to you?"

"We have all kissed her, ma," said Miss Maria, who was judging of the effect of the new bracelet on her own wrist.

"I didn't," contradicted Roderick, who perhaps felt he was too far advanced in years for such exercises to be considered becoming; "but I told her she was a jolly girl, and that I was awfully obliged to her."

"Roderick," remonstrated Mr. Wright, "where do you learn that incomprehensible style of language? Not from your mother or me, of that I am quite sure."

Now, if Mr. Wright had left out that statement, his utterance might have inspired his son with reverence. As matters were, the idea of either of his parents indulging in slang tickled Roderick's fancy to such a degree that he could only splutter out, "I don't suppose, sir, my language would be proper uttered in the pulpit; but it is quite comprehensible. All fellows understand 'jolly' and 'awfully.' I am sure you yourself know clearly what I mean."

"A new generation is about to reign," remarked Mr. Wright resignedly; "and you, I suppose, are one of the intended rulers."

He would have quoted Shakespeare at that moment anent young folks pushing elders from their stools; but he could not remember the text quite accurately; and, moreover, he was tying his white cravat, an operation which with him was one of exceeding care and nicety. Breakfast on Sunday morning at Fisherton Rectory was quite an imposing ceremony, and it is needless to say that on Christmas mornings all the resources of the establishment were brought into play.

Mr. Wright himself, in a snowy shirt and unexceptionable broadcloth, was indeed a spectacle to rejoice the heart of all good Protestants; and then there was Mrs. Wright, arrayed in her best bib and tucker; and the children, the eldest dressed out in their choicest apparel, the youngest soaped and towelled up to a state of the highest perfection, with well-oiled sleek heads, with wonderful chubby mottled-looking arms, with pinafores which rivalled the whiteness of their male parent's shirt, with little rosettes of bright-coloured ribbon tying up their sleeves, and a fillet of the same confining their hair.

It was not in Mr. Wright's human nature to refrain from casting a triumphant look at Colonel Leschelles when the troop ranged themselves round the table, and folded their hands preparatory to the grace, which their father, having a dislike to lukewarm tea, made commendably short.

As for Mrs. Wright, she held a fixed opinion that every one must be miserable, if not clearly wicked, who had not several children, and she made no secret even to the Colonel himself that she believed he was wretched because no fruitful vine and no young olive-branches graced his solitary board.

On occasions such as the present she was, therefore, wont to look at her children with a fond smile, which she suffered to fade away into sadness as her eyes rested on the unhappy bachelor. This little pantomime amused the Colonel immensely; and it was perhaps because she was the only one of the party likely to sympathize with his enjoyment of the position, that his glance involuntarily sought out Bella Miles, in whose face he saw something of mirth lurking.

Spite of her trouble—spite of the fact that she had cried herself to sleep overnight, and that her head was still aching, by reason of the conversation with her uncle on the previous evening, Bella could not help being diverted with both parents and children.

The latter were so satisfied with themselves, and the former were so satisfied with themselves and their offspring too, that the sight of the family trooping downstairs, followed by the admiring looks and approving words of the Rev. Dion and Mrs. Wright, was enough to have tried the gravity of any disinterested spectator.

"Ah," said Nurse Mary, in a discreet "aside" to Miss Miles, "they say stock is as good as money; but if I was in master's shoes, I think I could do with less of it than he has in hand."

On that particular Christmas Day Rosie was to make her *début* in church, and on the strength of this circumstance Bella Miles had presented the child with a prayer-book almost as big, and quite as bright and new-looking, as herself.

Already, with the assistance of Roderick, Rosie and Curran had looked up several services of the Church, publicly baptized her latest doll, married her to a man who was suspended on wires, and turned somersaults in a way calculated to make the beholder dizzy; and finally, having stretched her in an eau-de-Cologne case, buried her under the blankets of Rosie's cot. These rites and ceremonies satisfactorily performed, Curran and Rosie had a stand-up fight as to who should carry the prayer-book to church; and Nurse Mary finally conveyed the coveted article to Miss Miles' room, assuring her it had "stood a near chance of being torn to bits among them quarrelsome young divils. God forgive me for speaking such a word—though He knows I am not calling them out of their right names."

To describe the house when the young people were preparing and being prepared to go to church, it would, to quote Nurse Mary's lucid remark, "take the pen of a Job."

Maria had split her new gloves, and Roderick could not find the hat-brush, upon which Curran had seated himself in a sulk because his mamma would not let him have a mince pie before starting. One child was crying and another laughing. Colonel Leschelles was walking up and down the drawing-room, uttering a special thanksgiving all by himself. Mr. Wright, umbrella shouldered, chest well out like a pouter pigeon, sermon-case in his pocket, and peace and charity even towards his creditors in his heart—had wisely left the scene of action a quarter of an hour previously, and was walking with the gait and air of a bishop, sedately to church. Mrs. Wright had house-maid and cook, and a young woman from a former parish who

was in delicate health, all looking through her drawers for un-
findable articles of apparel. She did not do much herself,
except stand before the glass arranging her curls, varying the
proceedings by running to the door at intervals and exclaiming:

"Now, Bella, dear—now, Nurse Mary, you good soul—are
those children nearly ready? You know their papa cannot
bear their going into church late. And, Bella, will you lend
me a pair of your cuffs? and if you have a spare fall—don't
take yours off—any old thing will do for me. What a girl it is!
I believe, as Mr. Wright says, you would take the gown off your
back if you thought any one else wanted it."

At last, something like order being produced out of chaos,
the children trooped downstairs, and broke out into the drive.
Looking, though faded, pretty and ladylike, Mrs. Wright passed
into the drawing-room, and, seeing Colonel Lescheiles, said:

"I am so sorry to have kept you waiting, but there are such
a number of us to get ready. No, don't walk with me, please;
I must see to the little ones—and children bore you, I know.
I am sure they would me, if they were not my own. Bella—
Bella, love—Colonel Leschelles will take care of you. Rosie,
darling, come here, and mamma will hold your hand—there's a
dear."

"No," retorted the dear, clinging to Bella, who carried the
gorgeous prayer-book.

"*I'm* going to walk with mamma," said Curran, with a mental
eye to future mince pie and plum pudding.

" Me too !" instantly shouted the latest arrow in the rectorial
quiver, rushing off with infantile perversity to secure her mother's
disengaged hand; and thus, youngest son on one side, youngest
daughter on the other, with seven other pledges of affection in
front, and Colonel Leschelles and Bella in rear, Mrs. Wright
walked through Fisherton, to the admiration of all beholders.

"I think, Miss Miles," said Colonel Leschelles to his companion, "that I have had the pleasure of seeing you somewhere
before. Your face seems quite familiar to me."

Bella shook her head.

"You must be mistaken," she answered, looking up at him
with clear, honest, yet timid eyes as she spoke. "I should have
remembered you had I ever seen you since I was quite a little
child. I never did forget any one, I think,—unless it might be
the strangers who were about me when I had fever in New

York," she added, as if imagining he had possibly been one of them.

"I did not know you had been in New York," he remarked. "Are you American by birth, then?"

"Oh, no," she replied, and a swift, hot flush came up into her face as she said so. "I went there when I was quite young, with my uncle; but the climate did not suit my health, and so he sent me to a school near Paris, where I stayed till I came here."

"Then of course we have never met before," he said; "and yet I have seen your double somewhere at some time."

"It must have been a person like me; it could not have been me," she answered simply.

Upon that subject, at all events, Miss Miles had no reserves. As she owned, so far as she knew, no female relative save her mother, and as her mother was as unlike her as it is ever possible for a mother to be, she felt no anxiety on the subject of her accidental resemblance to any human being.

"Do you like Fisherton?" he asked, by way of turning the conversation.

"Very much," she said. "This is such a pleasant change after school life."

"I should have thought it very much like school," he remarked, with a significant glance ahead.

"You mean the children. Well, perhaps in that way it is. But then there are not so many of them, and they have not been drilled to one pattern. Even when they are naughty they are amusing—perhaps more amusing than at any other time. And for me this existence means freedom. One can run about and do as one likes—and one gets better things to eat—and one goes out to nice parties sometimes—and Mr. Wright is so kind—and Mrs. Wright has taught me so much—and indeed I shall always love Fisherton, to the last day of my life!"

"See how the old and the young sometimes agree," he said, with a little grimness in his voice. "I like Fisherton now very much better than I imagined it possible I should ever like any place again. But here we are at the church."

There they were indeed, and the bell had done tolling, and Mr. Wright was already in the reading-desk when the family proceeded up the aisle.

Still holding Rosie by the hand, Mrs. Wright entered the

square pew, which with some difficulty contained the twelve persons who now entered into possession of that well-cushioned, well-carpeted, well-hassocked domain.

Down on her knees beside her mother plopped the child, wondering exceedingly ; and on her knees she remained until the exhortation had begun, when Mrs. Wright, resuming an erect position, placed Rosie, whose eyes were round as peas with astonishment, on a footstool beside her.

Round and about went Miss Rosie's glances. She surveyed the roof, the organ-loft, the congregation, and with the intensest curiosity followed the movements of the sexton, as he ushered late arrivals into their pews.

Then suddenly her eye fell on the clergyman, who was at the moment saying :

"With a pure heart and humble voice, unto the throne of the heavenly grace."

Miss Rosie, recognizing him, cried out in a shrill voice which reached the farthest corner of the church :

"Why, mamma, there's papa in his night-shirt !"

I am bound to say the congregation behaved nobly at this crisis. First they tittered, and then they coughed ; but, upon the whole, they confined their feelings to their handkerchiefs, which they stuffed into their mouths.

By the time every one was almost in convulsions it occurred to Rosie that she had misbehaved herself, and looking at Curran, who knelt beside her, she put up her finger inside her lips, and the pair laughed audibly, like the rest.

As for Bella Miles, she rose when the *Venite* commenced, but, unlike the others, she asked Roderick to open the pew door, and walked out of the church, looking like a very ghost.

When she reached home, according to Nurse Mary's account of the proceedings, she fell to laughing and crying on the sofa, —laughing till she cried, and crying till she laughed.

"Till indeed, ma'am, I thought I would have to put on my bonnet and fetch the doctor from the sermon."

CHAPTER XXI.

FISHING FOR INFORMATION.

ROSIE's misbehaviour cast a gloom, so far as Mr. Wright was concerned, over the chastened festivities of Christmas Day. He did not like being the occasion for laughter to others. Many persons are similarly constituted; and though the prattle of children is doubtless a delightful music, still the Rector opined that when it played such a tune as his youngest-born had elected to raise in church, it was quite possible for there to be too much of a good thing. But the next day he recovered his good spirits. He saw some of his parishioners, and they spoke of the "dear little creature's" speech in a way calculated to soothe his ruffled feathers. Further, by the morning's post came a letter from Mr. Irwin, in answer to one Mr. Wright had posted to him a few days before, enclosing a whole half-year's payment for Bella, which amount, indeed, made up the payment for a whole year, *plus* the fifty pounds originally lent to the Rev. Dion.

Now, as heretofore, Mr. Wright was eating his corn before it was ripe; but, so long as evil could be staved off and present necessities provided for, little recked the Rector and his wife of the future. With fifty pounds in his pocket, no sickness in the house, and a clear conscience, as he himself would have said, who more happy than the Rector of Fisherton? who more ready to laugh at the misadventure of Christmas Day, and remark:

"You, my dear Colonel, know nothing from experience of these sorts of thing; but I assure you parents find them of daily occurrence"?

And then he went on to tell a case which had happened, to his own knowledge, of a child who, seated on a small stool in the drawing-room, heard her mamma remark, concerning some visitors who were driving up the avenue, "How provoking! here are those tiresome H——s again!" and so forth. Changing her tone, however, as the ladies entered, she said, "Dear Mrs. H——! this is an unexpected pleasure! I am so delighted to see you!" Whereupon the *enfant terrible* interposed: "Mamma, she observed solemnly, "how can you tell such untruths? It is not three minutes since you said she was a prosy, gossiping, ill-natured old woman, and that she was always calling upon people who did not wish to see her." "Thank you, my dear," said Mrs. H——; "I have heard truth spoken for once in this house;" and so, exit, with a stately curtsey. Exit also the child, a moment after, not of her own free will.

Also he spoke of another sweet darling, who, at luncheon, asked an old lady, from whom the family had great expectations, when she was going to die, as Aunt Helen wanted her diamond ring; and brought forward, in fact, many statements to prove that children have a pernicious habit of saying the right thing at the wrong time, which, if he had only been aware of the fact, was a truth concerning which Colonel Leschelles entertained no manner of doubt.

Passing from the subject of children to that of unseemly interruptions of public worship, Mr. Wright quoted some curious though not particularly amusing instances in point. As most of these occurred in dissenting places of worship, and in remote districts, he was naturally led to speak of the extraordinary remarks sometimes made from the pulpit in cases where the clergyman was noted for eccentricity; instancing, for example, the text Dean Swift selected when asked to preach a sermon to the tailors of Dublin, the first of which set the then gay city laughing, and the next sent his audience indignant from their seats; also the observation of a well-known minister in the north of Ireland, who, not wishing to be personal, went on to say that in a pew, sixth from the door, on the left-hand side of the aisle, there was a woman seated—a woman in a red shawl—who was laughing, and otherwise misbehaving herself. All he had to say to that woman, to whom he should feel loth to direct attention, was, that if for the future she did not conduct herself properly, he would have her turned out. He was sure that slight hint would be enough, he added, and then went on with his sermon.

But when he got to the religious utterances of some of his friends, the dissenters—good men, but imperfectly educated—Mr. Wright, who really could, when his mind was at ease, still tell a story well, made Colonel Leschelles laugh. Not with bad effect, he repeated part of a sermon he once heard delivered on the Prodigal Son. "He came, no shoes to his feet, no coat to his back, in his shirt-sleeves, and *them* grimed with dirt! his beard grown and matted, his hair uncombed and wild-like, his trousers just hanging together, all in rags and tatters, dirty with living among swine. You know what pigs are, my brethren, and they were no cleaner at that time in the Holy Land than they are in Ulster now. Well, in this plight he came back to his father's house; and his father fell on his neck and kissed him. Ugh! I wonder how he could!"

More marvellous still, however, was the prayer Mr. Wright stated to have been offered up by a staunch Presbyterian for Queen Adelaide:

"O Lord! save Thy servant, our Sovereign Lady the Queen. Grant that, as she grows an old woman, she may become a new man. Strengthen her with Thy blessing, that she may live a pure virgin before Thee, bringing forth sons and daughters to the glory of God; and vouchsafe her Thy blessing, that she may go forth before her people like a he-goat on the mountains!"

To these and other anecdotes of a similar description—notably to that of the old lady parishioner, who, being told by her minister that the "Lord had called him to labour in another part of the vineyard," answered, "And ye'll be getting better pay, no doubt; for sure am I, if you had not, the Lord might have called long enough and loud enough before ye'd have heard Him."—Colonel Leschelles would doubtless have lent a more appreciative ear, had he not been hungering and thirsting to ask some questions about Bella Miles.

At length, despairing of introducing her name naturally, he inquired: "Is that young lady who is now staying at the rectory a countrywoman of yours?"

"Of mine?" repeated the Rev. Dion. "Certainly not. I should be very glad to claim her, for she is a charming girl; but that is impossible. Her coming to us was the most extraordinary thing in the world—for us, I may say, providential. Though at first I dreaded having a stranger in the house, she has been a blessing to it in every respect. It was all brought about in an extraordinary manner. Her uncle was almost unknown to us, when, one night last summer, I found myself in a serious difficulty. I won't distress your kind heart by explaining what the nature of the difficulty was. I need only say that I did not know from hour to hour whether Selina and the children might not find themselves houseless and homeless."

"Dear me!" ejaculated the Colonel, as Mr. Wright, after this reticent statement, paused to regain composure.

"I was at my wits' end," resumed the Rector. "I felt I had better give up the useless struggle of trying to keep a roof over our heads. I felt beaten—and I think you know I have some fight in me still—when Providence put it into my head to ask this stranger—who had taken Sir John Giles' house while they were abroad—for help. He gave it, sir, instantly. I never before met with such delicate generosity from one on whom I had not even the claim of acquaintanceship. He wrote me out a cheque then and there; and I was so overjoyed, that when I found myself out in the night, and all alone, I could have sobbed like a child. As for Selina, poor dear!—but I need not tell *you* all that creature had suffered."

"No, indeed," remarked the Colonel.

"So that is how I came to know Bella's uncle intimately," said Mr. Wright, finishing his narrative.

As Colonel Leschelles was aware it was the way in which the Rev. Dion had come to know a great many people intimately, he only remarked, "And how you came to know Miss Miles too, I presume."

"Well, yes. At the time, Mr. Irwin happened to be looking out for a suitable family in which to find a home for his niece, then at school in France; and it occurred to him that the money he meant to pay would be of use to us, and that we could be of use to his niece—and I trust we have been of use to the dear girl. Selina has taken immense pains—wonderful—in forming her; and she has improved to an extraordinary degree since she came amongst us. Her uncle is quite delighted with the change. I had a char-ming letter from him this morning—char-ming! I have it in my pocket. No, I must have left it at home," added Mr. Wright, colouring a little; for he remembered it might not be prudent to exhibit Mr. Irwin's statement of accounts to his companion.

"Her uncle is wealthy, then?" said Colonel Leschelles interrogatively.

"One of the merchant princes, my dear friend," answered Mr. Wright unctuously, which statement would considerably have astonished Mr. Irwin, had he chanced to hear it.

"Did you say he was married?" asked the Colonel.

Mr. Wright had not said so, but probably imagining he had, replied, "Yes."

"Is not it strange that he did not take Miss Miles to his own home?"

"Evidently," thought Mr. Wright, "his suspicions have taken the same turn as mine. He imagines Bella to be Mr. Irwin's daughter." But he knew better than to let his companion see he comprehended what was passing through his mind, and answered :

"So far as I apprehend the matter, Mr. Irwin has at home a wife with a temper."

"Poor devil!" said the Colonel compassionately.

"And I think it is very possible she might not care to have a handsome, accomplished girl distracting attention from her. Remember, this is only my idea. All I know for certain is, that she is a very rude sort of person. Why, when Selina called upon her at Riversdale she was 'not at home,' and never—positively never—returned the visit."

"How singular! Then, I presume, all arrangements respecting Miss Miles are made solely with Mr. Irwin?"

"Solely with Mr. Irwin. I have never spoken to his wife, and I have only seen her driving past in her carriage."

"Does Mr. Irwin resemble his niece? She is very peculiar-looking, you know, and must inherit her face from some one."

"He is not like her in the least. He is fair, with blue or light grey eyes, I cannot be quite certain which—a long face, light brown hair, a high forehead, a man of an ordinary type—a man who impresses me, I am sure I cannot tell why, with the idea of having risen from the ranks, and been somehow worsted on the road—a man inclined to be melancholy, and weak—yes, decidedly weak, I should say. He has nothing of the high-bred look which, no doubt, you have noticed in Bella. He does not alternate as she does, poor child!

'From grave to gay, from lively to severe.'

He is never very cheerful, and never very dull. Perhaps he 'does not digest,' as Sydney Smith used to suggest. The state of a man's spirits is generally governed by the state of his liver; and I attribute Bella's customary vivacity to her superb constitution. I never saw a girl enjoy such perfect health. I

thought my dear children were pretty well blessed in that respect;
but certainly Bella excels them there."

"Yet she had a bad headache on Christmas Eve, and was
hysterical yesterday," objected Colonel Leschelles.

"True; but her uncle came down, if you remember, on
Christmas Eve, and evidently entertained the girl with all sorts
of dismal subjects. He talked, I have no doubt, about her
dead parents and his unhappy home, and other matters of the
same kind."

"Do you happen to know who her mother was?" asked the
Colonel. "Forgive me for putting so many questions; but the
girl's face seems perfectly familiar to me."

"Her mother, she says, was Mr. Irwin's sister; and, in answer
to an inquiry of Mrs. Wright's, she stated that she believed she
resembles her father in appearance."

"And who was he?—what was he?—where did he live?—
and where did he die?"

"I do not know. He died abroad somewhere, but where I
am sure I have no idea. As to where he lived, Bella gives
little information. I suspect, however, from her knowledge of
localities about that part of London, that they resided in
Clerkenwell."

"Where on earth is that?" asked the Colonel.

"Well, it lies between the Goswell Road and Farringdon
Road—between Snow Hill and Pentonville. I do not think I
can give you any nearer clue to its whereabouts."

"Oh, indeed!" commented the other. "Perhaps he carried
on some trade or business there. Do you know what he was?"

"Ah! now you puzzle me altogether. 'That is your own
question, and you must answer it yourself,' as my countryman
remarked."

"And may I inquire upon what occasion it was that your
countryman made the polite observation you have quoted?"
asked Colonel Leschelles, a little irritably.

"Well," answered Mr. Wright, laughing at his friend's touchi-
ness, "he proposed a game, one of the conditions of which
was, that if any one of the players could not answer his own
question he must pay a forfeit—Pat himself leading off with the
inquiry how it happened that a rabbit made her hole without
casting out any earth. None of the company being able to
account for the phenomenon, the Irishman explained that 'she

began at the other end.' Whereupon some one, utterly amazed, cried out, 'But how does she do that?' 'Ah!' said Pat, 'that is your own question; answer it yourself!' And that is precisely what I am obliged to say to you. If you can obtain from either Mr. Irwin or Miss Miles the slightest clue to the nature of Mr. Miles' occupation while on earth, where he came from, and who his father was, you will be much cleverer than your humble servant."

Colonel Leschelles, knowing that, as regarded recondite researches concerning the antecedents of any human being whose histories they wished to investigate, many talents had been given to the Rev. Dionysius Wright and Selina his wife—talents which they had not kept hidden in a napkin—made no reply to his friend's exhaustive statement. He felt, where they had failed, he was not likely to succeed; and for some reason, unintelligible then even to himself, he was very anxious to know more of Miss Miles' past and Miss Miles' progenitors than he seemed at all likely to ascertain.

"It must be a little unpleasant for you," he said at length, referring to the fact of having such a mystery boarding, washing, and lodging at the rectory.

"I do not feel any unpleasantness now, I assure you," said Mr. Wright, cheerfully beating a tattoo on the front of his topcoat, inside of which lay, crisp and snug, Mr. Irwin's letter and his welcome cheque. "You see, she is such a dear, good creature; and one hundred a year is one hundred a year, to a man with twelve children, an appearance to keep up, and a position to maintain."

"The uncle pays you a hundred per annum, then?" interrogated Colonel Leschelles.

"That was his own offer, and I need not say I did not urge him to reduce it," said the Rector.

"No, I suppose not," said his companion, looking with his outward eyes up and down the flat, marshy, uninteresting valley of the Thames, as it presents itself to the beholder at Fisherton —vainly searching mentally for some small fish to attach itself to his hook—and finally coming to the conclusion that no fish, whether great or little, was to be landed by means of any bait he could present.

CHAPTER XXII.

THE COLONEL MAKES A DISCOVERY.

THERE is an uncertainty about fishing. It is curious to consider how one's experience varies according to the locality in which one resides.

At a remote period of my life I should have said positively that, given any decent sort of weather, a fisher need never have returned from a fishing expedition empty; but in that case he had to seek his prey in the sea.

Recently, I know it is very possible for a man to spend hours —days—weeks—months in this enticing occupation, and catch nothing. Not far from where these lines are being written, there is a bridge, described in the local guide-book as being of stone, and very handsome; and indeed it is a graceful and substantial structure. It spans a river, part of which is dear to anglers, and from it a near view is obtained of a pretty village and a church.

On that bridge there stands perpetually a man fishing. No one has ever known him to bring anything from the lower depths up to his own level, though it has been rumoured that he was once heard informing a friend of some special good fortune, in which a jack of five pounds weight played a conspicuous part.

Which brings me back to my own sheep. Not a stone's throw—a child's stone-throw, I mean—from our accustomed sitting-room there is another bridge over a stream.

The stream is neither very wide nor very deep, and the bridge is consequently not handsome or built of stone.

Nevertheless, it is very pretty. It is covered and festooned with ivy; and on a favourable day, when one stands upon it looking down into the wider water lying riverwards, one can see plenty of fine fish making circles and ripples, and then disappearing, to re-appear, a few minutes after, a little farther off.

In this water, which would seem to present a fair prospect to an angler, a certain youth undertook to lure, with cunning hand, perch, dace, jack, and roach to land.

He fished and he fished. He began early in the morning. He was still hopeful at midday. He stood calmly expectant on the bank in the afternoon, and evening found him unwearied with his ill success.

For indeed he never caught any creature worth calling a fish —since it is not easy to cook a piscine baby about a day old, and consisting of a head and tail and no body. Of these useless innocents he would have made a collection in a large waterbutt, had they not been summarily turned back into the stream; but the wiser and older fish refused to listen to his wooing.

Nevertheless, he persevered. He tried all baits and all hooks, and had perfect faith, if he failed to-day, he must have a full basket to-morrow.

In especial he pinned his hopes on a certain jack, which he represented as residing amongst the weeds and eating its smaller neighbours. According to his statement, this jack was a creature of enormous size—a sort of Daniel Lambert amongst pike; and he never lost his bait, nor had his hook carried off, but he declared the jack had been at his line again.

Had his statement been correct, that pike would have been as full of hooks as a Christmas pudding is of plums.

Once a girl, curious to know what really was at the end of his line, picked up the rod he had laid on the bank, and found an unfortunate perch, about two inches long, well hooked. Releasing it, she threw the foolish creature back into the water; and when the angler returned, he solemnly declared, "That jack has been at his old tricks again!"

On another occasion, the whole household was solemnly asked to assemble and see the landing of the big pike. "I've got him at last!" said the angler, hauling away with eager hands. „There!—there!—don't you see him now?"

Some of the spectators were polite enough to say they saw the prey, and others were truthful enough to say they saw nothing of the kind. Nevertheless, every one believed the pike's hour had come, as the line was drawn slowly in—slowly and carefully —with a great bunch of weeds!

After this it was necessary to speak plainly, and say, as it was impossible to live upon the faith of a supposititious jack, some fish must be caught—caught, too, by a particular day.

The day came, and though three animals, which might have looked well through a microscope, were brought in, no human being out of a lunatic asylum could have thought of cooking them; and the domestic atmosphere was clouded when there came—from a non-preserved part of the stream, observe, where Dick, Tom, and Harry are free to spend their Sunday mornings and all the many other idle hours Satan allows them for recreation—a basket full of the finest fresh-water fish eye could desire to see.

It is a melancholy fact that successful angling, like kissing, goes by favour.

You may woo the stream patiently, skilfully, perseveringly; you may be constant in season and out of season; and not get enough in return to pay for your tackle; and then there comes along some careless stranger who casts his line at random, or some impudent, ragged young varlet, armed only with a crooked pin and a piece of twine, and you shall see him carry off the prize your soul has longed for—the ewe lamb out of the water you had almost come to consider your own.

Which brings me to the moral I desire to draw. People who go fishing on land often find themselves much in the same condition as those who go angling in streams and rivers. They bait with likely questions—they choose their time, place, and opportunity, and the result is generally *nil;* and then suddenly, when they had no thought of getting what they want, their fish is hauled to land, and lies on the bank beside them, waiting for the fatal blow.

Colonel Leschelles proved the truthfulness of this theory. He angled with a light line and delicate flies in the uncertain waters of Mrs. Wright's nature, and the only treasure he produced from those depths and shallows was, that Mrs. Wright did not like Bella Miles.

"I am very sorry for her, of course, poor child, and I would do her any service in my power; but for me to love, it is necessary I should understand, and I confess I do not understand Bella—I wish I did."

"The uncle might have saved *his* money," thought Colonel Leschelles. "The niece's investment will, I think, turn out better."

Then he tried Miss Miles, by asking her leading questions and endeavouring to surprise her, and came out of the encounter

a defeated man. Miss Miles was prepared at all points. There
was nothing to be got out of her.

Ere long also he had an opportunity of making Mr. Irwin's
acquaintance; but Mr. Irwin proved a greater mystery than his
niece. He traced back his career to the earliest period, only
to find nothing in it beyond the common, unless, indeed, it
might be that the man's cleverness had somehow compassed
success.

Of his antecedents Mr. Irwin made no secret. He and his
sister, being early left orphans, were obliged to shift for themselves, and did so, she as nursery governess in the house of a
relative, he as apprentice, clerk, manager to a firm of die-sinkers
in Soho, where he remained till he went to America.

His sister met her husband at the house where she was governess. He took a fancy to her, and she to him, and they were
married. That was the true and straightforward story, my dear
friends, you will perceive, such as is told us every day by some
one. Not a word in it which could not have been verified on
oath, and yet conveying a series of false impressions to the
mind of the hearer.

Only one more piece of information did Colonel Leschelles
essay to obtain, and he obtained it in this wise:

"Mr. Miles was a doctor, was he not?"

"Oh, dear, no!" answered Mr. Irwin. "He was a jack-of-
all-trades."

"And——" suggested the Colonel.

"Master of all," was the reply; "or at least, pretty nearly so.
A clever man—so clever a man that I think he might have done
anything he chose, had he only made up his mind to a certain
course and followed it. Veering and changing about were his
ruin."

"Ah!" said the Colonel, and, fairly beaten, dropped the subject.

"What a stupid creature the world makes a fellow!" he
thought. "Here am I, who ought to know better, suspecting
a mystery where evidently none exists. The father was a 'ne'er-
do-weel,' doubtless, and perhaps came from some poor, wicked,
half-mad old stock, which accounts for Miss Bella's beauty,
talent, and eccentricity. Besides, why should I try to unravel
the antecedents of this uncle and niece? What are they to me?"

Which would have been a prudent question once, but was now

incapable of receiving a suitable answer; for the Colonel was in love with this girl, and pulses which for years had throbbed slowly and regularly, beat rapidily when she entered the room where he sat, or walked beside him along those dull, endless, muddy Fisherton roads. For which reason—seeing she was in her teens, and he, Heaven only knew how near threescore and ten—he would thankfully have received the news that she was illegitimate, or that her father had been hung, or her mother divorced.

All he wanted was Bella; and he dimly grasped the truth that, unless there was something very questionable about Bella's antecedents, about the life-story of her father and mother, he might want that young lady for a very long time.

Not twenty, exceedingly beautiful, amiable, accomplished, owning one rich relation at all events, it was not in the slightest degree likely she would cast a favourable eye on a man capable of being her great-grandfather; and yet—and yet the Colonel had his ideas and his hopes, and so went fishing from day to day. And still he landed nothing; and it was in a moment of utter despair that chance gave him the clue after which he had so long been searching.

"His dears," as Mr. Wright complaisantly called his children, had all been bidden to a Twelfth Night party. They were all well goloshed and warmly wrapped up to walk to the entertainment, attended by Mr. Wright, and that gentleman had rushed out of the dining-room to see that his general attire was as scrupulously perfect and utterly clerical as usual, when Bella Miles entered the apartment, and walked up to the table without perceiving that the Colonel sat in shadow beside the fire, which was burning low.

"Oh!" she said, when she did see him; "I beg your pardon. I did not know you were here."

Whereupon he laughed, and asked if he were such an ogre that his presence should prevent her entering any room in which he happened to be.

He had never before seen her look so handsome or so remarkable. Her white dress, knotted up with black ribbons, for she wore slight mourning out of respect to Mr. Irwin's memory; her round arms clasped by jet bracelets, lent for the occasion by Mrs. Wright; her shoulders covered by a red opera cloak, trimmed with white fur, the hood of which, drawn close about her face, enriched it with a setting of soft, snow-like down. As she stooped a little forward, the hood fell back from her head; and with a sudden exclamation, Colonel Leschelles rose astonished, and said:

"Why, it is Molly Barthorne you so much resemble! Standing as you do now, I could fancy she herself had stepped down from her frame."

And then he stopped, for the flowers had dropped from Bella's fingers, and she was looking at him with dilated, frightened eyes.

"What is the matter?" he asked anxiously. "Are you ill?" And he hurriedly poured out first some water, and then some wine.

"No," she said, rejecting both; "I am not ill, thank you. Who is Molly Barthorne? Where does she live?"

"She does not live anywhere now," he answered. "She was a celebrated Court beauty once upon a time, however; and you might be her sister, so great is the likeness between you."

"Oh! don't," entreated Bella, "don't say so to anybody but me! Colonel Leschelles, don't be vexed with me, please; but may I trust you never to mention this to any one else? I cannot tell you why I ask; but will you do me this kindness?"

She held her hands out to him appealingly, and he took them, as he answered:

"My dear, you might trust me with your life. I would do anything on earth for you. A word of this shall never pass my lips. Now, gather up your flowers and go; Mr. Wright is calling you."

Which, indeed, was true. At the top of his voice Mr. Wright was saying, "Bella! Bella! Bella! Where are you? We are all ready; don't keep us waiting the whole evening."

"Here I am," said Bella, coming out of the dining-room, and interrupting the pastoral, Mr. Wright, imagining her to be upstairs, was delivering from the bottom of the flight. "I did not know you were ready. I was only getting a few flowers."

And drawing her hood over her head, she stepped out into the darkness, that Mr. Wright might not see her face.

CHAPTER XXIII.

SLIGHTLY IN ADVANCE.

"Selina," said Mr. Wright next day, "I have bad news for you."

Mr. Wright imparted this intelligence at luncheon, whilst engaged in carving the dilapidated remains of a fowl which had done duty on the previous night. Mrs. Wright looked inquiringly at her husband over the cruet-stand, and Colonel Leschelles, knowing what was coming, fixed his eyes on the tablecloth.

"Yes, very bad news," repeated the Rector, finding his better half remained mute. "Our dear friend is obliged to leave us to-morrow."

"No, surely not!" exclaimed Mrs. Wright, with a start, and an expression of decorous tenderness directed towards the veteran Colonel. "I thought—that is, I hoped——"

"I know you are goodness itself," remarked the Colonel, as she did not finish her sentence; "and I would impose upon your kindness a little longer were it not absolutely necessary for me to leave Fisherton. When a man of my age," added the Colonel bravely, "finds any business to attend to, he is foolish not to do so at once."

"Of your age indeed!" exclaimed Mr. Wright, with a jolly assurance, calculated to make an elderly gentleman fancy his memory must have been playing him tricks.

"I think you grow younger every year, Colonel," added Mrs. Wright mendaciously. "I am sure you will never seem old, you have such a bouyant nature and such boyish spirits."

"You have a genius for saying pleasant things," remarked the Colonel in answer to Mrs. Wright's implied compliment.

"Truthful things, I trust," she answered, with a plaintive smile. "It seems to me that truth should always walk first, and pleasantness follow after."

"Admirable!" said the Reverend Dion, who never failed to applaud his wife's artistic utterances.

"But I cannot deceive myself any longer," went on the

Colonel, as though neither host nor hostess had interrupted his sentence. "Like many another, I have gone on through life, forgetting time was running on too ; and now, when I suddenly awaken, I find, what my friends have doubtless known for many a day, that notwithstanding my bouyant nature and boyish spirits, as you, Mrs. Wright, are good enough to call them, I am an old man—'terribly old,' so Curran informed me this morning."

"The naughty boy," exclaimed Mrs. Wright ; "I will punish him for his rudeness."

"I hope you will not punish the child for speaking the truth," said Colonel Leschelles a little sarcastically. "Moreover," he added, watching Mrs. Wright furtively while he spoke, "Miss Miles read Master Curran a very pretty lecture on politeness in general, and respect to his elders in particular."

"Oh, indeed ! I was not aware that Miss Miles considered herself competent to instruct any one."

"Tush, my dear !" said Mr. Wright, who, though not above being affected by small matters himself, did honestly despise what he called the babbling and bubbling of women's trumpery jealousies. "Bella Miles is as true a lady as I should ever desire to meet, though I grant you she may be a little ignorant of some of *les convenances.* She is a good girl too, kindly, un- selfish, generous ; and if she did scold the young rogue, I'll be bound he deserved every word of it."

"Master Curran is young, and time will doubtless temper the present extreme frankness of his manners," remarked Colonel Leschelles ; "but I cannot help saying that when out of the softening influence of his mother's society, the child is somewhat apt to be uncivil."

"I am very sorry," answered Mrs. Wright, "that any son of mine should ever appear rude to such a valued friend as you are."

Whereupon the Colonel rejoined, "Dear Mrs. Wright, do you imagine that truth could ever offend me? Few, indeed, have the art of presenting literal and unpleasant facts in a coat- ing of sugar. Yourself and Mr. Wright have the happy knack of making deformity itself look beautiful ; but then in that, as in most other things, you are thorough artists. "

"I trust not—I hope not," cried Mrs. Wright. "We are sincere. Whatever our faults may be, we are utterly sincere, I can assure you."

"There is no necessity for you to do so, dear," interposed Mr. Wright. "The Colonel knows all that."

"Indeed," said the Colonel, "there is no one knows better than I how sincere Mrs. Wright is."

In reply to which ambiguous speech Selina impulsively presented her thin ladylike hand to the Colonel, who pressed it, and bowed, and then returned it to the whilom Dublin beauty, with all the decorous gallantry of a race now well-nigh extinct.

"Now, Leschelles," said the Rector, who, after trying in vain to satisfy the cravings of a healthy appetite with the drumstick of a patriarchal cock, had fallen back upon bread, washed down by a few glasses of the Colonel's admirable sherry, "I will only let you away on one condition, namely, that you come back for our confirmation. It will be a very pretty sight, and I should like you to meet the Bishop."

"And our two girls are to be confirmed," added Mrs. Wright.

"And Bella Miles," supplemented the Rector. "You must promise to come to us. You have never been at Fisherton yet in decent weather."

"Fisherton in any weather," Colonel Leschelles was beginning, when Mr. Wright cut across his speech.

"Come, come, that is no answer. Say we may count on your company. You will not regret honouring us with it. The confirmation will, I assure you, be a very pretty sight — very pretty indeed."

The Rector had been at great pains to pronounce the word pretty — usually a snare to his countrymen — correctly, and having eschewed the pitfalls represented by "pratty" and "prutty," into which Irish people generally tumble, he had finally arrived at the conclusion that there was only one correct way of uttering pretty, viz., to make the *e* the same as in pet.

Quite convinced he had at length conquered the difficulty, Mr. Wright aired the word on all possible occasions, and with an emphasis which of course drew attention to it.

"My sister is going to present Maria with her dress for the occasion," went on the Rector, "and very pret-ty she will look in it, though, perhaps, I ought not to say so."

"She gives great promise of beauty," said the Colonel, who was considered, and who considered himself, a judge in such matters. "She grows very like her mother."

"Oh! Colonel," exclaimed Mrs. Wright, with a little modest

bridling and graceful deprecation of the implied compliment
that reminded Mr. Wright of the days when he could not eat,
or drink, or sleep for thinking of her countless charms.

"She is not so pretty yet," continued the Colonel, calmly;
"but I think she will be.　She is certainly a nice-looking girl."
Then, without allowing Mrs. Wright time for further protest, he
proceeded to ask if the Bishop were a judge of wine.

"I don't think any man deserves to be a bishop who is not,"
said Mr. Wright jocosely.

"Then in that case, if I bring myself, I should like to be
allowed to bring the wine also," explained Colonel Leschelles.

"Bring yourself—that is all we want," answered Mr. Wright.

"I shall certainly do that," answered the Colonel; "but I
should like to hear the Bishop's opinion of some port I had sent
to me just as I was starting for Fisherton."

"Do as you like," agreed Mr. Wright.　"We understand
what you mean—don't we, Selina?　The Colonel would not
object to see his old friend's lot cast in even more pleasant
pastures than Fisherton."

"I should like to see you a bishop," rejoined the Colonel,
who certainly thought the sight of Mr. Wright as a "my Lord,"
and Mrs. Wright as "my Lord's Lady," would have been cheap
at fifty pounds a head.

"You are a friend in need to us," said Mrs. Wright, who had
been exercising her mind, as had also the Rev. Dion his mind,
on the subject of wine for the successor of the Galilean Fisher-
men.

In the privacy of the conjugal chamber they had decided to
invite the Colonel to the episcopal feast, hoping he "might offer
to send a little wine."　It had been quite beyond their calculation that he would honour the feast himself, and provide all the
wine.

"We may as well make a luncheon party," suggested Mrs.
Wright, when talking the matter over the same evening with her
husband.　"Luncheon need not cost us a great deal.　People
do not much care what they have to eat, so long as they have
plenty of good wine."

Which observation argued a considerable amount of worldly
knowledge on the part of Mrs. Wright.

"And his wine is A 1," said Mr. Wright, nothing loth to give
honour where it was due.

"Some of it is almost as old as himself," remarked Mrs. Wright, who could not forgive Colonel Leschelles' strictures on Curran. "My dear Dion, how touchy the poor man is about his age."

"To a thoughtful man, even if he be sufficiently religious, age is a very serious thing," answered the Rev. Dion, who never had a finger ache without wondering how Selina and the little ones would get on if he were taken from them.

"He is certainly looking, to quote Curran, 'terribly old.' When I see his poor lean body buttoned up so tightly in that close-fitting top-coat, I feel as if some day when he unfastens it he will drop to pieces. How absurd he is still to affect all the airs of juvenility."

Which remark of Mrs. Wright's was indeed quite true; but how hard a matter it is to grow old gracefully! After all, it is not easy to greet sorrow, or poverty, or reverses, or dishonour with a smiling face. And there are many people to whom age seems less endurable than grief, or shortness of money, or the cold looks of friends and acquaintances. For grief may be subdued, and in lieu of lost fortune another may be found; while if old friends have no cordial greetings, old acquaintances no longer wear bright faces, the wise man understands precisely how to value their former professions and kindnesses, and turns his attention to new people, who may be pleasanter and more faithful.

But for old age—ah! my friends, we must have grown very weary of the road, very tired of the inns by the way—very, very sure that all earthly good is vanity, before we can feel quite thankful and satisfied to know youth, sweet, bright youth is gone, and may return never more—that manhood's prime is past like-wise—that the morning sun and the midday have shone their last for us, and that we shall never behold more any radiance save the solemn glory which prefaces—night.

Colonel Leschelles did not feel all this then, and Mrs. Wright found fault with him for refusing to look at the clock.

She did not know he had a dream that the pleasantest part of life might still be in store for him. She had not the faintest idea that the while his thoughts should have been on wills, they were dwelling on wives.

If she had, having that beautiful maternal eye, of which we hear so much, directed to the interests of her children, it is scarcely likely she would have parted with the Colonel with all the touching interest she did.

"God bless you!" said the Rev. Dion, as his visitor stepped into the fly which was to convey him to Fisherton Station.

"Good bye, good bye," echoed Mrs. Wright from the steps, while the children clustering about, shouted, "Good bye, Colonel!" and waved their mites of handkerchiefs, as did their mother her French cambric adorned with lace.

In truth, Mrs. Wright was delighted to see the last of their visitor. She had been on drill for so long a time, that she longed for the matutinal cup of tea in bed, the easy lounge before the drawing-room fire, the scrambling meals, the cosy *tête-à-tête* with Dion after the children were all in bed.

Not a strong woman naturally, and less strong in arithmetical proportion to every young Wright who, in the midst of harass and distress, had made his or her way into this wicked world, the strain of a martinet visitor in the house tried her more year by year.

"I have *never* been so tired of the Colonel before," she said, breaking into an hysterical whimper in her husband's study after the visitor's departure.

"My dear, he is a prince," answered Mr. Wright; and he handed her a cheque for five and twenty pounds.

Selina took it.

"To which of the children do you think he will leave his money, Dion?" she asked.

If you consider, my reader, women are proverbially ungrateful. I am afraid Mrs. Wright was.

"To none," answered the Rev. Dion.

It so chances, my reader, that occasionally men are gifted with a wonderful foreknowledge.

Intuitively Mr. Wright felt the relations between himself and Colonel Leschelles had changed.

He could not have given any reason for the faith which was in him, but he was sure.

He comprehended, vaguely perhaps, but still certainly, that the Colonel had passed beyond him, and would spend no more Christmas Days in his house.

He did not know the disturbing influence was Bella Miles; but as one vaguely feels the presence of thunder, he felt there was a fresh element at work. And, indeed, how should he know? There was Miss Bella, as kind, as ready, as inscrutable as ever. There was the Colonel absent.

How on earth was the Rector, whose thoughts never wandered very far afield, to comprehend the Colonel was going to Abbotsleigh to hunt up the Barthorne lineage?

In the course of the next three months the Colonel did not find all he had set out to discover, but he discovered enough to induce him to take a furnished house at Daceford, and write thence to his friends at Fisherton :—

"I am located here by my doctor's orders for a few months, and shall hope to run over to the rectory, and have the pleasure of seeing you and Mrs. Wright at my little cottage whenever you have a spare afternoon to waste upon an invalid."

In reply Mr. Wright shook hands on paper cordially with the gallant Colonel.

He was delighted to have him for so near a neighbour; but why did he not come and take up his abode at the rectory—or, if not at the rectory, why not at Simpson's Retreat? Simpson's Retreat was the perfection of a country snuggery, and he might have had it for a pound a week.

However, both regrets and reproaches being in vain, Mr. Wright would take an early opportunity of calling on his friend.

Selina, he regretted to say, was ill—very ill. The doctors had ordered her to the seaside; but how she was to get to the seaside Mr. Wright professed himself unable to imagine.

Things had, however, turned up miraculously for them (himself and Selina) so often, that it seemed a mere doubting of Providence to doubt now.

To this very palpable hint the Colonel did not respond immediately.

"There is an obtuseness about the man I do not quite understand," observed Mr. Wright to his better half.

"My dear Dion, he is getting very old," said the lady, with a little sob. She had set her heart on going to the seaside, and she was not well—far from it, indeed.

When Easter had passed, however, and Lent, as a matter of course, also (it may not be quite amiss to remark that every day during Lent Mr. Wright thanked Heaven there were no leanings to Popery about him), the Colonel began to think Mrs.

Wright would really be better away from Fisherton, and, having arrived at this conclusion, he one day took Mr. Wright aside, and "hoped he would not feel offended if he asked him whether pecuniary matters had any share in preventing Mrs. Wright having the change she so greatly needed."

In answer Mr. Wright wrung Colonel Leschelles' hand, and saying with effusion, "he could have no secrets from such a friend," told him precisely how they were situated, the result of which touching confidence was that twenty pounds changed hands, and Mrs. Wright and her very latest baby, accompanied by a servant, and Rosie, and Curran, started for the nearest seaport on an early day.

As a natural consequence Mr. Wright was much at Daceford, and Colonel Leschelles very much indeed at Fisherton Rectory, where, the young ladies of the Wright family eschewing the task of entertaining their papa's friend, Miss Bella Miles was usually charged with the burden of receiving and amusing him.

Did she object to undertaking it? By no means. In those days of unrestricted intercourse she formed a very sincere liking for the officer—no longer young. Had she been a different sort of girl, she might even have gone the length of imagining she loved him.

And in truth she did love him, though not in the way that he desired.

When, in the time to come, she summed up her opinion of him, it amounted to this:

"He is the truest gentleman I ever knew, and the staunchest friend woman could desire in her extremest need."

And that was all? Yes, all there could ever be.

The girl beheld the years stretching between them the man had forgotten, and never for one moment did it enter into her mind that he could regard her save as grandchild or daughter, till he asked her to be his wife.

When—but I anticipate.

With Mrs. Wright at the seaside, and the household moralities uninfluenced by Selina's gentle presence, events occurred at the rectory which never could have happened had she been at the helm.

When she returned and discovered the chaos her absence had wrought, she said plaintively, "I must never leave you again, Dion."

"No, my dear," answered the Reverend Dion, "you had better take the whole responsibility the next time. No matter how things turn out, be sure I will not blame you." Which was a slight rap over the knuckles administered by the Reverend Dion; for Mrs. Wright had blamed him most severely for his management of matters during her absence.

"If you had only given me a hint, I would have come back, even had the journey killed me," she said.

"How could I give you a hint when I had not a suspicion myself?" he answered.

"She is a bad, designing girl," said Mrs. Wright, "and I always thought so."

At which juncture the Reverend Dion remained judiciously silent.

—◇—

CHAPTER XXIV.

"NOTHING COULD BE BETTER."

FISHERTON was looking its best—its very best, indeed—though Mr. Wright, with that tendency to differ from other people, which was a way he had of asserting originality of opinion, declared Fisherton was only perfect in August, when every garden presented a blaze of colour—when the orchards were full of ripened fruit—when the creamy flowers of the magnolia showed them-

selves from amidst the green polished leaves—when the myrtle
buds were opening, and the gum-cistus unfolding its beauties
one hour and scattering them on the earth the next.

"At that season," pronounced Mr. Wright, "I first beheld
Fisherton.   At that season the place is perfect."

And the Fisherton aborigines hearkened to the voice of this
Solomon who had come to sit in judgment upon the beauties of
their native village, and were well pleased with the Rector's
dictum.

"Though I will still uphold," said one ancient pensioner,
sturdily, "that Fisherton be main pretty when the May is all
a-bloom, and smelling so purely sweet, and the throstle a-singing
his throat out, and the lads and the lassies wandering through
the lanes shaded with green limes—sweethearting, as I used to
do myself once ; but that is an old story now."

His love-making might be an old story, but the man's notion
that Fisherton was "main pretty" in May and the early summer
chanced to be still quite true.   No pooh-poohing of the Reverend
Dion could rob the hawthorns of the white glory which covered
them, or take the scent of the May from the clear air, or retard
the opening of the dog-roses, or remove the buttercups out of
the meadows, or the bright green, the pure, bright spring green
off the foliage.

After the winter floods—after the snow and frost, and rain and
hail—after grey skies and lowering fogs, Fisherton always came
forth beautiful in the spring, as if newly created.   Verdure everywhere—the fresh smell which comes with the rising sap, the
songs of birds, the hum of bees.   A sweet valley when the
waters had subsided—when the Thames flowed quietly within
due bounds on his way to the sea.   Yes, then, before the summer
droughts had parched the earth—before the reaper had cut the
corn—while there was still bud, and promise of fruit, Fisherton,
set around with May, and lilac, and laburnum, with chestnut-
trees bursting into flower, with the red hawthorn and the redder
japonica all ablaze in the cottagers' gardens, looked its beautiful
best.

It was afternoon, and two young men who had been fishing
sauntered idly up from the Thames, and turned their steps towards the village.

One was the son of a rich man, who had a few months previously bought Fisherton Lodge, the great place of that small

neighbourhood; the other a Baronet, whose acquaintance Mr. Morrison's heir had made at Oxford, where parvenus go to make friends.

The first young fellow was clever, and short-sighted; for perhaps both of which reasons he disfigured himself by constantly wearing a glass screwed up into his eye. The second was not clever in the ordinary sense of the word, and not short-sighted; but he had an advantage over his fellow—it was only needful to look at and to like him.

A man fleeing for his life, and coming unexpectedly upon the pair, would at once have said to himself, "I can trust you," meaning Sir Harry; "I will not trust you," meaning Bob Morrison; and yet there can be no doubt that Bob Morrison would have helped him loyally, had he seen his way to rendering assistance; only he would first have wanted to know so much, that any poor wretch in a difficulty might scarcely have relished his cross-examination.

With Sir Harry, on the contrary, he would have helped the man on the instant, and possibly never asked a question.

Foolish, no doubt; and yet, as we know, Providence takes care of drunken people and fools. Providence had taken remarkably good care of the young Baronet.

So far, though he had been cheated more than once, and disappointed as regarded the antecedents of his *protégés* over and over again, Sir Harry's memory held no shameful secret, recalled no enormous iniquity.

Left very young fatherless, brought up by a mother who idolized him, adored by his pretty cousin Edith, flattered by his private tutor, surrounded at Oxford by those who would gladly have let him walk over them had he expressed a desire to that effect, Sir Harry had fallen no prey to sharks or flatterers. When men talked about his faults and follies, no scandalous flutter of petticoats disturbed the air. He had not run into debt to such an extent as seriously to embarrass his estate. His transactions with those good Jews who kindly look after the pecuniary welfare of young Christians were confined to two little bill affairs, in both of which he had lent his name to a friend, and lost his money. He had made no great success at college, but neither had he made any great *fiasco;* and as time went on, there was only the same story to be repeated of his life.

His mother wanted him to go into Parliament, and marry his

cousin; but Sir Harry did not seem inclined to pleasure her Lady-ship as regarded either whim.

Nevertheless, with that pertinacity for which even the gentlest women are remarkable, Lady Medburn felt quite certain her dear Harry would yet add his wisdom to that of the rulers of the people, and make Edith mistress of Cortingford (the name of the family seat), and his poor mother happy.

Edith was the daughter of Lady Medburn's only sister. That sister had run away from her father's vicarage with a handsome young ensign, who speedily left her an almost penniless widow, with one little girl.

On her death-bed she bequeathed this child to Lady Medburn, and Miss Edith's life had consequently proved a most desirable affair ever since she wore short white frocks and long blue sashes.

Lady Medburn had no sons or daughters save her Harry, and there was no Miss Medburn to make a wearisome affair of exist-ence to the young dependant, for which reason she, though utterly penniless, had grown up with all the assured certainty of position which might have become an heiress of the house.

Yes, it had long been decided at Cortingford that Edith was to be the next Lady Medburn; and if there were those who said Sir Harry would never be more to her than cousin, the majority opined he would settle down some day, and marry Miss Selham, if only to please his mother.

At seven and twenty, however, the Baronet seemed as far off settling and matrimony as ever; and it did not occur to Lady Medburn and Miss Selham, on that particular day when Fisher-ton was looking its best, that there was any especial need of their prayers to avert the calamity of marriage from so heart-whole a young man.

"What's all this?" exclaimed Mr. Morrison, as he and his friend, turning a corner, came in sight of the church. "Car-riages—servants—children, of course. Oh! the confirmation! I had forgotten it, though I saw three washing-baskets full of flowers, sent in honour of the occasion, yesterday. Let us stop, Medburn, and have a look at the girls as they come out."

They had not long to wait. Already the ceremony was over, and the little bustle of leaving commencing. Coachmen were bringing their horses up to the gate of the churchyard, footmen were flying from the porch to the road, and from the road back again to the porch. The feeble, aged women at the almshouses opposite were shading their eyes with one hand, and holding back obstreperous little urchins with the other. On the tiled roofs the pigeons plumed themselves, as if waiting for the congregation to admire their beauty. Glimpses were caught at intervals of the Rev. Dionysius bustling about on business connected with his Lordship the Bishop; and all this time people were defiling out of the church, singly, by twos and threes, forming groups amongst the grass-covered graves, or walking away solitary and silent, having no one to whom to speak. Even at a village gathering one may always see a few lonely and neglected inhabitants.

At last came the girls, the commonalty first, the *élite* last—a goodly company.

There was naughty Polly Prickley, the most audacious romp in Fisherton, looking as demure in her light cotton dress and plain cap, coquettishly worn, as if she had spent every hour since babyhood in reading tracts and reciting the Psalms. There was Victoria, daughter and heiress of Sir John and Lady Giles, of Riversdale, tricked out like a bride, with everything on her a milliner could suggest and wealth and vanity secure, and an expression on her face which said plainly:

"Good people, look at me. Though I am so charmingly dressed and so handsome, and though I am the only child of my papa, Sir John Giles, and though he is going to give me a splendid fortune, I have just renounced the World, the Flesh, and the Devil. You may be surprised to hear the news; but it is true. Ask the Bishop if you are inclined to disbelieve me."

"Gracious heavens!" exclaimed Mr. Robert Morrison, as he beheld this young lady ambling along in her papa's carriage, "would any other woman except Lady Giles have sent her daughter out dressed for such an occasion like a May Queen? No, my dear, it is of no use your looking so graciously at me. I am engaged; and if I were not, I would never marry you, Miss Vic. Do regard that young person, Medburn, and contrast her with the lilies of the field, which she only resembles in so far as she neither toils nor spins."

But his companion would not regard Miss Giles. His attention was fixed on three other young people, who walked slowly and decorously out of the porch—the very last to leave the church.

"Morrison, who is that lovely girl?" asked Sir Harry. Hearing which question, Mr. Morrison adjusted his eye-glass, and surveyed the group.

"That—oh! that is our Rector's eldest daughter. Pretty, undeniably, and the dress becomes her. Maria Wright. The Rector has a baker's dozen. Mrs. Wright is at Southsea with the latest addition to the family. Now, the show is over, shall we be going home?"

Their homeward way led them past the line of carriages, and Mr. Robert Morrison had to raise his hat frequently, and to pause often when some demonstrative lady beckoned him to her side.

From a distance, however, he was at length hailed by his father.

"Hallo! Robert," shouted that worthy, "what are you doing here?"

"We have been following the occupation of the first disciples, and admiring the doings of their descendants," was the reply.

"In other words," added Sir Harry, who saw that Mr. Morrison looked puzzled, "we have been fishing, and we have been admiring the young ladies of Fisherton."

"Well, it was a pretty sight," said Mr. Morrison, who had stayed away from a committee meeting in order to support Mr. Wright on the occasion, and meet the Bishop afterwards.

"I saw one very pretty sight," agreed the Baronet.

"He means Maria Wright," explained Mr. Robert, compassionately.

"Now, do not be ill-natured, Robert," entreated his parent; "the girl is pretty, very much so indeed. Looks quite like a what-do-you-call-it, in all that light drapery."

"I suppose you mean a seraph, sir?" suggested his son.

"She is not in the least like a seraph," said Sir Harry, as if there were something especially derogatory in the comparison.

"My dear fellow, she shall be like anything you please," Mr. Robert Morrison was saying, when a movement on the part of Mr. Morrison's footmen indicated some arrival of importance, and Mr. Wright, walking forward, began:

"Allow me, my Lord, to have the honour of introducing my very good friend and most liberal parishioner, Mr. Morrison. I am proud to have so public-spirited and generous a gentleman located in this parish. In whatsoever place he may have chosen to cast his lot, he has always proved himself a staunch pillar of the Church."

The Bishop, who, being a most quiet and unpretending individual, looked, but for his dress, much less like a Bishop than Mr. Wright, expressed himself truly delighted to make Mr. Morrison's acquaintance, and shook hands, with much impressiveness, on the side path, to which Mr. Morrison had promptly descended.

Then his Lordship stepped, with an air of dignified accustomedness, which was not at all assumed, into the carriage, and Mr. Wright, at Mr. Morrison's solicitation, was about to follow, when his eye fell on the two young men, who had fallen a little back when the Bishop appeared on the scene.

If Mr. Wright had met Calcraft in his Sunday clothes wandering about Fisherton parish, he would have raised the rectorial hat in greeting. The practice had often served him in good stead, and he was not going to deviate from it now; so he greeted Mr. Robert Morrison and Sir Harry Medburn with affable condescension, and they, as in duty bound, returned his salute.

"My son, Mr. Wright," said Mr. Morrison, senior; "lately returned from Egypt; and Sir Harry Medburn," added the millionaire.

Whereupon the Rector seemed to expand, physically and morally. He could not tell Mr. Robert Morrison how charmed he was to see him at Fisherton. He could not express to Sir Harry Medburn how delighted he was to make his acquaintance.

He trusted they would both come on to the Rectory and partake of luncheon. Only a few friends to meet his Lordship. No ceremony, just a glass of wine, a slice of meat, and a biscuit. With Mrs. Wright absent, he could offer little, but that little he hoped the young men would honour with their presence. Nothing loth, the young men availed themselves of the invitation.

"Send the carriage back, please, sir," said Mr. Robert Morrison to his father; and then the carriage referred to, containing the Bishop, Mr. Wright, and Mr. Morrison, senior, drove off, the Rector returning the salutations of his parishioners in a "king by the grace of God and defender of the faith" manner.

The meagre glass of wine, the modest slice of beef, the vague biscuit of which Mr. Wright had made mention, proved to be simply figurative expressions, really representing a feast that need have shamed the table of no modern Belshazzar.

On the board appeared everything in season, and many things out of it. Each guest, with the exception of the Bishop, had contributed something to the feast, which thus came really to assume a little of the character of a picnic. Spring chickens, as large as young turkeys, came from the yards of Sir John Giles, whose "lady" had made poultry a study, and sold sittings of eggs at fabulous prices. Fruit and flowers were contributed by Mr. Morrison ; the Rector's churchwarden, who had never before found himself in such grand and good company, had sent in enough butter and cheese and bacon from his little farm, as he modestly called eight hundred acres, as would, Bella Miles and Nurse Mary calculated, last the family for three weeks. As to the other churchwarden, who said he was a plain man, and did not want to intrude on the Bishop or anybody else, he dispatched from his warehouse in town, which warehouse happened, "providentially" Mr. Wright said, to be of the description called Italian, such a supply of foreign delicacies that the Rector's heart softened towards the sometime recalcitrant parish representative, and blessed him for all the dainties he should now be able to take to the seaside, snugly packed, when he next ran down to see poor Selina.

Never, out of a great man's house, had the Bishop beheld such preparations in his honour, and as it was part and parcel of Mr. Wright's nature and politics to give unbounded honour where honour was due, his Lordship soon understood that the entertainment was rather secular than clerical; that the luncheon was but a series of gifts laid at his own admirable feet, and his soul inclined to the man able, at this time of the world, to draw such admirable offerings from the cellars, and forcing-houses, and dairies, and warehouses, of his friends, in order to do honour to his ecclesiastical chief.

Especially in the matter of that port. The Colonel had struck by accident his Lordship's weakness.

He was no *gourmand*, or *gourmet*. Like most wise people, he liked good things when they fell in his way; but he was moderate in, and not over-particular concerning, his fare, as became a bishop.

"But if he must drink wine," this was what he said himself, "if people would insist on offering him something out of a decantei, instead of a tumbler of honest Bass—a beverage good enough for an emperor—he did not care to swallow a decoction of blackberries."

And no doubt the poor man had often been forced to taste the products of some even less natural vintage, for which reason his Lordship appreciated the outcome of Colonel Leschelles' cellar, and was gracious to him accordingly.

Now, this pleased Mr. Wright. The Colonel was, *par excellence*, his friend, and not his parishioner. The Colonel held a different position from that occupied by any one else round and about the table. Further, the Colonel and Sir Harry Medburn had at once discovered they knew each other intimately; knew far more about each other, in fact, Mr. Wright could see plainly, than the Baronet knew of Mr. Robert Morrison.

"Really exceedingly gratifying," the poor Rector thought, mentally planning his evening letter to Selina. "Gratifying in the extreme."

But gratifying as the luncheon proved, the tea-party on the lawn, to which several ladies, anxious to say they had met the Bishop, were bidden, proved more gratifying still. His Lordship praised the grounds, and their state of excellent cultivation.

"Well, it is no credit to me, my Lord," said Mr. Wright, "and very little expense either. As curate, I naturally moved about a good deal, and in each place where we settled my dear wife found some sickly gardener, or weakly labourer, or pensioner past regular work, whom she was able to help—for it is marvellous how little does help the poor—and now they come to us, first one and then the other; and when they do, they take off their coats and begin to put things in order. And they send us, those who are in situations, roots and plants, the things coming with their masters' compliments; and it is wonderful, it is really," finished Mr. Wright, "how our garden has grown and been kept passably tidy."

The Bishop thought the state of the garden spoke highly for all parties concerned; which was very natural, seeing his Lordship had not provided the beef and mutton, and arrowroot, and tea, and so forth, these poor creatures needed, and been forced to wait months and years for his money, like some of the tradesmen Mr. Wright benefited by his patronage.

And then, when the Bishop praised the coffee, Mr. Wright

said it was a present from his good kind friend, the parish war-
den, and made by one of his girls.; but he did not mention that
the girl's name was Bella Miles.

Indeed, during the whole of that evening Bella passed muster
as one of the family.

Even Robert Morrison, who having seen Maria talking to
his mother concerning the clothes-baskets of flowers, knew only
her amongst the Rector's daughters, remained under the same
delusion, until, happening to remark how little Miss Bella resembled her sister, Lady Giles informed him the girl was not
even a relation of the Wrights, but some orphan, whose friends
paid Mr. Wright " only a hundred a year for the inestimable
advantage of living at the rectory."

This with a sneer; for Lady Giles, who was no match for
Mrs. Wright either in cleverness or rapartee, disliked that lady,
as is the pleasing manner of her pleasing sex, for no reason in
particular.

She and Sir John had met the Morrisons abroad—had, indeed, first directed their attention to Fisherton Lodge as a
desirable place to purchase—therefore she and Mr. Robert
stood on the basis of old acquaintances; and her Ladyship
hoped Robert—familiarly called Bob—might marry her daughter Victoria, occupied at that present moment in scolding her
maid for malpractices in the matter of folding up dresses.

For Miss Victoria's name had by some mischance been left
out of the list of invited guests—greatly, to say the truth, at the
instigation of Miss Maria Wright; and as it would have seemed
a special insult to Lady Giles to invite other unmarried ladies
and exclude her daughter, no unmarried ladies were present—
always excepting the Rector's family (including Bella Miles)—
save those who, by reason of there remaining no matrimonial
prospect whatsoever, were as good as married, or, by reason of
lack of daughters, better.

Miss Miles did all that lay in her power to make the afternoon pass pleasantly. The Bishop complimented Mr. Wright
on his charming family; and Mr. Wright bowed his delighted
acknowledgments, and said:

"My Lord, though I say it, who perhaps should not, throughout England there is no more united household than mine."

"And your eldest daughter seems a treasure in herself," remarked his Lordship, referring to Bella.

"She is the image of her mother when I first saw her," said Mr. Wright, referring to Maria.

"How remarkably unlike," thought the Bishop, "are the rest of the children to the mother."

After that a wonderful thing happened. The Bishop, while talking to Bella Miles, forgot that his train left at a certain hour, so actually supposed he must wait until the next.

To fill up the interval, some one suggested "music;" and Mrs. Wright being absent, and Mr. Wright knowing perfectly no one present but Miss Miles could satisfy the ears of a bishop, asked her to play.

And Bella did play. With all the power God had given her —with all the veins of her heart—she brought harmony out of the misused piano that night, and told to more than one of her auditors something of the force and passion in her nature.

"It is marvellous!" said the Bishop; "it is indeed. I could not have believed so young a girl capable of playing as she does. I congratulate you. It is long since I have spent so profitable and pleasant a day—a day, I may truly say, of unmixed satisfaction. I am so much obliged!—thank you most earnestly."

And with the last conventional sentence on his lips, exit the Bishop in Mr. Morrison's carriage, Mr. Morrison seeing him to the station.

"What a wonderful girl that eldest daughter of our friend seems to be," said the Bishop, speaking on the subject just then nearest to his mind.

"She is extremely pretty," agreed the millionaire, who shared the tastes of his son, and who considered Maria Wright a much "sweeter-looking creature" than Miss Miles.

"And what an admirable musician!" observed the Bishop.

"I am told all the Rector's children are clever in that respect; but I am no judge of music myself."

"Your friend the Baronet is a little attracted in that quarter, or I am much deceived," said his Lordship, a little slyly.

"Yes; my son made some remark to a similar effect," answered Mr. Morrison, still playing at cross purposes; and the next time he met Mr. Wright, he asked him some absurd question about Sir Harry, and told him even the Bishop had noticed how deeply the young man was smitten by Miss Maria's pretty face.

Out of pure mischief Mr. Robert Morrison had, after the

Bishop left, managed to draw Mr. Wright apart, in order to enlarge on the same theme; and accordingly, between champagne—a good deal of that wine being drunk at a late and very cosy supper, at which only Colonel Leschelles, the Rector, Mr. Robert Morrison, and his friend were present—the remembered affability of the Bishop, the success of the day's proceedings, and visions of rank and wealth for Maria, Mr. Wright went to bed jubilant.

Not, however, before he had written to his better half. The Reverend Dionysius never neglected her. If he had remembered few other promises in life, the vows made at a certain little country church in Wicklow were religiously kept by plausible, well-intentioned, selfish, careless Mr. Wright.

He had never been selfish towards Selina: she and the children were always considered first, and himself last; and if sometimes he did, as he could not help doing, enjoy a day thoroughly in her absence, there always succeeded to his pleasure a sense of wrong, as if his happiness had been purchased at the cost of a certain disloyalty to her.

For this reason, ere he slept, Mr. Wright penned the following letter to his absent wife :—

"Dearest S."—(it was thus Mr. Wright, in the sacred familiarity of matrimonial correspondence, usually addressed his Selina)—"Late as it is—*One* A.M.—I must write you a line to say everything went off splendidly. The confirmation —the luncheon—all a *complete success.* His Lordship was *more* than gracious. He was condescendingly familiar; indeed, many a rector *we* have known has been far less affable. The girls looked lovely—simply lovely; Maria in especial, saint-like and angelic, reminding me of *you know who*, on the day which made me the happiest man in the three kingdoms.

"Her dress suited the dear child to perfection, and the solemnity of the service imparted a look of sweet thoughtfulness to her face, which endued it with a *finishing charm.* I am not alone in this opinion. Parental vanity has not led me astray on this point. The dear girl was universally admired. Good, kind, charming Bella looked quite plain by comparison. The simple, modest attire which set off the retiring beauty of the one failed to suit the very different style of our child by adoption, who proved herself to-day all you could wish.

"And now, my dear, I come to the pith of my story. Our Maria has made a conquest. Of course it is not for any poor fallible human being to tell how this may all turn out; but a certain Sir Harry Medburn, staying with the Morrisons, has—so young Morrison assures me—quite lost his heart to our pretty one. He seems a very nice fellow, and, I find from Dod, is the patron of two livings!

"According to Morrison, he has thirteen thousand a year; and Leschelles, who knows him well, says he will be heir to a Sir Alexander Kelvey, who made heaps of money out in India, and who has no other near male relative. You will not, dearest S., take all this for more than it is worth; but I do think our sweet child stands a very fair chance of being asked to become my Lady—God bless her! Leschelles has invited Medburn to stay with him when he leaves the Morrisons'. I have said nothing to Leschelles about Maria. *He is odd* in his notions, as you have often remarked; and I think the least said in such a case is soonest mended.

" Enclosed is half of a five-pound note. It is my last, and I do not know where any more is to come from at present; but the hour before dawn is the darkest, and I trust our dawn is near at hand.

"I wrote to Mr. Irwin, asking him for fifty pounds—just another poor fifty—*nothing* to him, health to you, and ease of mind to me; and what do you suppose he did?—sent me a *statement of account*, bringing me in one hundred and sixty-five pounds overdrawn—as if, even supposing he never received that amount, it could repay us for our loving care of that poor child, who is so grateful for our kindness. He explained that business was dull, and money scarce, etc., etc.—the *usual trade cry*, with which time has made us so well acquainted; and he said he must really beg me to excuse him from making any further advances at present. After all, my dear, as you say—I beg your pardon, you do not say anything so vulgar—but as you imply, there is 'a dirty drop' somewhere in Mr. Irwin, and that *will show itself.* The longer I live, the more fully satisfied I feel that *blood* cannot associate for any length of time with *bone.* If you could only see the difference there is between young Morrison and his friend Sir Harry! But, of course, you will see, and, as usual, draw your own admirable conclusions.

"Don't buy anything this week till you see the hamper un-packed, which I shall take down the day after to-morrow.

"Every one contributed to to-day's feast. We have had in our lives, spite of much anxiety, my dear S., great cause for thankfulness; and could you have seen the success of to-day, you must have called it a *complete victory*. Nothing could have been better. I do not believe his Lordship ever sat down to a better luncheon, better served, in his life.

"Good night—or, rather, good morning, darling. Kiss the young master for me. What do you think of Leschelles and Medburn for godfathers, with Bella Miles for godmother? The conjunction might please even W. C. I., and be beneficial to the rogue hereafter.

"Ever yours devotedly,

"Dion."

Having addressed and sealed up and stamped which epistle, "hers devotedly Dion" put on his hat, and, whistling softly to himself, walked up to the little village shop that served as post-office, in order to drop his love-letter in the box.

It was a beautiful night, tender and mild, with refreshing perfumes pervading the air, the sky laden with a suspicion of light from the coming day.

The Rector extended his walk, and strolled on past Fisherton Lodge, to Riversdale, and thence home.

"Our dear Maria," he thought, "shall be mistress over a finer establishment than either of these. And there have been people who thought they could crush *me*. Ah! they did not quite understand the Rev. Mr. Wright!"

CHAPTER XXV.

A CONJUGAL TÊTE-À-TÊTE.

IT was not that time of roses which old-fashioned writers had in their mind when gossiping about the pleasant seasons, and to which modern poets—all honour to them for their constancy—have remained faithful.

The fragrant cabbage-rose, the picturesque York and Lancaster, the little button-like *des mois*—which name children used to alter and improve into *des mots*—the pure white clustering amid green on great trees, not mere bushes; the pure white in which, in warm summers, the rose-beetle reflected its brilliant colours to the sun—all these, and many another rose, the beauty and perfume of which delighted our grandmothers, had shed their despised leaves, once considered precious, and collected carefully by dainty fingers for preservation in great china jars, and still the modern standards in the rectory garden, bunches of colour surmounting long bare stems, went on blooming, unmindful of their dead fair kindred.

It was late summer in the rectory garden, where were beds all aglow with scarlet geraniums; borders decked by the Rev. Dion's grateful dependants, with all possible variations of that monstrosity, ribbon gardening; plots left by good fortune to chance old seeds and the children, and so growing flaunting poppies wreathed by many-coloured diversities of the nasturtium tribe, with here a tuft of mignonette, and there an almost wild growth of sweet peas and French marigolds—a flower which bids fair soon to become as extinct as the tremulous harebell and the deeper-blued gentianella.

Other beds there were telling of the work of a careful hand directed by a different head.

Here is one, a centre of fuchsia, surrounded entirely by heliotropes, well pegged down; here is a second, a bed filled with ivy geraniums and many-coloured verbenas; and then what could the heart of man desire to behold more beautiful than that wealth of gladioli surrounding an arbutus dwarf—as, un·happily, arbutus insists on growing away from Killarney?

Yes, the old rose month had long gone by, and that time which the Rev. Mr. Wright declared was the prime of the whole year at Fisherton was come, bringing with it hot days and sultry nights, the perfumes of all rich odorous flowers; and at inter·vals, too, the first faint scent of autumn's fading leaves.

Mrs. Wright sat by an open window looking out over the garden sloping to the Thames. From the river came the occa·sional plash of oars, and sometimes the sound of some distant party singing "Row, brothers, row," or a sentimental love ditty.

It was a calm peaceful scene on which the twilight deepened; but Mrs. Wright did not feel calm or peaceful.

She had come home expecting to find that everything was going on satisfactorily, and behold nothing was going on as it ought.

For weeks Sir Harry had been hovering about the rectory, —now staying with Colonel Leschelles, and accompanying him in his visits, then taking up his residence at a riverside inn, some three miles distant, and rowing down to Fisherton; again rush·ing off to Devonshire, and returning thence accompanied by hampers containing rare fruits and exotics for Mrs. Wright, and within a day or two running up to London, whence he brought gifts that caused the breasts of the younger Wrights to leap for joy under their white pinafores.

Nor were the elders forgotten. Mrs. Wright could not men·tion any want which the Baronet failed instantly to supply. He gave Mr. Wright a handsome writing-table. He presented the Demoiselles Wright with brooches, which those young ladies displayed next Sunday in church.

There was only one person to whom Sir Harry gave nothing, and with whom he seemed a little shy—Bella Miles—and she was usually very silent when he spent the evening at the rectory.

At that time she did not, however, talk much to any one. The only person in whose society she evinced any pleasure was that of Colonel Leschelles. She always left Sir Harry and the girls to amuse themselves, and stole away to the side of her elderly friend, who seemed in some danger in those days of being neglected by all the Wrights save the Reverend Dion.

Openly Mrs. Wright expressed an opinion that Colonel

Leschelles was acting as a spy on their younger visitor's movements.

"It is no business of his," she commented, "but I am quite certain he does not want Sir Harry to propose for Maria."

"I am not altogether of your opinion," said her husband. "The other morning, just to hear what he thought of the matter, I pointed to Maria and the Baronet, and remarked, 'I think our friend is pretty far gone in that quarter.' 'Do you mean in love with your eldest daughter?' he inquired. 'Well, yes, if you will put the case so strongly,' I answered. 'I am afraid he is not,' he said, with a solemn shake of his head."

"Old simpleton!" interrupted Mrs. Wright. "I wonder what he and Bella Miles are talking about so perpetually. She never seems happy except when she is strolling off with him somewhere. Do you think, Dion, there is any likelihood of his leaving her all his money?"

"I do not know. He might make a worse disposition of it," said the Rector.

On this point, however, Mrs. Wright did not agree with her husband. If Colonel Leschelles left his money to Bella Miles, to what purpose had the latest arrival been christened Archibald Harry Miles Wright, Sir Harry Medburn, the Colonel, and Miss Bella having all stood sponsors for him?

"With a fortune, Bella would be sure to marry, and then the Colonel might as well never have been—never have enjoyed their hospitality at Christmas. It was most provoking," Mrs. Wright said, beginning to have strong opinions about taking in strangers, about "whom one knows nothing," to the privacy of a refined and delightful home.

Something to this tune Mrs. Wright sat by the window thinking. Away in the distance, by the river's brink, two people walked—up and down—up and down—till their monotonous pace made Selina feel quite irritable.

"Curran," she cried, at last, to that young gentleman, who was disporting himself on the lawn, "run and tell Bella I want her."

But Curran pursed up his lips and shook his head.

"Run this instant, you naughty boy!" persisted his mother.

"Shan't," said the naughty boy. "Shan't. The Colonel told me to go away and play, and when I once happened to get near them again, he spoke to me, oh! so cross—just as pa does when

the butcher has been here for money."   Curran, in the excitement of making this communication, approached incautiously
near the window, and was rewarded for the simile so ingeniously
introduced by a smart slap, which had the effect of sending him
off howling to the kitchen, where he was solaced with bread and
jam, and had the pleasure of telling his tale to an appreciative
audience.

"She's just bewitched, that's what it is," commented Nurse
Mary, while Curran swallowed his jam and his tears together.

"Surely you never think she would be——" the housemaid
was beginning, when a look from Nurse Mary stopped her.

"Isn't it wonderful," said that privileged domestic, laying her
hand on the side of Curran's head, "how the length of children's
ears differs?"

With which profound observation she diverted the talk from
Miss Miles and her "old veteran," as she called the Colonel.

Already the kitchen understood that which the parlour failed
to see.

"I'm thinking she'll take him," Nurse Mary mentally decided.
"Well, that will be spring and winter, if you like.   The man's
old enough to be *my* grandfather, for the matter of that."

Mrs. Wright put a shawl over her head and stepped out into
the garden.   In the distance she could still see Colonel Leschelles and Bella Miles, but they were now standing still under
a willow which grew beside the walk, and at that point almost
concealed every one sheltered by its drooping branches.

Yes, they were standing still ; but what was Bella Miles doing?
Mrs. Wright could not believe the evidence of her senses.

She had taken the Colonel's left hand and was kissing it—
Mrs. Wright felt capable of making affidavit on that point—while
the Colonel, not to be behindhand in civilities of so questionable
a nature, had laid his right hand on her hair and was speaking
to the girl earnestly.

Mrs. Wright turned and went back to the house ; she had
seen too much—more than she felt she could trust herself to
repeat to the Rev. Dion—then, at all events.

When the rest of the household had retired, and Mr. and Mrs.
Wright were left to enjoy that solitary hour of uninterrupted
conversation which the twenty-four contained, the lady began :

"Dion, I want you to do something for me, or rather two
things."

"Fifty, my dear, if I can," answered the Rector, gallantly but judiciously.

"Bella is very fond of you, I know."

"Poor thing!" remarked Mr. Wright, treating the remark as a compliment, and deprecating it.

"She has a high opinion of your judgment, and would be likely to listen to any advice you might give her."

"I am sure, my love, it is very good of you to think so," said the Rector, who would have felt much more comfortable had he understood whither his wife was driving.

"It is true," returned Mrs. Wright solemnly. "Every one must see how partial the girl is to you."

"She is jealous," thought the Rector; "I knew how it would be sooner or later." But he only remarked aloud that he believed Bella was partial to all of them. "She has good cause to be fond of you, at any rate," added the worthy Rector, who never missed an opportunity, at home or abroad, of sounding Selina's praises, "for you have made her what she is."

"In some respects I hope not, Dion," answered Mrs. Wright. "I have done my best for the girl. If I were on my death-bed to-morrow, and I have been too lately lying on what seemed very like my death-bed to——"

"Now, now, now, my dear," interrupted her husband, stretching his hand across the table and clasping it kindly in her own, "you must not talk in this way. You were very, very ill, but not so bad as that, thank God! And while you were laid up, Bella, I am sure, did credit to your teaching. She was like a mother to the children——"

"I daresay," interposed Mrs. Wright, hastily wiping the tears from her eyes, and turning very red at the comparison the poor Rector had so innocently instituted: "I daresay she did take a good deal on herself while I was so ill, and away. She is very fond of taking on a little brief authority. Any one, to see her doing this, that, and the other about the house, might imagine everything had been neglected hitherto."

"Well, well, Selina, she is young, remember, and young people are not all blessed with the tact you possessed even at twenty. Make allowances for her, my love; for in some way, though I confess I cannot tell in what way, she has been unfortunately placed. And there can be no doubt but that her progenitors have been very common sort of people; and we know, you and

I, that the old proverb which says, 'You cannot make a silk purse out of a sow's ear,' is as true as that 'You cannot draw blood out of a turnip.'"

"I do make allowances for her," answered Mrs. Wright, putting aside the Reverend Dion's popular quotations as irrelevant to the matter in hand, "and I am sure I bear no ill-will to the girl, though she does try to make much of herself, and throws our dear ones into the shade. The way she went on playing last night, when Sir Harry was here, I considered perfectly disgusting."

After all, there are two sides to maternal affection : one which is very beautiful, and another which acts as a reminder of the savage pecks a hen is wont to administer to a chicken not her own. Poor dear Mrs. Wright was amiability itself to any girl who did not poach on the manor of her charming flock ; but her eyes were very sharp indeed to notice the faults, real or fancied, of that youthful maiden who stood to intercept the sunshine falling upon the rectory daughters.

Said the Rev. Dion, answering his wife's parenthesis :

"Perhaps Bella did play a little too long and too much last night ; but we ought not to find fault with her, as it enabled our young friend to devote himself exclusively to Maria."

"I am not quite sure of it," replied Mrs. Wright. "That sort of professional playing is very distracting to many people. I know I never can even write a letter when she is performing. In my opinion, the music annoyed Sir Harry : he looked quite out of sorts all the evening."

"What is it you want me to do?" asked the Rector, understanding that this sort of discourse might go on indefinitely, unless he pinned Selina to one subject. "Am I to ask Bella not to exhibit her accomplishments, or to suggest that she makes herself too busy about the house?"

There was a certain bitterness in Mr. Wright's tone as he put his question, which happily dearest S. failed to notice, so eager was she to answer :

"No, nothing of the kind. I want you to advise her not to be quite so familiar in her manner towards Colonel Leschelles."

Mr. Wright set down his tumbler. He had been, when his wife spoke, in the act of putting it to his lips.

"Towards Colonel Leschelles!" he repeated. "What on earth do you mean, Selina? What cat is with egg now?"

"I wish, Dion, you would not use such low expressions. If you accustom yourself to employ them when alone with me, you may say what you would be very sorry to think you had said in public. And there is nothing to cause such expressions of astonishment. Bella Miles is—well, we don't exactly know what Bella Miles is; and Colonel Leschelles is a vain old simpleton, who could be flattered into leaving his money to a charwoman, if she only knew the way to take him."

"I wish I knew how to take him," said Mr. Wright, plaintively.

"We are not the people to do a thing of that kind," objected Mrs. Wright, plaintively. "We are too honest and too straight-forward to condescend to tricks that are but every-day weapons in the hands of mere worldlings. Bella Miles comes from no one knows where, and belongs to no one knows who; and if you are blind, I cannot shut my eyes. She is wheedling the Colonel into a belief of her utter simplicity and amiability; and I repeat, you ought to speak to her, and say, though you are certain she means nothing by her manners, still they are not so circumspect as you could wish them to be."

"Why not speak to her yourself?" asked Mr. Wright.

"Because she thinks, wrongly, that I am prejudiced—because she understands my standard of propriety in a woman's behaviour is very different to hers—because she likes you better than she likes me, and would attach importance to your advice, and none to mine."

"You are quite wrong in your idea, Selina," returned the Rector; "but I will speak to her, if you consider it well for me to do so. What is the next thing in her conduct to which you object? It may be as well to include all her sins in one lecture."

"I have nothing more to say about Bella *at present*," answered Mrs. Wright, with an ominous emphasis on the two last words. "What I want you to do further is to get some sort of an explanation from Sir Harry. It is not well for him to be hanging about the house and making no sign. If he admires Maria enough to come here three or four days a week, and two or three times a day, he ought to say so in plain English. We cannot have a young man, even if he be a baronet, amusing himself at our expense. Maria is very pretty, we know; and if he thinks her pretty enough to fall in love with, he ought to ask your permission to propose for her. If she is not pretty enough

to be Lady Medburn, she should not be flirted with—of that
there can be no doubt. You must speak to him, Dion. You
ought to tell him how difficult our position is here, and how
necessary we find it to have everything straightforward and
clearly understood. He should have seen this himself without
any hint from you ; but as, like all English people, he seems
utterly destitute of tact, we must show him that affairs cannot go
on much longer as they are."

The Rev. Dion rose from his seat and took two or three
hurried turns up and down his study. He had a man's natural
reluctance to force his child upon another man's acceptance ;
and yet, still knowing Selina's view of the affair was correct, he
did not dare to shirk the task assigned to him.

Nevertheless, he tried to temporize. "Do you think, dear,"
he asked, once again taking possession of his chair, "that it is
necessary to ask Sir Harry for an explanation at once? He is
not a worldly man, as you see ; he is not a man who has mixed
much with worldly people. Supposing we give him a little
longer law? The fact is, Selina," finished Mr. Wright, "that I
don't know where to turn for money ; and if I speak to Medburn about Maria, I can't ask him for a loan."

"I should think not," said Mrs. Wright, scornfully.

"Then how am I to keep the wolf from the door? It is
very close upon us again, remember."

"How should you have kept it away had you never seen Sir
Harry Medburn?"

Which was one of the speeches poor dear clever Mrs. Wright
considered trenchant, and yet which was really as absurd as if
she had asked the Rev. Dion how he would have reared his
family had he never seen her.

"I am sure I cannot tell, Selina," answered her husband.
"All other doors seem shut, and this about the only one which
is open."

"Can't you go to Mr. Morrison?"

Mr. Wright shook his head. "You know, dear, I have never
yet applied to a man *certain* to refuse me."

"And you think he would?"

"He would, without doubt. If I wanted the church restored
—if it were necessary for new schools to be built—if there was
anything, in fact, to which he could sign his name, Samuel
Morrison, and thrust it under the eyes of the public, I should

not have to ask in vain ; but as regards giving in private, or lending to a man in straits like myself, he would just as soon fling his money into the Thames. I have taken the latitude and longitude of Fisherton, Selina, pretty well, and know there is only one way of navigating our craft in these waters. If I may not ask Medburn, I tell you candidly, I don't see in which direction we are to turn."

Then Mrs. Wright's maternal feelings rose triumphant, and she became sublime.

"We must not be selfish, Dion," she finished. "At whatever cost to ourselves, we must consider our dear child. If by doing anything unwise, or leaving anything wise undone, we prevented Maria becoming Lady Medburn, I should never forgive myself, and I am certain neither would you. Besides, if he once proposes for her, we shall be able to get money. In that case, even Mr. Irwin might let you have what you want. No, Dion, I may not be so clever as some women—though you have told me you would trust my judgment and penetration beyond that of any man you ever met—but I am right about our dear child. Speak to Sir Harry to-morrow. You know how to put such a matter, if any one does."

"Very well," said the Rector, evidently unconsoled by this compliment, however ; "but remember, Selina, I don't think speaking is good policy. I should not have liked being spoken to when I was first in love with you."

At which remark Mrs. Wright laughed outright.

"You dear old Dion, you would only have been too glad had any one thought of such a thing ! You know you never for a moment imagined papa and mamma would allow me to think of a poor curate."

"That is true enough," agreed the Rector, with an affectation of humility and a sly twinkle in his eyes which belied his tone. "You see, at that time I did not know on how little money your father was keeping up appearances ; and I was always a man who entertained a low opinion of my own merits."

"I think," suggested Mrs. Wright, "that we had better go to bed."

CHAPTER XXVI.

MR. WRIGHT IS ASTONISHED.

DURING the course of that night the Rector slept uneasily, and awoke often.

Whenever he awoke it was with a start, and a feeling that something had gone very much amiss.

First he thought—long experience of such miseries having tended naturally to lead his imagination into that and similar channels—that a guest, not invited and not desired, was occupying a certain " chamber on the wall " of the rectory, and, between dreamland and consciousness, he struggled to remember "at whose suit" and for what amount he was there—whether the sheriff's officer was a man he knew, and who knew him, and similar gropings after light.

Then his notion would change, and he felt certain something dreadful had happened to Selina or one of the children; and when he had cleared his mind of these fears, he recollected suddenly that he was bound within a very few hours to remonstrate with Bella Miles on the forwardness of her manners, and to hint delicately to Sir Harry Medburn that Maria and Maria's mother, and, inclusively, Maria's father and all her family, to the hundredth cousin, had been waiting so long for his expected proposal that they were tired of waiting much longer.

" I can't stand any more of this," thought the Reverend Dion, when, after waking for about the twentieth time, he found the sun making his morning investigations into every corner of the apartment, and he exorcised his dream-devils by getting out of bed and passing softly into his dressing-room—after folding the bed-linen with tender hands over the wife who lay, her pale, worn face a little in shadow, sleeping soundly.

And, lest the sound of sponging and splashing might disturb her, the Reverend Dion dispensed with his bath, which he loved, and dipping his head into the basin, at once enveloped it in a towel, and dressed himself very noiselessly, and went downstairs, where he found the servants beginning to creep reluctantly

about that morning work which servants hate with an intensity
worthy of a greater grievance.

"Ah!" considered the Reverend Dion, "they don't tub.
How different even poor faithful Nurse Mary would look if she
could be persuaded to step out of bed into a cold bath!"

As poor faithful Nurse Mary had probably never been washed
all over since babyhood (if then), she would have received a
friendly suggestion about stepping into a lake of fire and brim-
stone with equal favour; but the ideas evolved out of the spectacle of Mary's heavy eyes and unkempt hair served to beguile
Mr. Wright's attention till he was out of the rectory grounds,
and off for a long morning walk, along one of those hideous
roads which intersect the valley of the Thames.

On his return he found the servants a little wider awake, the
children rampant, breakfast ready, and Mrs. Wright—to whom
a restorative cup of tea had been administered in bed half an
hour previously—just down, looking ill and languid.

"You do not seem very well this morning, Selina," remarked
the Rector.

"I have passed a miserable night," answered his better half.
"I felt quite thankful when it was time to get up."

Mr. Wright was far too astute to controvert this statement,
which, rendered into English, he understood to mean: "Remember, I have all this harass about Maria's affair to keep me
awake at night," and, understanding, he girt up his loins for the
impending interview with Sir Harry.

But first he had to remonstrate with Bella Miles, who wondered during the course of the morning much concerning the
nature of the fresh anxiety which caused Mr. Wright to beat his
chest so often, and exclaim with such doleful unconsciousness,
"Hi! ho! hum!" when he helped himself to butter or cut
Selina a slice of bacon.

Was another unwelcome guest expected? There had been
one already in Bella's knowledge of the rectory, and during his
twenty-four hours' stay she gathered that such visitors were not
uncommon where Mr. Wright pitched his tent.

The Christmas presents and her own small stock of jewellery
had then gone on a hurried journey to town; and while she
drank her tea and meditatively ate her toast, Bella was considering whether Sir Harry Medburn's offerings would follow in
the way which Mr. Wright's valuables seemed to affect.

When, therefore, after breakfast, the Rector said to her, "One moment, Bella, my dear," and opened the door of his study for her to enter the only place safe from intrusion in the house, Bella, my dear, made up her mind that Mr. Wright was in sore pecuniary distress, and about to ask counsel—and help, of course—from her.

"Sit down, sit down," exclaimed the Rector brusquely; and, thus commanded, she sat down and watched him while he drew down the blind, which hung crooked, and then pulled it up till it hung straight.

"I have something disagreeable to say to you, Bella, and I don't know how to begin," said the Rector, turning away from the window and walking towards his writing-table, on which lay the materials for the next Sunday's sermon, waiting Mr. Wright's skilful manipulation.

"If you are in trouble," answered the girl, "surely it does not matter how you begin.   I hope you can trust *me*."

Her voice trembled a little.   Short as the years of her life had been, they were long enough for thought to travel back over and recall the trust she once held and fulfilled bravely.

"My dear, it is not that," said the Rector, softened at once. "I am in trouble.   I shall always be in trouble till I am tucked up with a spade in the daisy quilt; and if it were not for Selina and the children, I should not care how soon that event came to pass.   But it is not any worry of my own that is teasing me at this present moment.   What I want to say concerns yourself."

"Myself!" she repeated; and the hot tell-tale blood came flushing up into her face, hanging out its crimson colours from each cheek.   "Is it anything about Uncle Walter?"

"I assure you Mr. Irwin is quite well—at least, he was quite well when last I heard from him.   All I have to say need cause you no great distress, though I confess it vexes me to have to lecture you; but the fact is—yes, the fact is—you are still so much a child—of course no thought of wrong has occurred to your mind—I understand this perfectly—that Mrs. Wright considers you ought to be a little more—how shall I phrase my sentence so as not to give a false meaning to my words?—a little more—suppose we say—reticent in your manner towards strangers."

The worthy Rector had honestly tried to avoid offence, but

in doing so fell into another error—that of obscurity—bewildering Bella Miles to such an extent that she could only stare at him in blank astonishment.

"I confess," blundered on Mr. Wright, "the idea of there being anything in your innocent frankness likely to give rise to misconstruction would never have occurred to me; but no doubt Mrs. Wright is entirely correct in her opinion. She thinks people who do not know you as we do might imagine your manners to be a little too easy and familiar for so young a girl. I repeat, such a notion never crossed my mind. At the same time, my dear Selina is so admirable a judge of the niceties of feminine deportment, and of all shades of propriety, that I have thought it only my duty to mention the matter."

Poor Bella had seen too little of the world to controvert Mr. Wright's statement concerning the infallibility of his dear Selina's judgment on all subjects, etiquette included, and accordingly she sat silent—stunned and mortified—feeling that if once she opened her lips to reply she should burst into tears.

This silence encouraged the Rector.

"I trust, Bella," he said, severely, "you are not cross. Believe me, Mrs. Wright and I have but one object in any remark of this nature—your good. Do you suppose it has been a pleasure to me to find fault with you? Do you think, had duty permitted, I would not much rather have remained silent for ever?"

"I am sure of that," she answered bravely, and then broke down, asking, while sobbing as if her heart would break, "But what is it I have done? Towards whom have my—my—manners been too familiar?"

"My dear girl—my dear child," said the Rector, laying his hand on her shoulder, a little more tenderly than Selina, with her accurate opinions about *les convenances*, might altogether have approved, "pray, pray calm yourself! Remember, *I* did not say you had done anything. It was only Mrs. Wright, whose motherly apprehensions are always awake to your interests, who thought, that is to say, feared——"

"What did Mrs. Wright fear?" inquired the girl, her eyes still cast down, her cheeks still aflame.

"She only feared that others might not understand you so well as we. She only imagined that perhaps the exceeding friendliness of your manner towards Colonel Leschelles might

draw censorious remarks from those likely to forget the extreme
simplicity of your nature."

"Colonel Leschelles!" repeated Bella : and she drew a long
sigh of relief.   "He is a good man, Mr. Wright.   I wonder if
you know one-half how good he is ?"

"I think I do," answered the Rector dryly; "at any rate, I
am sure I ought to know.   Waiving that question, however, for
the present, it may be just as well for you to bear in mind that
he is a man, though not a young one, and not your grandfather,
though old enough to be so twice over."

She had done blushing now, and she winced at his words no
longer.

"I am sorry," she said, "to have grieved Mrs. Wright; but I
think—I do think she might have spoken to me herself."

Now, this was precisely what Mr. Wright had also thought;
but, loyal ever, he replied :

"My dear girl, you may rest satisfied that Mrs. Wright understands these things better than you or I, and—but run away
now, child, and hide your red eyes.   Here come Sir Harry
Medburn and Maria."

And as he conjoined the names of the Baronet and his daughter, the Rector's shirt-front swelled out perceptibly.   He threw
his head back, he ran his fingers through his hair, in view of one
of Sir Harry's livings as a step, and a bishopric as a goal; he
turned over the pages of future manuscript lying on the table ;
yea, even when Bella was gone, he hummed to himself a few
bars of some tuneless air.

At that moment Mr. Wright believed that Fortune was smiling
upon him, and he, courteous as ever, smiled back at her.   But
Fortune, as we know, is apt to be deceitful.   Fortune was deceiving Mr. Wright, while he was thinking how to receive her
advances with becoming modesty.

Down the avenue came Maria and the Baronet, Maria looking
"very pret-ty indeed," looking very much like her mother, so
Mr. Wright thought, when Selina was in her happy teens, ignorant of the cares of a family, and knowing very little about dress
and bills, Mr. Curran, with that pride which distinguished his
character, taking these domestic burdens upon his own ample
shoulders.

Certainly Maria was pretty, a girl "fitted to adorn any sphere," decided Mr. Wright, as, stepping to his study window, he welcomed the Baronet.

"What a superb morning!" said the Rector, in rich, rolling tones of approval. "Come in, come in;" and he grasped Sir Harry's hand, and made him free of the study, and the chairs and tables, and books and shelves, all of which had been so often held in trust by a man from Reuben's.

"He has proposed," Mr. Wright said to himself, as he saw Maria disappear and beheld the Baronet suitably seated for a *tête-à-tête.* "Well, well! it is a long lane which has no turning, and God knows my lane has been long enough and weary enough to entitle me to some change at last."

So reflected the Rector, while Sir Harry pulled the ears of a sorry mongrel, once the property of a disreputable costermonger in the New Cut, who had presented the creature to Mrs. Wright as a delicate acknowledgment of various kindnesses done by her to a woman who perhaps should have been his wife, but who was not.

"Charming weather," said Mr. Wright, finding his visitor made no sign, uneasily moving his sheets of paper. "Just the very best part of the year for Fisherton, eh?"

"I dare say it is," agreed the young man; "but I am going away."

"Going away!"

With a sudden jolt Mr. Wright found himself precipitated from his air castle on the bosom of mother earth.

"Going away! Well, you do astonish me! But only for a short time, I suppose? You will be back ere long?"

"I do not think so," was the reply. "I do not think I shall ever see Fisherton again. I wish to heaven I had never seen it."

"Something has occurred to annoy you?" suggested the Rector.

"Yes," was the reply; "but I need not trouble you about my private affairs. You and Mrs. Wright have been very kind to me, and so I— I—thought I could not go away without calling to thank you, and to say good bye."

"You are not going to slip out of my hands so easily as all that comes to," considered the Rector; then, after a short pause, added aloud: "My dear young friend, I am about to say something to you which I feel sure you will take in the spirit in which it is meant. You will not feel offended, for instance, if I——"

"Go on, Mr. Wright," said the Baronet, as that gentleman stopped and hesitated. "I shall not feel offended at anything you may choose to say."

"Precisely what I expected. You know, Sir Harry, a person has often to say things he would much prefer leaving unsaid. For my part, I think a man should be disassociated from his words in many cases. The words are the world's words, and oftentimes one most unworldly has to become the world's mouthpiece."

"I don't know—I dare say. If declaring I quite agree with you will make matters any easier for you, pray believe that I agree, so far as I have the slightest comprehension of your meaning."

Mr. Wright bit his lip. The Baronet had no idea how much he helped his mentor when by these light words he put him on his mettle and dug spurs into the flanks of his self-love.

"You have alluded, Sir Harry, to the fact that Mrs. Wright and myself have been able to show you some slight attention during your stay at Fisherton."

"I can never forget your kindness," murmured the Baronet.

"It has given us the greatest pleasure to receive you here," went on the Rector. "We have felt honoured by your visits; but, at the same time, we were not so vain as to suppose we owed the happiness of your society entirely to any attractions possessed by ourselves."

He paused, but his visitor did not answer. He kept his eyes fastened on the floor, and continued caressing the costermonger's mite.

"In short," proceeded Mr. Wright, "we felt that what the world feels in such a case must be true. When the world sees a young man visiting constantly at a house, it concludes he must have found some very different loadstone, in that house, from a middle-aged lady and an overworked parson."

"And for once, Mr. Wright, your opinion and the world's are in unison?" suggested the Baronet.

"Even from a Christian standpoint the world is not always wrong," remarked Mr. Wright.

"The world and you being in unison and right," said Sir Harry, "what then?"

"Why, then I say as the world would say, that frequently as you have come to this house, there is something else you ought to have done before bidding me and my wife good bye. Be candid now : don't you think so yourself?"

"Certainly ; but it seems to me we are playing at cross purposes. Evidently you are not aware that I have proposed—that I have been rejected."

"Nonsense !" exclaimed Mr. Wright.

"It is very bad sense to me, nevertheless," said the young man.

"Impossible !" vociferated the Rector.

"Perhaps so, but it is true, nevertheless."

"My dear Sir Harry, there is some terrible mistake; you must be labouring under some great delusion. She never could —she never would—oh ! it is too ridiculous. You must have been deceived by her shyness—her beautiful timidity; you must have startled her. Why—why did you not take me into your confidence first? But it is not too late, thank God ! her mother shall talk to her; I myself will ascertain what it all means. Think of her youth, have patience with her inexperience ; why, she is little more than a child—a tender, innocent child. It will be all right, and I shall yet have the happiness of seeing our beloved Maria united to the noblest of men."

In his enthusiasm, Mr. Wright stretched out his hand; but Sir Harry did not grasp it as the Rector intended he should. He only laid his own left hand on it, and said :

"I am so sorry ; oh ! Mr. Wright, I cannot tell you how grieved I am. I admire and like Miss Maria, but it is not she who has refused me."

"Who has, then, in Heaven's name?" inquired the Rector.

"Bella."

"Bella !" gasped Mr. Wright, then added in a bewildered aside, "What will Selina say? And Bella, too ! and that poor dear child ! Well, well ! well, well, well !"

"Colonel Leschelles, sir," announced the housemaid at this juncture, and so exit Fortune with a gibing smile, and enter the Colonel, tall, thin, erect, closely buttoned up as ever.

"I will bid you good morning, then," said Sir Harry Medburn, rising hastily. "Pray make my adieux to Mrs. Wright and your family."

"Do you go up by the midday train?" asked the Colonel.

"Yes, and shall but have time to catch it," answered the other, looking at his watch. "Good bye, Mr. Wright, good bye, Colonel." And he was gone.

For once the Rector's presence of mind had forsaken him and he was stricken dumb. He could think of no form of words which might undo the evil Bella had wrought and the wrong Maria had sustained—poor dear Maria, who had looked so like Selina in her best days while she walked down the drive with Sir Harry sauntering at her side.

It was all over—the doubt, the hope, the fear, the uncertainty; everything was assured now save this—

What would Selina say?

If the reader remembers, Mr. Wright had asked himself the same question when he first beheld Bella Miles.

And now Bella had spirited away the lover who otherwise might have made the fortunes of the Wright family, and the Rector had very good reason indeed for wondering what Selina would say.

CHAPTER XXVII.

MRS. WRIGHT'S EYES ARE OPENED.

UPON principle, Mr. Wright never drank water when any other beverage was procurable. His was a comfortable creed, which contained no mention of asceticism—which, setting forth as a starting-point that God had provided an infinity of good things for the use of man, argued that an indifference to or abstinence from partaking of the Almighty's manifold bounties amounted to a positive sin.

Aware of his friend's principle, carried, as he knew well, into practice with an admirable fidelity—such being, indeed, the sort of principle which a man does carry out faithfully—Colonel Leschelles was astonished to behold the Rector fill a glass of water from the caraffe, which, as a matter of form, always stood on the study table, and swallow its contents.

"I have had a dreadful shock," said the Reverend Dion, in explanation of this unwonted procedure, and speaking of his shortcoming apologetically.

His visitor had no difficulty in imagining the nature of the shock referred to, so only remarked that "he was very sorry indeed to hear it."

"I may say," observed the Reverend Dion, "that, in the whole of my experience as a clergyman, my confidence in mankind has never—I say it advisedly—*never* .been so shaken as this morning."

Colonel Leschelles sympathizingly answered that this was indeed speaking strongly.

"Not too strongly," said Mr. Wright, striking the blotting-pad with his open hand. "I trusted him, Colonel, as I might have trusted a son. I believed in him as if he had been my own flesh and blood," added the Rector plaintively, labouring evidently under the delusion that his flesh and blood were different and better from and than the flesh and blood of other people.

"I hope I am not indiscreet in remarking that I presume the 'him' to whom you are referring is Harry Medburn?"

"The Baronet—yes," replied Mr. Wright dramatically; "and Selina does not know anything about the matter as yet—and how I am to break the news to her, God only knows."

"She will be very much disappointed?" said Colonel Leschelles interrogatively.

"Disappointed!—that is not the word to express what her feelings will be; in fact, there is no word capable of conveying even an idea of her distress. We have been deceived, fooled, betrayed—yes, betrayed," finished the Rector in a tragic tone of voice, and with a stony expression of countenance.

"I do not think Medburn betrayed you, at any rate," observed the Colonel. "I have long believed his attraction here was Miss Miles."

"Then why did you not say so?" demanded Mr. Wright.

“ Do you consider you acted a friendly part in sitting by while
we were being made fools of ? ”

“ Gently—gently,” entreated the other, as if he were soothing
a vicious horse. “ The young fellow never took me into his
confidence, and I had no better means of obtaining information
than such as were open to yourself. From the first day he came
here, you made up your mind—why, I never could imagine—
that he was in love with Maria ; and when once, in answer to a
remark you hazarded concerning his being pretty well over head
and ears in love in that quarter, I said I feared such was not
the case, you seemed rather offended at my frankness.”

“ But you never told me you thought he was in love with
Bella.”

“ You never asked me my opinion on the subject,” returned
the Colonel dryly.

“ I don’t know how I am to break the bad news to Selina—
I don’t, really,” said Mr. Wright, harking back to that part of
the subject.

“ Do you mean to say no suspicion of the actual state of the
case ever crossed Mrs. Wright’s mind ? ”

“ Certainly no idea of the kind ever occurred to her. How
should it ? ”

“ I cannot tell. It occurred to me ; and I should have
thought that very likely Mrs. Wright might have elicited from
her daughter whether so constant a visitor was making love to
her or not.”

“ Ah ! you know nothing of Selina. She would not for the
wealth of the Indies speak on such subjects to one of our girls.
‘ Let them be innocent children as long as they can,’ she has
often remarked to me. ‘ It is easy to rub the bloom off the
peach ; but who can replace it ? ’ ”

“ A very nice feeling,” said Colonel Leschelles.

“ She is full of nice feelings, poor dear,” answered Mr. Wright ;
“ and I am afraid what will hurt her in this matter, more than
anything else, may be the idea that Bella has not behaved quite
circumspectly. She has, as you know, taken vast pains to improve Bella—to model her, in fact ; and she will, I fear, feel
hurt at the notion of a love affair having been conducted under
our roof so secretly and, I must say, so slyly. The girl ought
to have taken counsel with us. One word from her would have
prevented my being placed in a most difficult, and I may add,

humiliating position. We have had nothing hidden away from her in holes and corners. If there was adversity, we informed her of the fact; if prosperity, we were always pleased to make her a sharer in our happiness. No daughter was ever more *au fait* with her father's affairs than Bella has been with ours; and this is the thanks we get! Well, well, well—oh! dear, dear me!"

"I don't think you ought to be too hard upon the girl," suggested Colonel Leschelles. "Like Mrs. Wright, she may feel a delicacy in talking about a lover, more particularly when she had evidently made up her mind to reject him."

"But why did she make up her mind to anything of the kind?"

"I think you had better seek information on that point from head-quarters," was the reply.

"What more could she ask?" went on Mr. Wright, unheeding the Colonel's advice. "In the name of Heaven, what more could she want than a man—young, rich, handsome, a baronet? Does she suppose a royal duke is going to propose for her? Does she imagine, so long as she lives, she will ever get such a chance again?"

"I really do not know," remarked the Colonel. "Once again, I can only counsel you to put these questions to the young lady herself."

"I do not understand it—I really cannot fathom the mystery. Why, he is a man *any* girl might feel proud to marry. Speaking for myself, and putting poor dear Selina out of the question for the present, I may say, if Bella had accepted him, I could have borne the disappointment better. I have always felt like a father towards Bella. She has been very near to my heart. She has seemed like a dear elder daughter. She knows all about our position. I could have asked her to do anything for me; but, as matters are—as matters are——"

Colonel Leschelles looked curiously at the Rector as he suddenly broke off the end of his sentence, and gazed out of the window.

The waters were flooding him again, and no way of escape presented itself. He had trusted in Sir Harry Medburn to help, and lo! Sir Harry Medburn was gone, taking the sting of a rejection with him.

Even while he talked of Selina's disappointment, he had been veering round from the thought of Maria and her mother, and considering how Bella might have brought him ease of mind.

Supposing Sir Harry, instead of going away a rejected suitor, had remained engaged to Bella? Everything would have seemed very different to what he hoped, of course, but everything would not have been lost. Out of common gratitude, Mr. Irwin must at once have signified his readiness to convert himself for the nonce into a good milch-cow; whilst the Baronet's purse would have been at Mr. Wright's service, and a future living in Bella's power to bespeak.

"The girl is mad!" he said, at last, considering his own position as he spoke—"stark, staring mad! How could she refuse such a chance? Why, it is just as if I flung away the offer of a bishopric."

"Mr. Wright," here broke in the Colonel.

"Did you speak?" asked the Reverend Dion.

"Yes; I want to know if you are again in pecuniary difficulties."

"Again!" repeated Mr. Wright, whom disappointment and despair conjoined had startled out of his usual habits of caution. "Have you ever known me clear of pecuniary difficulty? Have you ever seen me when my mind was not occupied with the thought of where the next ten-pound note was to come from?"

"Well, yes," replied Colonel Leschelles. "On last Christmas I do not think you were doubtful as to where to turn for a much larger sum than that"

"True," agreed the Rev. Dion, recovering himself. "Last Christmas I was for the moment easy as regards money matters. I had lulled myself into a false security. I was depending on a REED, believing it to be an oak; and the reed has failed me; that is all: and I am a ruined man. But why, my dear, kind friend, should I distress *you*, who have proved a most generous friend to one most unworthy, but not ungrateful? No, no , believe anything of me rather than that——"

"I presume," said Mr. Wright's "most generous friend," "that Mr. Irwin confines his payments strictly to one hundred per annum?"

"Not precisely," answered the Rector, who never told a deliberate falsehood, though he frequently implied one. "Strictly speaking, he does not limit his remittance to that amount, but it comes to the same thing. Remember, I do not complain; I have no right to complain. Business, I know, is business, and a bargain is a bargain, and I don't complain. All I can say is,

Selina and I did not think of business, or of adhering to a mere bargain, in our treatment of Mr. Irwin's niece."

"I am sure you and Mrs. Wright are the last people in the world to adhere to a mere bargain," remarked Colonel Leschelles soothingly.

"Thank you, thank you," said the Rector, with effusion. "You are a true friend. But you understand us."

"If I do not, I ought to be ashamed of myself," answered the other, "for I have known you for a long time."

"Yes; and the longer we know you the better we like you," replied Mr. Wright, who felt that his friend must have some decent sum burning his pocket, or he never would have spoken in such wise; and gratitude with the Rector was very prospective. "Now, that is not the case with myself and Mr. Irwin. I thought at first he was charming. I said to Selina, after our first interview, 'I could take that man into my confidence, no matter what trouble overtook me, and feel certain of help.' I was mistaken in my impressions. My dear wife was not mistaken. When she received his first letter, she said, 'That man has the soul of a bookkeeper.' She was right."

"And so—to return to our sheep—Mr. Irwin will not assist you beyond the hundred a year he pays for the advantages his niece enjoys at Fisherton Rectory?"

"That is what it comes to, though I am in Mr. Irwin's debt."

"Yes, I suppose so. We need not, however, go into the pounds, shillings, and pence question. Broadly, Mr. Irwin refuses to allow you to draw further upon him?"

"You express the position exactly."

"And consequently you are once again in difficulties?"

"I am," agreed the Rector solemnly.

There was silence for a few moments, which the Rector would not break, because he wanted to land his fish gently, and which the Colonel employed in thinking how he had best say what he wanted to say.

"It must be very miserable for you to be in such continual hot water," he began at last.

"Yes," agreed Mr. Wright; "the life is killing me—mentally, I mean. The eternal consideration of ways and means is enough to break the spirit of any man; and the worst of all," he added —remembering that his latest visions had been dispelled—"is that I begin to feel *hopeless*. This living seems to have stranded me. Wherever else we have been placed there appeared a chance of better days to come; but here there is no prospect. I am shelved. Yes, with the very best intentions, my kind patron has spoiled my life. I feel stultified at Fisherton. Of what avail is it to preach a good sermon to the dolts who come to hear me? I give you my honour, Colonel, I might buy my sermons for sixpence apiece, and my congregation would like them just as well as those to which I have given thought, time, study. When I came down here I imagined I was coming to peace; but I find it is the peace of stagnation, broken only by the occasional advent of noxious reptiles, out of whose reach I trusted I had passed for ever."

"It is very sad," said the Colonel; and in truth he thought it all was very sad; "but don't you think—excuse me if I seem impertinent—that things might be better if you took a comprehensive view of your position, and looked your affairs straight in the face?"

"They have such a sweet face, it ought to be a pleasure for any man to look straight in it!" answered the Rector grimly.

"Still, don't you think it would be wise to make the attempt?" urged Colonel Leschelles. "Were I placed as you are, God only knows what I should do; but I know what I ought to do, and I know what you ought to do. You should put down your income, and you should calculate your expenditure. You should say to your creditors, I can spare so much a year to clear off all my debts: but I must have time to do it. There is not one of the people to whom you owe money who would, I believe, refuse to meet you on these grounds, and you would be then able to live without this everlasting consideration of ways and means, which is enough to take the spirit and energy out of any one."

Mr. Wright smiled. He understood now that if the Colonel meant to do anything for him, he meant to do very little indeed, and he felt for once in a mood to speak plainly—perhaps because there was little or nothing to be gained by speaking diplomatically.

"Your advice," he said, "is very good; but, like advice generally, it is better to give than to take. Were you in my position to-morrow, you would understand how impossible it is for an embarrassed man to make terms with his creditors. If I had houses, and lands, and shares, and a variety of other things,

which I could assign, these harpies would take security and give
me time, doubtless; but that is not the position. I have no
houses, no lands, no anything save this living; and I tell you
quite candidly, we cannot make both ends meet upon my income,
to say nothing of paying off old scores."

"Do you mean to say," asked the Colonel, "you cannot live
upon the income you receive here?"

"That is precisely what I mean," replied Mr. Wright. "Calculate the pecuniary question for yourself. The living here is
estimated as worth three hundred and fifty pounds a year. As
a matter of fact, it is not worth quite so much; but with fees
and one thing or another, probably that amount is nearly made
up. Including house and so forth, a good living, as livings go,
which is not saying much. Very well: divide this wonderful
living by fifteen—I am now leaving out our three boys, other·
wise provided for, who, nevertheless, cost me something—and
the result is twenty-three pounds six shillings and eightpence a
head for maintenance, out of which has to be deducted rates
and taxes, travelling, wages, dress, subscriptions, and so forth.
What do you make of that, Colonel?"

"It seems very little," answered the person so addressed;
"but yet some people do live on such an amount."

"Precisely what I have often said myself. I have remarked
to Selina that there are people able to make the two ends meet
on so small an annual income, and she has inquired, 'How?'
I echo that inquiry. I suppose one ought to live within one's
income; but I confess—always bearing in mind that an appearance must be kept up—I do not see how it is to be done. Now
look at this house, Colonel. Look at it!" and Mr. Wright
paused in order to enable his auditor to take in at one compre-
sive glance the rectory and its domestic economy. "I put it
to you, Do we wallow in luxury? Rather, is not our expenditure calculated upon a system of the closest economy? Is not
our butter, as a rule, Dorset? Are not our eggs the produce
of foreign farmyards? Do we ordinarily indulge in the luxury
of wine—except in case of illness, or when a friend sends us in a
few bottles? Of course the children must be fed and clothed,
and the servants fed and paid. It is essential I should be
respectably dressed, but I am not extravagant. I wear a coat
till it assumes quite the character of an old acquaintance. My
life has been one of shift and struggle, I admit that. First or

last, I have never done justice to the talents God gave me. They have lain buried among writs, and lawyers' letters, and bills, and suchlike. If it were my last word, Colonel, the Church is the only sphere in England where a man like myself has no chance—no chance at all. Look at the fools who get deaneries and bishoprics, and all the great prizes, and then consider me. By Heaven, if it were not that my faith is built on a rock, it is enough to make me turn infidel to-morrow!"

"Or to-day," said Colonel Leschelles cheerily. "To-morrow you will probably take a different view of the position."

For he quite understood that Mr. Wright, being occasionally natural and unaffected, his utterances merely meant, he felt disappointed at the result of the morning's conversation with Sir Harry Medburn.

Had things gone right as regarded the Baronet, how differently Mr. Wright would have discoursed concerning the Church and her mode of bestowing benefits !

"I shall never take a different view of the position," said Mr. Wright determinedly. "In any other profession I might have made a fortune."

Colonel Leschelles looked him over, and doubted the truth of this statement; but he only answered, rising from his chair and buttoning up his coat :

"I have very little money available now. Of late, owing to circumstances with which I need not trouble you, it has been necessary for me to expend a considerable amount. Nevertheless, if a cheque for a small sum can be of any assistance to you——"

Majestically Mr. Wright repudiated the idea of a cheque for any small amount being of the slightest use to him or his.

Almost with tears he refused Colonel Leschelles' proffered kindness.

"Why," he asked, "should I take your money down into the abyss of ruin I see yawning before me? Why should I encroach further upon the kindness and generosity of one of the kindest and most generous of men? Why should I lay a fresh burden on my already overburdened memory?"

"Pooh!" interposed the Colonel at this juncture, drawing pen and ink towards him. "You are not a ruined man yet— you will look at life with different eyes to-morrow. And as for this," he added, blotting off the cheque and laying it, folded, on a side of Mr. Wright's manuscript paper, " though it is but little, still it may prove a nest-egg. ' Many a mickle makes a muckle,' remember."

And he held out his hand, which Mr. Wright pressed with tenderness, as though he would have implied, " The world is not worthy of you ; " and he walked up the drive with his guest, and bade him another adieu at the gate ; after which, with considerable rapidity, he retraced his steps to his study, where he at once seized and scanned the neglected cheque.

" Come," he said, " this is not so mean after all. Courage, courage, Mr. Wright ! something may be made of a bad business yet."

And, fired with some sudden inspiration, he pushed aside the memoranda of his intended sermon, and, taking note-paper and envelopes, forthwith wrote and addressed two lengthy epistles, which he finished just as Mrs. Wright, gently opening the door, said :

" I could scarcely believe Nurse Mary when she told me you were alone. Why did you not come to me at once—surely you knew how anxious I must be ? "

" Well, yes, my dear, I did," answered the Reverend Dion, " and that was the very reason I stayed away ; because——"

" You do not mean to say you have not spoken to him ? " interrupted Mrs. Wright.

" Oh! I have spoken," was the reply. " I went straight enough to the point, you may be sure ; and he—yes, he came straight enough to the point also ; but the fact is, Selina, we made a little mistake, and I am afraid you will be dreadfully disappointed when you hear what it was."

" Surely he never said he meant nothing by his visits ! " cried Selina wrathfully.

" No, not exactly ; but nothing as regards Maria."

" What did he mean, then ? " asked the lady.

" He meant—the fact is—now, don't excite yourself—pray don't. He came after Bella ! "

" After Bella ? " gasped Mrs. Wright.

" Yes ; and, to cut a long story short, she has refused him, and there is an end of it."

Then it was that Selina indulged in those remarks previously mentioned. Then it was that she went into a long fit of heart-breaking sobbing ; then it was that Mr. Wright tried to soothe her, first with wine, and that proving ineffectual, with water; then it was that, finding she alternated between scolding and crying with a somewhat monotonous regularity, he summoned Nurse Mary to his assistance, and, giving Selina into her charge, went out to post his letters.

After some time, Maria, coming to see what ailed her mother, was received by that lady with tears and an exclamation of " My poor, poor child ! "

" Nonsense, mamma ! " retorted Maria, with the ingenuous *brusquerie* which formed such a contrast to her pretty young face. " We all of us knew from the first Sir Harry cared for no one but Bella, only we did not like to say so for fear of putting you out ; and besides——"

Here Maria stopped and looked significantly towards Nurse Mary, who took up her parable on the instant.

" Ay, ye may well feel ashamed to finish, miss ; for it is a thing not to be believed unless a body seen it with her own two eyes. To think of a young lady sending away a handsome gentleman like the Baronet to foregather with one who might be her great-grandfather ! "

" What do you mean, nurse ? " asked Mrs. Wright, speaking quite in her natural tone.

" Just what I say, mem ; that it is unnatural—it 's witchcraft —he has put a spell on her, or sure am I Miss Bella would never think of marrying the Colonel."

" The Colonel—which Colonel ? " inquired Mrs. Wright.

" The only one that comes here," retorted Nurse Mary, defiantly.

" What is the woman talking about, Maria ? "

" It is quite true, ma," answered Miss Maria, not without a certain comic relish of the position. " Colonel Leschelles worships the ground Bella walks on ; and Bella—well, we cannot tell whether she is going to marry him or not."

" And this has been going on under my very eyes ! " cried poor Mrs. Wright, " and there was not a creature about me honest enough to open them ! Go away, both of you—leave me—my cup is full."

CHAPTER XXVIII.

MR. IRWIN REVIEWS THE POSITION.

IT was a very hot day in London. Down at Fisherton the dust lay thick on the unwatered roads, and there was not a suspicion of shade along any one of the treeless and almost hedgeless highways that intersect the valley of the Thames. Nevertheless, indoors, with blinds down and windows open, it was possible to keep, comparatively speaking, cool. Not so in London. From the freshly-watered streets a steam rose as if the drops had fallen on a hot plate. Into the City offices not a breath of air seemed able to find its way. Even in the narrow lanes, where grateful shadows always fall across one side of the pavement, there was not any relief from the close oppression of the atmosphere.

A day when people rush off madly to partake of iced drinks; when messengers are to be met with hat in one hand, and a handkerchief, with which they wipe their foreheads, in the other; when white waistcoats are the rule, and a man with a red face and purple nose appears in the light of a personal offence—an aggravation of the height of the thermometer; when human beings feel as if they were so many drooping shrubs, and wanted rain; when City folks think longingly of distant mountains, and shores on which the waves plash gently. An intolerably hot day—exceptionally hot, even for London and the time of year.

So said Mr. Irwin, seated in his office, to Colonel Leschelles, who sat opposite to him, looking as thin, as precise, and, save for a slight moisture on his forehead, as cool as ever.

"Yes," answered the Colonel, "it is very warm indeed— almost as warm as India. And that," he added, reverting to what he had been previously talking about, "being my opinion, I thought I would mention the matter."

"It is very kind of you," replied Mr. Irwin, pushing some papers away from him with an irritable gesture. "I am quite sure you are right; and, indeed, in any case, I should not have allowed Bella to remain at Fisherton—only, what to do with her I do not know!"

"Medburn has been with you?"

"Yes, twice; yesterday and again this morning. I told him Bella was quite right. Good heaven! who would have imagined that such a misfortune could happen in a dead-and-alive place like Fisherton! And then, to crown my annoyance, Mr. Wright sends me a letter, pointing out all the advantages such a marriage would secure to my niece, and asking for a further advance, as he has been put to considerable expense during the stay of Sir H. Medburn and Colonel Leschelles in the neighbourhood."

Colonel Leschelles laughed outright: he could not help doing so.

"The Rector is incomparable and unconquerable," he remarked. "If his wife resembled him as much in character as she does in extravagance, Fisherton might still prove a pleasant enough residence for Miss Miles."

"I should not allow her to remain under any circumstances," said Mr. Irwin. "I am fond enough of the girl—fond as I am of any one of my own children—but I cannot continue to spend as much money on her as I have done. I am willing to pay handsomely for her board and so forth; but the Wrights are not willing to abide by the terms of their agreement, and I am not willing to put up with the continual annoyance of Mr. Wright's appeals."

"And yet, as Mr. Wright would tell you, Miss Miles has had the chance at Fisherton of marrying better probably than she could in any other house in England."

"But what is the use of that?" demanded Mr. Irwin.

"Not much, apparently; but still you must have had some vague idea of her marrying when you placed her under Mrs. Wright's motherly wing."

"I do not believe an idea of the kind crossed my mind. What I wanted then was a comfortable home for her—a home where she might learn things she never had a chance of learning previously."

"It is more than a year since, and you have much to occupy your attention; but still I think, if you will try to recall the evening when Mr. Wright first asked you for a loan, you will find that something to the following effect occurred to you:

"Here is a well-educated, gentlemanly sort of man, filling a highly respectable position, but burdened with a large family, and poor ; his wife has the character of being a very sensible woman. Suppose they all take to my niece, and she to them, and that hereafter one of the elder sons falls in love with her, and she with him——"

"Go on," said Mr. Irwin, as his visitor paused.

"You probably can supply the finish of my sentence for yourself."

"As you chose to begin it, Colonel, I think you ought to end it also."

"Very well. The view I imagine you took of Mr. Wright at your first meeting was, that given a young lady with a little money and a relation with more, he would not, in the event of his son caring for her, think it necessary to inquire into the antecedents of her family."

"You are wrong there, at all events," answered Mr. Irwin "The Rector made very particular inquiries concerning Bella's legitimacy before he consented to introduce her to the notice of his dear Selina."

"And took you in, no doubt, by his expressions of propriety; the fact being that the man would receive the whole Foundling Hospital with effusion, providing the governors sent plenty of money. But this is beside the question. It is not of what Mr. Wright thought I am talking ; it is of what you thought when the notion of sending your niece to Fisherton first entered your head."

"May I ask you, Colonel, without giving offence, what business it is of yours what I thought on the occasion when, unfortunately for me, I made Mr. Wright's acquaintance ? "

"Certainly ; it is my business so far as this, that I fancy we have both travelled, mentally, the same road, arriving, however, at slightly different results. A year ago, it strikes me, you considered a marriage with one of Mr. Wright's sons might form a not undesirable finish to the story upon which you were just entering. Six months ago, I foolishly began to hope that a marriage with me might end many a difficulty both for you and your niece."

"With you !" repeated Mr. Irwin in astonishment.

"Yes ; I am not young, it is true——"

"No——," agreed Mr. Irwin, who was really too much amazed even to think of politeness.

" I am not young," repeated the Colonel steadily, though **a** faint red tinged his cheeks as he made the assertion, " and she is young—very young ; but, knowing something of her story, I thought it not impossible she might learn to cling to a man even as old as myself, in whom she could confide thoroughly, and who would have tried, God knows, to make her happy."

" I am sure you would," agreed Mr. Irwin heartily ; for he was touched by the simple modesty, by the unaffected candour of the suitor, who had hoped in his age to possess treasures that belong only to youth—who had dreamed in his winter that spring-time can come twice in a human life, and that in dreary December it was possible to gather the flowers of May.

" I am sure I would," repeated the Colonel, slowly. " So far as lay in my power, she should never have repented becoming my wife. I am not a poor man. Quite lately I have fallen into some property in Wales, which largely increases an income which before was not contemptible. I could have given your niece many things which money could buy, and many things which money could never buy ; but it is of no use talking of all that now."

" No," said Mr. Irwin once again ; but he was not thinking about the Colonel's rejected suit, or his appointment. He was only wondering what he knew of Bella's story, and whether he was aware how largely his—Walter Irwin's—life had been mixed up with that of Miles Barthorne.

The past came forth and stood before him like an actual pre-sence. He was back in the cottage at West Green ; he was spending his best energies to make a fortune unlawfully. He might not actually have been a thief, but he had been a partner with one. Like a receiver, he had asked no awkward questions, but taken his share of the spoil and the profit with a virtuous equanimity. Since then he had lived and struggled and pros-pered ; he had worked hard ; he had found means to silence the tongue of the solitary enemy who was capable of injuring him very materially. His father-in-law's death had left him, to a certain extent, pecuniarily independent of what any one could say. And yet, when Colonel Leschelles stated he knew some-thing of Bella's history, the man's heart seemed to stand still, and the whole phantasmagoria which once haunted the vigils of darkness and the hours of day once more danced before his eyes.

Not knowing what he did—unconscious that he had twice essayed to speak and his tongue refused its office, he mechanically poured himself out some water and drank eagerly, like one in the first stage of fever ; then turning to Colonel Leschelles, who had watched him closely and with surprise, he said :

" May I ask how you came to know anything of Bella's antecedents? and, for the matter of that, what you know?"

" I know why she refused Sir Harry Medburn."

" Did she tell you her reason?"

" No ; I had discovered the cause of the mystery connected with her past, poor girl, and having hinted as much, she confessed to me that, for reasons to which we need not now further allude, it was impossible for her to marry any one."

" And you——"

" I advised her to tell Medburn the story, and let him decide ; but she refused to do so. I asked her to let me tell him ; and she implored me, with tears, not to betray her secret. So I let him go, though I am afraid I did not act rightly by either of them in doing so. And yet I do not know ; I do not see how he could——"

" Marry her father's daughter," finished Mr. Irwin, as the Colonel paused and hesitated, "although you would be willing to marry her yourself," he added, a little bitterly.

" I am differently situated from Medburn," answered Colonel Leschelles simply. " I have no relations whose prejudices I am bound to respect ; I have no family traditions binding upon me ; I care nothing for the world's opinion ; I have no title to transmit ; I can afford to do what I choose, without thinking of the feelings or considering the likes or dislikes of any other human being. Further, I do not consider that a daughter is answerable for the sins of her parents ; and I would willingly devote the remainder of my life in trying to make her forget her dead father, or think of him as of one who had much to forgive, if he had also much to be forgiven."

Mr. Irwin rose, and walking to the door of his office, opened it, and looked out on the landing, to see that no eavesdropper was lingering there ; then he closed and locked it, and, resuming his seat, said :

" I see Bella has told you nothing about her father ; it was not likely she should. If you knew more about him, I think you might advise me concerning her future. I want help ; J want to take counsel with some one; and though you cannot be her husband, I am certain you will stand her friend. Tell me first what you know about Barthorne, and how you came to know it, and then I will tell you where my difficulty chiefly lies."

"What I learnt was first by pure accident," answered the Colonel. "I was struck by your niece's extraordinary likeness to the portrait of a once celebrated court beauty, whose face has been copied often enough to render it familiar to those who, like myself, are fond of wandering through galleries of paintings; and, being surprised to think who it was she resembled, exclaimed, 'Why, you are the image of Molly Barthorne!' I had not the least suspicion of her being in any way related to the lady in question, and was therefore astonished at the effect my remark produced."

"Yes," said Mr. Irwin, reverting to his favourite expression.

"Of course," continued Colonel Leschelles, "I had always felt there was a mystery connected with your niece. When a girl of her age confines her reminiscences strictly to school life; when she makes no mention of father or mother, of home, of relations, of holidays, of friends, of pets, of any one of the hundred things which constitute the memories of childhood, we naturally assume there has been something curious associated with her parents."

"Naturally," agreed Mr. Irwin.

"Up to that evening, I need not trouble you by explaining what my theory had been. From that evening I devoted myself to solving the enigma presented for solution by the difference between your niece's position and her antecedents, her appearance, and her friendlessness."

"Why did you do this?" asked Mr. Irwin hoarsely. He comprehended that along the road one man had gone another might follow.

"Because I was fond of her; because I hoped to make her my wife; because I thought, if there was any shame connected with her birth—any story you and she wished kept secret——"

"You would hold your knowledge of the shame or the story over her."

"No, by Heaven!" exclaimed Colonel Leschelles. "You must have been brought up in a very bad school to be so ready to impute dishonourable motives to one who only sought full knowledge of her antecedents in order to serve your niece more thoroughly."

"I have been in many bad schools," was the answer; "and it is the knowledge there acquired which makes me comprehend that though a man may ferret out the secrets of another human being's life to serve his own turn, he never does so purely and simply for the sake of befriending his fellow-creatures."

There was a pause; then said Colonel Leschelles:

"I am afraid you are right. I imputed too good a motive to my own actions—judged myself, as one rarely judges another, too leniently. But it is not too late to retrace my steps; the story, so far as I am concerned, can be as if it had never been. I shall never cease to take the deepest interest in all that concerns your niece, but that interest need not be active."

"Sit down," exclaimed Mr. Irwin; for his visitor had risen with the evident intention of leaving at once. "You have seen so much of the world," he went on, speaking with unusual *brusquerie*, "that you must know, or at least ought to know, no man can ever go back one step of the road he has travelled. You cannot undo what you have done; you cannot make yourself the 'one person less' acquainted with my brother-in-law's story. You can, however, as I said before, tell me how much of that story you have heard, and how and where you heard it; and possibly you may help me, or rather Bella."

"I heard the story by chance—thus far," answered the Colonel, swallowing his wrath, "that I had given up the search as hopeless, when I met with my informant. I went down to the neighbourhood of Abbotsleigh to prosecute my inquiries. The family were away, and I was able consequently to see on the walls of the picture gallery a portrait of the beauty, and satisfy myself as to the strong resemblance subsisting between her and your niece.

"But beyond this it seemed impossible to get. All the bygone Barthornes, male and female, were satisfactorily accounted for, either in the family vault or the family traditions. There was no record of a ne'er-do-weel amongst them—no story of any son or daughter cast out from the ancestral home for any indiscreet marriage. You are getting impatient, however, I see, and I hasten on. The very morning I made up my mind to leave Abbotsleigh, fortune threw me in the way of an old sexton, who had previously narrated to me circumstances connected with the

deaths and burials of many generations of Barthornes. I met
him beside the stream which runs through Abbotsleigh, and as
he was going up to the garden, I walked with him till we came
to a spot where the ha-ha separating the park from the lawns
commences. I had before noticed its unusual width, and remarked upon it to my companion.

"'Ay, it is uncommon wide, sir," he answered ; 'but I once
see a boy of eight clear it on his pony.'

"'He must have been plucky,' I remarked.

"'A daredevil—that's what he was, sir. God knows how it
would have been had the estate gone to him, as many a one
thought it would. He was a plucky one, child, boy, and man,
and, base-born or not, free and generous. He had hard lines
of it. I have always said that, and always will.'

"Little by little I got the story out of the depths of the old
man's memory. I heard of the boy being brought up to be a
gentleman, and then cast out and apprenticed to a common
trade. I heard of his proud application to that trade. I heard
how he and his master's wife could not agree—heard how he
left to come to London, and how well he prospered—how he
married, and had one child, a daughter.

"'But at last, sir,' finished the man, 'something or other went
wrong. I never clearly knew the rights of it ; for friends, and
all who had kept up any correspondence with him, were dead
or gone away ; and it was only a sort of rumour came down here
that Barthorne had stood his trial, and been sent beyond seas.
Some said it was the old Squire's son, and others said no—it
was no kith or kin. I cannot tell who was right. All I know
is, news of him has never come here since.'"

"And that is all you know?" commented Mr. Irwin.

"Not quite. In the records of the Old Bailey I found that
in the year 18— Miles Barthorne, aged —, had pleaded guilty
to stealing from a house at Enfield Chase, and was sentenced
to seven years' transportation. I did not care to pursue the
matter further. I had learnt all I wanted to know ; and I may
candidly tell you what I had learnt filled me not merely with
the deepest pity for your niece, but also with an, if possible,
stronger desire to make her my wife. It was folly, if you like ;
but I felt that, whether as my wife or my widow, it would be
well for her to have my name shielding her from the consequences of her father's act."

"You were very generous," said Mr. Irwin.

"Not so; I was very selfish. I saw what she was. I knew that for gratitude, for remembrance of my love, my care, she would try to give me back something—the fondness a daughter has for a father, perhaps—and come in time to mistake it for affection. I built my castle cautiously. She grew to like and trust me. And then Medburn came; and I know it was better so. If he had come after marriage, and she had then learnt to care for him—true though she is, faithful as I am sure she would have been—it must have proved a worse trial than—this——"

"It must," sighed the other. He was thinking of his own marriage, without love or happiness. Out of the depths of that experience he comprehended what love might have proved to Bella, had she come to understand its meaning after marriage. "You have had an escape, Colonel, though I do not think——"

"She would ever have accepted me," finished the other.

"Though I do not think she would marry any one, remembering her—story."

"But when I knew it—not when I told her, as I have told her—there is no feeling in my heart save compassion for that dead man—that Ishmael, who, cast out from the house and lands he expected would be his, fought his battle bravely, until temptation—what form it took I never inquired—proving too much for him, he fell, and suffered."

"That is the idealized view of Miles Barthorne," remarked Mr. Irwin. "Shall I tell you mine? A man with an enormous capacity for evil, and little for good; a man who, let him have been what he may as a boy, grew so soured and envious as the years rolled by, that he would stick at no crime to compass wealth and success. A terrible man," added Walter Irwin— sometime Chappell—"clever, cunning, plausible, wicked. Colonel Leschelles"—and the successful London merchant, leaning forward, laid his hand on the officer's arm—"if you knew one-half so much about Bella's father as I do, you could never again even think about marrying her."

"I wish she would give me the chance," was the prompt reply. "What do a man's sins signify to man when he is lying in the earth, answerable for his shortcomings to God, and God only?"

"But Miles Barthorne is not dead."

"Not dead!" repeated the Colonel, with an involuntary expression of repulsion. "Well, what does that matter to me?" he added, after a pause. "If she will only give me the right to stand between him and her—between her and the world—she may be as happy as I can make her."

"But she won't give you the right; and she cannot stay at Fisherton, and she must not come to me; so I want your help. How am I to find a lady of limited income with whom the poor child shall be happy? I tell you candidly, I am not so well off as people think. When my father-in-law died I thought myself a rich man; but the profits from the business are not so good as I supposed them to be; and further, he had engaged in contracts and speculations which have crippled the firm considerably.

"Of all this I knew nothing when I left Bella with the Wrights, and it is a fact I cannot afford to continue to pay a hundred a year for her. Besides, if anything were to happen to me—if I were to fail, or die, or——"

Colonel Leschelles cut relentlessly across this list of possible casualties by saying:

"You want my advice—it is this: Permit your niece to earn her own living. Virtually she has been doing so at the Wrights'; only they let her work hard, and received a large sum of money for graciously allowing her to perform it."

"I should not like her to be 'put upon,'" answered Mr. Irwin, reverting to a phrase culled out of his early vocabulary. "I am so fond of Bella. You do not know what we two have gone through together."

"And she so young, poor girl!" said the Colonel, pityingly. Mr. Irwin had been thinking of himself when he spoke. Colonel Leschelles thought of Bella as he heard. "It is quite clear," he went on, "that, even if you had no fancy to continue to act the part of generous patron to Mr. Wright, your niece would find life at the rectory somewhat unpleasant. Mr. Wright's dear Selina is, as he himself would admit, but a woman, after all; and she has a good many feminine weaknesses, amongst them jealousy, which is a quality that does not usually promote domestic happiness. Of course poor Mr. Wright felt the loss of the Medburn lands and beeves dreadfully; but he almost got over his annoyance whilst I was talking to him, and began to consider, if your niece married the Baronet, he might still make a good thing out of him. With Mrs. Wright, however, the case will be different.　To the last day of her life the wound will rankle; and, her own time for conquest being over, she will dislike and distrust a girl who has proved herself so formidable a rival against her daughter."

"I can see all that," remarked Mr. Irwin impatiently.　"What I cannot see is where I am to place her."

"I have sounded your niece as to her wishes," answered the Colonel.　"Her first idea was to return to the French school, and make herself useful by teaching English to the younger children.　'Thanks to Mrs. Wright, I think I should be able to do that now,' she said.　Evidently she is anxious not to be more of an expense to you than can possibly be avoided.　I cannot tell you how sweetly she spoke of your love for and kindness to her—how earnestly she assured me you would share your last shilling with her; but the refrain of everything was, 'I want to work.　I shall be happier when I am very, very busy.'"

There was a little break in the Colonel's voice.　If he had been selfish, still he sorrowed for Bella's sorrow with as true and tender a sympathy as ever mother felt for the heart's grief of an only child.

"To cut the matter short, we decided that, with your approval, I should write to a friend of mine who is looking out for a young lady to act as amanuensis and companion.　She is one of the most amiable persons I ever knew—a thorough gentlewoman, who spends her life and income in trying to do good. With her your niece would be safe from all impertinent questioning; and I trust, in time, she may be happy.　Before I left home this morning I wrote this letter.　If you read it, you will see how I have put the matter."

Mr. Irwin took the enclosure out of the envelope and read; then, with a sigh, he said, "Nothing could possibly be better. Poor child!—poor Bella!"

"I will see you again in the course of a few days," remarked the Colonel, rising.

"Thank you—and I will let Wright's note remain unanswered until then."

"You will have another from him," suggested Colonel Leschelles.

"Probably two or three.　The man has a mania for scribbling."

"He makes a very good thing out of it, I fancy," was the

reply ; and the pair shook hands, and the Colonel went out of the hot office into the hotter streets, leaving Mr. Irwin to consider the interview and Bella's position.

"He would marry her, knowing all about the public scandal. As for *the other matter*, that is between Bella and myself. There is a great deal in what Leschelles said about a man's sins being little to any one when he can sin no more ; and if it were not that I am so mixed up in the business, and that Barthorne may return at any minute, I would tell the Baronet all about the matter, and let *him* decide."

If Colonel Leschelles had heard this sentence, he could not have formed a more accurate opinion of Mr. Irwin than he did.

"There is more in that old business than I know or than he told me," thought Bella's elderly suitor. "Mr. Irwin is keeping back something which concerns himself. And as for being so fond of his niece—pooh! He is proud of her ; but the man has not it in his nature to be one-half so fond of any other person as he is of himself."

CHAPTER XXIX.

FORTUNE AGAIN FAVOURS MR. WRIGHT.

In November, Fisherton, as a residence, was not a place to desire.

Gone were the flowers of May and the glories of August, and in their stead water reigned supreme—the fields were swamps— the roads muddy—the aspect of Nature gloomy to a degree beyond description. Even Mr. Wright, whose cheerfulness was proof against almost anything except a visitor from Reuben's and who had an affection for a good London fog, declared at breakfast on one particular Sunday morning that the weather was enough to " depress a kitten."

The younger children and Mrs. Wright having colds, Mr. Wright intimated that he considered they would be much better at home than "in that damp church ; " to which arrangement Selina, nothing loth, assented, and perhaps, as he stepped out into the cheerless weather, Mr. Wright felt he also would have preferred a seat by the fireside to the atmosphere that sent a chill through his bones. A miserable morning—cheerless, raw, heavy; not at all the sort of morning any one would have selected on which to preach, to almost empty pews, a sermon which, for its production, had required both time and thought.

So many persons had evidently been of one mind with the Rector, that they were better at home, as to render his congregation a very limited one. Nevertheless, bad though the weather might be, it had not deterred one stranger from venturing to church—a modest, unassuming kind of man apparently, who resolutely refused all offers of a prominent position, and sat in a dark corner under the organ-loft, an attentive listener to Mr. Wright's utterances.

When the service was over he did not leave with the rest of the congregation, but sauntered up the aisle, his hands crossed behind his back, looking around with the air of one interested in the architecture and general appearance of the building. Finally he found himself close to the door of the vestry-room, which he opened without ceremony, and so came upon Mr. Wright, who was buttoning up his top-coat, preparatory to venturing out into the rain, which by this time had begun to fall heavily.

" How are you ? " asked the stranger, stretching out his hand.

The Rev. Dion, looking a little surprised and somewhat displeased, replied that he was very well.

" You don't remember me," suggested the other.

" Oh, yes, I do, perfectly ! " answered Mr Wright, " but it is a very long time since we met."

Which sentence was true so far as it went.   Mr. Wright did recollect the face in which he stared, though when he had seen it last he could not decide. He knew a long time had elapsed, of that he was certain; but he was unable to call to mind whether it belonged to a money-lender, to an attorney's clerk, to a sheriff's officer, or to a pawnbroker.

The other, looking on, laughed and said:

"Come, Wright, confess you don't remember me. You may recollect you have seen me somewhere, but you can't imagine where. Well, I suppose I am changed. I have had lots of ups and downs, and the downs don't made a fellow look younger. As for you, I'd have known you anywhere. If I'd met you out in Africa, I'd have said, 'Holloa, here's Wright, turned missionary.' If I'd seen you with your head shaved, and no end of frippery adorning your person, officiating in Rome, I'd have said, 'Here's Wright, turned Papist.'"

"And pray, sir, may I inquire who you are, who would, under the impossible circumstances you mention, have made the remarks just quoted?" asked Mr. Wright, drawing himself up, and swelling out perceptibly at the breast pockets of his top-coat.

Though he had a keen sense of humour, he writhed under even the suspicion of being ridiculed. This is an anomaly, I am informed; but if so, it is one frequently to be met with.

"That will do, Wright; that is capital," went on the stranger, whom the Rev. Dion mentally anathematized as a "brute." "Nothing could be better; that is the style I want. By-the-bye, I did not think much of your sermon this morning; it was fair —yes, above the average, certainly; but not what you used to deliver in the jolly days, when you were lecturer at old Innocents. Lord, what times these are to look back on! I can do my champagne every day if I like, but it never tastes as the familiar 'bitter' did then."

"Good gracious!" cried the Rector, with a tragic start, as the other finished, "you must be Ned Cahoon."

"At your service," said the gentleman with the four-honourable-professions-already-mentioned cast of countenance; and then the pair shook hands again in a much more friendly manner; and Mr. Wright, who had pricked up his worldly ears at the little word about champagne, said:

"My dear fellow, I am delighted to see you; who would have thought of your turning up at Fisherton? Come and dine with us. Pot-luck, you know, and a hearty welcome for sauce."

"All right," answered Mr. Cahoon, slipping his hand under the Rector's arm, and in this affectionate manner the pair walked beneath the shelter of two umbrellas along the roads of Fisherton, which were by this time of the consistence of Thames mud, back to Selina and the children.

" Beastly place this," remarked the visitor, who was possessed of an admirable, if occasionally disconcerting, frankness.

" We cannot always choose our places in this world," said Mr. Wright, with the air of a man who, having modestly asked only for daily bread, felt intensely disgusted at nothing better being given to him.

" Nor in the next, if all you parsons say is true," retorted his companion ; "which brings me back to what I said in the vestry. You 've gone off in your preaching, Wright : how does that happen ? "

" My dear fellow, who do you suppose could preach in such a hole as this ? " answered Mr. Wright, emulating the candour of Mr. Cahoon.

" Well, there 's something in that, to be sure," observed the other reflectively. " Fill the house, turn up the gas, let the organ peal loud enough, and the singers shout till they could be heard at the gates of the seventh heaven.   That is the sort of thing— eh, Wright?—to stir up the eloquence of a fellow who has any eloquence at all.   What congregations you used to draw at Innocents !   Do you never feel, old boy, like the racehorse, who, having once sniffed the battle afar off, longs to break loose from his paddock, and find himself in the thick of the *mêlée* once again ? "

Mr. Wright paused. Though the rain was then pouring down, he stopped in the middle of the miry side-path, and said :

" My dear friend, you are quite correct.   This place is killing me, mentally and physically.   But why should I complain? What would be the use of my complaining? I am here because it is good for those dearest to me that I should be here, where I am likely to remain for the rest of my natural life."

" No chance of preferment, then ? " suggested Mr. Cahoon.

" Not the slightest.   A few months ago I should have made a different answer ; but that is all gone and past, and I am left stranded.   I feel now just like a ship which, after waiting and waiting for a tide never destined to come, remains on some inhospitable coast till it drops to pieces."

" Humph ! " said the other.   " I did not myself know ships were sentient creatures ; but that sort of thing is your business; and I have no doubt you have mastered the complexities of the metaphor thoroughly.   I cannot say I understand your simile, but I do understand that Fisherton has disappointed you."

The Rector paused before he replied.　" Be frank if you can, but prudent always," was one of the maxims Mr. Wright would have engraved in a good, gentlemanly, clerical sort of hand, had he been invited by an enterprising publisher to eliminate from his experience and imagination a series of maxims likely to prove useful to the rising population of Great Britain ; and accordingly the Rector was prudent now.

" I cannot say," he answered at last, " that Fisherton has disappointed me.　I knew when I came here the amount of the emolument to be expected.　If I did not know how far such a honorarium would go with a man in my position, it was not the fault of Fisherton, or—I suppose—of myself."

" Certainly not," agreed his companion cheerfully.　" Fisherton, no doubt, has been accustomed to having its religious wants attended to by a clergyman either of very ample means, who treated it superciliously, or by a clergyman of no means or brains, accustomed to look at every penny, who treated it indifferently, and did just as little work for his salary as an honest parson might ; but of a person like yourself, possessed of many preaching talents and no money, Fisherton, misguided, unsophisticated, behind-the-age, sleepy, stupid, proper Fisherton, has really no knowledge."

" That is true enough," answered the Rector ; " though I cannot imagine how you come to know so much about our village.　And that reminds me that I have never asked you how you happen to be here ? "

" I am here on a little matter of business, but it can wait for awhile," was the reply.　" Now tell me all about yourself, and the children, and Mrs. Wright, and so forth."

Mr. Wright did not consider the finish of his friend's sentence as strictly respectful, but as he knew that, whatever other virtues Mr. Cahoon might possess, any clear knowledge of *les convenances* was not amongst them, he condoned the offence, and still walking jauntily along the muddy roads under the driving rain, he gave his companion a *résumé* of his history since the old days when he lectured at Innocents, and Ned Cahoon was the life and soul of an amateur choir and sang bass with the best, and was often asked by Mr. Wright to walk back with him and partake of a cut of beef and a glass of " bitter "—procured from some confiding tradesman who felt quite satisfied that, although

the Reverend Dion had so many children, he could, nevertheless, pay his debts.

In those days Mr. Ned Cahoon was managing clerk to a
solicitor of doubtful reputation and large practice, who finally
leaving his clients to take care of themselves, and carrying off
with him a considerable amount of money which he probably
imagined might have caused some worldly anxiety to its owners,
Mr. Cahoon was thrown somewhat suddenly out of a situation
and a character.

People were shy about employing the ex-manager. "Like
master like man," they probably remembered ; and Mr. Cahoon
must have starved had his clerical friend not come to the rescue
and found him a small situation in one of those Religious
Societies which are supported by a philanthropic public apparently for the laudable purpose of paying salaries to persons who
might find a difficulty in earning salaries elsewhere.

Tiring eventually of this employment, Mr. Cahoon procured
for himself an appointment in the north of England, and Mr.
Wright lost sight of him.

But that fact made little or no difference in the pleasure with
which the Rector recognized his old acquaintance. Cahoon, who
was well learned in every shift and subterfuge of the law, had
in former times assisted Mr. Wright in many an ugly difficulty,
and more than once he helped that gentleman to make, *sub rosâ*,
a few pounds in a gentlemanly way.

Though never rich enough to lend, he was good enough to
put Mr. Wright in the way of obtaining loans, and in many cases
also he had instructed the guileless Rector how to avoid payment
of loans already incurred.

Further, Mr. Wright knew the signs and tokens of a prosperous man, when such an individual presented himself to his
observation, and already the Rector had taken note of the
cut and quality of his old friend's new top-coat, and could have
told to a sovereign the value of the clothes he stood up in.

More than this, he saw, as he himself said afterwards, "that
Mr. Cahoon wore rings of considerable value, that his studs
were not those which a poor man would have selected. that his
handkerchief was of cambric, and scented with some refined
and superior perfume."

Add to this that his hands—given to habitual griminess in
the days of "Innocents"—were now of a colour and quality

which Selina herself might have approved, and the reader will comprehend that so acute a reasoner as Mr. Wright drew satisfactory conclusions.

"We have only very humble fare to offer you," remarked the Rector, as they drew near the gate affording entrance to "REPOSE," as Mr. Wright had once entitled his latest residence when writing to his noble patron.

"That is of no consequence," said Mr. Cahoon considerately.

"Only a leg of mutton, boiled," explained Mr. Wright.

"Boiled leg of mutton will be a pleasant change. I never get it at home now."

"You are prosperous, Cahoon, I hope," said the Rector, looking him over with fond clerical interest.

"I can't complain; but I will tell you all about it after dinner. You have not afternoon service, I hope."

"Oh, dear, no!" answered Mr. Wright; "two sermons a day are enough for any man. Afternoon service, in any case, is an entire mistake. It is a sort of——"

"Two o'clock performance at Drury Lane," suggested Mr. Cahoon, as the Rector hesitated.

"Well, very much the same thing," agreed Mr. Wright jovially. "But here we are, here we are, and there are the children, God bless them! Don't run away, dears; or if you do, tell mamma I have brought an old friend to see her. She will be astonished, won't she, Cahoon?"

With his lips Cahoon said, "No doubt Mrs. Wright would be very much astonished to see him," but in his heart he considered it would be somewhat difficult to surprise either the Rector or his wife.

He had known Selina when the airs of youth still sat gracefully enough upon her, but he never could remember her as genuinely unaffected, or other than a ladylike humbug. Mr. Cahoon had taken the moral measure of so many men and women, that the Rev. Dion and Mrs. Wright were not likely to present any insuperable difficulties to his observation.

"Now guess who this is, Selina," said the Rev. Dion, unfurling his dripping umbrella, and presenting his friend to the admiring gaze of half a dozen children in the foreground, with Mrs. Wright standing in the drawing-room doorway, forming an elegant point of perspective in the near distance.

From the Rector's genial tone Selina took her cue.

"Oh!" she said, holding out her hand and advancing one step forward, "if I am to recognize who you are, you must stand where I can see you," and thus exhorted, Mr. Cahoon walked towards the drawing-room, and, smiling somewhat awkwardly, surrendered himself for contemplation ; Mr. Wright meanwhile uttering with silent lips "Cahoon," for the benefit of his wife, who, being in some respects a cleverer man than himself, exclaimed :

"I know you quite well, but I cannot recollect your name. Speak to me, that I may try if I can remember it ; but first let me say how glad I am to see you."

"Thank you, Mrs. Wright," said the new-comer ; "you made me welcome often in times gone by, and I don't forget your kindness to a struggling man."

"Why, you are—yes, certainly you are, Mr. Cahoon, who used to sing so beautifully at Innocents. Oh ! I am *so* glad to see you again. Mr. Wright and I have wondered often and often where you were, or what had become of you."

And then Selina, with an engaging smile, and a little lift of the left shoulder, which had been once considered captivating by officers and others, shook hands with Mr. Cahoon again, and welcomed him to Fisherton.

"Snuggish sort of place this, ma'am," observed Mr. Cahoon, as after being made free of the Rectory, he walked from window to window, and looked out in all directions upon acres and acres of submerged country ; "at the same time, I should prefer less water myself. It is a matter of taste, however."

"It is not a matter of choice here, though," struck in the Rector. "Whether we like the water, or not, we are bound to have it."

"This has been an exceptionally wet season," said Mrs. Wright, in kindly excuse of the forlorn landscape, "and one cannot have the pure air of the country without some of its disadvantages."

"Humph !" observed Mr. Cahoon, in a tone which caused the Rector to inquire whether he would not like to step up into his dressing-room before dinner.

"Warm water, Mary," cried the Rev. Dion, from the top of the kitchen stairs, whilst Mr. Cahoon stood half-way up the next flight, looking over the banisters, and smiling to himself.

Upon the whole, dinner was not an entire success. Dinner

rarely is when children have to be carved for at the same time as adults.

Mr. Cahoon made himself as pleasant as he could, and talked as much as was compatible with perpetual interruption from the darlings clustering round the board.

Unfortunately the familiar friend · had selected a day for his visit when, owing either to the state of the finances, to some crisis with the servants, or to one of those fits of utter carelessness and mental aberration to which both Mrs. Wright and Nurse Mary were subject, there was not a thing in the house fit for any one to eat. The mutton was tough and almost raw. The turnips were hot as Eastern pickles, and porous as sponges. The butter tasted of everything of which butter should not taste. The caper sauce was manufactured out of the berries of the nasturtium, and there were no potatoes.

The housemaid waited, however, very well, and Mr. Cahoon, in the absence of food, no doubt solaced himself by observing that the attendance was conducted upon the most correct principles.

As for poor Mr. Wright, he could have wept with vexation when he cut into the obnoxious leg, and felt the truth of its exceeding hardness unmollified by any careful culinary processes.

Nor did his heart grow lighter after the mutton disappeared; the joint only vanished to be replaced with an enormous apple dumpling, the crust of which was quite an inch thick.

"Dear, dear! dear, dear, dear! you cannot eat that, Cahoon," exclaimed the Rector, as he saw a helping of this remarkable pudding handed to their visitor.

"Can't I!" replied Cahoon cheerily, sprinkling as he spoke some of the coarse brown sugar which Mrs. Wright, who was wont occasionally to take inconvenient economical fancies into her head, had decided was quite good enough to be served with apples defended by such ample bulwarks; and Mr. Cahoon did try, working his way manfully through fruit, and cloves, and syrup, and pastry, till at length Mr. Wright, thrusting his own plate aside in disgust, desired the maid to take it away, adding,

"Don't make a martyr of yourself, Cahoon, out of any mistaken idea of politeness. Follow my example, and have some cheese."

At which juncture the housemaid, very red and flurried, looked at Mrs. Wright, and Mrs. Wright, apparently a little put out, said :

"I am sorry, dear—but when the cheese went down from supper last night——"

The Rector waved his hand and rose to his feet. He knew what was coming. Selina rose likewise, meekly and gracefully drooping her head. With a clatter the children dropped to their feet and folded their hands.

"For these and all Thy mercies," said the Rev. Dion, "may the Lord make us truly thankful !—Now, Cahoon, come into my sanctum, and have a comfortable tumbler."

"Heaven send there may prove no hitch about that !" thought Mr. Cahoon, as he walked into the Rector's study.

"I must apologize," began Mr. Wright, as he mixed the modest glass calculated to inspire happiness in a stranger even at Fisherton Rectory.

"Pray don't !" entreated his visitor. "You know I have been used to roughing it; and now that I am better off, my appetite is not one-half so good as it used to be. Nine times out of ten, rich people eat and drink only to please their cook and their butler. Now, what I like is this"—and he held up the familiar "Irish" between himself and as good a light as Fisherton, on that day, could offer to visitors.

"I can recommend it, at any rate," said Mr. Wright, relaxing.

"So can I. And now to business. I want to talk 'shop' to you, though it is Sunday. I suppose, however, your shop is not shop, even on a Sunday."

"Cahoon !" observed Mr. Wright impressively, "I just want to make one stipulation : do not be irreverent—do not speak lightly on sacred subjects."

"All right !" answered the other, with an appreciative twinkle in his eyes. "Usually, I am as grave as an archbishop ; but the sight of you has carried me back to times when I was younger than I am now, and—not so prosperous."

"You have been prosperous, then ?" said the Rector, who considered youth quite an indifferent subject in comparison with money.

"Or I should not be here," returned the other.

"Now, now, now ! don't be so unjust," exclaimed Mr. Wright in his most soothing tone.

"I am not unjust," returned Mr. Cahoon. "I never said,

nor thought, you would refuse me a welcome, even if I came
to you without a coat to my back. It is not that ; only, what
is the use of one poor devil going to bother another as poor as
himself, with an account of his pecuniary troubles? I have
had my ups and downs, as I told you before, but I am not
going to enlarge on the subject of the downs, as I am up now,
and mean to keep up."

"Always under Providence," suggested Mr. Wright, somewhat in the tone in which mothers admonish their children to
say "please," and "thank you."

"Implied, Wright. Pray consider all that sort of thing implied. You need not trouble yourself to question the soundness
of my doctrines. I have gone in for everything which is purely
and thoroughly respectable ; and I am bound to say the policy
has paid remarkably well."

With a deprecating wave of his hand Mr. Wright put aside
this remark. He could not allow it to pass quite unrebuked,
but he was too anxious to come to the real purport of Mr.
Cahoon's visit to venture upon any verbal argument.

"Yes, it has paid," repeated Mr. Cahoon. "You remember
how poor I used to be in the old days at Innocents. Well, perhaps you may have heard of Huntingdon Park—a few years
since, meadows, afterwards brick-fields, after that a suburb of
London covered with handsome villa residences, much affected
by City gentlemen able to pay long rents. Well, that estate is
mine ; and you may guess I am drawing a pretty penny out of it."

"Bless my soul !" cried the Rector, "is it possible? From
the bottom of my heart I congratulate you. No man ever
deserved success better. And yet I am astonished !"

"You cannot be more astonished than I am," was the reply.
"As for the deserving part of the business, however, perhaps
the less we say about that the better. I have worked hard, it
is true, but——"

"Don't malign yourself, my dear friend," interposed Mr.
Wright, who beheld in imagination a cheque handed to him as
a thank-offering for mercies vouchsafed.

"To come now to the point," said Mr. Cahoon. "A church
is badly wanted on the property ; and it has occurred to me
that, if you wish a change, there is the very opening for you."

"Thank you !" answered the Rector. "It is very good of
you to think of me—thank you greatly."

But he uttered the words in a crestfallen tone, and sipped his punch less in triumph than by way of consolation.

"If you don't take kindly to the notion——" suggested Mr. Cahoon.

"It is new to me—it has come upon me by surprise. A person situated as I am is obliged to be very cautious. When a man has given hostages to Fortune, he cannot afford to play at pitch-and-toss with Success."

"That is very true," agreed Mr. Cahoon. He knew his man of old, and understood perfectly what was the matter with him; for which reason he refrained from further observation, and turned his eyes, with an appearance of much interest, on the Rector's bookshelves.

"How much, now, do you suppose," began Mr. Wright at last, "what do you imagine the value of such a living would be?"

"Anything you could make it between two hundred and fifty and twelve hundred a year."

The sound of that twelve hundred a year was pleasant to Mr. Wright, but he would not confess the fact.

"You see, one would have to give up all one's independence," he remarked.

"Do you think so?"

"Under the voluntary system, one can only live by currying favour with rich men."

"Humph! It seems to me much the same under any system. But no doubt you know all about the matter much better that I."

"You see—to give up a certainty for an uncertainty," said the Rector coyly.

"Yes—all such steps require consideration. So far as I am concerned, the matter stands thus. We must have a church on the estate, and I thought that such a church might suit you. We can put up a temporary iron structure as a beginning, and then build a permanent church when enough money has come in for the purpose. Of course I should guarantee you, or any other likely man, a certain income until the pews were all let; and when the church is built, no doubt some arrangement could be made to include a suitable parsonage in the scheme.'

Before the Rector's eyes that scheme seemed to be growing brighter and brighter still; but, diplomatical'y, he remained from showing how fair the prospect was beginning to appear.

"I suppose you don't want an answer to-day?" he said.

"I don't want a decision, if that is what you mean," answered Mr. Cahoon; "but I should like to know whether you mean to consider the matter. If not, I must, of course, turn my attention elsewhere."

This was bringing affairs to a crisis; and any other man except Mr. Wright must have felt compelled to face it. Mr. Wright, however, rose equal to the occasion.

"Let us consult my wife," he suggested. "She is twice as clever in worldly matters as I am—although she is the most unworldly creature living."

"You cannot do better than consult Mrs. Wright," was the reply. But Mr. Cahoon laughed to himself as he uttered the words, and remembered how utterly in accord he had found Mr. and Mrs. Wright on almost all worldly subjects in those bright days at Innocents, long departed.

Mr. Wright rang the bell (he was determined Mr. Cahoon should see there was no collusion between him and Selina), and desired the servant to inquire if Mrs. Wright could come to the study for a few minutes.

"Selina, my dear," he said as Mrs. Wright entered the room, "we want the help of your clear head."

"Yes," added Mr. Cahoon, with a bow, handing her a chair as he rose, "we have got into a little difficulty, and we shall never creep out of it unless you give us the benefit of your opinion."

Hearing which, Selina—who had already telegraphed a look to her husband, asking, "Is anything wrong?" and receiving another look in reply, which said, "All right; money to be made" —accepted the proffered chair with graceful ease, and then, glancing at Mr. Cahoon with a languid smile, gave it to be understood that her "clear head" was at the service of anybody who chose to make use of it.

"By Heaven! she is the best man of the two," thought Mr. Cahoon, as he saw how thoroughly she went into the subject. "Wright is but a fool to her. It is a pity she won't see after the cooking, though—thinks herself a cut above it, I fancy. Well, we can't have everything, and she is a woman no fellow need feel ashamed to say is the wife of his parson."

"It would be so desirable an arrangement for the boys, Dion," she remarked.

" I never thought about that.   See what it is to have a wife, Cahoon."

" Most strongly I advise you to consider the matter in all its bearings," she continued.

" Very well, my dear; I will, then.   Meantime, Cahoon, I am most grateful to you for bearing me in mind."

" There was a great deal of selfishness mixed up with my friendship," explained Mr. Cahoon with needless frankness.

" Tush !" said the Rector.   " We know how much selfishness there is about Edward Cahoon—don't we, Selina ?"

" You are a mass of selfishness, are you not, Mr. Cahoon ? You never went out of your way to serve a friend ; you never worked night and day for those unable to repay you in any way. Oh, yes, indeed, you are a mass of selfishness—for you are kind, and good, and generous, only to serve your own purposes. We understand that perfectly."

And then, with a little gasping sob, Mrs. Wright put her handkerchief to her eyes, and her hand towards Mr. Cahoon ; who, taking it, said :

" Upon my honour, Mrs. Wright, if I had not believed your husband would do well at Huntingdon Park, I should never have mentioned it."

" Poor dear Ned Cahoon !" remarked the Rev. Dion that night to his wife, " he is just the same as of old."

" Yes," she agreed.   " But he has much more in his power than formerly."

" That place might be made worth a thousand a year," said Mr. Wright.

" At least," agreed his wife.

" Though it would not have done to seem too much elated, I feel that, at last, fortune has relented in our favour," observed the Rector.

" But what about the debts ?" asked Selina.

" Cahoon must see to them."   And, having thus spoken, Mr. Wright fell asleep.

CHAPTER XXX.

ON THE WAY FROM CHURCH.

On the very same day as that on which the Reverend Dionysius Wright found, to quote Selina's version of the affair, that "Providence had opened another door of escape from their difficulties," Bella Miles, towards whom the Rector's thoughts had more than once during the progress of dinner turned regretfully, walked, under a November sky, from the house of her new friend or patroness, to church.

She had thought in work to find distraction, but she was far less happy with Miss Grahame than at Fisherton. Her life was outwardly peaceful enough, it is true, but it was, to quote Mr. Wright, the peace of stagnation. Existence, so far as events or interests were concerned, seemed suddenly to have come to a standstill. In Miss Grahame's home the routine of one day was the routine of that which preceded and that which should follow it. Externally there was no difference, except such as might be caused by the state of the weather or of Miss Grahame's health. If she was pretty well, she read prayers in the breakfast-parlour; if she was not well, she read prayers in her dressing-room; if she was very ill, Bella read prayers to the assembled domestics, all old and feminine, in Miss Grahame's bed-chamber. It was the home of a good and Christian and charitable woman, who out of her abundance gave liberally, and who led the calm, monotonous life which is at once so eminently respectable and so painfully dull, that girls who "have nothing to complain of, and are only discontented," beat their hearts out in vain struggles to escape from its bondage.

To Bella such an existence seemed simply a living death. From her father she had inherited some of his excessive vitality; and the sluggish waters of the life on which her own vessel now lay becalmed, filled her soul with an unspeakable despair.

Between herself and the gentle invalid, who, having early lost her lover, relinquished the world and all its pleasures forthwith, and lived the life of a hermit for the sake of memory, there yawned a gulf which all the girl's sympathy was unable to bridge across.

Her early memories, her later experiences, her young quick pulses, had nothing in common with the pensive lady who could think of little save her dead, her religion, and her poor; whose only recreation was almsgiving; whose only pet was an old, half-blind, half-deaf, wholly disagreeable King Charles; who having, at the time of her lover's death, stopped all the clocks of her life, could not understand how other people were able to bear the ticking caused by natural interests in their own; who had never had any secret to keep in the whole of her life, and who was as innocent of the world and the world's ways, of its sins, sorrows, pleasures, disappointments, as a dead baby.

Amongst other feelings which she had outlived was curiosity, and Bella was consequently left in perfect peace as regarded her antecedents. Colonel Leschelles having informed Miss Grahame that some sad circumstances were associated with the young girl's earlier years, she found herself accepted as one who had a few melancholy memories, concerning the nature of which, however, inquiry never was made, less because Miss Grahame happened to be a gentlewoman, than because she had survived the power of being interested save in the condition of the poor and the state of her friends' souls.

Coming from the bosom of a clergyman's family, the lady had anticipated much holy pleasure in holding intercourse with a young saint; but it may readily be believed that from Mr. Wright Bella had, on the whole, acquired more worldly than spiritual lore; which, indeed, can well be understood when we remember how far unconscious teaching excels that of line and plummet. Miss Grahame, therefore, being unable to exchange sentiments with her young companion, was fain to improve the girl's spiritual state by making her read aloud volumes of good books—which Bella did with an edifying composure, her thoughts meanwhile being miles distant. Of the girl's passionate longings to be able to do right—of the struggle she was maintaining against herself —of the stern resolves she was always making, that if her parents had done ill, she would try, Heaven helping her, to do well— of the utter conviction of her own weakness in being unable to cast the memory of her lover out of her mind, and of her own wickedness in sometimes falling into daydreams concerning him, from which she always awakened, as if she had been really asleep, with a start—Miss Grahame, of course, could have no knowledge.

She never saw anything but an extremely pretty girl with a thoughtful, downcast face, whom Colonel Leschelles wanted to make his wife, and who, no doubt, would some day marry him, when she became sufficiently a child of grace to care little whom she married, so long as he could help her to do the Lord's work.

"Crucifying our vile affections" was a favourite phrase on Miss Grahame's lips; but it seemed never to occur to her that all the best years of her life she had spent in offering up worship to a dead idol, and making unto herself a god of her early love; for which reason it came to pass that Bella Miles led at Miss Grahame's a life calculated, morally, to do her even less good than the life which she had experienced at Fisherton.

It was an introspective life, which is usually a weakening life to the moral sense; it was an idle life, which is trying to physical health. She had nothing to take her out of herself, her past, her future; of all the hundred interests she made for herself at Fisherton, not one remained. Servants did everything for Miss Grahame except read to her, and write at her dictation; if she were more than ordinarily ill, it was her maid who sat up with and nursed her, the cook who prepared the jelly and the beef-tea; and there seemed, therefore, little for Bella, once busy Bella, to perform, save the part of spectator in this drama of still life.

Not even Bella's superb constitution could stand up against the monotony of so terrible a dead-and-alive existence. She grew thin, her cheeks lost their roundness, her eyes their brightness. When Miss Grahame could dispense with her presence the girl went down to the seaside, and, sitting on some rock overlooking the lonely expanse of waters, would cry as if her heart were breaking,—cry for the loneliness of her life, cry for the loneliness of the life she felt it was only right hers should be.

From the thought of mother and father she shrank with equal dread. In her childhood it may be imagined she had met with but scant kindness from either. In such leisure time as his life boasted, her father had occasionally, even towards the latter part of his West Green life, been able to bestow a good-natured word and kindly look on his only child; but of her mother, Bella's longest memories were of scoldings and slappings, and such other indignities with which a disappointed woman is too apt to vent her temper upon the nearest and most helpless object.

Every day in her short experience had since her separation from her parents been removing her farther from them. If she had ever loved them, she loved them no longer; if she had ever wished to be reunited to those to whom she owed what gratitude might be involved in the gift of birth, that wish had long ago given place to utter dread of some still indefinite period when they and she would in the ordinary course of events resume, but with a difference, their old positions.

What she wished for, what she desired, it would have proved utterly vain to explain. What she said to herself was that somewhere far, far away, her father and mother were well and—happy. Beyond that she dare not go in the matter of self-examination, for otherwise she would have found the one vehement desire of her nature was never to look upon the face of either evermore.

At Miss Grahame's she had ample time to consider her position, to think how it would fare with her if, with wealth at his back, her father returned and claimed his only child.

Strange to say, she never thought of him as poor; she had never seen him in any grievous strait until that night when, through her mother's folly, his life was placed in jeopardy; she had faith in his talent, his brains, his readiness, as one might have in the strength of a strong man whom one has never seen reduced to weakness.

To her he was a mental athlete; to her he always so remained in memory, through every hour of her life in which memory recalled him. But she did not love her father: with a terrible grief she, in her lonely life, realized this fact; if she had ever loved him, the love was dead and gone, and dread alone lived in its place.

And Bella hated herself for not loving her father. There are parents for whom under all circumstances it is possible to retain an affection; on the other hand, there are parents to whom it is possible to retain an affection under none.

Sentimental writers ignore this last possibility, but matter-of-fact authors are compelled to acknowledge that it is quite possible for a parent to hate a child and for a child to dislike a parent.

In the midst of Bella's self-communings, however, there came from the outside world one of those facts which rouse people from the contemplation of artificial evils.

"I have news from Australia," wrote Mr. Irwin. "Your father is dead. He was robbed and killed when bringing gold to Melbourne. Your mother it is who sends me the tidings.

"She talks of remaining in Australia for the present; I trust she will marry again, and stay there permanently. I will run down the first opportunity, as there are several matters it is ecessary I should discuss with you."

That was all. As in a mirror, Bella beheld reflected in her uncle's letter the thoughts which had been filling her own heart. She saw he felt her father's death to be an unutterable relief, and that he expected her to share his feelings. She had got her wish now: one parent, at all events, would trouble her no more; and then, in an agony of remorse, Bella wept sore for the father whose faults, so far as she was concerned, were blotted out by the hand of death.

It was at night this letter arrived; and next morning the girl's heavy eyes and pale face attracted Miss Grahame's attention.

"What is the matter with you, Bella?" she asked. "Are you ill? has any one vexed you, or have you any bad news?"

It was one of Miss Grahame's good days, and consequently the foregoing exhaustive inquiry was made at the breakfast-table.

Then, after one or two vain attempts to answer, Bella so far mastered her voice as to say that she had heard of the death of a near relative; whereupon Miss Grahame, after condoling with her in a gentle and useless manner, said:

"I trust, dear, you have comfort in this matter, and that she died in the Lord."

"I don't know," answered Bella, covering her face with her hands, and sobbing out her explanation. "My uncle gives me no particulars of that kind: and it was not a woman, Miss Grahame—it was a man. At one time he did not lead a good life—and—and oh! may I go to my own room, please?"

That was all the plaint she ever made to any human being. Even when her uncle came down, he found she could talk as quietly and rationally about the matter as he himself. "It was better," she agreed; and then, in the watches of the night, she cried and fretted till her health began to fail, and even Miss Graname s anxiety was aroused concerning her.

"I am afraid, Bella, this place is too dull for you—that you are not happy here," she at length suggested.

"Oh, Miss Grahame!" was the answer, "I am as happy here as I could be anywhere. I am far happier than I deserve—than I could be in most places."

"As to the deserving part of your sentence, no doubt you are right, dear," said the lady in her soft, plaintive tones; "all lives are happier than they would be if strict justice were meted out."

"Not all, surely," pleaded Bella, "not all?"

"All," repeated Miss Grahame, with as much sternness as it was in her nature to assume. "And yet, still," she added, "as in this world the lot of some girls seems to fall in pleasant places, I could wish, child, that your lot were more free from trouble than appears to be the case at present. You are so young," she went on, with a little pathetic break in her voice, "and you try to be so good."

"But I am not good," said Bella, with a fresh memory of her unspoken sins recurring to her.

"You will try to be good, I know," remarked the kindly though unpractical lady, who might, had she been wise as a serpent, have done Bella much benefit at this precise juncture; "and God, in His own good time, will help you to find His eternal peace."

Which, being translated into plain English, meant that, sooner or later, Miss Grahame trusted Bella would marry Colonel Leschelles, and occupy herself in works of charity and of religion. Life had at last narrowed itself into the smallest dimensions compatible with retaining the slightest interest in the well-being of others; and to dispense soup and flannel petticoats, to distribute tracts, to subscribe liberally to missions, to swallow quantities of medicine and dwell upon her physical ailments, seemed to the invalid the whole pleasure and duty of woman. And all the time Bella's young heart was protesting against the useless monotony of such a grey existence, the quietness and peace of which might once have seemed to her desirable enough.

Through the winter months Miss Grahame never ventured out, and accordingly it came to pass that on that particular November Sunday when Mr. Cahoon made his proposition to Mr. Wright, Bella walked alone to church.

It was not raining, as at Fisherton ; but a leaden sky hung over land and sea, and the waves came rolling sullenly in upon a dreary, desolate shore—a scene and a day calculated to depress any one: but there was something in sympathy with her own thoughts in the sad expanse of sea and the gloomy canopy of sky ; and seating herself upon a great stone, Bella, looking with her outward eyes over the waste of water, let memory and imagination take her whithersoever they would.

Through the still, heavy air came the sound of the church bell, tinkling as if it were hung round the neck of some old ram. Not a living creature within sight, for, the shore being shingly, few persons cared to walk that way, for which reason Bella usually selected it in preference to the shorter and more frequented route.

At last she rose and wended her way to church. It was a small building, inside and out of the barn fashion, with an old red-tiled roof, with something resembling a dovecote in place of spire or tower ; with bare whitewashed walls inside, relieved by a few stained and discoloured marble tablets ; with a low gallery for the choir ; with square windows filled with small diamond-shaped pieces of greenish glass ; with a high pulpit, and without the smallest adornment of any kind, sort, or description. But, possessing a clergyman who could write a good sermon, and deliver it well afterwards ; who, though he had for audience, as a rule, few except farmers about as intelligent as their own cattle, and labourers a little less intelligent than the animals they tended, still brought his best Sunday after Sunday, and gave it to them freely, casting his bread upon the waters in faith, that if it never returned to him, some fasting soul might, at a minute of dire extremity, eat of it and live.

Bella Miles loved that whitewashed old barn. Some of the best lessons she ever learned were taught her within its walls, although she oftentimes rebelled against the truths, the stern, unflinching truths, she heard uttered there.

Anything more widely different from Mr. Wright's style it would be impossible to conceive ; but the clergyman preached a truer, and higher, and holier religion than Mr. Wright, who, always groping after light, never really discovered it. Always, less or more, Mr. Wright preached himself ; always his older and, it may be, in some respects less gifted brother, preached God's Word to the best of his ability and understanding.

On that particular Sunday which brought about a change in Bella's life the Vicar took for his text these words: "The sins of the fathers shall be visited upon the children."

What he made of his subject it is no part of this story to tell. All that need be said is that to Bella Miles his sermon was full of a sad and terrible significance; and as she walked homewards, after the service was over, she pondered the mystery with that increasing thoughtfulness which had wrought so great a change in her.

She chafed under her lot. It is the misfortune of strong natures to be long in learning how to bear troubles meekly; and with this girl the one ever-recurring question that eternally perplexed her was, "Why should I suffer? What have I done, that life, before I am twenty, should appear so terribly hopeless? How shall I ever endure the length of the weary, weary years to come, when the last few months have dragged on so slowly? I must get away from this place. I was happy enough at Fisherton; I was very happy there until——"

And at that point she would break down. She had been happy until she understood precisely how the sins of her father affected her own life. Yes, the sins of her father were being visited on his child. Pitiless as the sea, changeless as the great hills, was the law which declared that, in this world, at all events, the evil a man does shall not lie down with him in the grave, but continue to live and sting long after his own career has ended.

There is nothing vaguer than the theology of youth—nothing at some times blinder than its faith—nothing at others more daring in its questionings; and as Bella walked by the seashore, an idea, which had often occurred to her before, presented itself once more, namely, the terrible similarity there often seems between natural and Divine laws; unchanging and unchangeable, remaining ever the same, while man frets out his little day and spends his strength for nought.

Unconsciously almost, she repeated aloud part of a hymn which had been sung before the sermon—repeated it with the sea moaning an accompaniment, and the grey sky making the scene one of utter gloom.

> "Yet with the woes of sin and strife
>   The world has suffered long;
>   Beneath the angel strain have rolled
>   Two thousand years of wrong."

Two thousand years—making due allowance for the exigencies and exaggeration of poetry !

Two thousand years of people sinning and suffering, sowing wickedness, and garnering themselves, or leaving others to garner, the evil grain !

Two thousand years, and she, an unit amongst the millions who had lived and sorrowed—she, a mere mote in the sunbeam of that weary stretch of time, was adding her mite of trouble to the giant mountain already accumulated by the efflux of time and the accession of wrong and misery !

At bottom she was a good girl—a good and a religious—but she could not help, as all this occurred to her, sending a wail across the sea.

"Why was I born? why should I ever have lived here if I am to suffer more and more, as the years go on, for a sin I did not commit?" And then the tears came welling up in her eyes, and her heart grew softer, and she prayed a quiet little prayer that she might become thankful instead of thankless—able to remember the mercies vouchsafed, rather than the trouble permitted.

Then slowly, while the sea kept sobbing and fretting, and the grey sky looked down upon a sombre earth, she walked homeward, steadfastly determined to begin from that day a better life, and to be content with the lot which seemed most fitting for her.

"When I grow older," she thought, " I will go out and nurse the sick, and try to comfort those who have met with trouble. I will try to forget the foolish past—my own past, with its dreams and its pleasures. It is right I should work, I like working hard, and some day I shall surely be able to find out what my hand was meant to do. Meanwhile——"

She stopped at that point, suddenly—stopped, while her face turned first red and then white, for, as she rounded a little jutting rock, she suddenly met the man who had never, poor child! been absent from her thoughts since the days which were so happy and so miserable at Fisherton.

If he had ever felt doubtful concerning her feelings towards him, he must have been blind indeed had he then failed to read her secret in her eyes. Never had mortal beheld so glad a light in them as did he when she recognized him; and then, fast as it had sprung to life, the happiness faded out of her face, and the old look of trouble he remembered so well crept over and took its place.

"What have they been doing to you?" he asked, holding her cold hand in his, and looking anxiously at her. "Are you ill?"

"No," she said; "only not quite well; that is all, indeed."

"Miss Grahame told me you had gone to church, and that I should probably meet you if I walked by the shore. Will you sit down for a few minutes, or are you afraid of catching cold?"

"I am not afraid," she replied, and sat down on the same stone whence she had gazed over the sea a few hours previously; while he, leaning against the rock, began to speak.

CHAPTER XXXI.

THE FAMILY MOTTO.

"I could not keep away."

No answer. Only the far look-out seaward.

"And indeed I think it was high time for me to come and see after you."

Still no answer; but a deeper gravity settled down on the sorrowful face.

"My dear" (he did not draw nearer to her, except by voice, as he spoke), "will you give me the right to see after you always?"

Then she answered—not looking at him, but still over the sea:

"I hoped you had forgotten all about that long ago."

"Hoped! did you?" he said, and there ensued a dead silence. Sir Harry broke it.

"Bella," he began, "if you can only say truthfully that you do not like me—that you could never like me—I will go away at once."

"You had better, much better, go away," she answered.

"Not till you assure me that you do not care for me—that you could never care enough for me to marry me."

"I shall never marry any one," she said.

"My child, you are only fencing with my question. You evade replying to it because, as I hope, you do like me a little. And, oh! Bella, if it is as I believe, why should you make two lives miserable because of some foolish scruple or absurd obstacle which exists only in your own imagination?"

"You do not know—you do not know," was all her answer; but the waves caught it, and flung back a wailing response.

"And I do not want to know," he added, "unless, indeed, the knowledge might better enable me to combat your fancies. Take a case—I do not say a probable, but just a possible one —that you had got entangled with some person you discovered subsequently to be unworthy of trust, and that he had held a threat over you that you should marry no one else. I am just supposing such a case were yours, my dear. I have such faith in you—I have such faith that, if I knew for a certainty, now, some scoundrel was trying to trade on your fears, all I should ask would be the right to protect you from him—to stand between you and the world."

In her amazement at this speech she turned her head towards him. When he had finished, she said, "I do not understand what you mean."

It was difficult for him, after having spoken in the heat of excitement, to explain to her what he did mean in cold blood; but he managed, somehow, to tell what he had fancied—what he had feared might have been the case; and then Bella laughed.

For the first time in all their later interviews, he saw her eyes dance and her cheek dimple.

"Oh! no, no!" she exclaimed. "At the *pensionnat*, though some of the girls might be a little silly, such things were impossible quite for any one; while, as for me, I thought never of being cared for till I went to Fisherton; and you know all about that time, as I do."

She always, when excited, reverted to the French idiom, and her lover had never thought it so charming as at that moment, though she went on to add:

"My trouble had nothing to.do with love, neither with love-making, till you came ; and if you will only go away and forget me, I will bear it as I am able."

He was beside her now.

"My darling," he said, "I will never go away again. I will haunt you till you say 'Yes.' I have all most men would consider necessary to make life valuable, but without you I can honestly say life to me is valueless. Before I came down here your uncle told me the great obstacle to the gratification of my hopes had been removed. Do not waste your life and mine in dwelling upon imaginary difficulties. Marry me, and let us share whatever trouble the future my have in store together."

She remained silent for a long time—for so long a time that he felt tempted to speak himself, and would have spoken, but that he felt he might serve both better by possessing his soul in patience.

At last, almost with a gasp, she drew her gaze back from the sea over which her eyes had been wandering, and looking fixedly at the sand, asked, "Did my uncle tell you what the obstacle was which had been removed?"

"Certainly not. He might have done so had I inquired; but I did not want to know."

"It is better you should know. The obstacle he meant was my father—my father, who is dead."

Sir Harry stood amazed. He would not ask a question, but he was so evidently trying to comprehend her meaning that Bella said:

"When I met you at Fisherton my father was not really dead. He has died since I came here."

"My poor darling."

"Shall I tell you about him? Shall I tell you the terrible story?" she went on, rising. "I should be thankful to do it, though I know you will go away and leave me. But spare my uncle. Never repeat what I am going to say to any one. Let it be between us—you, I, and the great sea."

"You shall not tell me," answered her lover. "Whatever his sins or short-comings may have been, he is dead. No doubt he has suffered, so let everything concerning him now **rest.**"

But at that moment Bella felt strong enough to tell him the tale of sin and sorrow which had cursed her life. Her lips were opened, her tongue unloosed, and she began, not with any idea of making him her arbiter, but simply of telling him that which should part them for ever.

"You must hear me—I will tell you everything—everything When you know all, you cannot be sorry to leave me."

"Sorry to leave you, no," he interrupted; "for I never inten to leave you now. Let your father have been what he will, love his daughter, and I mean to marry you and try to make you forget the past. I want to hear nothing about your father —no matter what sins he committed. Being in his grave, if you can remember any good about him, do; if not, try and forget his faults. What rests between us to-day is a question relating solely to us two; not to my mother and your father, but to you and me—to me who love you so much; and to you, who I think love me a little. Marry me, dear, and end all doubts, all difficulties."

"I cannot," she whispered.

"That is what you say," he answered. "What I say is, you can. See, Bella, unless you are married already, you can marry me at once. Now, are you married?"

"Oh, no—no—no!" cried the girl. "I wish it were anything like that—anything of my—mine own—anything in which I had been wrong myself—I could then say all without trouble."

"And I wish nothing of the sort," he finished gravely. "So long as it is not your affair personally—so long, in fact, as you belong to no one else—I feel you belong to me. I don't care about father or mother, or brother or sister, or uncle or aunt— I care for you, and you only. I shall marry you, and you only. If I never marry you, I shall marry no one."

"Oh! let me tell you all," she pleaded. "After you hear what I have to say, you will be glad enough to leave me, and try to forget my name."

"Whatever you might have to tell, I should not leave you," he answered, "and you shall not tell me anything. Hereafter you must feel no pangs of conscience about having spoken of a father's shortcomings to your husband. All I want is you. If your father sinned, he is dead; let his sins die with him. My dear, you are morbid. You are young, you are ignorant of the world, and the follies, not to say crimes, men commit in it every day; and it is just because you are so young, so tender, so ignorant, so sensitive, that I long to call you my very own, and shield you for the future from every worldly blast which blows."

He was right; she did know nothing of the world; not even vaguely could she grasp all of sorrow, all of humiliation in the future, her father's sin might mean to this man who loved her —nay, so ignorant was she, that although she understood to some extent how far he was stooping from his high estate to love her, she had yet not the faintest comprehension how mad an act the world would consider his marriage.

So far Bella had thought of nothing save her father's sin as a barrier between them. As in the presence of a great light all lesser lights seem but darkness, so under the horrors of Barthorne's crime all other social considerations dwarfed themselves before his daughter's imagination.

Sir Harry had been much talked of at the rectory, but so had the lord to whom Mr. Wright owed his promotion, Colonel Leschelles, Mr. Morrison, and innumerable other people; and Bella had yet to learn the enormous distinction there is between bestowing your right hand in friendship, and linking your name, your fame, the honour of your house, the welfare of children yet unborn, with the antecedents of a total stranger.

What Montaigne says is right. Translating his meaning into decent English, other deities besides love should be present at a marriage which is likely to prove happy for the contracting parties. Love certainly; but prudence, and respect, and assurance of position, to say nothing of several matters too numerous to mention.

Ah, yes, of all these Sir Harry—generous, trusting, honest, honourable Sir Harry, who was as far above suspicion as he was above deceit, lost sight, as by the sea he pleaded his suit—not unsuccessfully.

She was so young, she could not but show that she loved him. She was so young, that when she began her story he found no difficulty in stopping its recital. She was so young, and this trouble was so new, she failed to conceal its effect upon her.

Well, well, what need is there to dwell longer on this part of the story?

Eventually Sir Harry carried the day. She agreed to refer the matter to her uncle. Her uncle, when referred to, saw openly no obstacle in the way of the marriage, and wrote privately to Bella that she would be worse than a fool to refuse the goods the gods sent her. Which remark disgusted Bella, and might have broken off the affair altogether had she not loved her lover.

Loving him as she did, she only stipulated that for a year there should be no talk of marriage, and that for the aforesaid period Sir Harry should not "consider there was any engagement, so as to know his own mind."

To which latter condition Sir Harry, knowing his own mind, and perhaps wishing the engagement kept secret, assented without reluctance, while to the former, considering the dead man was her father, he felt he could offer no objection, and so the affair drifted on through the winter. And spring came once again over the fields, through the woods, adown the rivers. Spring—bright, beautiful, heart-gladdening spring, burst in all her simple beauty upon the sight of men.

CHAPTER XXXII.

GOING WITH THE CURRENT.

BRINGING even to sick-rooms some of the freshness of reviving nature.

From her closely shut-up apartments Miss Grahame looked out with brighter eyes on the spectacle of a world waking after a winter's sleep. And what a winter it had been! Hail, rain, frost, snow, wind. At Fisherton the meadows lying near the Thames still lay a foot under water; while as for the Fisherton

roads, Mr. Wright said, " A man should have an extra hundred
a year for wading through them."

But it is not with Fisherton our concern is at present. Near
the sea the frost had not, of course, continued, or the snow
lain so long, as in the valley of the Thames ; but all the winter
through the rain had rained, and the snow fallen, and the wind
blown great guns in the district where Miss Grahame's house
was situated.

Therefore she felt, even in her heated, unventilated, stifling
rooms, something of happiness when the winter storms sank to
rest, and sunshine, though it was only the capricious sunshine
of the early spring-time, succeeded to storm.

" My dear," she said to Bella, as the girl arranged the pillows
in her easy chair, and wheeled the table, on which stood a vase
filled with violets, close to the window that commanded a view
of trees already beginning to put forth their leaves, " my dear,
should we not thank God for His seasons ? "

" I think we ought to thank God for everything," answered
Bella ; " but it is sometimes very hard to do so."   And then,
with a tender gesture, she drew the invalid's shawl closer round
her, and opened a window on which the spring sun shone
beneficently, and, after stirring the still welcome fire into a
blaze, took up one of the books Miss Grahame loved, and was
about to commence reading, when that lady stopped her.

" Come here to me for a minute," said that lady ; and Bella
obeying, Miss Grahame pushed the hair back from her forehead, and, looking at her steadily, asked—" What has changed
you so much during the course of this winter ? "

" Am I changed ? " asked the girl.

" Yes. You used to be sad ; now you are restless. You
have always been thoughtful for me, but you are more thoughtful
now. Your ways were from the first soft and gentle, but they
are gentler and softer now than they ever were before. Further,
you seem to take an interest in serious matters to a greater
extent than previously. Is it, dear, that you are forgetting the
world and its vanities, and seeing more clearly that nothing
except religion can confer peace here and give happiness hereafter ? "

For a moment Bella stood with a conventional phrase on her
lips ready for utterance. She had told herself over and over
again it was of no use talking to Miss Grahame as she might

to most people, and that it was better to humour her whims than to provoke discussion; but as she mentally repeated the conventional phrase over again, her better nature asserted itself, and she said:

"No, Miss Grahame, I am afraid I have not forgotten the world or its vanities either. If I am softer and more tender—I did not know I was either—it can only be because I am at times happy—oh! so happy. If I am more serious than I used to be, it is only because at times I am more miserable than you can imagine. I have promised to marry, and I am afraid—oh! I am so much afraid I have done wrong."

She covered her face with her hands as she finished, but Miss Grahame drew them away gently, and said:

"You have done quite right, my love. Think how happy you can make him."

"If I were sure of that—if I could only be sure of it," murmured Bella.

"Then I can assure you," persisted Miss Grahame. "In point of years it may appear an unsuitable match, but in everything else it seems to me eminently desirable. When did you write to him, my child? When did you end the long suspense? I suppose we may expect him back by the first possible steamer."

Then it all dawned upon Bella, and she cried out, "Oh! Miss Grahame, you are thinking of Colonel Leschelles, and I was talking about Sir Harry Medburn."

"About whom?" asked Miss Grahame, severely.

"About—the—the—gentleman who has called here two or three times during the course of the winter."

"What, that friend of the Colonel's?"

"Yes," rejoined Bella.

"Who is this Sir Harry Medburn? Get me Debrett, that I may see for myself."

With fear and trembling Bella got the book, and, opening it at the page where the glories of the Medburn family were set forth, handed it to Miss Grahame.

When she had read all Debrett had to say, she remarked:

"And so you have promised to marry this young man?"

"I have," Bella answered firmly enough.

"And may I ask how long all this has been going on?"

"It was 'going on,'" said the girl, "before I left Fisherton."

"Does your uncle know anything of the matter?"

"Everything," replied Bella, a little stiffly. "I have no secrets from my uncle."

"And he approves?"

"Entirely. I wish he did not. I wish he would look at the matter from the same point of view as I do."

"Are you not fond of this Baronet personage, then?"

"Not fond!"

She only repeated these two words, and yet Miss Graham understood that love had come upon this girl—as she said to herself—like an armed man, and taken her captive.

It was an unsuitable match; and yet, looking at Bella as she did with her poor weak eyes at that moment, Miss Grahame could not but acknowledge the Baronet might be excused.

Before her was the girl standing in one of those attitudes of unconscious grace which artists are sometimes able to transfer to canvas--standing, as that evil-famed ancestress of theirs might have done when, the devil leaving her for a time, the better part of her nature could assert its existence.

With no trick of attitude—with no affectation of expression—with a soft, dreamy light in her eyes and a little tremulous smile playing about her lips—she looked so fitted to be loved by any man, no matter how high his station, that Miss Grahame hesitated for a moment before she said, with a sigh:

"I hope you have asked for Divine guidance in the matter, my dear. Remember, the welfare of two lives is at stake. I do not usually attach much weight to the world's opinion, but when it says unequal marriages rarely prove happy, I am obliged to agree with it."

"Unequal?" repeated Bella, involuntarily.

"Yes," said Miss Grahame. "Of course I have no desire to speak slightingly of the great gifts wherewith God has endowed you. You are beautiful—you are accomplished—you are clever—you are amiable—but, as a rule, a man of high station, or, at all events, his friends, look for more than beauty and talent in the wife he presents to them." And then the lady was proceeding to state at length what the friends of a man in high station did look for, when Bella stopped her by saying:

"I know what you mean. I did not think of it before; but I see it all now—I see it all now."

"I hope you are not vexed with me," observed Miss Grahame. "I could not conscientiously have said less."

"Oh! no; not vexed. Only sorry I never thought of that before. I thought of other obstacles, but not of that. Shall I read to you now?" she asked abruptly, as if desirous to end the discourse.

"Not this morning," said the invalid. "You had better go out for a walk. Send Hughes to me, and do what you like until luncheon; but kiss me before you go, and say again you are not vexed."

"I am vexed with myself—only with myself," was the answer; and then the girl stooped and kissed Miss Grahame's withered cheek indifferently, as though her thoughts were hundreds of miles absent—as, indeed, they were.

By the afternoon's post there went two letters—one from Miss Grahame to Colonel Leschelles, then in America; the other from Bella to Sir Harry Medburn, to say the engagement must be considered at an end—that she had never thought as she ought to have done of the difference in their position until Miss Grahame put it plainly before her; and, now it had been put before her, she understood how wicked she would be to allow him to sacrifice everything for her sake.

The letter, written in hot haste, with the sting of Miss Grahame's remarks rankling in her heart—with all the old sorrow brought to life again and a new one superadded, was very earnest in its unstudied phraseology, in its singleness of purpose, and in its perfect and straightforward truth.

From her heart she wrote, without preamble, or disguise, or diffuseness more than ordinarily attaches itself to the productions of women.

It was for his sake—for his dear sake she indited the epistle; and whatever else may have remained obscure, no one reading her letter could fail to see that she loved him so utterly, so boundlessly, that self for her had, as far as he was concerned, ceased to exist.

"Yes, she would for his good give him up." She said so to God that night, weeping, on her knees, such tears as the very young alone can shed—tears which bring a virtue of relief with them. She said so when, braiding her hair and tiring herself next morning, she looked out on life—as life, she believed, must henceforth present itself.

But she thought he would answer to say farewell, at all events; and he did not answer. No word, no line came in response.

"He sees it now as I saw it all along," said the poor girl to herself, wandering by the seashore, beside which Miss Grahame's kindness gave her free leave to ramble and bewail her grief.

The days passed by, and still Sir Harry made no sign. Miss Grahame's hopes rose high. With all her soul—such portion of it, at least, as could still take part in mundane concerns—she hoped that eventually Bella might he induced to marry Colonel Leschelles.

When people grow elderly, their prejudices are generally in favour of the old. Concerning the probable doings of a man of twenty-five there must be always doubt; whereas the character of a veteran of above sixty may be considered formed.

Thus Miss Grahame argued, perhaps unconsciously. So many advantages were combined in such a match! If she had youth, he had money. If he were old, her belongings had no connection with the "upper ten."

Miss Grahame, a thorough Christian, entertained a Christian respect for gentle blood, and never, even by implication, had Bella suggested her relation to any one better than a nobody.

Thus, whichever way the matter was looked at, a beautiful sense of proportion obtained: on her side there was so much weight in the scale—on his side so much, all exquisitely balancing, and all eventually capable of resolving itself into a church being built somewhere, or a tribe converted somehow.

That was the broad view Miss Grahame took of life—missions here or missions there.

For the compassing of such purposes every life except her own was to be sacrificed. Did it matter in what weary schools human hearts were disciplined, so long as her medicine was regularly dropped into the stated amount of water? To her, most certainly not. Did it matter who lay cold in this world, so long as her pet converts were prevented from entering fires of an inconceivable heat in the next? Very little indeed.

Nevertheless, it is only fair to say that the conclusions she drew from entirely wrong premises were perfectly right. This is a fact worth noticing in connection with the conclusions generally of very silly people. By means of some mental road not given to wise men to follow, she decided the girl ought to marry Colonel Leschelles and ought not to marry Sir Harry Medburn. In which idea she was, unfortunately, correct; though she could not, between sunrise and sunset in a midsummer day, have given a sufficient reason for the faith that was in her.

Nevertheless, even while she believed her wishes were about to be compassed, she felt sorry to see Bella moping—poor dear Bella, who had nearly brought her to believe some things left in the world might be worth thinking about—who was never too tired, nor too sick, nor too sorry to attend to her lightest wish, and who had lightened her sombre home with youth and beauty.

The days passed by—there came no letter, no message of any kind. Was there ever so dreary a spring? thought the girl. She complained of the sunshine dazzling her eyes, of the glittering sea making her head ache, of the wind being too high, of the dust blowing along the roads. She felt as if she would have given anything to escape from Miss Grahame's even babble of inane talk—from her kindly-meant platitudes. For her even nature had lost its beauty. It was right for her to release him from so unequal an engagement. It was well for him to accept that release ; but he might have written one line. He might have sent her a note of farewell—something to keep her heart from starving—something on which in the future she could stay her pride.

But no note came. Bella moped about the house, and Miss Grahame, watching her, thought what a pity it was Sir Harry had ever crossed the girl's path.

As unexpectedly, however, as he had arrived some months previously, the young man appeared once again—this time asking to see Miss Grahame, and remaining closeted with that lady for more than an hour ; while Bella, unaware of his return, was slowing pacing the sands beside the sea. In ten minutes he had silenced Miss Grahame's arguments against unequal marriages, though he entirely failed to alter her opinion. He had all his life been accustomed to have his own way—so had his father before him—so had his father's father, and many another Medburn besides.

Fortunate was it for the family that their way was, upon the whole, a good one. Had the road they wished to travel led direct to ruin, they would have travelled it just as determinedly.

Wives and daughters and mothers had influenced the Medburn counsels only in the very smallest degree. In all matters the males had followed the bent of their own inclinations; and the women soon learned that their wisest policy was to stand aside. To her husband Lady Medburn had always deferred; and now she had given up the dearest wish of her heart, in order to please her son.

It was a shock at first to find every hope of a marriage between her son and his cousin must be abandoned. Little as her wishes had ever received in the way of encouragement, she never believed the project futile till her son told her he did not love the girl she wished to see his wife, and that he did love a total stranger.

Ill of a disease which must prove fatal eventually—which might take a sudden turn for the worse any day or hour, she resolved to speak seriously to her son concerning marriage—to tell him it was the wish lying nearest her heart to see him and Edith husband and wife before her death. And she did speak to him. In one of the pleasant rooms of the house where she had passed so many happy years, she talked of the death she was travelling on so surely to meet—of Edith—of himself— talked so tenderly and so solemnly, that, though he would fain have kept his secret from her, he could not do it. He was forced, almost against his will, to tell her that he loved, not Edith, but another, and that he would never marry unless he could wed Bella.

He broke his bad news tenderly and gently, as had ever been the fashion of the Medburns, even when they were crossing the wills of those nearest and dearest to them. But no tenderness or gentleness could greatly lessen the extent of the blow. Under it Lady Medburn sank, and her illness assumed so serious a character that for a time her life was in danger. It was during this period Bella's letter arrived, and when he read it Sir Harry took his resolution.

The moment he could leave his mother he would go to Mr. Irwin, explain his position, and obtain the sanction of Bella's uncle to an immediate marriage.

"There has been too long a delay already," he considered. "My darling must not be at the mercy of every old woman who conceives it to be his or her mission to see that the upper ten thousand do not marry imprudently. Once she is my wife.

no one dare speak to her of inequality of rank. Inequality, indeed! Why, she might be a princess! I won't write to her, though—I will take my answer to her myself. I will say nothing till I can say in person: 'My dear, I never mean to give you up; and I shall not leave the neighbourhood till you are my wife.'"

And so he waited day after day until the doctors should pronounce his mother out of danger for the time at least.

"I won't vex her any more about the matter," he thought. "I will get married, and then tell her. She will soon reconcile herself to the fact when discussion is useless."

But the rare tact which love teaches—even if nature has not been beforehand as an instructor—enabled Lady Medburn to save her son from committing an act he would always afterwards have regretted.

"I have been standing on the brink of the grave, Harry," she said, "and I would not that, when I am laid there, you should be able to remember I had ever thought of my own wishes first, of yours last. If she is good and true, and can make you happy, take her; only be quite sure, my dear, dear boy, it is you she is fond of, and not your title or your money."

For answer, he placed Bella's letter in his mother's hands. No studied epistle could have touched the lady as did that hurriedly-traced scrawl, containing words written in bitterness of spirit, straight from her heart.

"She loves you, Harry," was Lady Medburn's comment, when she had read to the end; and with a sigh his mother folded up the note and gave it back to him.

"My dear boy, I hope it will all prove for your happiness;" and she sighed again, and then added, "I will write a few lines to her—a few lines of welcome to my daughter that is to be."

So Sir Harry carried his point, as his father before him had been in the habit of doing; and it was an understood thing between him and his mother that he should endeavour to persuade Bella to marry him at once.

"I hope you will be very happy, Hal," said his cousin, after she had bid him good bye the morning he left for London. "Here is a little present worked by my own hand. Will you take it to her, with—my love?"

Her voice faltered a little; but she looked up at him with tearless eyes.

"God bless you, Edith!" he answered; and then he did what he had not done before since she was quite a little girl— stooped and kissed her.

Almost involuntarily she drew back, flushing painfully; then remembering, she touched his cheek with her lips, and repeating her former sentence, "I hope you will be very happy," flitted away.

Having carried the day with the ladies of his own household, Sir Harry's next anxiety was to gain over Miss Grahame; but Miss Grahame was not to be so easily won. He could silence her, and he did; but he failed to convince her. All he could extract in the shape of compromise was a promise to maintain a strict neutrality. She would not try to influence Bella one way or the other. She would place no obstacle in the way of the girl, and she trusted the marriage, if it took place, might be overruled for good. Concerning Bella herself, she had nothing to say except in her praise; but she observed she believed much unhappiness arose from people marrying out of their own rank in life. She advised Sir Harry to consider the matter yet a little longer, and then, when Bella returned, she left them to arrange their future without let or hindrance from her.

Which they effected, after much objection on Bella's part, as follows :—

The sins and shortcomings of all her family were never to be mentioned any more for ever. The question of difference of rank Sir Harry pooh-poohed altogether. There was no dif- ference. A lady could only be a lady, were she a duchess. As for money, he had enough for both. He hoped he could make her happy; he knew she could make him happy. His mother was longing to welcome her; his cousin would be as a sister to her. He himself—well, what was there Sir Harry did not feel he would be to her?

And as regarded the marriage, Sir Harry would have liked to be married that minute. Such precipitancy being, however, impossible, he pleaded hard that the wedding should take place in a fortnight; and finally it was settled that Bella should try to be ready in a month.

From that moment time sped by to Bella as if she were in a dream.

Once launched upon the undertaking, Miss Grahame entered into it with spirit. She sent her own maid up to London; she wrote to tradespeople; she inspected silks, and held interviews with dressmakers. Out of her own stores she produced wonderful laces of unfamiliar appearance, and quaint jewellery, "which I shall never wear again, my dear," she said with a little sigh over departed vanities.

Mr. Irwin gave *carte blanche* with regard to the *trousseau;* while Sir Harry poured in gifts, though Bella entreated him not to make her any more presents.

For the first time, the girl began to realize what a great match she was making; and the knowledge frightened her so terribly that, when olden memories cropped up, as they did with terrible frequency, she felt as if she must run away from all the grandeur so unsuited to her antecedents, and hide her head in some remote corner of the earth.

Time after time she opened her lips to tell her lover the whole weary story; but her tongue refused its office. She could not go back now; she could not bring misery on him, shame on herself; and she felt it would make no difference in the absolute course of events, now she understood Sir Harry would marry her no matter what the consequences might be. Already she was beginning to accept the position all women related to them adopted, sooner or later, with the Medburns. When he was near, she had no will but his; her own identity seemed to have become merged in his. Love him! Ay, indeed! fondly enough to satisfy fifty mothers—but not well enough to save him from the misery of an ill-assorted marriage.

And yet, perhaps, she was right after all. Through the trouble, and the sorrow, and the agony to come, Sir Harry never repented having made her his wife—never, he can truthfully say, once.

It was to be a very quiet wedding. The state of Lady Medburn's health precluded the idea of any other than the most private ceremony which could be performed; and accordingly one pouring wet morning a very small party entered the church by the sea, and, in the sight of only Mr. Irwin and a few of the parishioners who had obtained intelligence of the approaching ceremony from Miss Grahame's servants, Harry Medburn and Mabella Miles were made man and wife.

When, on a subsequent occasion, the Rev. Dionysius Wright, finding himself in the neighbourhood, took occasion to examine the registry, he found that Miss Miles' father was described as "of Tottenham, Gentleman."   "Humph!" remarked Mr. Wright, and closed the book, feeling that he had not made much progress in his investigation.

When the party returned to Miss Grahame's, the first person they encountered was Colonel Leschelles. He looked older and greyer, and he had a sad, anxious expression in his face, which seemed to Bella to reproach her for her conduct. But if his expression reproached her, his words did not. The first moment they were alone together, he asked :

"Have you told him?"

"No, I could not ; and, besides, he would not let me."

"Then never tell him," he said earnestly. "Keep the secret now, if it can be kept, for ever. And one thing more," he added, as she was gliding away. "So long as I live, remember, if you need a friend, I shall always be a friend in need."

"And you—are you going away again?"

"No," he said gravely ; "I shall take no more long journeys till I go upon that from which there is no return."

CHAPTER XXXIII.

AT HIGHGATE.

AFTER more than a year spent on the Continent, Sir Harry and Lady Medburn were back in England. It was quite the end of the season, but as the Baronet had business to transact in London, they remained there for some weeks ere travelling westward.

Why they had passed such a length of time in foreign travel is easily explained. Lady Medburn never seemed so happy as when they were moving about from place to place; and the doctors having said that this fancy must be humoured, Sir Harry for once in his life put his own wishes aside, and consulted only the likings of his wife.

After the death of the dowager, which occurred shortly after Sir Harry's marriage, Bella fell into a low, nervous state, for which the family medical adviser felt quite at a loss to account, so he had recourse to the formula generally used on such occasions.

"Lady Medburn," he said to Sir Harry, "is of a highly nervous and sensitive temperament. She has been constant in her attendance in the sick-room. She has eaten little and slept little—in fact, taken no care of herself whatever. Unless she be removed from the depressing atmosphere of a house with which her first associations cannot have been pleasant, I fear she may fall into a nervous condition from which there will be some difficulty in rousing her. Change, my dear Sir Harry, change is the medicine she requires. Take her abroad, and you will find her health improve immediately."

Acting on which suggestion, Sir Harry took his wife abroad, and found her spirits and her health did both rally as by magic.

But after a year had gone by, the Baronet grew so tired of a life he detested that he asked Bella—or Mabel, as he called her—whether she thought she could now return to England.

He put the matter before her reasonably and kindly. He told her that, whilst he would do anything for her sake, he still should be thankful to know she could rest satisfied to reside quietly on the estate where his fathers had lived before him.

"I am not clever, like you, dear," he said; "I am not much fitted to shine in society; but I have a strong feeling of duty attaching itself to my position—of responsibility, when I remember how much has been entrusted to me. I think, if he possibly can, a man should reside on his property, know his tenantry, give employment to his labourers, and—don't think me absurd, Mab—ask stupid old squires and squiresses to dinner, and dine with them in return. You shall have as much pleasant society as we can surround ourselves with; but——"

At that point she interrupted him. "Why did you not speak sooner?" she said. "I want no society except yours. I desire nothing upon earth except your happiness. Let us start for England at once."

"There is one thing I want to tell you, Mabel. I am afraid you will find the Court fearfully dull. I always hoped Edith would live with us for a time at least, and now I find her great-uncle—mine as well as hers—Sir Alexander Kelvey, wishes her to reside with him and his sister."

Bella was seated by the window, her head turned a little aside, so that her husband could not see the expression of sudden gladness which swept over her face. Only when she looked at him and said, "No place can be dull to me where you are," he saw there was a light in her eyes and a smile on her lips he had missed for many a month past.

"Let us go home at once," she went on; "I am quite well now, perfectly well. I will do my part with the squires and squiresses; the stupider they are the better I shall like them. And as to the tenantry and the labourers, only say what you want me to do, Harry, and I will do it. All I desire is that you should be happy, that I should be able to make you so."

"I am happy," he answered; "but you, my love, but you?"

"As long as you are happy, I shall have everything I wish for," she said. "I have no 'self' left; you are me now—all I care for, all I ever shall care for on earth."

"Mabel, my darling!" Those were the only words he spoke; for a great pain seemed to stop his further utterance as he strained her to his heart.

Already a dread of what that something might be to which she and her uncle had referred was beginning to cast an influence over him.

Before marriage he felt inclined to think little of any domestic slur, of any family misfortune; but since his marriage Sir Harry, though, as he truly said, not clever, had learnt that you can no more travel, matrimonially, in peace with a person possessed of a secret, than you can walk with a lame person and fail to feel weary. Not that he ever suspected her—so he told himself perpetually; and yet, and yet he was glad, honestly, disgustingly glad, when on their way back to England his wife asked him to take her to the school where she had been educated.

"I do think they liked me," she said naïvely; "and oh, indeed, I did like all of them!"

So they went and saw her schoolmistress and some of her

old schoolfellows ; and the lady was voluble in her praises of the dear Bella. "Ah! that girl, so amiable, so docile, one of the very dearest girls—she might say, indeed, the very dearest —she had ever had the happiness to instruct. Behold how time made of changes so many! It was but three short summers, but three, since she lost her favourite, and now view that she was become a woman, *une grande dame*, married so suitably. *Bon Dieu!* united, made alliance with one in all ways so well-sufficient to make her happy."

Nevertheless there was something the dear old fussy madame failed to comprehend entirely. "In the good days—for her, but, oh! not good by so many, for the child once Bella, now Lady Medburn—there was no look, to be swept away, across her eyes—no trouble about the mouth. Was she ill? oh! *grand ciel!* had that fearful climate ravaged the constitution once so superb? had the fogs of Albion caused ailments in her who while in La Belle France had understood not the meaning of the word illness?"

At the moment he could see in fancy Bella amongst her old schoolfellows—his Bella whom he had known at Fisherton— whom he had never really seen since.

"My wife is not very strong," he remarked to his garrulous companion. "My mother's death proved a great shock to her, and she has as yet scarcely recovered from its effects. When she next comes to see you I think she will be perfectly well. She is very sensitive, as you know."

"Ah, Heaven! yes," answered the lady; "if one of our children cut its fingers, it ran to the English girl for help. If one was in disgrace, it went to her for comfort. She had a heart for all troubles. I was so sorry when her good uncle, saying the time had come, removed her. But I am sorry no more, monsieur. I see my dear child married so happily; and, as you say, I think her health may be made quite right—in time."

Soon after that they left Paris ; and with almost feminine tenderness Sir Harry watched over the wife most people seemed to think so delicate, as they journeyed.

Long since he had decided there was nothing much the matter with her physical health. Love makes even the blind see clearly, and in Sir Harry's case the miracle had been performed of causing a man who had never before drawn a conclusion to feel certain Bella's ailment was mental.

"If I had only let her talk to me that day on the seashore," he thought sadly, "my poor dear would by this time have been quite happy and strong."

Would she? Perhaps so; perhaps the man's love and the man's generosity might even in such a case have impelled him to marry her; and yet I think the human being who, knowing everything, could have taken Miles Barthorne's daughter to wife, must have been singularly constituted.

Passion, it is said, is all-powerful. Nevertheless, any one who in such a case should have so far forgotten all the traditions of his family as to suffer himself to fall irretrievably in love even with Bella Miles, had he known the nature of her antecedents from the first, must have been differently constituted from Sir Harry Medburn. And, indeed, the worst of the most trifling deceit is, that not merely eventually does it render any retrograde movement as difficult as travelling onward, but it invariably complicates matters for some other besides the deceiver.

But what, then, is a man to do? He must spoil his own life certainly, or take his chance of spoiling better lives possibly than his own eventually. On the one side is the Charybdis of speaking the truth, on the other the Scylla of telling a lie. Between the two poor humanity tries to steer in silence—blind to the fact that eventually shipwreck must come with a more precious freight on board than when the bark carried only itself and its personal fortunes.

Lady Medburn had not been married a month—nay, she had not been married a day—before she understood something of all this; and, understanding, tried to put her foot on the head of the serpent reared to sting her.

And she might have managed to compass some success in her endeavous but for Edith—Sir Harry's cousin—that girl with her tender tints of pink and white, with her great blue childish eyes, with her full red lips, with her brown hair flecked with gold, with her willowy figure and sweet gracious manner, and loving heart holding no secret but one that had no shame in it, which was only love for a cousin—always destined, as she supposed, to be her husband, but who had passed her by for the sake of a woman younger, certainly, handsomer to some tastes, no doubt, but whom she could not understand, who was to her totally unintelligible.

The missing leaves in the manuscript of Bella's life were

puzzling beyond measure to the girl who had never in all her life shaken hands with deceit. The missing leaves—the missing years concerning which no mention was ever voluntarily made, filled Miss Selham with a terrible fear, with a sickening distrust.

So well she loved her cousin that, though she always should have disliked the woman, still she could have given him over almost cheerfully into the keeping of any human being whose nature she comprehended.

She loved him so utterly, so entirely, she could have abnegated self had she felt such self-abnegation would make him happy; but with the subtle craft of her sex, which grasps in five minutes so much more than a man comprehends in five hours, she understood, the very first evening she talked to Bella, while she sipped her tea and sate in an easy chair the time Lady Medburn's maid brushed out her long, soft tresses, that there was something behind, something which *for ever* would prevent Bella making her cousin quite happy, quite content.

And Bella knew this ; for which reason her heart leapt within her when she heard Miss Selham was not likely to reside permanently under the same roof which sheltered herself.

And once again the heart, so often weary, grew hopeful. There was an enormous amount of buoyancy in Bella's nature, spite of all its sensitiveness.

"When we are living at Cortingford," she thought, "I shall be able to find so much to do and to talk about, that perhaps people may never find out my life has been different from that of any one else. I will read all the new works, as Mrs. Wright used to do. I will try to understand politics. I will see after the poor and the schools, and help the Rector's wife, and pay visits, and strive to forget all about those dreadful days at West Green. Why do they now come back to me so persistently in dreams, I wonder? I used never to dream about them — I scarcely thought of them, even in the daytime, till I went to Fisherton. Why should I remember when others can forget? I am quite certain uncle is able to banish the memory of that time. Why should I, who am so young, let it make me wretched?"

Thus Bella, who, with all her experience, was not old enough to know life could not be lived if, as years crept by, men and women were always brooding over the sins and sorrows and follies of the past. Concerning Mr. Irwin her surmise was quite right. From the hour when news arrived of Miles Barthorne's

death he resolutely and successfully thrust all unpleasant recollections aside.

The dread of his brother-in-law's return, which had been a
haunting presence for years, weighing him down no longer ; he
looked—spite of his ailing, discontented wife, and the anxieties
of business—younger than Bella could ever remember him.

Long before he had settled matters satisfactorily with the
attorney who threatened to "expose him," and no lion having
since arisen in his path, he pursued the tenour of City life, and
felt, in most respects, exactly like his neighbours.

As for his sister, she was still in Australia. All the money
Barthorne had saved Mr. Irwin sent out for her benefit.

"Bella shall never want for anything while I live," he told
her, "so do not be uneasy on her account. I have placed her
with a lady, and she is well and happy. She may now write to
you occasionally ;" but he forbade his niece to add her address
to any letter ; and when she was married he insisted that she
should say nothing about the change in her position.

"If she knew you were a baronet's wife we should have her
home by the first vessel," he observed ; "and then God only
knows what would become of us all."

Amongst the first visits of Lady Medburn, when she returned
to London, was one to the Wrights, who had long since left
Fisherton and transported themselves, and such of their worldly
effects as Mrs. Wright considered worth removing, to Huntingdon Park.

There Bella found them, living in one of Mr. Cahoon's villas,
with new furniture in the drawing and dining-rooms and library,
with new oilcloth in the hall, with new stair-carpets, with unre-
membered bedsteads in the best sleeping apartments, with
everything, in fact, surrounding them which the hearts of Mr.
and Mrs. Wright had always desired.

With outstretched hands Mr. Wright welcomed his "dear
girl ;" and though Mrs. Wright did not greet her very cordially,
she was gracious in her manners, and apparently willing, if she
could not quite forget past injuries, to make a pretence of for-
giving them.

Nevertheless, the studied way in which, spite of her guest's
remonstrances she called her Lady Medburn, never once falling back into the once familiar Bella, was very suggestive.

"I am so glad to see you so much more prosperous, and

looking so much happier and better," remarked Bella, out of the fulness of her heart, fondling Rosie, who, having quite forgotten her existence, had to be won back to fictitious recol·· lection of her old friend's identity with *bon-bons*, and presents of all sorts.

"Thank you," said Mrs. Wright coldly. "I am thankful for the change in our position also, I can assure you. Fisherton was in every way unsuitable for us. Mr. Wright's talents were buried there. Here he preaches to those who can appreciate his sermons, and he is in the way if any preferment should be open. In the Church, as everywhere else, if people are out of sight they are out of mind."

"Come, come, Selina," remonstrated her husband. "It was not out of sight out of mind with Ned Cahoon."

"Because he had a purpose to gain in remembering you," retorted Mrs. Wright. "If he had not, you might have waited long enough before he would have held out his little finger to help you. He is not a man, as you know, to give anything for nothing."

Which remark, having reference to certain binding arrangements in connection with pew rents which Mr. Cahoon had made, when he agreed to find money to relieve the Rector of Fisherton from the incubus of his old creditors, caused Dionysius to smite his chest and sound his roll-call, and remind Mrs. Wright that there was no necessity to worry dear Bella with their little trumpery difficulties.

"We are in much calmer water," he finished, "as you and your kind husband will be pleased to know, and things have worked together wonderfully for us—wonderfully," added the Rev. Dion in a tone which had once been so familiar to Bella, that she looked at him fixedly for an instant, and arrived at the conclusion that, spite the splendour of his surroundings and the general prosperity of his appearance, her reverend friend had found one very much crumpled rose-leaf in his new couch.

And the Rev. Dion was quite as sharp to notice the change in her.

"Did you ever see a girl so altered?" he asked his wife, reentering the drawing-room after handing "dear Bella" to her carriage and assuring her he was "char-med" with—if he might say so, and he knew he might without giving offence—the improvement in her appearance. "I look upon you as a daughter," he explained; "and I must say you are more beautiful than ever."

"Thank you, Mr. Wright," she answered simply; "you had always a kind word for me."

But even as she smiled he saw there were tears gathering in her eyes.

Down the length of the new surburban road Mr. Wright watched the liveries, and the horses, and the carriage, till all disappeared from view, when he turned to Selina and delivered himself of the remark already recorded.

"She has gone off greatly in appearance," said Mrs. Wright complacently; "but then you must remember, Dion, those dark beauties never wear well." And Mrs. Wright turned to the drawing-room mirror and, with a simper, mentally pitted her faded middle age against Bella's youth.

"Yes, of course, dear," agreed the Rev. Dion, thinking at the same time that no congenital blindness could equal that of a woman mentally blinded by prejudice and vanity. "Still she is very nice and all that sort of thing—and it is a desirable connection."

"If you can use it," added Mrs. Wright, who, indeed, could generally, except in matters feminine, see farther into a milestone than her husband.

CHAPTER XXXIV.

AN OLD STORY RETOLD.

"I DO not, or course, wish to dictate to you, Bella," said Mr. Irwin to his niece, a few days after her visit to Huntingdon Park; "but if you care to follow my advice, you will not have much in the future to do with the Wrights. I think it is a great pity you called upon them. Take my word for this: when you are beginning a new life, it is better to begin it with new people; and if you encourage the Wrights, they will prove Old Men of the Sea to you every day throughout the whole of your future."

"They were very kind to me," remonstrated Bella.

"As for that, I don't know. They were kind to you as they would have been to a costermonger or an old beggar-woman, just because it is not in their natures to be very unkind to any one, except under great provocation; but when the provocation came—eh! Bella—what about the amiable Wrights then?"

"Mr. Wright was never unkind, uncle; and as for Mrs. Wright, I only care to remember pleasant things about people."

He did not answer for a moment; then, without any reference to what she had said, remarked:

"The whole matter as regards the Wrights was a purely business one. They were paid more than handsomely for all they did for you; and I am quite certain your husband would not wish to have them saddled on him for ever."

"How for ever?" Bella inquired.

"In the way of borrowing money, for instance," explained Mr. Irwin. "Mr. Wright says he has, through you, lost one of the very oldest and best friends he ever possessed—Colonel Leschelles, and in consequence he extracts from me many five-pound notes."

"But they are now so well off," suggested Lady Medburn.

"My dear girl, when people who have, say, five hundred a year, live at the rate of two thousand, how long shall they remain well off? Mr. Wright pestered me to such an extent that I went to his house-warming, as he called it—went for dinner and stayed the evening. According to his account everything was given him; but I do not believe that for a moment. The wines had no flavour of a private cellar; the flowers, I could swear, were supplied by a nurseryman; the game and fish came, I am satisfied, from a confiding local tradesman; and—and, to cut short my catalogue, eventually Mr. Wright must pay for these things; and he will either try to use your husband as a milch-cow or as a voucher for his respectability."

Lady Medburn sat silent for a minute, considering all the words of wisdom which had fallen from her uncle's lips; but after that thoughtful pause she said:

"I think you are right—indeed, I know you are. I will try in my own way to let them understand they are not forgotten; but it is, to quote your own remark, wise to begin a new life —with new people."

"And you are happy?" he said anxiously.

"No," she answered; "I am not. I have done a grievous wrong to the truest gentleman the world ever held, and I suffer accordingly. But we need not talk about that. The wrong has been done, and no one save God can set it straight, and not even God except by death."

"How you talk, Bella!" said her uncle.

"Foolishly you think, no doubt," she observed; "but," she went on, stretching out her arms, "how I have suffered! If you could only imagine the agony I have undergone—sleeping and waking—sleeping and waking. Death would be rest to me. I feel I have brought such disgrace on an honoured name, that sometimes I hate to hear myself called by it. If I had been brought up as a housemaid or a cook—but, dear, dear uncle, you did your best, and whatever comes—and I feel there is something coming—no blame attaches to you."

"My dear," he said, "disgrace can never attach itself to you or your husband so long as the story remains a secret, and there is no one to reveal it. No one has the faintest idea of who your father was except Colonel Leschelles, and you may trust him implicitly; and, besides, he does not know all."

"That is true," she answered; "and yet I live in constant dread. I wake at night feeling that some terrible trouble is on its way towards me. It seems to me that through the darkness I can hear its footfalls."

"If you do not strive to conquer these morbid fancies, Bella, you will bring on some serious illness," said her uncle severely.

"Perhaps illness may have something to do with the fancies," she answered. "Since we came to London I have not felt well. I shall be glad when we get out of town. Everything seems to weary me; and, kind as all my husband's relatives are, it is a misery to me to be with them. Now, we are going to dine with Sir Alexander Kelvey this evening, and, do you know? I quite dread having to talk to Miss Kelvey and Edith. Sir Harry ought to have married Edith. I wonder why it is that, out of all the millions of women in the world, he should have chosen me."

“With whom did you say you were going to dine, Bella?” asked her uncle.

“Sir Alexander Kelvey,” she answered.

“Oh!” and Mr. Irwin walked towards the window, and so hid his white shocked face from view. Was his niece right—was some trouble coming? After all these years, was the dead past about to rise up in judgment, and the sins of the father to be visited upon the child?”

“Do you know Sir Alexander?” asked his niece, marvelling at his sudden silence.

“No: the name, however, seems familiar. He is a judge or something of that sort, is not he? What relation is he to your husband?”

“Grand-uncle, I think.”

“Indeed? Well, you must try to get over your foolish fears, Bella. You will be better when you leave London. Good bye. I cannot stay with you any longer.” And then he turned, and for the first time she noticed the pallor of his face.

“What is the matter?—are you ill?” she asked anxiously.

“No—yes—that is, nothing is really amiss with me; only sometimes I feel faint for a moment.”

“Have some wine,” she suggested; but he shook his head.

“I shall be better when I get into the air,” he answered. “Wine would only make me worse. Good bye again, dear, and leave London as soon as you can.”

For the remainder of the day Bella puzzled herself about that singular and sudden indisposition. In all her experience of her uncle she had never before seen him look so ghastly ill; and, spite of his denial that he knew Sir Alexander Kelvey, she could not help connecting the change in his appearance with the mention of that gentleman’s name.

“I wonder,” she thought, “I wonder if he was judge on that trial?” In her ignorance she imagined he might have sat on the bench in England after his return from India. “I must ask uncle; anything would be better than this suspense. I shall keep fancying all kinds of horrors till I have seen him again.”

But she was not destined to wait long for information. After dinner, while Miss Kelvey was indulging in her evening nap—the imputation of which she so strongly resented that at last no one dare venture to suggest the soft impeachment—Miss Selham and her cousin’s wife strolled out into the garden and looked down on the Great City, the hum of which was distinctly audible where they stood dreamily surveying the scene.

"What a sweet place this is!" said Lady Medburn, at last breaking the silence. "I do not wonder that Sir Alexander likes it so much. If it were mine I should be as fond of it as he is."

"Well, I do not know," answered her companion; "the house is comfortable and home-like, and the grounds are certainly very beautiful, and the view magnificent; but still I confess I do not like Hillview. The thought of that murder makes me feel chill whenever I pass the spot. I knew the poor old man from the time I was a little child, and it was just like losing a relative by violence. I am sure when the news reached Cortingford, we all felt as if some one very near and dear had been killed."

"What murder?" inquired Bella.

"Has Harry never told you about it?" said Miss Selham. "How very odd! I thought everybody had heard of poor M'Callum's murder. Let us walk round this way, and I will tell you the story. Here is the spot—the very spot where the body was found; his brother pointed it out to me time after time. He used to be butler here, but after the murder he sank into a state of utter despondency, and became so useless that my uncle was obliged to pension him off: he lives in a cottage not very far off."

"But about the murder?" asked Lady Medburn.

"The poor old man was found one morning lying where you are standing now, with his head split open. He was quite dead. At the time no one could imagine the motive for such a crime; but it afterwards transpired that a great quantity of plate and other valuables had been stolen out of the strong-room, and it is supposed that M'Callum, having met the thief, was murdered to prevent his giving any alarm. I have often heard his brother describe the scene.

"'It was the loveliest morning ever broke, miss,' he told me; 'the sun was shining, and the birds singing, and there was a light, pleasant breeze, and the flowers were all in bloom, and everything but one looked bright.

"'And there, out in the sunshine, he lay; his grey hair dabbled with blood, his right hand clenched; a frown on his face—but that went away afterwards.

"'His eyes were wide open! It was an awful sight!'"

"And the person—who—killed him?" asked Sir Harry's wife.

She knew what was coming—she had known it almost from the first; but she could no more help putting the question than she could help the horrible deadly sickness she felt creeping over her.

"He has never yet been brought to justice. The presumption was that one of the workmen employed in executing some repairs was the guilty person; and Sir Alexander had his house searched in order to see if any of the stolen property could be discovered. Nothing, however, was found to connect him with that crime; but other goods were discovered, and I believe he was transported in consequence.

"M'Callum still declares he, and no other, was the murderer. 'Out of them all,' he says, 'Barthorne was the only man who refused to touch the body. He was afraid to do it! But my brother's blood will be avenged yet! I know it; I feel it!' —Mabel!"

With that exclamation Miss Selham broke off her narrative. On the grass where David M'Callum had lain in the bright morning light, Lady Medburn lay in the gathering night, totally insensible. She had, grasping the branch of a tree, fought against the deadly faintness till it conquered her, and then her hold relaxed, and she fell in a heap to the ground.

In another minute the whole house was in confusion. Miss Kelvey, aroused from her slumbers, was inquiring whether the house had taken fire: Sir Harry was carrying his wife across the quiet garden; servants were rushing off for doctors; the housekeeper hurried into the drawing-room to render assistance; —and through all the uproar Bella lay insensible—lay like one dead.

At last a doctor came, and, after what seemed to the anxious husband an eternity, Lady Medburn's eyelids trembled, then slightly unclosed, and, with a sigh, she began to return to consciousness—began to take up the burden of existence once more.

"Tell me the truth, doctor," said Sir Harry, as he stood with one of the medical men summoned in the hall. "What is the cause of this swoon?—what is really the matter with my wife?"

"I do not think you need make yourself uneasy about the

matter," was the reply, uttered with a significant smile. "Though alarming to witness, these attacks are not dangerous, I assure you—not at all uncommon under the circumstances."

"Under what circumstances?"

The doctor smiled again, and then explained his meaning more fully.

"You must not allow Lady Medburn to over-exert herself," he finished; "the more quietly she lives, for some little time to come, the better."

With all speed Sir Harry arranged the business which had detained him in London, and carried his wife off to Devonshire. There she would be able to keep perfectly quiet; there her child should be born; there, in the quaint old church where so many Medburns had been baptized, the heir he hoped for should be christened. About Cortingford Sir Harry walked a happy man. He was not now uneasy about his wife: her despondency—her restlessness were at last accounted for.

The one thing was coming his happiness had lacked; and all the time Bella was breaking her heart to remember that the heir of all those broad acres—of that good name—could not, if he were a child of hers, be ever other than the grandson of a murderer.

The sins of the father were being visited on the child. But Bella did not lament on her own account; it was always and ever for Sir Harry and his unborn infant she prayed.

"Punish me, O Lord!" was her moan, "but spare them. I have brought it all on myself. Let me have all the suffering."

One day, when Sir Harry was entering the lodge gates, he met one of the grooms riding, with a scared look on his face, at full gallop down the drive. At sight of his master he pulled up.

"My lady is very ill," he explained, "and I am going for the doctor."

Ill!—and she had been perfectly well when he left home. With a sinking heart Sir Harry drove on as fast as his horses could go.

"How is she?" were his first words when he entered the house, and the answer he received was:

"My lady is alive, but the child is dead."

What was the cause of it all? No one could give him any information.

An hour previously, when her maid took her up a letter, she was apparently quite well, and spoke of going out for a short walk. Immediately almost, however, her bell was rung sharply, and when her maid answered it, she found Lady Medburn sitting in a chair, "looking like death itself, and trembling from head to foot."

The doctors, when they came, were unable to account for the attack ; and, subsequently, Bella herself declared she could give no information about the matter.

She was a long time in recovering her health. People said she fretted over the dead child and the bitter disappointment, and Bella never undeceived them. It was only when she was quite alone that she turned her face to the wall, and talked to her own heart about her misery ; for the letter she had received on the day when she was stricken down so suddenly was to tell her that the tidings of Miles Barthorne's death had been false —that he was in England !

CHAPTER XXXV.

MR. WRIGHT AGAIN IN TROUBLE.

"After all, there are two sides to everything except a banknote. There is always unlimited satisfaction to be got out of that."

The speaker was the Reverend Dionysius Wright, who, while uttering the foregoing sentence, looked at a crisp bit of paper lying before him which had probably suggested his sentence.

Mrs. Wright, who was engaged in crocheting a baby's boot for an impending bazaar, looked across at her husband, and smiled pensively.

"I think, dear," she said, "there is a reverse side even to a bank-note. I never see one without remembering how short a way it goes."

"With us," agreed the Rev. Dion. "Other people manage somehow to make money go farther than we seem able to do."

Remarks of this kind had of late become somewhat common, so Mrs. Wright resumed her occupation with a deprecating grace which proved on that occasion very gall and wormwood to her husband.

"I often wonder," he resumed, "that is, I have often wondered lately, whether the game has been worth the candle, Selina. I look back through years and years, and strive in vain to recall the memory of a single easy hour. I have worked hard. In my own way, I think few men have worked harder. From one source and another we have had large sums of money, and yet we have been only able to keep our heads above water. It has proved an eternal struggle even to do that."

Mrs. Wright took her crochet-needle out of her work, put it to her lips as if engaged in profound reflection, looked out of the window, and sighed—then once again stuck her hook in the wool, and made a few stitches.

"Now, here is this living," continued Mr. Wright; "it brings me in already—say half as much more as Fisherton ; and I ask you—I just ask you candidly, Selina, are we one bit better off than we were there?"

Selina, suspending her operations for a moment, said she "hoped they would be in time. She did not see how they could expect to be in a much better position till they were out of the hands of such an impracticable person as Mr. Cahoon."

"Well, I'm sure I don't know," answered Mr. Wright; "sometimes I begin to despair. Cahoon said the other day we had always been trying the impossible feat of living at just double our actual income; and I'll be hanged if I don't think he is about right."

"If you are going to adopt the opinions of Mr. Cahoon, of course you cannot expect me to sympathize with you," observed Selina, her head a little on one side, and a spot of red beginning to show on each cheek.

Like most people, Mrs. Wright was somewhat susceptible to criticism, and Mr. Cahoon had lately not been sparing of it.

"Undoubtedly," she added, after a momentary pause, "in many respects Fisherton was preferable to Huntingdon Park. There, at any rate, one did not live within a stone's throw of all one's creditors. We cannot, however, go back to Fisherton, even if we wished to do so : a thing you, I am sure, do not."

And Selina closed her mouth and went on with her work.

"But don't you think "—the Rev. Dion was terribly in earnest at that moment—"don't you think we might manage to retrench —to live in some respects more economically?"

Mrs. Wright laid down the red wool and the crochet-hook, and, crossing her hands on the table, said:

"Do you know, Dion, what retrenching and living economically means? It means always doing without something—it means eternal self-abnegation—it means stinting yourself, and your wife, and your children. It means being afraid to give away a basin of soup or a bottle of wine to the sick and dying —it means a constant thoughtfulness about pence and halfpence —it means that a man has decided to trust himself rather than the Almighty, and that he must therefore grub along with his face always turned earthward. We have had great trouble, to be sure ; but I think, if you will look back, you will find Providence has always helped us at the critical moment. For my part, remembering how wonderfully we have been supported, I could not doubt now but that we shall be supported to the end."

If Mr. Wright had spoken out his mind at that juncture, he would have said, "And what is there exceptional about us, Selina, that Providence should go out of its way to attend specially to our affairs?"—but he was wise, and held his peace.

Once he had ventured to make some such observation, and being then met with an inquiry as to what he thought of the Jews, for whose sake so many miracles were wrought, and a further inquiry as to whether he did not believe much more would be done for a Christian, he decided it was better to allow his wife to air her theories unopposed ; so he only looked gloomily out of the window, and said nothing.

"You dear Dion," remarked his wife, "what is the matter? We have nothing pressing now except that overdue bill ; and I am sure Mr. Cahoon can settle that little matter for you if he likes—and he will like. He has sense enough to comprehend your value. Much as I dislike the man personally, I do admire his thorough appreciation of you."

"I wish, Selina," said Mr. Wright, "you would not show your feelings so plainly as you do. It is playing the——I mean, it makes things very difficult for me when you and Cahoon are at sixes and sevens. The fact is," added the Reverend Dion, "I am afraid this place has uplifted us all too much, and that we shall have a terrible fall in consequence."

"My dear," said Mrs. Wright, with judicial calmness, "I should be so thankful if you would see Dr. Boyd. You know you never look at things through smoked glass except when you are ill."

To which the Reverend Dion made no reply.

The husband and wife were sitting in a room overlooking that which, to my thinking, is the wretchedest sight on earth—a new garden in a London suburb.

The late September sun threw its beams across no trees laden with fruit, no well-grown evergreens, no creepers already turning from green to yellow and from yellow to red ; but fell instead athwart an enclosure which looked, spite of the wretched grass-plot and the scarlet geraniums planted in the few star and crescent-shaped beds, as if it had been that hour, that instant, fenced in from the original brick-field.

No doubt, had the so-called garden been left to nature, she would soon have covered the dreary soil with sufficient verdure by means of docks, burdocks, nettles, chickweed, and other plants admirably adapted for clothing naked places possessed of unpromising soils ; but Mr. Cahoon, having an objection to nature's management, had, over burnt clay and a little gravel, laid sods, and created a space of burnt-up greenery which he called a lawn, and in which he carved out wonderfully-designed beds, that looked as if cut with a series of paste-cutters. In these he or his tenants put a few geraniums, while over the grass a limited number of standard rose-trees were stuck, which bore a resemblance to a flamingo standing on one leg, without any resemblance to the flamingo body.

The walks were covered with reddish gravel, well rolled, and the garden was surrounded with aggravatingly new brick walls, too low to train anything upon, and yet still so hideously ugly that even the young Wrights had felt impelled to sow nasturtiums, convolvuli, and other such cheap, flabby annuals around the borders, in order to break the dead monotony of the brick and mortar, on the top of which the domestic cat prowled by day and woke the echoes by night.

The Rector had a certain love of things beautiful and soothing. Like most men who lead an anxious and restless life, he felt a grateful peace in looking at greenery—at rich foliage, at a wealth of flower and leaf. A field full of buttercups had ere then sent him home in a happier frame of mind. Soft, shaded light in a drawing-room, the subtle scent of hothouse blossoms, ay, even the familiar look of old, dark furniture, of worn carpets, of an accustomed chair, of bookshelves edged with a remembered leather, had all in turn, some time or another, quieted his nerves and eased the throbbing of his temples.

At Fisherton, though the quietness wearied him, and the change from an exciting to an utterly still life proved too violent to be accepted patiently, still the Rector had never felt anything of the irritation which occasionally overmastered him in Huntingdon Park.

What had he there? A brand-new house; a house freshly painted and papered; a conventional house, with plate-glass windows and stone-coloured Venetian blinds relieved by red tapes, broad steps leading to the front door, wide steps leading down into the area; a strip of desolate garden in front, ornamented with a starved laurel and a wretched yew, the slip of ground already described at the back; a house with new carpets in the drawing-room, dining-room, and library; a house smelling of varnish; a house where his old books looked as much out of place as his old coat did; a house which, though Mr. Cahoon charged them only a very moderate rent, had one way and another cost Mr. Wright more than he had the slightest right to spend, and which was likely to go on costing till he died or became bankrupt.

And what added to his trouble was that not even in his church had he now any comfort. It was of iron, and consequently a more hideous building than even modern architects can eliminate out of their imaginations. Most clergymen have the same pleasure in officiating in a beautiful church that a musician has in playing on a fine instrument. But pleasures of that kind were not for the Rev. Dion. He could not even think of the new church, "chaste in design, admirable in its proportions," which was in course of progress, without a shudder.

He could not sleep at night, he could not relish his food by day. When he talked and laughed, at parties, his talk and his laughter sounded to him like those of another man. For once he had borne his trouble alone; for once Selina and he were playing no little game together: but looking out on that cheerless bit of garden, and thinking of all he had left behind when he left Fisherton, Mr. Wright felt he could carry his burden no longer in silence—that it was time his wife took some share of the knowledge, at all events.

"I am afraid, Selina," he began, "that there is a considerable amount of truth in the saying that there are no such fools as clever people. You and I are clever; but we do not seem to have done much good for ourselves after all."

"Perhaps you would still like to be a struggling curate," commented Mrs. Wright, sarcastically.

"I should like to be anything, even a day labourer, if I could have an easy mind," said the Rev. Dion. "Don't you see, cannot you understand, Selina, that in a life like ours, the better our social position the more dreadful it is to contemplate losing it? And every upward step we take makes it harder to undo any false step taken at the beginning. If, when we came here, we had come as comparatively poor, struggling people—"

"We might have gone on struggling to the end," interpolated his wife.

"I don't believe it, Selina; the longer I live, the more I doubt whether there is any real benefit in keeping up false appearances. The public will read an author's book if it be worth reading, whether he lives in a garret or dines with dukes every night of his life; and just the same the public will come and hear a man preach, if he is able to preach, whether he have hemp carpeting on his floors, or dresses in purple and fine linen, and fares sumptuously every day."

"And do you think the man could write as well, or preach as well, if he lived on bread and water instead of on beef and mutton, and Bass and Guinness?"

"Under certain circumstances, yes. I consider an easy mind one of the essentials to success, in middle life at any rate. I do not believe any man stands a chance of reaching the winning-post if care be always sitting behind on the crupper."

"Well, I do not know," said Mrs. Wright plaintively. "I am sure I thought we were managing admirably. Here we have very good society, of its kind; we need never from necessity spend an evening at home. Our boys have fair appointments in the City; our girls may marry well; you preach to an intelligent and educated audience, while, as for me, I have not felt so strong for many years."

"That is the only comfort I can see about the matter; for all the other benefits you have mentioned the price paid has been fearful. I have kept our last trouble from you as long as I could, but I can keep it no longer. Unless, in a very short space of time, I can manage to raise a large, an extremely large sum of money, I shall be not merely ruined, but disgraced."

"What do you mean, Dion?" inquired his wife.

Then he told her how, having received subscriptions for the new church, he had, under pressure, withdrawn the money from his bankers, and employed it for the settlement of pressing claims, believing he should be able to replace all sums so taken long before he was called upon to hand them over.

But suddenly a day of reckoning came—it always does come when least expected—and Mr. Wright was called upon to make up his accounts, and deliver the money collected by him to the trustees.

For a period he pleaded pressure of parish work as an excuse for delay: then stated he had not received all the money promised; that he would lose no time in writing to those who were thus lagging behind, and have everything ready to lay before the committee ere long.

Eventually, however, as he did not lay everything before the committee, or, indeed, any part of it, he had received a letter from the secretary, civil, indeed, but pressing, stating that as it was necessary for the accounts to be made up immediately, he would feel obliged by Mr. Wright favouring him with a statement of the amounts he had received, not later than the 21st of October.

"And now it is getting towards the end of September," said Mr. Wright, rising, and pacing the room, his hands crossed behind his back; "and God only knows what I am to do."

For once, Mrs. Wright did not suggest that Providence would open some road for them. She sate, her work lying idly in her lap, her eyes wandering over the arid garden, utterly silent, stunned by the weight of a trouble as tremendous as it was un-expected.

"Selina," said the Rector, and his voice shook as he pronounced her name—was her manner a premonitory symptom of how the world would receive the story of his fall?—"I would have spared you this if I could."

She pressed her hand across her eyes as one who comes suddenly into the light after walking through darkness, and looked at him for a moment like one dazed: then she rose equal to the occasion, and answered:

"Dion, we must not sink under this; we must face the difficulty. You can get the money somehow. Why did you not tell me before? I could have helped you. How much do you want? Why do you not go to Mr. Cahoon?"

"I have been to him," explained the Rector.

"And what did he say? Did you explain the matter to him?"

"I did fully; that is one of the advantages, or disadvantages, of having to do with a man who is not easily scandalized. He expressed no astonishment; indeed, I believe he had suspected something of the sort; but he declined to help me."

"What excuse did he make?"

"Well, he made several. One, that previous arrangements with me had entailed a good deal of trouble. Another, that as he had befriended me, he thought I might have compelled my children to be ordinarily civil to his; and a third, that he did not believe any human being could keep us out of debt.

"'You have been in debt and in trouble ever since I knew you,' he said, 'and you will be in debt so long as you are not in jail or your grave. Time teaches a little to some people, but time has taught nothing to you. King Solomon expresses an opinion that "Though you should bray a fool in a mortar among wheat with a pestle, yet will not his foolishness depart from him;" and I am inclined to think King Solomon was about right.'"

"The profane wretch!" murmured Selina.

"I humbled myself," continued the Rector. "I give you my word, I never so prayed and besought a favour from a human being; but I might just as well have entreated that chimney-piece. I reminded him of the long years during which I had worked; I spoke of the disgrace to my children; I pleaded on your behalf; I implored him by the memory of old times; I——"

But here Mr. Wright broke off with a sob, to the intense dismay of his wife, who had never seen him so utterly disheartened before.

"Dion!" she cried, "for pity's sake don't give way now! We shall get through this trouble somehow, if you only face it boldly. We will write to every one we know. Bella, I daresay, could get her husband to help us; and then there is Mr. Irwin, and—and plenty of people besides."

For answer, Mr. Wright unlocked a drawer, and pulling out some letters, handed them across the table.

One—the first Mrs. Wright unfolded—was from Bella herself, hurriedly written and expressed, enclosing all the money she had at the moment—thirty pounds—and saying that when Sir Harry, who was out of town for a few days, returned, she would beg him to give her twenty more to make up the fifty Mr. Wright wanted.

"Why did you not ask her for a hundred?" inquired Mrs. Wright, a little scornfully; "you would have got it just as easily."

"Read on," was Mr. Wright's reply.

The next letter proved to be from Sir Harry himself, apologizing for a delay in writing, occasioned by Lady Medburn's dangerous illness, and begging to be excused from sending the cheque requested.

The wording of this epistle was icily cold; nevertheless Mrs. Wright said:

"I do not attach any importance to that. Naturally the man was in an ill humour at being disappointed of the long-expected heir. It was wretched management on Bella's part, in some way—of that I am quite sure."

"Very likely, my dear," agreed the Rev. Dion, who had never been disappointed in that way himself; "but read on."

Mr. Irwin's refusal came next. After that Colonel Leschelles'; after that, half a dozen more.

"That is the state of the case, you see, my dear," remarked Mr. Wright resignedly.

"At present," said Mrs. Wright; "but I will get the money out of some one, if I have to ask for it on my knees."

It was noticeable that the lady made at that time no further reference to the especial care she believed was exercised by Providence over her husband's affairs; though it was not long ere she declared that, from two most unlikely quarters, help had been coming all the time—and that she always had firm faith help would come, though she felt scarcely justified, under the circumstances, in expressing such an opinion.

" For you know, dear, we ought not to do wrong that good may come of it," finished the graceful self-deceiver.

" Yes, Selina, I know that, perhaps, a little better than you," answered the Reverend Dion, somewhat brusquely.   After all, it was he who had sinned, he had sinned for her sake, and that of his children; and it was he who had borne the sleepless nights of care, the long, long days of struggle, the humiliations, the rebuffs, the sickening hope deferred.   And it had not been pleasant to hear Cahoon's remarks on his own folly and the incompetency of Selina.   To be told in plain words that he is a fool, and his wife another, is trying to the complacency of any man.   But Mr. Wright took his revenge.   When he was quite out of the wood, he preached two sermons intended to strike home to the heart of that purse-proud upstart, Cahoon.

People said they were wonderful sermons—so perhaps they impressed that "recreant" Cahoon, as the Rector loved to style him.

The only remark Cahoon, however, made on the subject was this—

" I believe, Wright, you would boil your own mother down if you ran short of literary stock.   I wonder if you ever had a feeling or an experience you have not turned into a sermon, or money."

" And," considered the Rev. Mr. Wright, as he turned his steps towards home, " now he speaks of it, I wonder if I ever had."

CHAPTER XXXVI.

MR. WRIGHT'S DIFFICULTIES.

THE first great deliverance accomplished for Mr. Wright was wrought through the death of his brother.

Never did Mr. Wright feel that he had loved that brother so well as when, close upon the 21st of October, news arrived that Mr. Horatio Wright had taken his departure heavenward from the obscure town in which for many years he dispensed medicines and practised as a fourth-rate surgeon.

In that town he mixed with people who were—so said the Rev. Dion—"entirely unsuitable;" but, upon the whole, Mr. Horatio Wright managed to lead, according to his lights, not a bad sort of life.

True, the doctor of the neighbourhood patronized him, whilst the gentry of the neighbourhood never even dreamt of asking him to their houses; but then Horatio did not owe one penny he was unable to pay; he contrived to put by a little money; he was burdened with neither wife nor child. He had an old maid to keep his house, who, always secretly hoping he would eventually marry her, devoted all her attention to compassing his happiness.

In the county no man was a better judge of whisky, and throughout the county no man could have been found capable of imbibing so much liquor at night and rising utterly sober in the morning; whilst as for fame, had he not his brother Dionysius?

That was fame enough for him. In a very dilapidated box were found, after his death, carefully packed away, "Sermon by the Rev. Dionysius Wright, M.A. Trin. Coll. Dub., Curate of St. Augustine-in-the-East, Lecturer at the Church of the Holy Innocents;" "Sermon on behalf of the Poor and Needy, preached at St. Mary's beyond the Precincts, by the Rev. Dionysius Wright," etc., etc., etc.; "A Lecture on the Congruity existing between Ancient and Modern Infidelity, delivered at the City of London Christian Improvement Society, Bevis

Marks, May, 18— ;" besides the *Times* of a certain date, containing an account of some meeting at which the Rev. Dion had flourished away on the platform; many local papers bearing testimony to the activity of that celebrated divine, the Rev. D. Wright; a copy of the *Middlesex Conservative* which gave a description of his induction to Fisherton and a sketch of his career—the last contributed ,by Mr. Wright himself; other copies of the same paper containing accounts of various meetings at which the Rev. Dion addressed a select audience, as well as paragraphs relating to local festivities in which the Rev. Dion and Mrs. Wright and the Misses Wright took honourable place.

Each of us takes a pleasure in something quite unaccountable to our fellows; and, next to whisky, Mr. Horatio Wright prided himself on his brother the parson.

Not that he would have lent him ten pounds, had that precise amount stood between the Rev. D. Wright and the workhouse; but he delighted in sending him the best whisky he could procure, which was, indeed, better than any money could buy, and talking to his boon companions about Dion, who was "hail fellow well met" with bishops and earls.

And his audience believed him—an Irish audience always believes in the success of a man who has gone to England—and Mr. H. Wright, the surgeon, derived a sort of reflected glory from the doings of Mr. D. Wright, the divine.

"They cannot hurry a man to make up his accounts who has just lost his brother," thought the Reverend Dion as he took his seat—back to the engine, second-class—at Euston Square. "Poor Horatio! Dear! dear! it seems only yesterday since we went poaching together in old Tracy's park; and now all the Tracys are dead and gone, and Horatio is gone too." After which tender tribute to his brother's memory Mr. Wright unfolded the *Times*, and began reading the leading articles.

Arrived in Dublin, without waiting, as he told Selina, "for bite or sup," he drove straight to the Broadstone Station, and arrived at the late Mr. Horatio Wright's residence about a couple of hours before the time fixed for the funeral.

"I have seen him," wrote the Rector to his wife. "His face wears a most peaceful expression. He was ill only twenty-four hours; but the clergyman who was with him at the la

who was good enough to call upon me immediately after **my**
arrival—says he had for some time past been directing his
attention to serious matters, and that he was fully prepared for
the GREAT CHANGE.   From the appearance of the house, I
should imagine he has been obliged to live with strict economy.
Poor fellow!   I wish I could have made his life happier; but
where he is now he will understand all my troubles, and it is a
comfort to think he has passed to a land where money can
neither make nor mar the happiness of its inhabitants.   I write
this before the funeral, as the post leaves at four o'clock.   I
shall look anxiously for a letter from you at Jury's to-morrow."

But when the morrow came Mr. Wright did not return to
Dublin.

The previous night he had indited another epistle to Selina.

He wrote it after partaking liberally of the whisky which
had — so said his companion, the local attorney—"never
paid the Queen, nor cost Mr. Horatio Wright, one halfpenny.
Ah!" continued the speaker, "your worthy brother had some
queer patients.   Up the hills and among the bogs there are
many who will miss him, and that was how he came to get
such good spirits."

"He was always a curious fellow, but the best-hearted
creature alive," observed the Rector.

"Well, perhaps so," said the attorney, a little doubtfully.
"Now, really I must be going.   By to-morrow at two o'clock,
then, Mr. Wright, I shall have gone fully into the matter we
have been talking over.   Good night.   Delighted to have made
your acquaintance, I am sure.   Pray do not come to the door;
I know the way far better than you do.   Good night again."
And the Reverend Dion was left standing alone in the hall, a
candle in his left hand, his right laid on his shirt-front, and a
look of happiness pervading his features.

"I hardly know, my beloved wife"—thus the Reverend Dion
began his letter—"how to find words to tell you the news I
have learnt since I dispatched a few lines to inform you of my
safe arrival.   Our dear departed was not straitened in his circumstances, as I supposed.   He died possessed of house
property to the value of about forty pounds a year.   This
amount he has left to *me*.   To his housekeeper he bequeaths
his furniture.   She is greatly dissatisfied, I can see, and hopes
I will do something handsome for her, which, indeed, I would

most gladly, were I differently situated; but, as matters stand, how can I? The lawyer who acted for H. spent the evening with me. He is a rogue, I believe, and he evidently thinks me a fool as regards worldly affairs; but, as it happens, his roguery suits my folly on the present occasion to a T. He wants to buy the houses, and I want the ready money, so he supposes 'that I could never be worried with looking after such a small property,' and I have agreed to sell if he can find a purchaser likely to give a fair price. *I shall settle the matter before I leave,* and you may expect to see me with the purchase-money in my pocket. Not a word of this to Cahoon, if you happen to see him. He knows too much about the state of my affairs already. I cannot tell you how utterly different a man I feel to-night. A load has been taken off my mind. I shall sleep sound for the first time for months. Poor H.! I trust saving was a pleasure to him, for I fear he must have stinted himself sadly to put by anything out of the wretched pittance he earned here. My heart is full—of gratitude, wonder, and relief!"

And indeed Mr. Wright's heart was so full, that, when he reached Dublin, out of the money paid him by the attorney—who did not deal more hardly by the divine than might have been expected—he purchased so many things for Selina, the children, and himself, that, on casting up the total expended, he found a considerable inroad had been made on the amount —originally only sufficient to cover the deficiency in his accounts.

"But never mind," thought the Reverend Dion; "if I give them this I will make some excuse about the balance, and ere long I shall be receiving money, and can then settle up everything."

Thus the lighted-hearted divine, who had not been able to sleep sound for months, slipped back into the waters of difficulty from which he was but just rescued; into shallow waters, perhaps, but still quite deep enough to drown him unless another miracle were wrought in his favour.

Back in London, however, Mr. Wright found that unless he immediately paid over every halfpenny he had left, he would find himself in an extremely awkward position; and, indeed, it was only by dint of telling more untruths than he probably ever uttered before at one sitting, that he could defer the evil day of accounting for the deficiency still remaining.

"And then there is that thing of Averill's," he remarked to

his wife. " I had entirely forgotten it ; but when the list is published he must find his name amongst the subscribers, or I know
he will make a fuss."

" I should let him make a fuss," said Mrs. Wright philosophically ; but the Reverend Dion shook his head.

" My dear," he explained, " there are things a curate can do,
and things an incumbent cannot do ; and I must refund that
money, or run the risk of a most unpleasant exposure."

" Well, all I can say is," remarked his better half, " that it is
a very hard case indeed."

" Perhaps so ; but fretting over spilt milk won't put it back
in the jug, Selina."

" You never go to Ireland but you come back with a number
of the commonest proverbs at your fingers' ends. I do wish,
Dion, you would be more careful."

" I wish I had been," muttered the Reverend Dion *sotto voce.*
The man was always a most repentant sinner when in trouble.

" What was that hitch about Averill ?" some over-curious
reader inquires. Just this. In days too remote for the Rector
to remember anything about the transaction till reminded of it,
he had once, when schools were wanted for a parish with which
he was temporarily connected, taken from a list of subscribers
to some other charities the names of various philanthropic persons, to whom he sent a moving circular, drawn up by himself,
stating the need of schools, the condition of the parish, and
various other matters upon which it is unnecessary to enlarge
here.

In reply he received some letters containing money, but not
sufficient money even to begin to build the schools; so he used
the subscriptions for his own purposes—meaning, of course,
ultimately to restore the amounts to the donors—and then
quarrelling with the Rector, just come home from foreign parts,
he left suddenly, and, having a judicious and well-balanced
memory, forgot all about the schools and the subscriptions.

But Mr. Averill had a better memory. When once again the
signature of Dionysius Wright lay on his study table, that gentleman, who was methodical and regular in his habits, referred
to his filed letters and well-kept correspondence-book, and
among them he found: "Rev. Dionysius Wright, curate in charge
of St. Lazarus-in-the-North, for schools, £25 ;" whereupon he
wrote to the incumbent of St. Lazarus to ascertain about the

schools ; and, finding none had been built, sent a letter to Mr. Wright, in which he remarked that he might apply the twenty-five pounds subscribed for the purpose of assisting the St. Lazarus Schools, which had never been erected, to the fund for "rearing that beautiful structure, the Church of the Disciples, Huntingdon Park." Having quoted which elegant extract from Mr. Wright's own circular, Mr. Averill proceeded, on his own account, to add, "I shall expect to see my name amongst your list of subscribers"—an observation full of significance, as the Reverend Dion comprehended.

"I must make up the whole amount ere long," he said, on an average about twice a week, in a tone of great conviction, and Mrs. Wright agreed that she supposed he must, with the air of an injured woman ; but months passed by, and still the account was not made up. Neither did there seem the slightest prospect of its ever being made up.

Out of each fresh payment Mr. Wright expected to receive, a certain sum was verbally and mentally subtracted to liquidate "that fearful debt," as the Reverend Dion styled it ; but, somehow, when the money came, the whole of it was found to go so short a way in even partially satisfying hungry creditors, that not a halfpenny could be spared to provide for the payment which had already been delayed so long.

Christmas came and passed. With one excuse and another Mr. Wright had staved off the evil day for months enough to have enabled him to find the cash by some means ; but at length, when February arrived, the secretary grew very peremptory—"very nasty indeed," explained the Rector ; "and there are now but three alternatives open for me—to pay the money, confess my real position, or be publicly and eternally disgraced."

"Oh, Dion !" exclaimed his wife, "do not despair. You will be helped out of this, I am sure. A man who has done as much for others as you have done will never, I am confident, be deserted in his hour of need."

"I am not quite so certain about that, Selina," he answered. "We have been helped wonderfully, it is true ; but I do think, sooner or later a man is expected to help himself a little, instead of lying a burden upon Providence. Upon my word, I often feel as if Heaven must be tired of assisting people who so eternally stand in need of assistance."

"If you are going to talk in that way," said Mrs. Wright a little severely, "of course we cannot expect assistance. If you mean to relinquish faith, and to become totally oblivious of and ungrateful for all the great mercies vouchsafed to us, we shall, I fear, be forgotten. But, Dion, what is the meaning of this change in you—of this unintelligible depression?"

"The meaning of it is, Selina, that I am tired, that I am sick of debt, and borrowing, and lying, and keeping up appearances when we have nothing to keep them up on. I would rather live in the meanest house, I would rather eat the humblest fare, than continue to endure the life of harass I have done."

"My poor dear," answered his wife, "I am afraid living in a hut on potatoes and salt would not mend the matter. We should want less money, it is, true, but we should have just as much trouble in getting it. If people have to live on their talents instead of a settled income, they must expect annoyances. But do not let this worry conquer you, Dion. I am certain a way out of it will be presented, and when you are a bishop you will look back and laugh at the troubles you now think so unendurable."

"When I am a bishop perhaps I may," agreed the Reverend Dion, "but I certainly do not feel inclined to laugh at them now. Suppose, for a change, Selina, you write to Lady Med burn. I really think, as you could put the need for pecuniary assistance, she might get her husband to help us."

But Selina declined. She would write to Colonel Leschelles, if Dion wished, but she could not—no, really she could not— ask a favour from Bella, "who was always your *protégée*, if you remember. I never liked the girl, nor understood her. In my opinion she is a sly hypocrite."

"Well, well, well, my dear," said Mr. Wright, which Selina correctly interpreting to mean that he courted no discussion about the matter, she swept out of the room with a languid grace, the skirt of her unpaid-for silk dress sweeping the dust out of the also unpaid-for library carpet as she walked.

"Dear me!" thought the Rev. Dion, as he watched her exit, "I wonder if anybody living ever paid so high for having nothing done as we do!"

The letters were written and dispatched. From Colonel Leschelles was reluctantly wrung a five-pound note; from Sir Harry Medburn a cheque for ten pounds, and a hint that, as Lady

Medburn had to give largely to local charities, he trusted Mr. Wright would not ask her to contribute any further sums to the good work carried on in the parish of "The Disciples."

Mr. Irwin refused to advance another penny, as did many more dear, good friends of the Wright family. In fact, all the Rector could scrape together was five-and-twenty pounds. "Not enough to pay for the time, trouble, humiliation, and postage," he said sadly.

"I will send it in, though, as Averill's subscription," he observed, noticing a look in his wife's face which warned him she had thoughts of annexing so useless an amount.

"Mr. Irwin ought to be ashamed of himself," said Mrs. Wright. "Why, his niece never would have been married at all had it not been for us."

"I wish he had done what I asked him," mused the Rev. Dion. "He could not have been a loser, and it would have proved temporal salvation to me. However," he added, striking his bosom with emphasis, "Mr. Wright is not beaten yet. If any one thinks he has beaten Mr. Wright, he is greatly mistaken." Which utterance, rendered into plain English, meant that Mr. Wright had bethought him of some other person, besides Mr. Cahoon, who might feel inclined to lend money on his pew rents.

"While I am about it I will ask for a couple of hundred," he thought; and meantime, to stave off the secretary, he sent him twenty-five pounds, *re* Averill.

It was a wet day on which the Rev. Dion sallied forth to try his fortune with the money-lenders; but he had come from a country where a downpour is considered of little importance, and, merely remarking to his Selina that rain, as a rule, meant "at home," he sallied out, took the first omnibus that offered— local trains were then almost unknown—looked benignantly on his fellow-passengers—some of whom whispered to each other, "That is the great preacher at Huntingdon Park!"—and travelled Cityward.

Arrived there, the very first man he met whom he knew chanced to be Mr. Irwin—Mr. Irwin, walking with a dark-bearded gentleman, whose face seemed, in some curious way, familiar to the Rector.

"How do you do?" exclaimed Mr. Wright, joyously holding out his hand, and standing quite at ease on the pavement as if the finest weather prevailed, umbrella jauntily poised, dress as neat and irreproachable as ever. "How do you do? What an age it is since I have seen you!"

Remembering that within a day or two he had refused the speaker pecuniary help, Mr. Irwin took the outstretched hand rather sheepishly, and shook it with a bad grace.

"All well at home?" went on Mr. Wright, as though he and Mrs. Irwin and the little Irwins were the dearest of dear friends.

"Thank you, yes; Mrs. Irwin and the children are pretty well."

"Rather wet to-day," observed Mr. Wright, glancing at the stranger as he spoke, and understanding he had "money" written on him from the crown of his head to the heels of his boots.

"Very wet indeed," replied Mr. Irwin, trying to move on.

"Have you heard lately from her ladyship?" asked Mr. Wright, still airily poising his umbrella.

For a moment Mr. Irwin hesitated; then he said, "I heard of her the other day: she was quite well."

"Dear, sweet creature!" ejaculated the Rector.

"I am sorry to say I must bid you good bye," observed Mr. Irwin; "I have an appointment."

"Good bye, then," said the Rector, in dulcet accents. "So glad to see you looking so well. Good bye! God bless you." And he was gone.

"Who is your rosy friend, Walter?" asked the dark and bearded gentleman.

"Only a begging parson, and a cursed nuisance," was the answer.

"And who is her ladyship?" pursued the other.

"A lady I met at his house, and to whom I have been able to prove of some little service," was the reply.

But as he replied, Walter Chappell Irwin could not help looking straight at his companion, who only remarked:

"Oh! indeed; you seem to have got into high company since we parted."

"I suppose so, though I have never been inside her doors."

"How very odd!"

"Not more odd than true."

CHAPTER XXXVII.

A FRESH INTERPOSITION.

STILL wet weather; still an even, industrious, apparently untiring downpour of rain, and the Rev. Dionysius Wright was no nearer an advance of money than ever.

The twenty per cent. men, and the thirty, and the forty, and the fifty, and the sixty, had apparently taken his measure, and either could not or would not advance what he wanted. Perhaps they did not think it was well to try to fleece a parson, more especially one so popular as the Reverend Dion ; perhaps they had unpleasant visions of police courts and brutal cross-examinations if they tried to extort their pound of flesh from a man in Mr. Wright's position. Whatever the cause may have been, the result was disastrous. He could not get the money. If he had offered all the tribes of Israel five hundred per cent., the answer would have been the same.

Since the time when Jacob, by subtlety, annexed the stronger of Laban's sheep, the Jews have rarely, save in their dealings with the Almighty, forgotten their own interests ; and, happily for themselves, they did not overlook those interests when Mr. Wright, suave, well dressed, prosperous-looking, plausible, went to ask for the advance of a mere bagatelle.

"It is a thing quite out of our line," answered, as with one voice, the descendants of Jacob's dozen sons ; and accordingly, at length, even Mr. Wright was fain to confess himself beaten.

"Really," he said to his dear Selina, after one of these unsuccessful journeys, "it is wonderful to see how totally insensible the Jews are to any Christian feeling."

"But the Christians are as bad as the Jews," sighed Mrs. Wright ; which was, indeed, so true, that one wet, dreary day the Rev. Dion found himself in Cornhill, still *minus* the money he required, very cold, very miserable, **very** much depressed.

"I will just turn into Birch's," he said, mentally, feeling at the same time if he had any silver in his pocket, "and have some soup and a glass of Madeira. Perhaps I might have been more fortunate to-day had I, before going to those creatures, partaken of some refreshment."

And accordingly he went into Birch's, sat down to the ordered soup and the well-remembered Madeira, his hair already turning grey, and his admirable appearance making a sort of clerical halo in that totally worldly room.

While he was breaking some bread, after three spoonfuls of the soup and a sip of the Madeira, he chanced to look across the narrow table, and saw the man with whom Mr. Irwin had been walking when last he met him. Already the stranger had recognized him, and consequently, as their eyes met, remarked

"I think I have had the pleasure of meeting you before."

"Delighted, I am sure, to have the pleasure of meeting you again," said the Reverend Dion genially. "Any friend of my dear friend Mr. Irwin must always be acceptable to me."

"You are very kind," replied the other, with a smile, which, as Mr. Wright afterwards observed, might, like Mr. Irwin's "Yes," have meant anything.

What it probably did mean was that he remembered the criticism of Mr. Wright's dear friend upon that gentleman, also that Mr. Irwin had not thought it necessary to introduce him.

They went on chatting for a time, in the intervals of soup and Madeira, concerning the weather, the City, the state of trade, politics, and various other subjects; and when they had paid the waiter, and gone downstairs, and passed through the shop, they continued to walk together towards Princes Street.

"I am going to the Joint-Stock Bank," observed Mr. Wright's new friend, "and shall soon have to say good morning; but I trust our acquaintance will not end here."

Mr. Wright trusted it might not either, and said he was charmed to have the happiness of meeting a gentleman possessed of such an amount of varied information, as was the case with his companion.

"I have been knocking about the world all my life," answered the other. "I have been in all sorts of places, and mixed amongst all sorts of people; and if a man keeps his eyes and ears open, he cannot well avoid picking up a good deal."

"Very true—very admirably put," commended the Rev. Dion, wondering whether pecuniarily he could pick anything out of one who had, he felt convinced, "knocked about" to some purpose.

"You, too, must have seen something of the world," observed his proposed prey; "enough, at all events, to enable you upon occasion to dispense with ceremony. Dine with me, will you, this evening? I know scarcely any one in London—no one, indeed, intimately except Mr. Irwin; and he, though doubtless a most excellent person, is not a very lively companion."

Mr. Wright remarked he could not listen to a word in disparagement of the very best man in existence; but his face showed at the same time that he understood the stranger had detected Mr. Irwin's weak spot, and appreciated his cleverness in doing so.

"You will dine with me, however?" persisted his companion.

"Indeed I will, if I can," answered the Reverend Dionysius with hearty alacrity. "Now just let me see," and standing at the door of the Joint-Stock Bank, he made a dive into his breast pocket, and extracting from its depths an immense memorandum-book, studied the last written page it contained attentively.

"After half-past six I shall be at leisure," he said at length; "that is to say, I can be at leisure."

"Seven, then, will suit you. I am staying at the Golden Cross."

And he was turning away when Mr. Wright stopped him.

"By-the-bye, to whom am I indebted for the honour of this invitation?"

"I beg your pardon. I quite forgot that neither of us knows the name of the other," and he pulled out a card and handed it to Mr. Wright, Mr. Wright following suit.

"Mr. Sanson," read out the Rev. Dion, "delighted, I am sure, to have made your acquaintance."

"A rough diamond," he remarked to Selina when he reached home; "but a gentleman—decidedly a gentleman; and, what is far better, I feel confident a very good man."

After he had dined, however, and found himself on the top of a Huntingdon Park omnibus on his way home, he was not, perhaps, quite so satisfied about the latter point.

Over a bottle of remarkably good port Mr. Sanson approached the subject at that moment nearest his heart.

"The first time I had the pleasure of seeing you, Mr. Wright," he began, "you made an inquiry concerning a friend of Mr. Irwin's."

"Ho! ho!" thought the Rector, "sits the wind in that quarter?" But he only said, with an admirable semblance of forgetfulness:

"Did I?"

"You old fox!" thought the other. Then he said out loud, "Yes; you asked after some one you spoke of as 'her ladyship.'"

"So I did, so I did," agreed Mr. Wright.

"Will you tell me the name of the lady to whom you referred?"

"Before I say yes, or no, will you tell me what passed between you and Mr. Irwin after I parted from him? You asked him the same question. What reply did he make?"

"An evasive reply."

"Exactly as I expected. Such being the case, I cannot tell you her name."

"But, sir, I must know it."

"Not from me."

"Why should you make a mystery about so simple a matter?"

"Why should you make a point of solving the mystery?"

"Because it is important that I should solve it; because for months past I have been trying to extract the secret from Irwin; because I hate being baffled. Look here, sir: if you understood me better, you would know I am a man who never yet really turned back from any enterprise on which I once embarked. Three times I seemed to have fortune within my grasp—three times fortune was swept from me. And yet I persevered; and now I am rich enough to buy a fine estate and take rank with anybody."

"Most creditable, I am sure," murmured the Rector; "quite an exceptional career."

"You would say so with more reason were I to describe it you," said the other, with an unpleasant smile. "My path has not been over roses and lilies, believe me. But to return to the point. I want to know who this ladyship is, concerning whom you maintain such secresy. She may or she may not be the person of whom I am in search; but, at any rate, I mean to find out where she is, and see her."

"If not an impertinent question, who is this person of whom you are in search?"

"That is my affair," was the reply. "Come now, Mr. Wright,

we need not beat about the bush any longer. I am determined
to find out what I want to know. Will you give the information at once, and greatly oblige me, or must I employ a detec-
tive? I would rather subscribe handsomely to one of your, no
doubt, numerous charitable undertakings than fee a spy." Which
sentence contained a great deal more truth than even Mr.
Wright imagined.

"You are very kind, I am sure," said the Rector; "and I am
greatly concerned to think I cannot comply with your request.
Mr. Irwin has been a dear good friend to me, and I really cannot betray his confidence."

"That means, I suppose, that he has assisted you pecuniarily,
and that you are afraid of offending him."

"No; I am not afraid of offending him. That he has helped
me materially, however, I am not ashamed to confess; and of
whatever sins I may be guilty, ingratitude is not amongst the
number."

"Of course; I understand all that; but between ourselves,
I don't think you owe Irwin much gratitude in the past, and
I believe he will give you little chance of being grateful to him
in the future. Be good-natured, therefore: tell me the lady's
name, and I will hand you over twenty-five pounds for any
charity you like to mention. Will that do?"

With all sincerity Mr. Wright said it would not. He *could
not think* of being a party to such a transaction. He would not
betray his dear friend for any consideration whatsoever.

"Not for twice twenty-five pounds?" asked the other, eyeing
him curiously.

"Not for twice twenty-five," declared the Rector firmly; but
firmly as he spoke, he was wavering, and the other saw it.

"Well, then, this is my last bid. If you refuse it I shall employ some one to-morrow who will not be long in worming out
the secret. If you tell me, without further trouble, where to
find her ladyship, you can have a hundred pounds. You won't
serve her by refusing to help me; and you won't serve yourself.
Be quite sure of that."

"Give me five minutes," gasped the Rector. Behold, here
was the amount needed ready to his hand. Why should he let
it go? What Mr. Sanson said was doubtless quite true. The
discovery now could only be regarded as a question of time;
and in any case Sir Harry Medburn and Mr. Irwin were rich

and prosperous, men well able to take care of themselves, whilst ruin and disgrace stared him, the Rev. Dion, in the face.

Nevertheless he hesitated. If ever a devil lurked in a handsome face, Mr. Wright saw it in Mr. Sanson's then. It seemed gibing at him as he looked helplessly at his tempter. It shone out of the dark eyes, and he knew, if the concealing hair were removed, he should behold it curling the resolute mouth.

Could he jeopardize Bella's happiness by telling this man where to find her? Could he, on the other hand, jeopardize his own position by refusing to avail himself of an opportunity so wonderfully offered?

"I must have time for consideration," he said at last. "Let me have four-and-twenty hours, and you shall hear from me, yea or nay."

"No," answered the other; "now or never. If you refuse to oblige me, I shall take other measures without delay."

"Do you know anything to her prejudice?" asked Mr. Wright.

"Nothing. What could have put such an idea into your mind?"

"And you do not want to trade on your knowledge of any secret connected with her?"

"No. I only wish to become one of the family party."

"But of what advantage can that possibly prove to you?"

"Perhaps some—perhaps none. Most likely I should never have wanted to see her again, had Irwin not made such a secret of the matter."

Another pause—another wrestle between the demon which had cursed Mr. Wright's life and his better nature, and he said:

"Give me the hundred pounds."

Without a word Mr. Sanson counted out the required sum, and laid it on the table, keeping a stern grasp on it the while.

"Now," he said triumphantly, looking across at his visitor, "let us exchange."

The Rev. Dion pushed a pencilled card over to his tempter, and, covering his face with one hand, placed the other on the notes.

"All right—take them," remarked Mr. Sanson; and then he pocketed the address, and Mr. Wright the money.

"She is pretty, no doubt," observed Mr. Sanson; but Mr. Wright refused to notice the suggestion. He simply rose, buttoned up his coat, said:

"It is time I bade you good night;" and so betook himself, as has been already stated, to the top of a Huntingdon Park omnibus.

Next morning he overslept himself. He had not designed to commit such an enormity; but, in good truth, he felt worn out, mentally and physically, and the consequence was that he had but just entered his study after breakfast when Mr. Irwin was announced.

"My dear, good friend," Mr. Wright was beginning, when the other waved him off.

"Read that," said Mr. Irwin imperatively, thrusting a letter into his hand.

"Dear Walter," so ran the epistle, "your clergyman deserved all you said of him, and more. He is a 'begging parson,' and a 'cursed nuisance.' Nevertheless he has served my turn. I start for Devonshire to-morrow. Why did you cause me and yourself so much trouble?

"Yours, MILES."

"How much did he give you?" asked Mr. Irwin; and Mr. Wright, smarting under the maddening influence of finding his dear friend had called him a begging parson, answered:

"One hundred pounds."

"I would have given you five hundred to keep her secret."

"Why, who is the man?" inquired the Rev. Dion curiously

"Her father, and the greatest scoundrel in England."

"Ah!" said Mr. Wright, "you should have been more explicit, and more liberal. But all that cannot be helped now!" which was the Rector's lament over Bella—and the lost five hundred.

"And yet he might never have paid it," he considered. "Really, when one comes to think over the matter calmly, there was not much generosity about Irwin. A mean fellow, like all self-made men. He was self-made."

"I shall acquaint Colonel Leschelles with the details of this most disgraceful transaction," observed Mr. Irwin at the end of his interview.

"Perhaps you will make Sir Harry Medburn acquainted with it also," said the Rev. Dion sarcastically. "No doubt it will afford him the keenest pleasure to meet, in the person of his wife's father, the greatest scoundrel in England.'"

Then Mr. Irwin understood he had in his haste and rage put a weapon into the hand of the Rev. Dionysius which that popular divine would not hesitate about using, should necessity arise for doing so.

CHAPTER XXXVIII.

LADY MEDBURN SPEAKS PLAINLY.

TIME went on. Considering time has been doing the same thing for six thousand years, or thereabouts, it is singular that people should be so much surprised to find it still does go on, making the young old, and the old older—bringing happiness, ʝaking happiness away—making all sorts of chimes and changes as it hurries along.

But the experience is new to each of us. Life is a fresh toy to each child born into it. Life is as a wonderful experience to each man and woman in existence. The life he or she enjoys or endures may not be much to speak of, amongst the millions; but still it is all that the individual unit has to make or to mar.

A five-pound note might not seem much to the possessor of three hundred thousand a year, but it appears a fortune to the struggling widow who loses what stands between her and beggary; and so it is with the little dot existence gives to some amongst us—when it is gone, everything is gone. In your eyes it seems but little; but, oh, friends, how much its loss may mean to me!

Vaguely Lady Medburn grasped this truth. Lives were being lived all around her for good or for ill; but the only life she really thought of was her own, so far as it affected herself, her husband, and her again expected child. People were suffering, people were enjoying, people were sinning, people were striving to do good; but she could not look over the fields where they were sowing and reaping, scattering the seed, garnering the harvest, because her own trouble was too near and too keen to let her eyes behold the troubles and joys of others.

If her husband had grown cold or neglectful, she might have borne the misery of her own deceit better; but, as matters stood, she never rested night nor day for thinking of that awful secret he should have known, which sooner or later, she was quite aware, she would be compelled to divulge. For she could not allow things to go on drifting—she could not peril the hopes and happiness of one after another, because her lips were slow to utter that which she believed would break Sir Harry's heart.

The county ladies thought that the "little upstart," as they called her, gave herself airs, because she shrank from society. The county gentlemen thought she must have had a previous lover, and thrown him over for the Baronet and the estate; while Sir Harry himself felt he could not understand her.

"It cannot be any sin of her own she is fretting about," he considered; "and yet what is wrong I am unable to imagine. I think she is fond of me, and God knows I try to make her happy; but she is uneasy when I am with her. She does not rejoice at the prospect of becoming a mother. She is wretched when that queer relation of hers, Sanson, is in the room with her; and yet the fellow tries to make himself agreeable, and there is no reason why she should feel ashamed of him. I wonder what that old story was she wanted to tell me before we were married? It had nothing to do with my darling—of that I am confident. For ever she shall stand 'Above Suspicion' with me."

As for Colonel Leschelles, who, coming from his new estates in Wales to visit his old friends, looked often dubiously from Mr. Sanson to Lady Medburn, he was more perplexed even than Sir Harry.

He had guessed the truth; but he could not understand Bella—could not comprehend how any woman should sit by and see the game played which was being played without uttering a word to prevent it.

At last he spoke.

"You notice what is going on, I suppose?" he said, one day as he and his hostess walked through the gardens together.

" I notice—yes."

" And shall you allow it to go on ?"

" No; but there is no necessity for hurry: she does not care for him. How, indeed, could she? If she could, I must have stopped it all long, long ago."

" Why do you not stop it now?"

She put her hand to her head while she answered :

" Because whenever I even think of speaking, such a pain here distracts me. At Fisherton Mr. Wright used to say how strong I was; but I am not strong now. It has all been too much."

" It has," he sadly agreed. "Shall I say what is necessary for you? Shall I take it all off your hands? You may be quite sure nothing can change your husband's heart towards you; but something ought to be done at once, my dear. Every hour you delay will make each minute of the future harder to bear."

" I know it," she replied. "But if he will go away quietly, who but you, and me, and uncle need ever be the wiser?"

" No one, perhaps; no one, I hope. But will he go?"

" I think so. I have something to say which may make him go. If that fail, I know what I intend to do."

" But why not do something at once?"

"I cannot," she answered; "not while I have this stupid pain; not while I have Sir Harry here, or you. But I promise to speak soon; I will—I will, indeed."

" Poor child!" said the Colonel pityingly; then went on : "I wish you would let me settle this matter for you; but perhaps it is better for it to rest between himself and yourself. Of course you have your husband to depend on in case of need; but if ever he should be ill or away, when you are in trouble, remember I will come at any moment—any moment," he added, with a lingering tenderness which sounded like the faintest echo of hopeful music, which once had been, but which was dead.

"I shall always remember," she answered, taking his hand and humbly kissing it. "You have been so good to me always —always so good."

Time went on, however. Colonel Leschelles left Cortingford. Sir Harry was here and there on business connected with a lawsuit then pending. Miss Selham was my lady's guest, as she had been for three months following Miss Kelvey's death and Sir Alexander's consequent absence on the Continent. Then suddenly he returned, claiming hospitality from his nephew in his nephew's absence.

As may be imagined, Lady Medburn, the most ill-starred lady who ever queened it at Cortingford, had now no gracious, winning ways, but she was possessed of a presence.

"I am so glad to see you, Sir Alexander," said the miserable wretch, copying the accepted formula. "It is most kind of you to come and see us."

"It is most kind of you to welcome an old man," answered Sir Alexander.

"Does that relative of Lady Medburn's live here?" he took occasion to ask Miss Selham the morning after his arrival.

"He is here almost constantly," was the reply. "He is looking out for a suitable property."

"Rich, I suppose, in that case?" hazarded the ex-Judge.

"Very rich, I believe."

"Humph!" said Sir Alexander.

Somehow he and Mr. Sanson could not stable their horses together; indeed, so indifferently did they agree, that Lady Medburn's relative betook himself to London, and would probably have remained there, but that once again a woman was influencing his life.

From the moment he first beheld her, he believed Edith Selham to be the most beautiful girl he had ever met; further, she belonged to an order with which he had previously had nothing whatever to do. He was for the time being like one intoxicated, with her and the atmosphere in which she lived. The luxury surrounding her, the flowers, the scents, the silent-footed servants, what these things proved to a man who, always yearning after wealth, and the things wealth can command, had yet been forced to pass through years of toil—years of shame— years of frightful companionship, may hardly be imagined.

He was no longer young, and he was ten times older in

feeling even than in age; and yet it is true that for the first time in his life he was in love—if, indeed, the passion he conceived for Miss Selham could be dignified by that name. For it was a love which cared for nothing, thought of nothing, but its own gratification—which, finding him a bad man, made him worse—which rendered him quite indifferent to consequences, providing only he could secure the prize.

And Lady Medburn remained silently watching, while the terrible pain grew worse and worse, and its agony seemed to numb her conscience as well as her tongue.

Relieved, however, by his absence, she experienced some slight ease. She talked more willingly; she did not sit so utterly mute; sometimes a faint smile appeared on her lips; and then he came back, and the shadow fell over her once again—a shadow which seemed to her like the precursor of death.

A purpose delayed is often a purpose frustrated; and so time passed on, and she had not yet spoken—seemed farther off speaking, indeed, than ever, when, one evening at dinner, there occured this conversation:

"I have bad news about M'Callum, Edith," said Sir Alexander Kelvey.

"Poor M'Callum! is he very ill?"

"He is ill no longer," answered Sir Alexander. "He is dead; and that reminds me of a letter I had from him when abroad. In it he stated that he had seen Barthorne walking down Highgate Hill, looking quite like a gentleman. He said he was so prosperous in his appearance, and so changed in some respects, he felt doubtful about his identity till he spoke; and then, though he denied being Barthorne, his voice betrayed him in a minute."

"Did you ever see the man, uncle?" asked Miss Selham.

"I may have done so, but I retain no recollection of him. M'Callum, however, knew him intimately. Nevertheless, though it is not impossible he may have have met Barthorne, whose term of transportation must long since have expired, I think the matter is open to doubt. M'Callum was a perfect monomaniac on the subject of his brother's murder. Poor fellow! where he is gone now he will know whether his suspicions were correct."

All this time Lady Medburn had sat looking at her father,

all this time he had sat staring defiantly at her. Then, in an instant, the pain she suffered seemed to cease, and her head grew clear and her mind collected.

For weeks previously she had been eating little, so that her lack of appetite attracted no attention. Only one thing Miss Selham noticed at the time, and recalled afterwards, viz., that she swallowed a glass of wine, which, as a rule, she disliked ; also that she made the signal for leaving table almost immediately dessert was placed.

Without entering the drawing-room, Lady Medburn passed straight on to the library, saying she had some letters to write.

"But the post has gone out !" exclaimed Miss Selham.

"No matter; I will write them to-night," was the answer.

An hour later, when she appeared in the drawing-room, there was a red spot burning on each cheek, and a glitter in her eyes no one had ever seen in them before.

Mr. Sanson, his chair drawn near to Miss Selham, was giving her a description of life in the bush and at the Gold Fields; and so engrossed was he in his subject that he started when Lady Medburn, coming behind him, said :

"I wish to speak to you for a few minutes. Will you come into the library?"

"Certainly," he answered, rising, and following Lady Medburn as she led the way.

"What is the meaning of this?" he said, watching her lock the library door. "If you had anything to say to me, why could you not have deferred saying it till to-morrow?"

"Because to-morrow I may not be able to say it ; because all this shall not go on twenty-four hours longer; because you either leave here first thing in the morning, or I shall tell Sir Harry who you are."

"And, consequently, who you are," he remarked.

"And, consequently, who I am," she agreed. "Do not deceive yourself. I have counted the cost. I know what telling the truth will prove to me, and to him ; but I mean to tell it, nevertheless."

"No, you will not," he said. "You are frightened now because of that drivelling old Judge's talk about M'Callum. The fellow was right, too. I did go to Highgate, and he did speak to me ; but he is dead, and there is an end of the matter. No fear of any one else recognizing me."

"It is not that," she explained. "If you had stayed here only for a short time, and been quiet and discreet, as you promised to be, I should never have spoken; but you have not kept your promise. How dare you, knowing what you are, think of trying to marry Miss Selham?"

"Dare!" he repeated. "That is rather an ugly word to be used by a daughter to her father. But if it comes to such plain speaking, how dare you, knowing what you are, marry a man who, when he knows the deception you have practised, will never forgive you?"

"I do not expect him to forgive me," she said. "I tell you I have counted the cost, and I shall speak the truth now, unless you leave here early to-morrow."

"That I will not do," he answered. "You seem to forget that I want to have some innings out of life as well as you, and that if I marry this girl, as I intend to do—for she has no money of her own, and will look kindly on mine in time, more especially as the only man she loves is married to you—it will insure to me position and respectability."

"But even supposing the past could be blotted out—that with your money you could begin a new life—supposing there were nothing about you which she ought to know, and which she shall know—you could not marry her while my mother lives."

"She may not be alive. Australia is a long way off. She may be married again, for aught I know or care. Perhaps also you are not aware that the fact of my—well, of my absence from the country, annuls the marriage."

"I do not believe it; but even if it were so—even if my mother were dead—you should not marry Miss Selham."

"Who says so?" he inquired.

"I do," she returned.

For a moment the pair looked at each other, and there came a wonderful resemblance into the two faces as they stood darkly defying—she him, he her. Then suddenly he dropped his eyes, and began :

"Mabel, what folly this is! Why should we not make our interests identical? Why should it profit you to cross my path, to ruin yourself, for the sake of ruining me? Can you undo what has been done—can you unmarry yourself? can you alter the fact that your child will call Sir Harry Medburn father? Don't be rash—don't, by one foolish word, curse your own life and that of your husband! 'Where ignorance is bliss'—you know; and if ever there was a case in point, it is yours. What you have to do is to hold your tongue. If I talked for a year I could give you no better advice."

"Will you go away, then?" she said.

"Not to remain away," he answered.

The red in her cheeks deepened in colour—the glitter in her eyes grew brighter—the dark determination of her expression became more intense as she repeated:

"Will you go away? For the last time, I ask whether you will leave me in such peace as I can ever know, or compel me to tell Sir Harry he has under his roof the murderer of David M'Callum?"

With a curse, he lifted his clenched hand to strike her, but, checked by something he beheld in her face—some reflection, perhaps, of his own nature—refrained.

"Tell what you like," he said. "Only remember there is nothing you can tell that will be worse for me than for you."

Then, striding to the door, he unlocked it, and quitting the library, left her there alone.

Contrary to his expectations, she came into the drawing-room before they all separated for the night.

"Do you leave in the morning?" were the last words she addressed to him.

Looking at her quite steadily, he said:

"No—I do not!" While Sir Alexander Kelvey, looking at both, said nothing, but thought a great deal.

CHAPTER XXXIX.

NEAR THE END.

LADY MEDBURN did not go to her own apartments when her guests had left her, but, ringing the bell, desired that Sir Harry's valet should be sent to the drawing-room.

"Can you catch the mail train to London, Ellis?"

"If I start at once, my lady."

"Do so, then," she said. "I want you to give this letter into Sir Harry's own hands. Do not allow any one else to see or touch it on any pretence whatever. And, Ellis," she added, as he was leaving the room, "tell your master I am quite well—do not forget."

The man assured his mistress the message should be delivered. He thought it a very curious message to accompany a letter, but he was a discreet and silent individual, and rarely, by word or look, gave an indication of what was passing in his mind.

For a minute after Ellis left the room Lady Medburn stood motionless, her eyes fixed on the ground. When she lifted them, it was only to look round the apartment with a weary, hopeless glance.

"The die is cast!" she said, unconsciously speaking aloud, and then slowly, but without once faltering, she walked out of the room she was not again to enter.

Next morning there was such consternation at Cortingford as had never agitated it before.

My Lady was nowhere to be found. My Lady had not been to bed. My Lady was gone without bag or baggage. No one had seen her leave. She must have made her way out of the park by a little-frequented path which led away to the uplands behind the house; for no gate had been unlocked except to give egress to Ellis, hurrying off to catch the night express.

Sir Alexander Kelvey telegraphed to London, begging his nephew to return by the first train, but already Sir Harry was speeding westward.

The old Judge was standing on the platform as the train drew in, and looked amazed to see his nephew alight.

"I did not think you could have got my message so soon," he remarked.

"I have had no message from you," was the answer.

And then Sir Alexander broke the news.

"I know why she has gone," was the answer. "No doubt she is in London with her uncle. I will follow her there—but I have something to do first at Cortingford."

They drove home in utter silence. Sir Harry never opened his lips, and there was a white despair in his face which told his uncle that he was battling with some sudden anguish that had, for the moment, almost mastered him.

"Can you tell me what it is?" the old man had said, as they walked out of the station; and Sir Harry had answered, "Not yet."

Arrived at Cortingford, the Baronet, after telling a servant to request Mr. Sanson's presence in the library, walked straight into that room.

"Shall I leave you, Harry?" asked his uncle, hesitating at the door.

"If you please," was the answer.

Not when he stood in the dock had Miles Barthorne looked more dark and defiant than was the case when he and the young Baronet faced each other.

"I had a letter this morning from my wife," began Sir Harry in a low voice, hoarse with restrained passion. "You can imagine what it contained. I have only one thing to say in reference to that letter now—leave my house—leave it at once !"

"Before I go——" the other was beginning, when Sir Harry interrupted him.

"Will you go?" he asked, furiously, "or must I order the servants to put you out? Is it not enough that you have driven my wife to tell me a secret I had better never have known— but you must strive to bandy words with a man who holds your very life in his hands?"

"The man who says so must be very tired of his own," retorted Barthorne, scarcely able to speak, because his lips were dry and cracked, and impotent rage was choking him.

"Will you go?" said Sir Harry, striking the table with a vehemence which caused every article on it to jump as if endued with vitality. "I am not master of myself—I cannot answer for what I may do if you stand there another instant. Go!" and, flinging the door wide open, Sir Harry pointed the way out.

So Barthorne went, and Sir Harry, his passion spent, sat down in the sorrowful silence, and wept like a child. Wept for the tarnished honour of his house, for his own broken heart, and the downfall of every hope a man can centre in his children yet unborn; but more—ay, far more—for the misery his wife had suffered, the misery he believed she would endure for evermore.

"Above Suspicion," he had said, he would ever hold her; but no loyalty, no faith, no future, no love could alter the fact that she he had taken to his heart was the child of a convicted thief, of an unconvicted murderer.

"Harry," said his uncle, entering the room softly, and laying his hand on the young man's shoulder, "can you tell me now what it is?"

"Not yet—never, perhaps. I must think it all over first. So far, I have not thought; I have only felt. Will you come back with me to London? I must go there by the first train."

But even while Sir Alexander was consulting the time-table, Miss Selham came to them, holding a telegraphic message in her hand. The word telegram was unknown in those days.

"From Colonel Leschelles," she said, and read:

"Lady Medburn is here, and very ill. Let Sir Harry know. Tell him to come at once."

Small need to tell him to hurry. Before his cousin had finished the message, he had seized his hat, and was half-way across the hall.

Miss Selham looked at Sir Alexander, who, answering her thoughts, said:

"We can follow him."

Instantly Ellis was ordered to pack a few things for his master and his master's uncle, whilst in like manner Lady Medburn's maid was hurried off to put up some necessary clothing for her mistress and Miss Selham.

"Lady Medburn has gone to Colonel Leschelles'," explained Miss Selham thankfully; for she did not know what the servants might have been thinking and saying. "Sir Harry knows all about it."

"My lady seemed to me last night as if she was going to have a fever," said the maid, as she passed and repassed from the trunk to the wardrobe. "When she spoke she appeared scarcely to know what she was saying. And when I was brushing her hair I could see in the glass that her cheeks were like two twin damask roses, while it is unusual for her to have much colour."

"She is very ill," remarked Miss Selham, still mindful of appearances, and anxious to encourage the impression which had evidently gained ground.

"Could not I go with you, miss?" ventured the woman.

"If she is not able to return with us, I will send for you," was the reply; but when they reached Colonel Leschelles' Miss Selham found that a very different attendant would be required.

"What fever is it?" asked Sir Henry of the doctors, when he saw his wife's convulsive struggles, and heard her cries.

They glanced at each other, and then the elder of the two answered:

"It is not fever at all—it is insanity."

For a moment the room seemed whirling round with Sir Harry. The faces of the doctors grew dim and indistinct, and their voices sounded as if heard from some immense distance.

All at once it appeared to Sir Harry that he was able to grasp what his wife must have endured, the agony she had suffered.

"My darling!—my poor darling! And you bore it all alone!" That was the one thought that took possession of him. In that supreme moment, pride, the love of self, the memory of the wrong done him, died out, leaving only pity in their place. His heart was so full of it that no space remained for a second feeling.

What she had suffered! not even Bella herself could ever have told that, for she herself scarcely knew. The sleepless nights, the wretched days, the constant suppression, the agony, the fear, the pain, the shame, had all culminated in this!

"But there is hope," he murmured, when at last, the room ceasing to reel round, and the doctors' faces becoming once more distinct, he could speak like a rational being; "she will be better soon."

They looked at each other again. Then the younger, taking up his parable, said:

"We should like, ere pronouncing a positive opinion, to

know how this attack commenced. Was it after a sudden shock of any kind, or had the patient been for any time in a low and despondent condition?"

"Both. She had been enduring a mental trouble for a long time, and at last she experienced a great shock," explained Sir Harry eagerly.

"Just so," said both doctors simultaneously, but there was no gladness in their voices.

"Is there madness in the family?" they asked, after a pause.

"I never heard of there being," answered the Baronet, thinking how very incompetent he was to speak as to the tendencies of his wife's ancestors.

"I think," said the senior physician, "that we had better be quite frank with you. There is a hope, and only one, for Lady Medburn. If after her child is born she recover her reason, she may live and do well; if not——"

"And if not?" questioned Sir Harry, clutching the back of a chair as he spoke.

"Why should we anticipate evil, and diagnose the worst?" here interrupted the younger doctor cheerfully. "Please God, Lady Medburn may yet be as sane as any of us—and live to be the mother of many children."

At which utterance Sir Harry crept away sick at heart. The wife was one thing, the children another. Thoroughly he understood why Bella had never seemed to desire daughter or son.

"My poor dear!" he said sorrowfully; "my most unhappy wife!"

He could not always remain in Wales. It was necessary for him now and then to make hurried journeys to Devonshire and to London, and during these absences Mr. Irwin visited his niece, and sometimes Barthorne his daughter!

Of the blacker mark against Barthorne Colonel Leschelles was totally ignorant, and, considering Lady Medburn's condition, he scarcely felt justified in denying the man admittance.

"My whole future," explained Bella's father, "depends on her recovery." And how was the Colonel to know that he came to Wales solely in the hope of seeing Miss Selham, and being able to entreat Bella to plead for her father?

All he wanted was leave to stay in England. That Sir Harry would pursue him to the death he never for one moment imagined.

And so he came and went—sometimes seeing Miss Selham, who was evidently quite ignorant of the story, and sometimes seeing no one, not even the Colonel, who had suddenly grown an aged man.

All at once, however, his visits ceased. Colonel Leschelles told him he must not come while Bella's life and reason hung in the balance; and while he stayed away a child was born—the heir so long expected—alive, and instantly handed over to the care of a healthy Welsh matron.

But Lady Medburn's state did not improve. The mania was exhausted, it is true: and then the doctors said they understood her case thoroughly. She lapsed into childishness. For a fortnight they entertained some hope; at the end of that fortnight they were not chary of saying Lady Medburn would for the remainder of her life be imbecile.

The imbecility proved a harder trial than the mania. When she could get about she was found to be quite quiet and harmless; but amongst Colonel Leschelles' curiosities she found a foreign doll, which she kissed and fondled as she might a real baby.

Beyond the animal instinct which told her she had been a mother, no one could trace the smallest knowledge of human interests.

The doctors said, "Try to rouse her;" and her friends did try, all in vain.

To each and all she presented the doll, saying, "Is not my baby pretty?" and then she would push the short hair off her forehead, and remark that she had been ill lately, and she hoped her visitor would excuse her want of memory.

When she was in this state, down came Mr. Wright to see her.

At Cortingford he had been informed she was staying at Colonel Leschelles', and so, with a view of preferring a request, came westward.

"My dear Lady Medburn, I am indeed rejoiced to see you once more," he was beginning, when ushered into her room, but there she stopped him.

"You have come to see my baby; is not it a darling?" and she turned the glazed face of Colonel Leschelles' foreign doll towards the intruder, who fled, appalled.

"Selina," he said, on his return to London, "you never saw

anything so awful. I could never have believed a doll could attain dimensions at once so awful and so pathetic."

"As people sow, they must reap," said Mrs. Wright, sententiously. "As Bella sowed in our house, she is reaping now. I suppose she will never recover her reason?"

"The doctors say never," agreed the Rev. Dion, ruefully.

But for once the doctors' dictum was wrong; Lady Medburn did recover her reason.

She had been failing in health for some time, becoming restless, and evidencing a certain irritability and fretfulness, which caused those around her much anxiety, and made them inwardly marvel whether it might not become absolutely necessary to place her under careful and gentle supervision for the remainder of her life, when all at once she fell into a deep sleep, from which she awoke very weak indeed, it is true, but with all fever and mania gone, quite sane, reasonable, and collected.

"Where am I?" were the first words she uttered; and Edith Selham rose, startled at hearing the sound of her natural voice again.

"At Colonel Leschelles', love."

"At—Colonel—Leschelles'?" she repeated slowly.

"Yes; you came here the night you were taken ill."

"Have I been ill long?"

"A long time."

"And my husband?"

"Has been with you almost constantly. But now you must ask no more questions. Dear, dear Mabel! how thankful I am to hear you speak rationally once again!"

Just at the first the invalid spoke more than the doctors considered good for her, but shortly she lapsed into silence, and remained so quiet that Miss Selham understood she was trying to recall for herself the events which preceded her journey.

The only impatience she manifested was on the subject of Sir Harry's return.

"I wish he would come—I do wish he would come—I do so wish he would come!" she repeated, weakly and plaintively.

"My darling, your wish cannot be greater than his," answered Miss Selham; and then she would go to the window and look out over the hill-path she knew her cousin would be sure to take, because it was so much shorter than the road.

"Come here, Edith," said Bella, at length; "I know he will

not delay, and I will try to be patient. Sit down, I want to look at you."

Many a time in the after years Edith recalled that hour—recalled the sad expression of the wistful eyes that gazed upon her, as if trying to photograph each feature in her face.

"Smile, Edith."

She tried to comply, but the smile refused to come; instead, she broke down and burst into tears.

"Forgive me, Mabel," she said; "I am sorry to have been so foolish."

But Bella did not answer; she only put out her hand feebly, and turned her head a little from the light.

The hours went by, and still Lady Medburn lay so still that Miss Selham, thinking she must again have fallen asleep, crept softly from the room.

But Bella was not asleep. Her eyes were closed, it is true, but her mind was busy travelling back along the road so mercifully forgotten for a time, but again so well remembered.

Slowly and weakly she retraced it all, step by step, from the hour when in darkness and silence she left her husband's house, on the day of the Confirmation at Fisherton.

Once again she saw the young girls in their pretty dresses. She saw the chestnut-trees glorious with bloom; the scent of the hawthorn seemed floating around her. She saw the sunshine lying over the churchyard and tenderly resting on the lowly graves; the chatter and song of birds were in her ears; the figure of the Reverend Dionysius rose again before her. She could see the picturesque cottages, and the old women and children watching the sight. And then *he* came into the foreground of that peaceful, happy scene—he whose life she had marred—who had loved her—whom she had loved too much for the happiness of either.

It was not until the next day that Sir Harry arrived. He had started the moment the message reached him, but, being absent from Cortingford, he did not receive it until his return thither.

He found his wife very weak, very quiet, but with a look of rest on her face he had never seen since their marriage.

"Harry!" she said.

"My darling!" he answered; and then there ensued a dead silence, whilst, hand clasped in hand, they gazed at each other.

It was she at length who spoke.

"You forgive me, Harry?"

"Forgive you, dear! I have nothing to forgive," he said simply. "I love you."

"As much as you ever did?"

"More."

She gave a little sobbing sigh, and her poor thin fingers closed tighter on his.

"My poor Bella!" It seemed natural to him then to call her by the name first known, first loved. "My poor Bella, what you must have suffered!"

"Yes; but it is over now."

"Why did you not tell me sooner?" he asked.

"I wonder I ever told you at last," she said feebly.

"You must not talk any more now, dear," he declared. "The doctors particularly wish you not to exert yourself."

"Never mind the doctors. I know as well as they what I am able to do, what I must leave undone. I have very little to say. Still I should like to say it."

"So long as you do not exhaust yourself," he answered.

She lay with her eyes closed for a minute, then, partly unclosing them, murmured:

"The child——"

"Is dead, poor baby! He died a fortnight ago."

"Thank God!" she whispered, after a pause adding, "I hoped it was so when Edith never mentioned him."

Sir Harry did not answer, he only drooped his head. Her words brought back to mind all the shame and the sorrow, forgotten in the ecstacy of her recovered reason.

How in the future should it fare with husband and wife, when the mother thanked God for the death of her child!

Once again the weak voice began to speak.

"Have you told any one?" it inquired.

"No one; it all rests between you and me and Irwin."

"I wish them to know," she said. "Tell Edith and Colonel Leschelles and your uncle. They will advise what you ought to do. They will help you to bear it."

"Do you really mean this?" he asked in amazement.

"Really. Have no secrets from such true friends. I want Edith to know all now. I want her to understand to-night."

"She shall, dear—she shall."

"She will see then why I was so different from every one
else. She will know what life has been to me."

"She will love you the better for what you have endured."

"I think so—I believe so. And, Harry, I should like to
see my father. Don't be angry. You will know why I want
to see him later on. I will get him to go away—far, far away
—where he will trouble you no more. Send for him soon, will
you? Ask him to come at once."

"As you like, dearest—as you like, even in that."

"I am getting very tired now," she went on. "I think I
could sleep. Kiss me once again, Harry. I am so happy;
I have never felt so happy before in all my life."

Lingeringly he smoothed her pillow, drew the coverlet closer
around her, and left the room.

First, he dispatched the promised message to Miles Barthorne; and then, while his powers were strung up to tell the
story of Bella's father, he repeated it to Miss Selham and
Colonel Leschelles.

And while he talked night dropped down over the Welsh
mountains, and closed into the room where Lady Medburn lay
so peaceful and so happy. And in London, under the gaslight,
Miles Barthorne was studying "Bradshaw," and found it would
be quite possible for him to reach Colonel Leschelles' house
early the next morning.

"Recovered her reason—wants to see me at once," he said
to himself, repeating the sense of the telegraphic despatch.

"Wants, I suppose, to get rid of me for ever, is about the
English of it. What a fool I have been! Always a woman—
always—always a woman. Well, a woman shall work no more
evil for me. So now for Wales and my daughter Lady
Medburn!"

CHAPTER XL.

WHAT BARTHORNE SAW.

THERE is no such glory of sunrising as that over the sea and upon the hills; but to the opal tints of morning Miles Barthorne, striding along the path leading to Colonel Leschelles' house, was as indifferent as to most other wonders of nature.

Taking it round as a rule, a man must have a fixed income and a contented mind to enable him really to enjoy any one of the marvels our great Mother daily unfolds.

Artists fancy they alone can thoroughly appreciate sweet sights.   Artists, I conceive, are really the last people on earth who enjoy anything natural.   They cannot revel in the dews of early morning; in the sunlit fields of noon; in the gold and purple of evening, and the silvery bars of moonlight, without thinking how each would bear reproduction on canvas; and the man who has once, as regards the loveliness of nature, an *arrière-pensée*, can never look upon her face with the same appreciative fondness as that which sometimes touches even the dull apprehension of a hind.

And the same remark applies, though with possibly a difference, to the human being who has made for him or herself gods of things temporal—such as money, ambition, fame: ay, even fame, dear young friend.   Follow the leading of that vanity, which is usually considered a safe enough guide, and see where it shall land you.

Or rather do not follow it.   Keep, instead, to the old familiar life and the sweet home gods; and though the world ring with your plaudits, hardly cross your door-step to respond to the cheers of those who would just as soon, or sooner, hiss you to-morrow.

So when the end comes, the inevitable end, Nature will step in and help you to cross the last threshold over which your feet may ever pass on earth.   To the very confines of eternity she has great consolation for the children who have understood her on earth.

Since to a certain extent such children must have been true-

hearted, which Miles Barthorne never was; and yet—and yet
—as he crossed the hills, his heart recalled what he fain would
have forgotten.

There are times in a man's life when, whether he be willing
or not, memory insists on his reviewing the road he has travelled;
and one of these times came to Barthorne as he strode across
the grass still glittering with dew, and looked with his bodily
eyes on the gay patterns wrought by gorse and heather, on the
cloudless sky, up which the sun was climbing, on the sea lying
below, calm and quiet as some inland lake.

With all his soul he hated morning. The recollections he
held of it were none so pleasant as to cause him to give it a
cheerful greeting.

Mornings when he was running wild about Abbotsleigh. Ay!
they were mornings worth having, if you like. Early mornings
spent by the river's brink, watching the speckled trout darting
hither and thither through the clear stream, and then hiding in
dark places sheltered by the alder-trees; or with the game-
keepers in the woods; or clearing the ha-ha in the park; or
watching the men bark-peeling; or shouting for glee when, the
ice on the ground, the great logs were carted to the Hall.

Happy mornings, whether the sun were shining or the snow
falling! As memory gave them back to him, Miles Barthorne
felt his heart must break for very pity of himself.

After all, it is not necessary for a man to be of a very sym-
pathetic nature in order to feel for his own wrongs. And then,
after those days so blissfully long in the passing, so brief in the
retrospect, came other mornings of which Barthorne thought
with unspeakable disgust—mornings when he had to work at a
trade hateful to him; mornings when, with a scowl on his brow
and curses brooding in his heart, he had to stand, cap in hand,
before his father's equals, to be to them as some being of an
inferior race.

And then came his Tottenham experiences, when he used to
watch the sun rise over the flat marshes bordering the Lea—
when, from his cottage door at West Green, he beheld morning
coming across green fields bordered by rows of elm-trees.

Not so bad a life that, could he have made enough money to
satisfy his requirements without annexing his neighbours' goods;
but, good or not, it ended the mor ng David M'Callum was
murdered.

That was a morning! Lovelier, surely, than morning that ever dawned before upon the earth. Not a cloud in the tender blue sky—not a sound breaking the stillness. Far below lay the Great City—silent; each gilt vane and weathercock and cross glittering in the glorious sunshine. And then—but what boots it to go on with the chronicle, save as speedily as may be? Mornings when the sunbeams darting through barred windows roused him from blessed forgetfulness— mornings passed at sea—mornings on land while working out his sentence—mornings when at the first streak of dawn he was labouring away to find the gold afterwards stolen from him.

And there was one morning stamped upon his memory— when he woke to find himself bruised, battered, wounded, alone —left for dead. He lay there all day, and then all night again; and the sun rose once more, and he had scarcely strength left to unclose his eyes and look at it. He could not crawl from the spot—he could not cry for help; and yet help came, and he was nursed back to health, and had strength given him to make a better thing of life and the future than he had ever made of it in the past.

But he was incapable of learning. At the end, as at the beginning, he thought of self first, of duty last; and the natural consequence of such personal devotion proved that while he walked over the headlands he felt no delight in the sunshine flooding land and sea, no happiness in the remembrance of a daughter restored to reason, no resolves to lead a better life stirring within him—nothing save a craven dread of having to give up England and his hopes of position there—nothing save a mad anger at his plans having been thwarted and his schemes destroyed.

"I had better have left the girl alone," he said, lifting his hat from his head and letting the morning air play about his temples. "If that fool Irwin had not made such a mystery about the matter, she would never have been troubled by me."

Wherein he chanced to be wrong. But then, men like Miles Barthorne are in the habit of shifting the blame attached to their actions off their shoulders on to the shoulders of somebody else.

And so he went on, unheeding that placid sea, regardless of the grand old hills—on over the headlands, till he came to the point where the path dipped and led him, by a circuitous route,

to the rear of Colonel Leschelles' house.   Over the wicket gate
he found the Colonel leaning listlessly, wearily.

Barthorne stretched out his hand in greeting, but the other
affected not to notice the movement.

"Does the amendment still continue?" asked Bella's father
anxiously.

"She is well," was the answer.

"Can I see her?"

"Yes."

"Had I better send a message up?"

"No."

"The old room, I suppose?"

"The old room," assented Colonel Leschelles.

There was something strange about his manner, Barthorne
felt—something more than resentment against himself.

Were they sorry she had recovered her reason?   Did they
feel it a misfortune that his daughter should—sane, as he understood her to be—come between the wind and their nobility?

Without another word he turned from the Colonel and walked
straight through the open door into the hall.   Up the remembered staircase, at the head of which he paused for a moment
to note the extraordinary stillness of the house.

"The servants have overslept themselves," he thought, "and
no one except those attached to the sick-room are yet stirring."

Even while he stood thinking this, however, a light footstep
sounded along a distant corridor—it came nearer and nearer,
then suddenly Miss Selham appeared in the distance.   The moment she caught sight of him she turned and retraced her way.

There was nothing wonderful in that action, though Barthorne
smiled as he noted it, and smiled still more grimly at the involuntary gathering of her skirts about her, as if to escape the
possibility of the contamination of touch from such as he.

"She knows all.   The game is played out, my lady—but I was
very near winning it," he murmured, and then walked straight
on along another gallery to the rooms set apart for Lady Medburn.

Through the first apartment, where Mr. Wright had seen her
fondling the doll she imagined to be her baby—through the
dressing-room beyond, opening to her sleeping-chamber, this
man passed swiftly; but on the last threshold he paused—it
was so horribly neat, so orderly, so——

Through chinks in the closed shutters came some rays of light, otherwise the room was in total darkness; and yet Barthorne placed his hand so as to shade his eyes, as if he had been standing in the full sunshine.

What did he see?

Only a man and a woman—only a husband and wife—she with the sheet drawn closely up around her throat—he, sitting by the bedside, his weary head resting on the pillow beside her, fast asleep.

Ay, both asleep!

Barthorne advanced a step or two forward. As he did so, a stray sunbeam fell across the faces of husband and wife—across the man's, worn, stained with tears, wan and haggard with watching: across hers, white with a pallor no one had ever seen on it before, with the long dark lashes, which might never be lifted again, resting on her thin cheeks; with the mouth set in a smile which was terrible to behold; with the mark of the grave upon her; with death written, in Death's own stern caligraphy, upon every feature!

Out again, over the thick carpets, along the corridors, down the stairs, Barthorne groped his way like one blind.

When he came to himself, he was standing in the hall, holding fast by the rail of the banisters.

"My God!" he said, "my God!" uttering the words, as men do in their most grievous troubles and perplexities, all unconsciously; and then he wiped the cold dew off his forehead, and stood quite still till such time as he felt able to pass out into the open air again and face his future.

As he had left him, so Colonel Leschelles stood when he spoke to him once more.

"When did she die?" asked Barthorne, touching him on the arm.

"Yesterday evening," the Colonel replied, absently brushing the portion of his sleeve Barthorne had contaminated.

"Will you tell him I leave for America by the first steamer?"

"I will tell him," was the answer; but still Mr. Barthorne waited.

"Have you any further message you wish me to deliver?" asked the Colonel.

"None whatever."

"Then, had you not better go wherever you mean to go?"

"Certainly; I will adopt your advice at once." And with a mocking laugh, Barthorne took off his hat, said, "Good bye, Colonel—not *au revoir* this time," and went on his way across the hills above the sea, the sunshine flooding hill, and sea, and valley with gleams of golden light.

On, like a man drunk or delirious or in a dream, to his inn, where the first person he met was Mr. Wright, who speedily restored him to his senses.

"How is my good friend?" asked the Reverend Dion, holding out his hand and clutching Barthorne's with vehemence, even while keeping his head averted to prove that his feelings were too much for him. "How is my good friend?"

"If you mean me," answered his good friend, "I am quite well."

"My dear fellow," pursued Mr. Wright, "I cannot tell you how delighted I was at hearing such cheering news as I did from Mr. Irwin yesterday; I cannot indeed."

At that Barthorne turned upon him with the old cynical smile, and said:

"I suppose it is cheering news; but I confess I never before imagined a man would say he felt delighted at hearing it."

"Why not—why not, pray?" asked the Rev. Dion, looking very red, and ruffling up his clerical feathers for an argument. "Must it not be cheering to *all* her friends to know that our dear Bella—we always call her Bella still amongst ourselves—is in a fair way of getting strong again? And is it not doubly delightful to me to know that the sweet girl will at length be able to reproach her most devoted friend with all his sins of commission and omission?"

For an instant Barthorne paused, then he said:

"I suppose, Mr. Wright, you came down to congratulate my daughter's husband on the occasion of her auspicious recovery?"

"Most certainly I did," answered Mr. Wright, looking, at the door of the clean, quaint, but modest Welsh hostelry, a very great dignitary of the English Church.

"And I suppose you had no other errand in this part of the country—no wish, say, for ten minutes' private chat with Sir Harry or Colonel Leschelles?"

"I fail to follow your meaning," said the Rector, with a delightful assumption of innocence.

"I had only one object in making the inquiry," pursued

Barthorne with pitiless candour—"to save you trouble.   If, upon the strength of my daughter's recovery, you have come to see her husband about business, it may be as well to inform you she is dead.   She died yesterday evening."

"You are jesting.   It is impossible," gasped Mr. Wright.

"Sir!" said the father who had just left his dead child.

"Why, they told me," gasped Mr. Wright, "she had quite recovered her reason."

"I suppose she had—I know nothing to the contrary; and the first use she made of it, apparently, was to leave a world you and I, for instance, did not help to make happy for her."

"I always tried to make her happy," said the Rector.

"I have no doubt you gave me her address solely with that intention," agreed Miles Barthorne.

Mr. Wright was by far too old a diplomatist to continue this sort of discourse.   Instead, he put his hands behind his back, and with head bent down, began to walk to and fro, that all beholders might see his grief.

"Dear, dear, dear!" he said; and, spite of bailiffs, and duns and impending bankruptcy, or perhaps, indeed, because of them, his grief was very genuine. "Poor, poor Lady Medburn! It is the last thing I should have supposed possible ; but to God all things are possible, and, in His hands, probable.   Such a superb constitution, and yet first insanity and then death! Only last night!   I will go over and say a word or two to the poor husband.   At such a time language truer than any man can speak must be grateful to him."

"You can see," observed Mr. Barthorne, "whether anything you say is favourably received.   I am no authority on such matters myself, otherwise I might remark that I should have thought to intrude into a house of mourning is scarcely in good taste."

"In some cases, doubtless," returned the Rev. Dionysius; "but the dear creature was like a child of my own ; and, her bereaved husband knows that, and will understand how fully I sympathize with him."

"Very well, then, go," retorted the other.   "Do anything you like, in fact, except stay talking to me."   And he turned into the inn, followed by a caressing entreaty from Mr. Wright that "he would not stand on ceremony with him."

A little after noon the Rector reappeared.   Sir Harry, he

explained, had left for Cortingford, and Colonel Leschelles had treated him most scurvily.

"I suppose, sir, you would hardly credit the fact," proceeded Mr. Wright, "but, although Colonel Leschelles has stayed at my house for weeks and weeks at a time, and partaken of the best we had to offer, he never asked me to sit down, or to take a glass of wine. I never was treated so vilely in all my life before, never."

"You chose an unfortunate time for your visit," was the reply. "The next time you call Leschelles will probably give you the title-deeds of his estate."

"What are *your* plans now, my dear friend?" asked Mr. Wright, wisely ignoring his friend's last remark. "Do you purpose to remain here, or return to London, or what are you going to do?"

"I have no plans," answered Mr. Barthorne. "At the present moment I have only one intention, and that is, not to have you fastened on to me. If you are going to stay here, I will go to London; if you are going to London, I will stay here."

"Poor fellow! it is natural you should feel a little bitter, after what you have gone through this morning; but I need not tell you where consolation is to be found, and——"

"Now, will you stop all that," said Barthorne fiercely, "and just tell me whether you are going back whence you came, or whether you purpose remaining here?"

"I shall return to town," answered Mr. Wright, his clerical countenance wearing a look of sorrow, more than anger.

"Very well, then, I shall remain here," said the other; and taking his hat, he went out.

"I shall not leave until this evening," decided the Reverend Dion, as he watched Barthorne's figure growing more and more indistinct in the distance; and accordingly, having inquired for what time his friend had ordered dinner, he requested that something might be prepared for him at the same hour, and sallied forth for a walk.

When he returned dinner was ready, but Barthorne had not appeared.

"I will not go to London to-night," thought the Rector, after he had finished his meal. "In fact, I cannot go till he returns, for I have not enough money to settle with mine host. Dear, dear!—it seems as if money always went to the wrong person."

Evening drew on, night came, it grew quite late, and still no Barthorne.

"Perhaps he is staying at the Colonel's," suggested the landlord. "It is hardly safe for a stranger to cross the hills after dark."

"I suppose not. Very likely he is at the Colonel's," agreed Mr. Wright, thinking in his heart it was much more probable Barthorne had sought another inn.

Had he guessed where Barthorne really was, how differently would he have passed the night! How frantically he would have organized a rescue party—how he would have roused the village, and called for ropes, and men, and dogs, and lanterns—how he would have hurried hither and thither, shouting till the welkin rang again, for his dear friend to answer—to say where he was—to be certain there was help close at hand—his help, Dionysius Wright's!

It was a lost opportunity; but then, as the Rector said afterwards, "How could I know the man was lying at the bottom of a quarry?"

That was why Barthorne did not return. Wandering in the dark from the direct path, he climbed over what seemed to him a fence, and went straight down on the other side, a depth of some thirty feet.

For a time he lay insensible—for a long time it must have been, as when he recovered consciousness the stars were shining, and the moon, then in her last quarter, throwing a ghastly light across the sky.

He tried to move, but he could not—he strove to call out, but his voice failed him; and so he lay there thinking—thinking about his life—about the years piled up behind—about what he had set out to do—about what he had done, till he dropped off into a troubled doze, from which he woke, thinking David M'Callum was sitting on his chest, crying out, "I am avenged at last!"

He was found next morning by a shepherd, whose attention was attracted to the spot by his dog; but when, help being procured, they tried to lift him, he prayed them with such groans to let him die where he lay that the men drew back, and looked at each other in frightened silence.

Just then a doctor came hurrying up.

"He must be lifted," he said. "Never mind his cries; he will faint, and then we can take him to the inn."

And so it fell out: he did faint, and remained unconscious as the men carried him, carefully and tenderly as they were able, across the hills overlooking the sea, down the hillside, and so to the inn where the Rev. Dionysius Wright was regaling himself with a dish of excellent trout.

An hour afterwards the doctor stood in the street talking to Colonel Leschelles.

"You can send to London for a surgeon, if it will be any satisfaction to you," he said; "but the whole College of Surgeons, president included, could not benefit him. He may live for ten days or a fortnight; but if he died before sunset, it would be a merciful release."

Softly the Colonel entered the darkened room where Barthorne lay trying to bear his sufferings in silence.

"It is death, I suppose?" came slowly from the blue, trembling lips.

"I fear so. Tell me if there is anything I can do for you, and I will try to do it."

"Send Wright away. He adds a new terror to—— He will go if you give him ten pounds. There is more than that in my pocket-book."

CHAPTER XLI.

CONCLUSION.

WINTER'S snows and spring's showers have fallen often and often upon the earth, since, in the little Welsh hostelry, Miles Barthorne breathed his last.

The story I have told is now an old one, and, although her memory still remains green in some few fond hearts, the world has since her death gone on much the same as if the first Lady Medburn had never existed.

A mistress, fair, gracious, wise, has stepped into her vacant place; and if she is not able quite to fill Sir Harry's heart, he is, nevertheless, happy and content.

He can think of the dead wife with no pang of self-reproach. He can look on his living children, and feel thankful to remember that no shadow of the disgrace which once troubled him can cloud their future. But Bella is not forgotten. She never will be by him, till he is carried to the gloomy vault where they laid her to rest.

Under Miles Barthorne's will, the second son at Cortingford is amply provided for.

Sir Harry cannot disturb the arrangement if he would, and although he chafed about the legacy at first, he has perhaps (time being a great promoter of worldly prudence) become more than reconciled to the arrangement.

He allows Barthorne's widow a handsome income. She has long since returned from Australia, and been married for years to a dissenting minister, whose eloquence is much admired by his own congregation, and the members of his denomination generally. He is a great contrast to her first husband, and she is, in her own opinion, an important person now. She drives about in a neat brougham, she dresses in the richest attire, and remembers her daughter was Lady Medburn, a fact she never allows her acquaintances to forget.

She rather looks down on her brother, whose worldly affairs have not prospered since the time of Barthorne's return. He is considerably poorer than in the old Fisherton days; but his wife is dead, and he is probably better satisfied with life than formerly.

As for Mr. Wright, he has once been bankrupt, and once compounded with his creditors, during the course of the years intervening between this present and that morning when he beheld Miles Barthorne for the last time. He can still preach, however, and is apparently as genial and cheerful as ever. Nevertheless, in moments of confidence, he tells Selina that he feels he is getting old; that the wine of life has, somehow, not the flavour it once possessed, and that he believes the game so long played has not been worth the many candles burnt over it. With which opinion Mrs. Wright does not agree—for she preserves a firm and admirable faith in a bishopric, "which must," so she says, "come eventually to Dion," and with it five thousand a year!

THE END.

PRINTED BY J. S. VIRTUE AND CO., LIMITED, CITY ROAD, LONDON.

www.ingramcontent.com/pod-product-compliance
Lightning Source LLC
Chambersburg PA
CBHW051220120726
47905CB00004B/1203